PICASSO
BLUES

PICASSO
BLUES

A Ray Tate and
Djuna Brown Mystery

Lee Lamothe

DUNDURN
TORONTO

Editor: Matt Baker
Design: Jennifer Scott
Printer: Webcom

Library and Archives Canada Cataloguing in Publication

Lamothe, Lee, 1948-
    Picasso blues / wirtten by Lee Lamothe.

Sequel to the book: Free form jazz.
Also available in electronic formats.
ISBN 978-1-55488-966-2

    I. Title.

PS8573.A42478P52 2011   C813'.6   C2011-901861-6

1   2   3   4   5   15   14   13   12   11

Canada

ONTARIO ARTS COUNCIL
CONSEIL DES ARTS DE L'ONTARIO

We acknowledge the support of the **Canada Council for the Arts** and the **Ontario Arts Council** for our publishing program. We also acknowledge the financial support of the **Government of Canada** through the **Canada Book Fund** and **Livres Canada Books**, and the **Government of Ontario** through the **Ontario Book Publishing Tax Credit** and the **Ontario Media Development Corporation**.

Care has been taken to trace the ownership of copyright material used in this book. The author and the publisher welcome any information enabling them to rectify any references or credits in subsequent editions.

J. Kirk Howard, President

Printed and bound in Canada.
www.dundurn.com

Dundurn	Gazelle Book Services Limited	Dundurn
3 Church Street, Suite 500	White Cross Mills	2250 Military Road
Toronto, Ontario, Canada	High Town, Lancaster, England	Tonawanda, NY
M5E 1M2	LA1 4XS	U.S.A. 14150

Painting isn't an aesthetic operation;
It's a form of magic designed as a mediator
between this strange hostile world and us ...
— Pablo Picasso

Prelude

The woman lay buried in leaves and twigs on the marshy margin of the wide river through the night and wondered if she appeared dead enough that, after someone discovered her and the coroner took her away, they'd re-bury her alive, thinking she was already dead.

Her left eye was dislodged and twisted, looking blindly, impossibly, away. The right eye was frozen open, a fixed lens on a fresh blue sky cut with arcing seagulls. She felt her throbbing cheekbones swelling against her gums. There were teeth in her throat, and she was afraid to swallow her pooling blood and saliva in case she choked.

The logic of her senses told her she was alive. For her, sight was the most important and because there'd been no stars in the clouded night she'd feared she was blind and perhaps dead, until the eastern light began to glow on the periphery of her right eye. Scent and sound returned in that order; first the fecund odour of the river and of the musty cracked leaves over her face. Then the screaming madness of the gulls and the creaking of boat hulls, and in her ears the slow but lazy pulse of her indifferent heart.

Live interment was a basic human terror. When she was a girl down in Missouri, some schoolmates, experimenting to determine if it was possible to turn her black skin white from terror, had locked her in a root cellar that was so dark and absolutely still and warm that she didn't know where her skin ended and the dank air began. They'd covered her with a tarp and she couldn't tell if she was face up or face down. Until she gave up hope that someone would come to the cellar, she had tried to still herself, tried to keep away the thoughts of black snakes and spiders. She'd lain frozen, humming gospel songs her grandma had taught her. She was freed several hours later when her dad came down to the cellar to get a wooden barrel of pickles to sell at the family's roadside stand.

It would be like that to be alive in a buried coffin: an atmosphere humid with her own breath, strumming with her own sounds. When she'd done a student documentary at the city morgue, though, a hale and hearty attendant listened to her spooky concerns and laughed into her wide eyes. "If you weren't already dead, the autopsy would finish you off anyway." He shrugged, adding that he'd heard tales of caskets being opened years after interment and fingernail gouges found engraved inside the lids. "So, what do I know?" His morbidity was friendly. When he saw he'd spooked her, he said, kindly, "Best thing, Missy? Check off the organ donor box on your driver's licence. That'll do it."

Had life been at all real since she'd been in that cellar? Was she still under that tarp twenty years later, and all her life a dream delivered between two impossibly long, final heartbeats? There'd been no college over in Chicago, none of the boyfriends had been born or even existed, her cat hadn't lived and died, she hadn't met Quentin Tarantino at a West Coast film festival. She wondered in a series of abstract thoughts whether maybe this was what everybody's life was like: a dream in a wet womb of a woman who might have never existed in a place that never was. She wanted to examine that but the thought skidded away.

She knew the survival value of an active mind, but didn't think too much about the man who'd beaten her, methodically taking her apart until ... Horace acted and there was yelling and cursing and the man was just gone, not there any longer.

She'd studied film and video and knew her eye had now become a fixed lens and that a world of moments would pass in front of it, be recorded in the pixels of her grey brain. She thought of Michelangelo Antonioni's beautiful seven-minute tracking hotel scene. She'd rather look at a blurry photograph of Antonioni in a magazine than have drinks in person with Tarantino. She'd never met Luciano Tovoli but she knew from the moment the film closed that she'd love his eyes without reserve.

She studied the birds slicing around the sky. It was a perfect sky. For her graduation project *à la* Antonioni, she'd set up an old 8mm camera on a set of sticks and had her actors wander slowly across the frozen scene, talking or making love, or just standing a moment, then moving out of the frame as if their appearance was a sprocket in a longer journey.

For her new documentary she'd wandered the banks of the river looking for beaching points used by migrant smugglers who ran little canvas dinghies and rowboats across from Canada, depositing Chinese families in the land known in China as Gold Mountain. America. There had been deaths, bodies found the previous winter in their inadequate coats, an ice sculpture of mother and daughter together, hugging each other, a pair of young boys a month later a mile downriver, their malnourished bodies twisted and trapped and frozen in the rocks. And a week ago a sailor on a lake freighter spotted the floating body of an elderly woman with photographs in a fanny pack of grandchildren she'd never meet and a telephone number of a local East Chinatown restaurant.

The river was spooky at night. For comfort and companionship she'd brought Horace with her. The visit was taken without any equipment except her eyes and intuition. Before she had her mood, her vantage point, her voice, she wouldn't lug equipment; she was a previsualizer, panning her boxed fingers through the trees, feeling properly pretentious. Once she had her research done and some funding in place, she'd film, hopefully with a full winter moon in the froth of grey cloud. Some wind to make a sinister rustling, although the trees would then be bare. Now there was only her own breathing and her faint footfalls in the dark.

She had some rippling piano music in mind, a score she was composing. A little Keith Jarrettish, maybe. She would do nothing so cliché as blending a track of scripted migrants' cries for salvation before death to interplay with the cresting ripple of noir piano. She had been thinking of owls, loud warning hoots, maybe an explosion of one out of a tree that would bring first shock and then laughing relief to the migrants. There were ethical issues; she didn't want to do re-enactment, she didn't want to do dramatization. She wanted to document. She'd have to research if there were owls along the riverbank in winter.

When she'd seen flashlights bobbing on the water, she'd stopped. The Volunteers, come to defend the shoreline from Chinese migrants carrying all manner of disease and communism. When the lights were past she shook a cigarette from a pack, turned her back to the river to screen the flame, and lit it with a lighter in the cup of her hands. Before she could exhale she felt a huge mass slam into her. She was overwhelmed and her inner organs and her eyes and her breath and pulses seized in shock. She was rushed right out of her shoes and hoisted by the throat and held against a tree.

As the man grunted, she grunted, each in turn. He was measured, as if she was a punching bag and he was a boxer in training or he was a workman getting a chore of rote done. It seemed to go on for a long time. A punch and a grunted word, a punch and a grunted word and a punch and a grunted word, and she thought, Horace Horace Horace. Confusion then, as she went out, returning to being dragged by the hair down to the riverbank, him swearing, calling her a fucking dog, then dropping her into a depression in the ground. The sting of dirt and pebbles as he kicked at her. And then he was gone.

Alone in the aftermath she realized night wasn't quiet at all. There were hums of insects, faint stirrings of shrubbery, the lap of nearby water, and later as the sun rose, the screaming of birds that she thought would drive her mad in their intensity and pitch.

She hated those noisy birds.

She loved those noisy birds.

They spoke to her and validated that she was at least alive in some of her senses. A ship heading out into the lake hooted from the direction of the river; there were faint voices and boats were close enough that she could hear them creak at moor. There was a snatch of laughter. There was life and it wasn't far away. She had merely to attract it and plead her case to rejoin it.

He'd almost completely covered her with a kicking of leaves and stones and twigs. There'd been a rage in him as if he were kicking her entire existence off the surface of his planet.

Her left thigh was suddenly shot with feeling and she sighed happily at the pain, that she wasn't totally paralyzed. A girl in high school had fallen only a very short distance off a root shed and became paraplegic. Her classmates explored in that morbid but human

indulgence how they would handle being in a wheelchair
for life. Some said they'd kill themselves. She herself
had reserved judgement. In a wheelchair she could
still operate her camera off a tripod of sticks, could
direct her actors, could edit her video. A quadriplegic,
now that was another set of problems she'd have to
deal with if it came to that. She'd seen quadriplegics
operate their motorized chairs by blowing into a tube.
She could do that. A tube for panning, a tube for
zooming, a tube for dissolve. All was doable, if you
didn't surrender.

She believed. God had repainted black sky blue for her,
had populated it with those beautiful noisy birds to
make her senses jump.

She believed. God had planted the seed that grew
the tree that was butchered into timber and fashioned
into a boat that had a hull that groaned and creaked
nearby for her to hear.

She believed. God had made the clouds that made
the rain that made the ice that melted and made the
river that she could smell.

She believed God had let her keep this single lens
in her face and let life pan itself across it so that she
could record it for something.

And he'd created Horace, as if only to have him
save her. She wondered if the man had taken Horace
away with him. God wouldn't do all that unless there
was a purpose to the recording of it.

I'm going to live, she told herself.

She closed her eye and died.

But then, with the day alight and alive again, she heard a faraway voice calling, "Hey, Picasso. Yo. You got a reason for being here, Pablo?"

Chapter 1

The city was besieged.

An invisible and sinister mist had ridden in on a vicious breeze. The source of the deadly fog was the elusive Patient Zero, suspected to be an illegal migrant from China, a night horse spewing disease and spraying phlegm in a fifty-dollar dinghy, run across from Canada by a snakehead. At first no one had cared much: it was a vicious flu bug that seemed to only be attracted to Asians. But when the bug jumped races and whites, young and old, were infected, there were beatings and riots and arsons in East Chinatown. The Volunteers, formerly mere ad-hoc bands of crackpot racists, suddenly became prominent, more organized. They had a visible and public focus. A crude leadership emerged, and they manned the city airport, looking for international transfer passengers on flights from Chicago or Detroit. Night patrols ran up and down the waterway at the top of the city.

You could catch the bug by not washing your hands, or it was conducted through intimate contact, or it was in the ethnic foods, or it had an indefinite shelf life on banisters, telephone receivers, elevator buttons, or it was airborne and it gathered in pockets of clear vapour throughout the city, waiting to practise osmosis on hapless passersby. The conflicting information made a city of paranoia, of surgical masks and latex gloves and soap dispensers. People shook hands by touching elbows. Husbands and wives kissed each other near the ear.

The cops, who had to work in all kinds of medical weather, were hit hard. The few remaining moustachioed gunslingers from the robbery squad were twitchy. They cruised the downtown financial sector in heavily weaponed bank cars. Folks wearing masks on the streets triggered inside the gunslingers a genetic urge that they struggled to master. Except for Halloween, and that was iffy in some neighbourhoods, running the streets in a mask made you a magnet for a hollow-point. The gunslingers fought to control their tingling fingertips. Their frontier moustaches twitched in frustration.

The hammers of the Homicide Squad were almost wiped out; the bug had hit them hard in their dog-eyed wanders through the homes of murder victims and their constant presence in the dank halls of the stone courthouse. The hammers were reduced to chalking-and-walking or bagging-and-tagging, escorting corpses to the morgue where they told the fluorescent bleached clerks: You better stack 'em way back on the meat rack, Jack, 'cause I might come back in the black sack.

There was mindless violence. An unmasked Chinaman coughed in an elevator; he was stomped by fellow passengers. City buses became segregated: there were routes where all the passengers were Asian. Before boarding, non-Asian riders peered through windows to make sure they weren't embarking on the Fuzhou Express. There were luggar bandits at work: crews of Asian kids who slipped out of East Chinatown and shook down the city, threatening to spit toxic phlegm onto pedestrians if they didn't drop their wallets. Dim sum restaurants were bereft of clientele; the cart ladies had gone back to hoeing vegetables for street stands that nobody visited. In the subterranean massage parlours of Chinatown, the ladies danced naked except for their masks. Dreamy hand jobs came back into vogue for the lovelorn.

It was a humid dog day of summer and the bug breathed out a sigh, and a man in a black Chevy Blazer, his feet jammed into the detritus of around-the-clock surveillance, breathed it in.

Their skinner lived in a small brown post-war bungalow with an unhealthy undulating lawn and a sprinkler system that had gone on automatically an hour earlier. The house had grimy-looking beige curtains. A bouquet of flyers and envelopes poked up out of the black tin mailbox.

The spin team hadn't seen their skinner all day. He was clearly inside: early lights had gone on; a shadow moved from room to room. When children passed by the house on their way to school, a curtain cracked at the corner of the bay window. After the children had passed and the school bell a block away rang, the curtain twitched shut and the house went still. At four o'clock when the last knapsack-laden little potential victim had trudged past the house safely, the spin team would move on to their next spot-hit assignment.

"Maybe he snucked out," the wheelman said for the fourth time. "He gave himself his morning rub-and-tug at the window. It didn't satisfy, and he went out the back, around the block, and grabbed one of the kiddies up."

For the fourth time, the shotgun said, "Do I look like I give a fuck?" He rubbed his lower abdomen. "He could be ramping up his hard-on in the gym locker room, all we know, showing the kiddies what it looks like when it gets happy and spitting." He made a belch, forcing it. "Ah, fuck." He belched again. "Two guys doing a spin? What kind of fucking detail is this?" He shifted in his seat and pressed his hand to his diaphragm. "Geez, my guts." He moaned. "Ahhh, *fuck*." His stomach rumbled audibly. The air in the car took on a brown aura. "Donnie, I just shit my pants ..." He wobbled as if he'd lost his gravity, looking like he wanted to cry from humiliation but instead suddenly convulsed, jackknifing his face hard into the dashboard. His nose spouted blood. His knees jerked up into the racked shotgun under the dash. "Ahhhh *fuck*, *yack.*" He began vomiting spasmodically and continuously onto the jumbled mess of camera equipment, clipboards, crushed tin cans, and coffee cups at his feet.

The wheelman, without pause, locked his breath and stumbled from the vehicle. He said: "*Fuck,* Stanley, *fuck.*" He pulled a white surgical mask from the back pocket of his blue jeans and clamped it to his lower face with one hand while with his other he groped at his belt for his rover and yelled, "Ten Thirty-Fucking-Three."

Just before close of business on the day after Stanley the spinner blew his stomach all over the Chevy Blazer, the skipper of the Zombies received a rare telephone call at the Intelligence Bureau from a deputy chief at the Jank Center of Public Safety: "Cops are puking in Technicolor all over town," a clipped voice twisted at him. "The State's sending some troops. Meanwhile, dig up your bodies, we're letting those sad-sack motherfuckers walk the earth."

"I only got six guys on," the Skipper said. He paused carefully. "Ah, one of them is, ah, Ray, uh, Ray Tate? The gunner?"

"Fuck. Hang on." The voice from the Jank went away for a few minutes. "Okay. Dust him off, Harold. All hands on deck. Send him out. Better snap his trigger finger first, though."

Chapter 2

The fella was leaning against an ambulance, smoking a cigarette and dreamily examining the thin milky pre-birth of morning out over the lake. He ignored the indifferent enticement of the paramedics. The blood on his shirt was pretty much tacky three inches above the left pocket, where Ray Tate could see the outline of a cigarette lighter through the corduroy fabric. An angry scorch mark and flecks of burnt black gunpowder embedded in the fella's left neck and chin told the tale: up close and personal. In his right hand the fella held a package of Kool menthols; his left hand held the quarter-smoked cigarette elegantly near his face, straight up with an inch of ash on the end, leaning but solid. The knuckles of the hand holding the cigarette package were scraped raw. The fella was clearly a scrapper and he might have picked the wrong bar to carry a full bag of asshole into.

No nerves, no shakes, Ray Tate decided. There were guys like that. Take a small-calibre hornet a couple of inches above the red pump and yawn, go, Bummer, this is my favourite shirt. And he weighs the price of a new shirt against the expense of the lost art of invisible mending.

The road sergeant had a white gauze mask pulled down from his face while he mangled a stogie. He rolled his eyes and stepped away when Ray Tate nodded at him. The Road looked at Ray Tate's beard and biker garb and muttered to the ambulance crew and they all laughed.

To the fella, Ray Tate said, "Going to be a nice day. Hot one." He shrugged himself into a yellow vinyl raid jacket with POLICE printed in black block-letters across the back and vertically down the right chest.

The fella nodded and inhaled with confidence. "They said no rain, but I smell it. Maybe there's something over the water, there, coming down from Canada. Dunno." He took a careful drag on his cigarette and lifted his left arm a bit, testing. "How you think they get that job? Calling the weather?"

Rate Tate took a notebook from his back pocket. "Good guessers, I guess. They test you. You come down to the station every day for two weeks and wing it. If you're right enough of the time, you get a hairpiece, they bleach your teeth, and give you a suit from Bummy's."

"You think the weather guy gets to fuck the lady that calls the news?"

"Wouldn't surprise me." Ray Tate wrote the time and date. He glanced at the squat old row houses, looking for an address. The buildings' windows were about half lit up; it was a working neighbourhood where folks crawled out at dawn to factories and work sites to bust themselves a living. There were neat bags and recycling bins lined up in front of each stoop. No discarded furniture. It was the kind of no-bullshit neighbourhood where you threw nothing away until it had absolutely no function any longer and you could at least afford to make a down payment on a replacement. Some windows had bright flowers in bottles or vases. The sidewalk and stoops in front of the buildings were wet from a hosing down. A neighbourhood of prideful people working their way up, not falling their way down. If you attracted trouble here, Ray Tate knew, you must've been really looking for it. He doubted the fella had been shot where he was found.

A garbage crew paused their rumbling truck at the edge of the crime stage and the female driver was arguing through her mask with a blasé charger who wore his union baseball cap backwards, his uniform shirt limp and half-untucked.

Ray Tate wrote down the state of the weather. He always did, since a defence lawyer had questioned his memory in court. "You remember all those details about my client, Officer, but you can't recall if it was *raining* on your *head* that day?" So he led each incident note with the weather.

He looked around to see the numbers of the marked cars blocking off the stage. He wrote down the name of the road sergeant who'd voiced out on the rover without much hope for a response. The Road's badge number was 667. Everybody knew the road sergeant who said he was right behind the devil, Chief Pious Man Chan, when he signed up. The beast: 666.

"They say," the fella said, "that those people behind the big desk look like they're wearing suits or good outfits, but down below, out of camera range, they either got old blue jeans on, or they're naked. For laughs."

"I don't know about that." Ray Tate wrote down a thumbnail: white, mid-thirties, heavy-set, muscular, six-two, two-twenty-five or -thirty, blond and blue, soul patch, gold stud in his left ear, black corduroy shirt with blood and scorch visible on upper left quadrant, blue jeans, scuff boots, laces unfastened. Calm and relaxed, smoking. Swollen right-hand knucks. He didn't write *Moron*. "You been searched yet?"

The fella nodded.

Tate called to the sergeant. "Road, you India Delta off him?"

The Road shrugged. "No ID, he says. Smith, John."

"No doubt." To the fella, Tate said, "You want to break out something for me, John?"

"Not so much. I already know who I am." The fella knew his game and was pleasant with genial menace. "But thanks for asking." He seemed to be weighing a big thought. "They've all got big heads, you know? I saw that little Chink chick from Weather One down Stonetown last week. Nice hot little package, she's got it all going on. But she's got this big fucking plate-face. Guy she was with, I seen him on CX doing sports and he's got a big head too. What's with that? Big fucking heads?"

"The camera loves them, I guess." Ray Tate tried to think of something to ask that might wing the boomerang back to the shooting. Without taking his cellphone from his pocket, he fingered the camera function. "You got work, John? You a working man?"

The fella shrugged his right shoulder carefully. "You know. A little here, a little there."

"Where and what?" Ray Tate slipped the cellphone out of his pocket and snapped the fella's face.

The fella ducked too late, then faintly smiled. "Ah, you know, hog and pig man, that's me. Off-season, plumbing, mostly. Tuck and point. Shingle your roof." He leaned toward Ray Tate. "You get a good one?"

Rate Tate pressed a button, showed the screen to the fella. "Just in case the next guy shoots you shoots better. Souvenir." He put the phone away. "You pull any time, John? Craddock, out of state? Joliet?"

The fella seemed to ponder that. "Well, I got caught banging a hog one time, but they dropped the charges. The hog wouldn't testify. It was consensual, anyway." He stared at Ray Tate with a glitter. "You like pork chops?"

Ray Tate nodded pleasantly. He began steering the boat without much hope. He wanted the bullet. "Look, let's get down to Mercy, dig that bad boy out, okay? Fix you up. Just take a sec."

The fella said, *"Huhn?"* He turned around, careful with his vertical cigarette ash and showed Ray Tate a blot of blood on his upper left shoulder. "Come and gone." He looked closely at Ray Tate. "You think I could get a job like that?"

"What?"

"Calling the weather. Except that I don't got a big head."

"A good thing, maybe," Ray Tate studied his skull as if he cared and tried with no real hope to get off the skull-enhanced weather team and onto the shooting. "If you had the big head thing going on, they might've shot at that." He looked at the bloodstain on the shirt, remembering the pain and confusion when he himself had been shot the previous year. "That's gotta hurt, that, huh?"

"This?" The fella glanced at the blood. "This is nothing. Last time, they got me in the gut. That hurt. Hadda go to Saint Frankie's, that time. They took a mile of sausage casing out of me. I shit by gravity for a month."

"You been shot before? Like, how many times?"

"This year?" The ash fell from his Kool and he looked disappointed. "Or all together?"

"Oh-kay." Defeated, Ray Tate closed his note-book. "Have yourself a nice day."

Chapter 3

The cafeteria down the street was close enough to East Chinatown that it was empty except for the two grill men, the cashier, and two idle Mexican-looking bussers who looked for a horizon to jump when Ray Tate and road sergeant 667 walked in. The cashier and the workers wore white gauze masks and tilted away from customers so they wouldn't have to share breath. Someone had put a sign in the window: NO MASK NO SERVICE. Someone had added, *No Chineess Niether*. Under that someone wrote *Cracker Asshole*. And, beneath that in a casual scrawl: *Ahhh, Soooo solly, Chollie*.

The cashier silently pointed to a plastic bottle of hand sanitizer mounted near the door and Ray Tate and the Road pumped at it.

The Road knew the counter crew and he armed two stale breakfasts off the hot table and drew two mugs of coffee. He brought the tray to the window booth. The eggs were poached to rubber; the brittle toast under them was barely tanned; the bacon was pale lank flesh. But the coffee was coffee and it was hot, and, Ray Tate knew, at seven in the morning after a bad night there was no such thing as crappy hot coffee.

"So, Ray," the Road said, passing his notebook over for a scribble, "you like that mutt?" He made a toneless voice, "'You mean, duh, how many times I jerked off, like so far *this morning* or all day *yesterday too*?'" He laughed. "Fu-king mutt."

Tate signed his name and badge number and wrote the time under the Road's last notation, then drew a wavy line to the bottom margin, looping to circle the page number.

"What brings you out to the streets so early, Ray? I thought you were up in Intelligence Zombies?"

Ray Tate had been out and about because he'd painted through the night until early in the morning and then couldn't get to sleep with the whirling colours in his head and his ceiling fan indifferently shoving the humidity around his apartment. His morning assignment was to set up at the courthouse and monitor the release of a suspect on a homicide case. He'd gone on a cruise, riding the radio, killing time. When the Road voiced out for a scribbler, he'd snapped up the rover. With the bug gone wild and the chief's decree that a detective or soft clothes had to attend every crime stage with a wisp of gun smoke, everybody had to lift a little extra weight. There were stages, especially in the Hauser North Projects, that had been frozen for more than twelve hours because no one in a suit or designer windbreaker was inclined to run up there, stick their head in, and scribble in somebody's notebook.

"We should've probably taken him in, Road. If he goes south, we're going to wear it like the slippery brown hat."

"That guy, Ray, that guy looks after himself. You see his knucks? It looks like he got a few shots in. When we patted him down there was gun oil on his shirt, there, on his waist. He stank of gun smoke. I figure he had a heater of his own tucked away and he dumped it before we got there. Dumped his wallet, too." The Road picked up a piece of toast and tried to stab the corner through the poached yellow deadeye. The bread snapped like a cracker. "What the fuck we going to do, anyway? Arrest the guy for *getting* shot?" He gave up on trying to penetrate the deadeye and crunched on the toast. "I asked him. I said, 'Who shot you?' Fucking guy's worse than Bill Clinton. He said, 'Well, it depends what you mean by *shot*.'" He started laughing.

Ray Tate kept his raid jacket on and zipped. The cafeteria was cold with air conditioning; it was believed that the bug multiplied in heat and humidity. The windows looked up the damp street at the broken crime stage. Four bulky men in surgical masks and sports windbreakers, wearing red baseball caps, headed in the direction of East Chinatown, carrying golf clubs. Volunteers. A one-man ghost car trailed them at a walking pace.

The fella was standing around in the brightening grey dawn, scoping The Road's flashing cruiser and Ray Tate's unmarked Taurus. Waiting, Ray Tate thought, to retrieve his gun and wallet from where he'd dumped them when he realized those sirens were singing for him. The fella had a fresh cigarette in his mouth and his right hand was pressing a medi-pak to his left shoulder. One-handed, he dragged on a recycling bin and sat down on it, leaning back against the brown bricks to hang in for the long haul. People shuffled past him, all wearing surgical masks, all moving quickly. They each seemed stiff, holding their breath. No one headed into the plagued precincts of East Chinatown.

Ray Tate, who fancied himself a bit of an artist, felt like he was sitting in a moody Edward Hopper painting, looking out at an old pearly photograph of hopeful ghetto life. "How many guys you down?"

"With the bug? Out of my twelve-guy night leg, there's four left, plus me. I got three guys at Mercy, one of them on a lung. Timmy Harper. You know Timmy?"

Ray Tate nodded. When he'd come out of the departmental hearing that cleared him after he'd put down the second black guy, a television reporter said Congratulations, Ray, and handed him a lit cigar, trying to get footage of him looking like some arrogant gunner who'd got away with something, celebrating it off a *cubano*. Timmy Harper had grabbed the stogie and stabbed it at the guy, grinding the hot coal into his hairpiece. Timmy Harper lost a beat and went down to patrolman, getting badly stomped in the Racist Ray Tate riots. "Tell him I'm having a thought, right?"

"He'll appreciate it." The Road looked at the fella up the street, basking in the flashing blue and red lights. "Good that you're getting out and about, Ray.

So, how come, anyway, you're out so bright and early, on the rover?"

"This fucking heat. With the bug and the Volunteers, here I be." He rubbed his face. He had paint crusted on his fingernails. His hair was too long and greasy and he had an unshaped beatnik beard. He was going grey and his eyebrows seemed to be curling into his eyes. There was a benefit to the dripping hair: it obscured his missing earlobe, snicked off by a wild shot when he'd been gunned. His eyes were red from smoking out his apartment. Several gin and tap waters might have something to do with it. Under his raid jacket he wore a black leather biker vest with silver conches over a grey sweatshirt, black jeans, and scuffed short cowboy boots. The handle of his gun, riding in his boot, made a distinct bulge. His badge hung from a breakaway chain around his neck. "Yesterday they had me like this directing traffic down on the Eight while they untangled a wreck. One guy almost clipped me and I caught up to him in the gridlock and tinned him. 'What the *fuck're* you doing, man?' He said: 'You? A cop? Fuck, I thought you was gonna wipe my windshield. I lost so many wipers to those guys I got my own parking spot at Walmart.' Duh."

"What you do? You wallpaper him up?"

"Naw." Ray Tate shrugged. "If *I* saw me, badge or no badge, standing the middle of the Eight looking like this, I'd speed-dial my lawyer, lock my elbows and floor it, brace for impact. Anyway, I went down to Stores and checked out the jacket. Enough's enough."

Up the street outside the window, a short blue-and-white van with a caduceus stencilled on the side stopped in front of the shooting victim sitting on his recycling bin. Someone had spray-painted balloons from the forked tongues of the twisted serpents of the caduceus and filled them with FOK YU in stylized Chinese characters. A brisk young black woman wearing a mask and a nurse's habit climbed from the passenger seat with a handful of surgical masks dangling from her fingers. She stood at a good distance, speaking to the fella, then leaned and at arm's length held out the masks.

The fella reluctantly took one and awkwardly tied it to his face. After the woman boarded the van and it slid away, the man stared after it for a moment, then removed the mask and used the point of his cigarette to singe a hole in it. He waved it in the air to stop the burn, then tied it back on and stuck the cigarette through the hole, exhaling jets of smoke through his nose.

"Road, I'm rolling. Thanks for breakfast."

"No problem, Ray. Don't breathe in."

Ray Tate wanted a real breakfast even if he had to pay for it.

Prowling the streets, it was eerie still, seeing masked pedestrians and motorists making their way through the morning. The four big men in sports windbreakers and red ball caps sat on folding chairs at California Street, at the gates of Chinatown. Drivers had their windows up; cringing pedestrians avoided eye contact. A taxi driver sped by a well-dressed masked Chinese

man waving him down with a rolled up newspaper;
another taxi clipped by, wowing wide in the road. In
the rear-view mirror, Ray Tate watched the Chinese
man start the long hike up Harrison Hill, rhythmically slapping his newspaper against his pant leg in
frustration. At a coffee shop an Asian woman in business attire, holding her briefcase against her chest, was
blocked by a man in a white apron waving a spatula
over his head, shouting, "We're closed, we're closed."
Behind him through the street-front window, Ray Tate
could see the place was packed with hunched customers who lifted their masks to sip coffee or eat food.

Down at the waterfront where the river widened
into the lake, there were dozens of boats bobbing off
the city's edge. People believed the bug was landlocked
and those with sailboats or power monsters slept on
them, barbecued meals on deck, had rifles or pistols at
hand to repel the diseased. They kept an eye to the pen-
nants on their masts, ready to weigh anchor and head
for Canada if the wind changed. There was litter and
beer bottles on the riverbank where vigilant groups of
Volunteers had spent the nights, ready to go hand-to-
hand with any boatloads of Chinese migrants trying
to sneak in from Canada to steal the American dream.

He eased the Taurus down under the span bridge
and across the access road, turning where it lifted at the
waterfront. There was a bit of reluctant mist still locked
in the hollows. The sun was screened behind fading fog
that looked nuclear in the strengthening yolky light.
The radio muttered and he sorted calls and warnings
and requests with a casual inner ear. A fist fight at a

bus stop; all free units to the airport for a protest over rumours Asians were being routed from Chicago; a call to shots-fired on Marlborough in Stonetown.

Everyone was getting a little goofy with the two-and three-shift days.

"Any unit near Bradford and Queen?"

"Scouter four solo unit, right there, dispatcher."

"Report a naked male complainant covered in pythons. Possible mental incompetent. Ambo rolling."

"Repeat, dispatch? Did you say …" The voice rose to soprano, "*Py-py-py-py*-thons?"

"Ten-four, four solo. Pythons."

"Unable to respond, dispatch. I got ophidiophobia."

"Sorry, four solo. I meant to say … ah … spiders?"

"Okay, then, dispatch. Through counselling I've overcome my chronic arachnophobia. I'm rolling solo."

There were appreciative single clicks.

A disguised voice whispered: "All *yoo*-nits. Ray Tate's on the road with a pencil."

Ray Tate laughed. The Road.

"All *yoo*-nits," the Road whispered. "Ray Tate's looking to meet new friends. Call him up for an autograph."

A serious youthful voice came over. "Sergeant Tate, come up on the air, please?"

A female charger, sounding like a breathy beauty queen: "Oh, Sergeant Tate? Ray? I'm in the Hauser North, building four, tenth floor, south end of hallway. I'm real lonely, honey, my puffy pal is no fun. Knock twice and let yourself in. Do come and sign me out and we'll go part-tay …"

He ignored that call but was a little itched to take a run up there anyway, scope the thing out. She sounded fun, the kind of girl who could stand in human gases and be cute with a clothespin on her nose. Except for his ex-wife, who was a cop's daughter, in his adult life he'd only slept with lady cops and a nurse who wanted to become one. Except for a woman from an art class he'd taken over in Chicago, he hadn't dated in a year.

Another man's voice: "We got one down in the gun smoke at Hauser South. Sergeant Tate, come up on the air."

Another: "We got a gunfire stage on Branksome in Stonetown no victim. Sergeant Tate, come up."

The transmissions broke with three fast clicks as Ray Tate pulled into the waterfront parking lot near an abandoned bacon stand. He cranked the volume.

A level, unpunctuated voice, fast: "Urban Squad Two solo request backup transport supervisor seven-seven Marlborough Road holding one solo at gunpoint one-eight-seven no outstanding no ambo required supervisor detective required roll the catering truck."

A female voice came on. "You okay, U Deuce?"

Silence.

Four rapid responses: "Ghost ten rolling solo." "Ghost four rolling lonely." "Scout four wheelman stag on it." "Scout sergeant one lonely."

Ray Tate imagined the ghosters and scouts and prowl cars, wherever they were, turning and racing like iron filings toward the invisible pull of a violent magnet. There were a lot of lonelys, solo units, and stags on the road, wheelmen whose shotguns were down with the bug.

He unlocked the short shotgun racked under the dash and started a slow roll to the access road, sorting himself a fast route, leaning for his red Hello light in the passenger-side foot well.

A ghost car came over, the charger a melodious thespian. "*Ghooooos*-terrrr Ten *on* the stage, dispatch. *One* for the box, *one* for the bag, all secure, *break off*, units. *Con*-tinue the coroner's catering truck, *sil vous plais*."

"Ten four, ten. Thank you."

"No, my dear, *thank you* for this opportunity to *perform* for you ..." the stage voice giggled, "... and all the other *little people.*"

Appreciative single clicks.

Ray Tate listened a moment. When there was no further air, he rolled the Taurus back into the parking lot. He locked the shotgun rack, took off his raid jacket and got out, slipping his rover into his back pocket. He popped the trunk and took a sketchpad and some charcoal sticks from his briefcase, slammed the trunk and walked to the edge of the river and set up on a defaced bench under a parched tree. The gold buildings of Canada, across the way, were half lit-up by the struggling sun. The sails of the boats in the foreground were still in low dawn shadow, vague smudges. A moaning tanker eased like a relentless predator down the centre of the lake under a plume of screaming seagulls.

Gold buildings and trudging tankers weren't going to do it for him. He'd had it with the lack of flesh.

He waited for inspiration, something to engage him. It wasn't long in coming.

On a nearby sailboat a woman came above deck. She had long black hair twisted into a rope, wore a white bra and red shorts. She carried a bucket and looked around, then stripped off the bra and shorts. Balancing herself to the rhythm of the waves off the tanker, she bent over and dipped the bucket into the river and doused herself down with water. At the distance she looked undefined, a smear of light grey. Minimalist, of no detail, as though she'd already been sketched or painted.

It was a vision that stirred him on a lot of levels. It was human and sexual, obscure and specific; enough to allow him possibilities, to fuck a little with reality. He flipped to a blank page and clutched the short charcoal stick between his knuckles. He kept the woman's graceful shape but used the flat of the stick like a wide brush to make a perfect, small dark torso in graceful pose; he made her hair spiky, the hint of her eyes wide and Asian.

The voice of the female charger with the puffy friend at the Hauser North Projects rang in his inner ear. His homicide target was coming out of the court-house at ten. He decided if the Hauser North stage hadn't been broken up by the time the target was either down for the day or in handcuffs, he'd push the Taurus up that way, maybe get a date or at least a few laughs.

* * *

He finished the sketch and softly blew the charcoal dust off of the thick page. The shape of the small dark woman was a shadow, but he'd managed to get the idea of detail in there; she was recognizable. The buildings of Canada were bare suggestions of sinister mountains looming over her and the boat. The woman looked very small and isolated.

"Hey, Picasso, yo."

He knew what the voice was. He kept his hands still and turned his head slowly and waited.

"You got a reason for being here, Pablo?" The man was red-headed and almost too short to be a cop and he was grossly out of shape, comically dressed as a jogger, smoking a small cigar. He wore an unzipped fanny pack and Ray Tate could see his hand rested on the butt of a revolver. "You want to break something out for me?"

Ray Tate smiled. "I just said that to a mutt, myself." He identified himself as Intelligence and said he was heavy at the ankle.

The thick guy sat down and held his hand out. "Brian Comartin. Traffic. You got a better gig than me, the artist thing. They got me running up and down the Riverwalk, pissing in the weeds. Get us a boatload of Chinamen, they say, stop the invasion."

Shaking his soaking hand, Ray Tate saw his face was flushed. "You okay, man?"

"I haven't lifted more than a pencil in ten years and they come down to Traffic Flow and say, 'Hey, you're a cop again, get your fat ass down to the river, run around, and look for wet Chinamen. You see them, surround them, we'll get you some backup in, oh, about two weeks when we get somebody off the lung.'" He laughed but he was panting and looked a little frightened for his own well-being. "Jeez fuck. If I wanted to work, I wouldn'a become a cop."

"How many you guys down here?"

"Me and two others. One from Projections and one from Computer Enhancement. For four miles of Riverwalk, three miles of lakefront, and who knows what the fuck all in between." He shook his head. "This fucking city. You ask me, every illegal who sneaks over here is a vote for the American way of life. When I first came on, I worked Chinatown, I seen them working the sweatshops, fifteen-hour days, buck an hour, kick back a quarter to the boss, rent a bed for a couple hours sleep. No fucking way do I send workingmen back in the water. I see a bunch of Chinamen coming up out of the river, man, I'll take 'em home, give 'em a cash job painting my apartment."

Ray Tate laughed and got up. "I gotta go to court."

The fat man looked shy. He said, "Let's see, what you did? You do anything good?" He was embarrassed. He looked at Ray Tate looking back at him with suspicion. "I, ah, I got a thing, too. I'm into, ah, poetry."

Ray Tate thought for a moment, then flipped open the pad.

The thick man stared at the sketch. "Oh, okay. That's good, man, that's like art." He looked around as though imparting a secret. "You should be in a gallery or something."

"Yeah," Ray Tate held out his hand. "I should be in Paris in a beret."

Chapter 4

The State Police detachment in Indian country was a single-storey cement-block building with chicken wire over the windows and a heavy door with a keypad beside it. The face of the keypad had been ripped out; exposed wiring drooped like bright entrails. Access to the building was done by mobile phone or over the two-way talkies the detachment officers carried around the clock, on duty or off. Shotgun pellets pockmarked the fascia of the building and there was a flaring scorch mark like a triangular shadow where someone had incompetently thrown a Molotov cocktail, short. Concertina wire was looped around the entire roof of the building. Three Ford Expedition four-by-fours with peeling State Police logos were strategically parked around the entrance, backed in on angles to take up as much space as possible. Each truck had suffered damage, ranging from raw punctures from deer-rifle slugs

to graffiti that called for Red Rool. All the trucks had
the wiring for roof lights but they'd been shot out with
such regularity headquarters said *Enough* and sent
lighter-operated dash lights.

Inside the building, Djuna Brown sat behind a
desk pirated from the asbestos-laden schoolhouse no
one allowed their kids to attend. The desk was deeply
grooved with messages: RED ROOL ROOLS, STICK THE
MAN, RIP KOPS, SP DOA DJA OK. SP stood for State Police;
DJA stood for Djuna. She wore her authority as though
it were a secret she only shared with an unlucky few.

"You know," she said to the man opposite her,
back-handcuffed to a heavy oak chair, "you know
everyone's got a ... thing. You know? A *thing*? That
sets them off, makes them crazy? Cops are like that. I
know a guy just goes nuts at animal abuse, especially
dogs. Another guy comes down heavy on people who
speed near schools. Another cop goes off on guys that
beat their wives. You following? A *thing*."

The man in the handcuffs nodded. His head was
huge; standing, he was about six-five, just short of a
foot taller than Djuna Brown. His torso was thick and
his weight was two-fifty, she knew from his file, exactly
double hers. Both were dark-skinned: he with Native
skin and a lifetime in the sun, trapping, hunting, fishing; she being more an inherited brown Caribbean coffee with a good shot of cream.

She gave him a peek at her authority. "Ronnie, I
asked if you're following me?" Her voice had a bit of lilt,
just enough that if they were sitting in the dark, Ronnie
would still know she was from a southern island.

His voice was rough and deep, the tone a little petulant. "I follow you, Djuna."

"Sergeant Brown."

He brooded, not looking at her face. She saw a moment of shame there. Everyone called her by her first name except her troopers. They had single syllables for her.

She waited for him. Ray Tate had taught her to make time her bubble, create a different kind of life in there, wait things out. Chat endlessly and fill it with verbal free-form jazz.

"I follow, Sergeant Brown."

She nodded and smiled her tiny pearly teeth, then sat back and put her feet on the desk. She wore red satin slippers decorated with bits of bright metal and beading. He looked at them and smiled sadly. Her uniform pants dragged back, revealing dark blue ankle socks, above them smooth brown hairless skin. Her tunic was opened against the heat in the close room and she wore a pure white T-shirt over a red sports bra.

She wanted to tell him something, but she wanted him to tell her something first. "Well, I'm sure you've got a thing, too, right, Ronnie? Something that just takes you out of who you are and you want to go primitive? No rules, no mercy, because of the wrong of it?"

He pondered a while, then nodded slowly. "The hunters in the airplanes. The wolves."

"Right. The hunters and the wolves. Winter kill."

"Machineguns." He wagged his head. "The blood in the snow, they leave them there. Kill them, skin them, leave the carcass." His face gathered red anger. "I want to —" He looked up beyond the watermarked ceiling and struggled against the cuffs with his shoulder to try to reach up.

She saw he wasn't dull or stupid and she put her feet down out of respect. She wanted to uncuff him but there was no natural way to do it before she'd finished. She still didn't know if she was going to have to beat him. "All right, my thing is bleeding children. When I rolled by your place and saw her, I wanted to just beat you with a stick. If I needed ten guys with me, okay, I'd find ten guys, easy. And you know, Ronnie, I'm not like that, right? Since I came back up here from the city with my stripes, things are better. Not great, they'll never be great up here in our lifetimes, not for you, not for them." She nodded at the closed office door; from the other side her troopers were banging their boots and bullshitting loudly in the shift room. "But right now, there's no more Saturday night rodeos. No cops selling hootch to your people, catching the girls drunk, and banging them in the trucks. I catch a dealer from the cities slinging meth or crack, that guy goes for a walk on the traplines for an evening and when he comes back he's got some serious winter mosquito bites. It hurts me to do that, that's not who I am, but I try to make a difference."

He glanced up at her, then away.

She knew she'd lost him, gotten sidetracked, her riff had gone nowhere. She held her palms up at him. Her hands were tiny, her fingers long, her fingertips looking stupid for a cop, a result of the sloppy white French manicure she'd given herself the night before, drunk and talking aloud to the absent Ray Tate. "Start again:

I know this isn't about me, all this. But at your place with Misha? That *is* what it's all about. Your twelve-year-old. Beautiful girl. Smart girl. Broken nose, blood everywhere. For me, Ronnie, that's the blood on the snow, that's the wolves. That's my winter kill." She studied him and reached her right hand straight up. "I saw Misha and that blood, and I wanted to ..." She made a fist above her head and pulled it down, "... just pull you from the sky." She felt her face turn to sadness, the muscles going wherever they wanted. She didn't know, yet. Hadn't decided. He had to give her something. She glanced at the door. Instinctively, she had it. She gave him power without surrendering any of her own and stared at his face until he looked back at her. "Don't make me like that, man. Don't make me like them. Please, don't."

Ronnie sagged a little. He looked like, given the choice, he'd rather take the beating. "I'm sorry, Djuna ... Sergeant Brown."

"Don't tell me, Ronnie. Tell Misha." There was a thick cudgel with dark stains at the business end leaning against the drawers on her side of the desk where he couldn't see it. It wasn't hers: it was called the Abo-Swatter and it had notches in it where the guys had tallied their Saturday night rodeos. There were a lot of notches, but none of them fresh. When she'd come up from the city, transferred back and promoted, she'd lined up the guys and told them where to head in. No one spoke to her after that except about the work, but she'd gone the distance in the cop trade and killed a man in the line and that came with its own respect, if not friendship.

"How we going to do this, Ronnie? Me or the elders?"

He looked at her.

She smiled, her hair spiky and jet black. She looked like a backup singer in the videos broadcast through his satellite dish over from Chicago. The handcuffs weren't necessary. Everybody on the Rez loved something about her.

"Elders." He sucked his lips. "Elders. I'll take a tribal council. Okay?"

It wasn't strictly legal under state law. Self-rule and tribal councils made the pale jowls in the state capital quake, preventing them from dispensing human mercy as though it was a gift, as if fairness and dignity were special rights to be bestowed.

She nodded. "Elders, okay. What they say goes. I'll stand by it, you stand by it." She came around the desk in her slippers, seeming not much taller standing up than she was sitting down. Even removing the handcuffs let her reveal her technique: she placed a gentle hand flat on his shoulder while she operated the key. Ray, her city cop, had taught her that. She was ready to jump away from him if Ronnie went off, to get the stick from behind the desk, to hope her guys outside the door came boiling in when she called out.

But Ronnie just massaged his thick wrists. He didn't want to frighten her and waited until she'd stepped away before nodding his head and getting up off the chair. "I'll be home, when they want me. The elders. Sergeant … Brown."

As she pulled on her knee boots, she gave him a luminous smile of perfect little chicklet teeth and took her round hat from the peg by the door. "Ah, c'mon, Ronnie, man. My name's Djuna. I'll give you a drive."

She felt like a city suburban mom piloting the Expedition. She wouldn't let Ronnie ride chained in the cage in the back like a prisoner in case his Misha saw, although strictly speaking he was still in custody. The top of his head almost touched the headliner. He was silent beside her. There was a type, she knew, who went quiet, gathering in their mind the slights and grudges of the day, mixing them together like a violent brew that reached fission and the next thing you knew you were on the floor in incredible pain, going holy-fuck, and covering up your vital organs as the guy tried to kick you to death. She'd been there twice, each time when she walked into a Saturday-night bar powwow and sparked off some deep thinker for whom a uniform was the last crucial ingredient in the wild beverage percolating inside. Both times it was the Native men who waded in and got her free, protected her, wrestling the guy off her and out the door. They wouldn't hold him for arrest; things weren't that way and she had no right to expect that.

The Expedition knew the way. It smoothly rolled past the bent, perforated stop signs, heading out of town beyond the shacks and cracked foundations of the government houses. Djuna Brown drove with the big red ball on the floor behind her, but all the troops left theirs on the dash. She didn't, because she wanted people to know it was her coming.

Ronnie didn't seem to want to talk, so she let her mind muse, think about Ray Tate, something she'd thought she'd have stopped doing by now but instead did more frequently, wondering if he even remembered her.

When she drove off the rutted driveway of Ronnie's sloping shack he was on his knees, forehead to forehead with Misha. She seemed to be comforting him. Ronnie's mostly absent wife was in the doorway, a shapeless woman in a colourless shift dress, barefoot and pregnant again. There was cardboard over the windows of the shack. There was no uncontaminated water in the area and empty cardboard cases of state government plastic bottles were stacked up in the shade against the crumbling porch, shaped into a doghouse, a long, twitching snout poked out.

She took the long way back, looping dirt roads through some of the most beautiful country she could imagine. She'd been told Canada to the north was even more stunning, but she couldn't imagine that. At the lift of a rise, she stopped the Expedition in the middle of the road and stared sadly down into a river where a creek bled effluent that looked like noxious green tea, now that the lumber mill up the other side, out of sight, was back in operation. A sign on the mill's office said WO/NR. Ostensibly, it meant Work Office, Northern

Initiative. In reality it meant Whites Only, No Injuns. The sawmill workers were tough but they found their own places to water themselves after a shift; the grim ramshackle bar in town was a little too edgy for them, so they drove thirty miles the other way and Djuna Brown's guys had had to yank a lot of wrecks off the road and pry bodies out of windshields.

Above the feeder creek the water was pristine and thick with beautiful silver fish. Below, in the morning sun, it was fouled with fish with bulging eyes gasping on their sides.

But Ray would love it here, she thought, slipping the truck into gear. He'd be a mysterious striding ghost, climbing the folds of the hills and sinking into the shadows of the valleys, an easel over his shoulder and his clutch of paintbrushes and charcoal sticks in a hip holster. She imagined him talking to himself. Back when they were partners down in the city looking for the X-men, the traffickers who sold party drugs, she remembered him driving the bosses nuts with his rambling soliloquies. The Natives wouldn't bother him because they recognized a slightly crazy soul, the spiritual worth of it.

They'd planned, after they got fired for thoroughly fucking up the X-men case, to take what buyouts they could negotiate and head to Paris, where he'd paint and she'd ... well, she was sure she'd find some creative muscle to exercise. She didn't see herself as an artist's moll, stretching his canvases and darning his old denim shirts. But Ray loved his city streets, the young chargers for whom he felt responsible, strange for a doorstep baby who'd been raised in the grim cycle of state

foster homes where the only loyalty was to survival.
And they never got fired anyway. Ray took some bullets
and closed it down for the shooter, a psycho ex-city cop,
and Djuna Brown became a hero, crossing the thickest
of lines and leaving a fat pervert dead in the dirt, a killer
drug network broken, and a kidnapped girl rescued. A
movie production company had flown her out to Los
Angeles but she was too modest about her exploits to fit
their dramatic needs, although a mannish script assis-
tant swore true West Coast love for Djuna Brown's little
red slippers.

Two miles outside town she passed a trio of Native
men walking along the highway, each carrying a long
tube of rolled newspaper with thick moss poking out
the ends. They turned at the distinctive sound of the
Expedition engine and for a moment they showed fear,
ready to head into the bush. Then they recognized her
and nodded, and she slowed and offered rides. One, a
slim man with a potbelly, declined politely. They didn't
have fishing rods or poles; from one man's vest pocket
she could see a length of fishing line looping out. The
edges of the man's hands had deep scars where the
tackle lines had been grooving for decades, hand over
hand to retrieve the fish. They all remained in easy
silence for a few moments, then one of the men, she
couldn't tell which one because no one's lips moved,
made the perfect caw of a raven. She laughed, slipped
into gear, and eased the truck away.

The raven's call kept her smiling the rest of the way into town.

She'd been invited to a sweat lodge after she first came back, an offer rarely made to a woman, never mind a black one. It was a low den, smoky with smouldering willow branches, with cracks in the woven tree limbs above her. Glowing hot rocks were carried in on forked sticks and gently laid in a small depression in the earth floor. A man set up a worn concave stone full of water, and another man, with a broom tied of brush and leaves, sprinkled the water onto the hot stones. There was chanting; she stripped off her T-shirt and shorts and sat naked in the humid almost-dark, surrendering.

She'd felt as if she were suffocating, the sweat rivers pouring individually from each scalp follicle and down her back. As she sweated something out of herself, she saw in the middle of her mind the sweat, black threads of thoughts and confusions, turn to silvery estuaries as her spirit cleansed itself, purified. It might have taken hours but she didn't know, because she was stoned on herself and the smoke and the rhythmic murmurs of the three men in there with her. It was rancid with human seepage and the little tied bundles of tobacco and herbs smoking on the hot stones, and she seemed to not blink for five or ten minutes at a time, not until she remembered to. The lodge was very dark and close and she'd been told it was called the Mother's Womb.

One man had asked: "What are you, sister?"

She said, for no discernable reason, "Raven," the image, not the word, flying itself into what remained of her drained mind.

"Go outside. Now."

One man held the thick blankets back from the doorway and she ducked out as naked as birth into the first cold day of creation, lit by a new light and populated with unheard sounds and unrecognizable colours and she heard every leaf rustle against itself, heard the individual microscopic boulders of sand shifting under a soft breeze. There in front of the low lodge was an inky raven perched on a mossy stone. It called to her and she laughed in return, a laugh her breath had never created before.

She was thinking of that day, of imagining a raven and then finding one, as she pushed open the door to the detachment office and her corporal handed her the printout of an email. Before she took it she had a sudden unbidden image of Ray Tate's face in her mind, and the email said the State Police were assisting the city during the epidemic. Manpower was requested.

"Right," the corporal said. "As if."

She said, "You're Acting. You're in charge until I get back."

He, who she'd overheard identifying her only by the monosyllabic name of a body part, smiled and said, "Yes, Sergeant Brown."

She saw his smile was genuine and appreciated that he was just a kid, an untested boy-cop who'd lose a lot if he ever had to cross the thickest of lines, inhaling his own gun smoke, watching someone die to death at his feet.

* * *

She was packed and at the detachment office, and her lieutenant said there were lots of cars down in the city. "They don't have a problem of vehicles, Sergeant, they're parked all over the fucking town. What they have is have a problem of no one to drive them. Take the nine o'clock Amtrak." He flipped her a State credit card and stared at her. "You sure you want to go? They got this plague going down there, I guess you heard? They're quarantining people. They're gonna have riots. That place is finished."

Her corporal silently drove her to the railway station. After she dragged her carryall from the back of the Expedition, she leaned in the window. "Look, you don't have to be afraid, you know? Go out, talk to them. They're just people, same as you and me. Ask them where the good fish are, where the good hunting is. Ask a question, even if you already know the answer. Give them that, at least." She stared at him. She wasn't sure she was getting through.

He nodded and looked away through the windshield. She thought he was going to laugh: a midget black girl sergeant telling a buff farm boy how to bale hay. But when she spoke he had to at least listen: she'd killed a gunman in the line and it entitled her to a measure of respect. She got her stripes by smelling her own gun smoke, not down in the capitol with her legs open.

She was fearful for the people up there, what might happen if she wasn't around. *This must be how Ray Tate feels about his kid cops.* She started to try again, "Tom, listen to me just one listen, okay, you got a toolbox —" She gave it up and made a sad little smile. "Good luck, Tom."

He put the Expedition into gear.

She stepped back, and when he drove away, she made a complex hand signal at his departing truck and went into the train station.

Chapter 5

In front of the old cut-stone courthouse on Soldiers' Square, Ray Tate sat on his balled-up raid jacket and studied the bird droppings on the wide steps. His artist self and his detective self engaged one another: the splashes of the runny avian stuff had a natural textured aspect that appealed to his abstract painterly eye; the velocity, direction of spatter, and thickness spoke to his deductive talents as well as to his appreciation of crazy Jackson Pollock. One particularly wide glob, a little shiny and red and with no drag to any direction, told him the bird had recently perched on one of the eaves, held its ass over the edge, and bombed one straight down, perfectly vertical. Another sample had extreme fingering: the bird had been in flight north at a good speed. He deduced that the caked bird shit had been dropped at the end of the previous spring, when a lot of the birds headed north full of southern berries.

Uncoagulated blood was thinner than bird shit but the principles were the same. On the walls of the academy training house, and at real crime stages afterwards, he could tell which way a knife had swung, what velocity a baseball bat had picked up in its travel. Spatter was the murderer's brush stroke: it spoke to the miscreant's enthusiasm and talent.

The gunshot fella had been wrong. The sun had burned off the dawn into a sharp, still morning. The stars-and-bars hung from the flagpole, limp as a rag. In front of the courthouse, the morning parade of miscreants lounged in the sunlight on the steps, unintelligibly welcoming each other with *yo-bloods* and *huhs* and slapping boneless high-fives. They talked bail and jail with depressed, drooping lawyers in sagging suits and bad haircuts. Three members of the Flying Fukienese Dragons, in black sateen gang jackets with Mandarin collars, wore white surgical masks decorated with toothy shark's mouths, lifting them only to take drags on cigarettes or to spit dangerously near passersby. A haunted bum clutched his chest and bent over, coughing sputum near the war memorial while four plainclothesmen backed away in a pack, looking back as though they wanted to kick his lungs out.

Back in his uniformed days, Ray Tate had liked being in court. It was the culmination of his work. He was good on the stand. He gave good fuck, the prosecutors said. When a clerk offered him the bible and asked if he swore to tell the truth, Ray Tate held the book with reverence, crossed himself, said, "I do so swear," and bit his knuckle. He stood erect in the box in his uniform, his hat on the ledge, hands clasped either front or back, but usually back because it gave a less defensive posture, and spoke exactly enough words to answer the question asked. Every second question, he'd answer directly to the judge or jury. Whenever he was asked about an action or statement of the accused, he'd glance over at the dock while answering, essaying that his answer applied to this specific accused and no other individual on earth. His entire posture said Nothing Personal; he seldom needed rehabilitation by the Prosecutor. The defence lawyers usually got him out of the box as quickly as possible.

The fingerman from Homicide was late. Ray Tate used the time to wander his mind through Paris, where he'd never been. *It would be like this*, he thought: observing passersby, a glass of something cool and European as his elbow rested on a round metal table, a snobby waiter hovering in the background. A thick coil sketchpad would be awaiting inspiration. His fingernails would be caked with primary colours, his knuckles black with charcoal. Cobblestones would be an endless slick geometry, diminishing into the vanishing point of coffin-shaped rocks, defined and perfect and endless into infinity.

Djuna Brown would've been in there too. He imagined swaggering narrow Frenchmen leering at her cocoa skin, at her spiked shiny hair poking from under a cocky beret. She'd wear a scarf looped at her long throat and would look as exotic as Paris itself.

He didn't make a picture of himself, but his garb wouldn't be faux biker or the blue suit with chevrons on his arms, although he loved that old blue bag. There'd be no holster in his boot, no badge chained around his neck. He cherished the badge, but sometimes it had come to feel like an anchor, preventing him from soaring someplace. And with his earlobe shot off he fancied himself as an amusing half-a-van Gogh.

"You're a bit of a junkyard dog, Ray," Djuna Brown had said after she got her stripes and visited him, convalescing in his apartment, a tube in his hip and a wad of gauzing on his ear. "You look like that little guy in the cartoon after the blunderbuss went off."

He saw she was dodging something, that her smile and teasing eyes were a mask. "So," he'd said, feeling bleak and hopeless, knowing. "Paris?"

Beatnik life in Paris is what they'd promised each other.

She looked very sad. "No can do, buckaroo."

They'd just finished the X-men case. He hadn't done much, just went from place to place with her and somehow they'd stumbled on the chemistry set used by a degenerate businessman and a psycho killer. She whacked the degenerate and the tactical guys took down the psycho. Ray Tate hadn't even been there, because a jealous lesbian ex-cop who had a jones for Djuna Brown had come by his apartment and opened up on him. He left her dead in the doorway and afterwards he lay on his floor, waiting to die, glad, looking at the fresh pockmarks in the plaster ceiling, that he hadn't wasted money painting the place.

Djuna Brown had come to his apartment to tell him she was going back to her precious Indian country, to her shacks and shanties and Saturday night bust-outs. Originally she'd been assigned up there as a punishment because she was thought to be gay; now it was her reward for being a hero. Bodies hanging from rafters in despair; families wiped out by accident and suicide, by murder and the simple surrender of life. But there was also the fish wrapped in damp moss, the bloody hunks of deer or bear during the season, presented to her with prideful love and meticulous cooking tips. Teaching girls about their periods and pregnancy and boys about respect and responsibility. She told him all this so he'd understand her duty.

"This thing we have, Ray, it's portable, you know? You could come up there." They'd been laying on his futon looking up at the splotches in the ceiling where Ray Tate's daughter and her friends had re-plastered the bullet holes.

But just as Djuna Brown couldn't abandon her sad tribe, he couldn't abandon his cops, young chargers burst into a world with no supervisors, no one to teach them how to police, when to police. He imagined them dead on the road because no one told them not to lean on the cars they pulled over, not to disrespect a man in front of his family, to take a subtle step back, deal out some breathing room, to freeze a situation to give everyone a chance to get perspective, to get back to being human.

So she went to Indian country and he stayed in his streets. He didn't call unless he was drunk; she didn't call unless she had the deep blues. There was a lot of silence over the wires. He called less and less and so did she. It hurt too much. Then he just stopped, afraid that she'd find the combination of words and promises and dreams that would make him walk away from the city.

Once, after a bad day followed by a lonely night, he decided he'd had enough, he couldn't carry the water, didn't even want to. With a stub of charcoal, he parsed his early pension and his savings and the monthly payout to his ex-wife. He packed his car with clothes and paints and drove to an Amoco where he tanked up, meticulously cleaned the windshield, and bought a bag of snacks for the long drive north. He didn't call to tell her he was coming. He knew himself too well and knew he might fold at the last moment, before the last off-ramp to Indian country.

Just before he hit the Interstate north, his day-dreams of a life with a cocoa midget cop in the boonies evaporated in the slipstream of four screaming cruisers charging past him. He got in line, flashing his high beams, leaning his horn. On the Eight he climbed from his car, hung his badge around his neck, and waded through cruiser gridlock.

On the sidewalk a young charger with a bullet hole in his jaw lay grunting, comforted by his crying partner, a sturdily built young woman who looked barely out of her teens. Between them they seemed to have about fifteen minutes on the job. Ray Tate took control of the stage and set a perimeter. He ignored the three chargers who had the shooter down behind a dark blue van, stomping him.

The shooter screamed, "Why'd he let me do it, huh?" He gasped as he absorbed some boots. "What kinda fuckin' cop is that, huh?"

"He ain't wrong, Ray," a charger told him, catching his breath between bouts of the boots. "Kid was on the job about a week. He came up with a smile and hi-how-are-ya. So of course the guy shot him. He'd'a shot the escort too, except his piece jammed." He rubbed his hand on his slick face. "You want in, get a few licks for the team?"

"Another minute, Bobby, then I take him out of here. I'll need a car for prisoner transport."

"Ambo on the way, don't sweat it, Ray."

"Another minute, Bobby, I mean it, man, then you chain him up and read him the poem. You don't want to lose this in court."

Ray Tate carried the weight of dead bodies and the charger had to nod.

He drove home and unpacked his car. On his futon he twisted, not with the gunshot face of the charger in his mind, but the face of the downed cop's partner who'd repeated over and over: "What could I do?"

She had the gaunt brown face of Djuna Brown, the stressed old Djuna who'd come to the city as a basket case and left as a hero cop.

He thought about her all the time and he dwelled in the imagined grimy architecture of romantic Paris, sketching or painting her in the late nights, and in really bad times of temptation he unplugged the telephone and locked it in the trunk of his car.

But he never tried to leave again. A doorstep baby of the state who'd lived in the revolving doors of foster homes, the blue tribe was the only family, dysfunctional and protective, brutal and tender, that he'd ever had.

* * *

The bell tower above the courthouse sounded eleven-thirty. There was no sign of the fingerman from homicide. The gangbangers and sad lawyers and striding cops had abandoned the wide stone steps to the pigeons. Ray Tate gathered his raid jacket, rolled it inside out under his arm and went inside to the security kiosk. Subtly, he palmed his badge at the masked guards and went around the metal detectors. A masked court officer pointed wordlessly at the disinfectant soap dispenser mounted on a pillar. There were six pay phones studded to the wall in the gallery and each was in use, by people who showed no sign of hanging up any time soon. He headed for the stairs.

The noisy, crowded basement corridor was a moist lung. The bug, he thought, would like it here, in the humidity and sweat. Outside first-appearance court, he leaned beside the defaced docket thumb-tacked to the wall, waiting for court security to unlock the room. Most of the people churning in the hallway were relatives of suspects gathered up in a series of overnight crack raids. Most of them were black, and even with their masks on he recognized a few dealers from the Hauser Projects by the Ws shaved into their hair. There were only a couple of lawyers on hand, so the overnight arrestees would let the duty counsel sort their cases out and listlessly pitch for low bail. A man stared at Ray Tate briefly, then away, and then back, trying to penetrate the greying beard and combed-back long greasy hair. Ray Tate popped a kink from his spine, yawned, loudly sucked snot back into his throat, scratched his crotch, and slouched along the hall reading dockets, keeping an eye out for any well-dressed cop who looked like a hammer from Homicide.

When he checked up in the gallery again, the phones were still occupied. Ray Tate went outside and stood in the sunshine. A young blonde woman wearing a white mask climbed out of a taxi at the curb and crossed past the cenotaph, giving the hacking bum a wide berth. She peered at Ray Tate. "Sergeant Tate?" She kept her hands behind her back in case he wanted to shake. She stood eight feet away. She had pretty eyes and plucked, arcing eyebrows. Her voice was a little muffled. "Ray Tate?"

"I'm Tate." He started to drift but then disciplined himself, picturing her under the mask with a harelip, yellow teeth, and the firm shadow of moustache.

"I was told to tell you your target won't be coming out. He was taken from the lockup to hospital early this morning, DOA."

"The bug do him in?"

"Kinda. Someone wanted his mask and he wouldn't give it up. They stabbed him."

"Okay." He stood, shuffling his boots. "Ah, your guys still got that crime stage up, up in Hauser North?"

There was no ticket on the Taurus where it blocked a hydrant. There was no one to paper up the town; half the ninjas were out with the bug, the other half refused to get out and open their yellow tag books.

He backed out of the spot and went on the air, clearing the courthouse. "Desk, I'm rolling on a maybe, a couple of, ah, miscreants, in the vicinity of the Lite-Bite lunch."

The Desk played it straight, "Ten-four, sergeant solo. You require, ah, backup with that?"

"Negatories, Desk."

Her sweet voice almost put him into a reverie. The Hauser North stage was broken and gone, but he thought of heading up to the local sector and prowling in the paperwork, getting the name of the policewoman who'd voiced out for him. He could, he thought, find her on the road and apologize for not busting her stage, steering the apology into maybe a night out. He felt hangdog: when you fell into brief love with a pair of plucked eyebrows or a voice you were really hurting.

He was pulling into the lot behind the Lite-Bite when the dispatcher came back. "Ah, Sergeant Tate, come up on the air."

He responded.

"Yes, Sergeant, when you've finished ... investigating the two ... *hardboiled* suspected miscreants, you're to roll on headquarters, four-ten-s, ten-four?"

"Ten-four."

Room Ten at south end of the fourth floor at the Jank Center for Public Safety was the briefing room for the Chief's Squad for special projects. It could be anything: cold cases, maybe, a sensitive political operation or corruption. He hoped to get assigned to a target in a good part of town, where he could at least snaffle himself a good lunch on a patio while he surveilled whoever was in the chief's sights. If it was a police corruption case, he'd start coughing and reeling around and go for medical-off. He'd been targeted himself a couple of times over the years and been ashamed for the cops who would set up on other cops at the whim of Pious Man Chan, the lumpy, bald Chinese chief, the beast, badge number 666. He wondered what kind of mentorship they'd had.

He went into the Lite-Bite and ordered a Canadian bacon-and-egg sandwich on a bun and a coffee. The staff wore masks and some wit had tied one to the huge snout of a plastic pig mounted on the wall. He carried the greasy waxed-paper package out to his car and sat in the passenger seat, the door open, his legs out on the sidewalk. An elderly masked woman crouched near an overflowing trashcan, trying to tie a mask to her resisting schnauzer. He thought about his morning target, killed for not giving up his mask. Two Chinamen were on life-support after taking severe stompings because of the shape of their eyes. Cops were on lungs, doomed because they breathed public air.

He pitched his wrappings into a garbage can, got behind the wheel, and crept the curbs to the Jank. He'd forgotten his mask, hanging around his neck. Pulling it on as he drove, he heard the dispatcher send a solo unit to a critical collapse, a man in a dumpster. She made it sound like a sexy and inviting adventure. He decided that enough was enough. After his shift, he'd sit down and have a talk with himself, get past the dreams of

Djuna Brown and Montparnasse, maybe use the membership pass his daughter had given him, head down to the new art gallery and find himself a low-maintenance, Chardonnay-drinking divorcee who'd been to Paris.

The slat blinds on the windows of the Four Ten-S briefing room were closed to daylight. Fluorescent lights eliminated any real shadows, making a grey world of boring indifference. Half of the three dozen hard plastic chairs were populated by single-dimension, yawning slumped creatures. Someone was snoring. Conditioned air chilled the room. The ceiling was absorbent cork and the floor was gleaming green sheet-run faux tile. It was very quiet and grim, as if to not disturb the array of three women whose photographs were set up on a row of easels. Each easel held a smiling portrait of a victim in life, and beside it was a colour morgue shot of the same woman, although you couldn't be sure, because their faces had been taken apart and left unreassembled. The colours evoked avocado and eggplant and ivory, Ray Tate thought, deflecting with artistic distraction.

His ex-wife's father had been an ident guy. He'd told Ray Tate he saw everything in a single dimension and pretended he was photographing a photograph. When he was first on the job, he said, on bad jobs he shot the pictures upside down to give the victims less human shape and perspective, but he got over that. His ex-wife's father was a self-created tough guy who'd never pulled his gun but flashed it a lot under his jacket. He had a lot of imaginary cartoon adventures. Ray Tate marvelled that he'd once admired him. The old man's mantra was a shrug and a comment that it was all pensionable time, so who gave a shit?

Brian Comartin, the fat jogger who wrote poetry, was slumped in a middle row, rubbing his thumbs into his eyes. He saw Ray Tate slip in and pump soap from a dispenser, and waved him over. "Fuck, Picasso. Thirty feet from where we talked this morning, there was a girl under the ground. Thirty fucking feet. Now I'm wearing it because I was the senior guy on the detail. I'm fucking Traffic Flow. I'm not senior to nothing."

"That what this is about?" Ray Tate sat in the same row, a vacant seat between them. He heard people shuffling into the room behind him. A podium at the front waited.

"Yeah. Chief's special task force. They're saying someone might be taking off women, might be the same guy, might be different guys." Comartin shook his head. "Three fucking dead women and this is the first anyone hears about it. Now, for some reason it's priority one to shut this down. Someone said they think it's the Volunteers. Those women up there are all black."

"How'd the girl die, the one we stepped over."

"Well, she isn't dead. Yet. In some kind of a coma. Some people off a boat found her. They thought she was a goner, she was all beat to shit. Then she got semiconscious, then lapsed out." He put his elbows on his knees and his face in his palms.

"You okay, man?"

Comartin looked down at his running shoes. "Fuck, how'd I miss her?" He looked at Ray Tate and exercised raw cop sympathy. "Poor little bitch."

Ray Tate felt for him. "She able to give up anything? Before she lapsed?"

Comartin shook his head. "Naw, she said her dog or something saved her, then she yawned off to Nod."

A convoy of suits filed into the room and arrayed themselves at the podium.

Chapter 6

The city had taken a block of rooms at the Whistler Hotel in Stonetown. The lobby was frigid and none of the doormen or bellhops wore masks. The two women manning the check-in desk were clad in blue uniforms that resembled flight attendants' outfits. They were chic and cheery and wore scarves knotted at the collars of their white blouses. Neither had masks. The check-in desk was three feet deep and the air conditioning had been set to send a strong sheet of arctic air laterally across the marble top. There was little activity in the lobby. Staff inspected each other's tunics and brass buttons beside the antique wooden revolving doors.

"Good afternoon," Djuna Brown said softly to the nearest woman, showing her badge. "I'm Djuna Brown, with the State. They have a block?"

"Welcome to the Whistler," the woman said. Her name tag said "Front Desk. Gail." She didn't lean away, but she didn't get too close, either. She was pleasant but seemed to be examining Djuna Brown with curiosity. "The city has several rooms and suites on reservation for the State." She tapped into her computer. "Room, or suite? The suites, with mini-bars, full hotel facilities, are for, hmm, let me see ... oh, Inspector or above."

"Oh, that's me." Djuna Brown made a confident smile. "I was told a suite. I'm an inspector."

"Certainly, Inspector. We have a suite on the twelfth floor with a view of Stonetown. Will that be all right?"

"Perfect. How many of my people are here?"

The woman made a humming sound and scrolled on the computer screen. "Just you, so far." She continued tapping. "Will you need help with your bags?"

Djuna Brown shook her head. She dug into her purse. "Do you need an imprint?"

"No, Inspector. You're a guest of the city. No credit card required. You're all set."

"Yes." Djuna Brown smiled brightly. "I am."

The suite had a sitting room of deep red paint that looked like it had been lacquered on repeatedly and then buffed flat. The ceilings and wainscotting were thick cream. The lights were in sconces and there was a chandelier in the centre of the ceiling. On the floor was a woven carpet of intricate Middle Eastern or Asian design, and Djuna Brown thought she saw some Native symbols in the gold border. The pale window curtains were pulled back and tied with thick red ribbons; they sagged and glowed with heavy sunlight.

Bordello chic, Paris, 1920, she thought. "Not," she said aloud, "that that's a bad thing."

In the bedroom were framed reproductions of French paintings. The one above the bed was *Whistler's Mother.* The bed was wide with a vast engraved headboard and a telephone console on each side. French doors faced out onto a tiny Rapunzel balcony overlooking Stonetown. Far away, toward Canada, the green river wended north. A basket of fruit that looked like it was waiting for Matisse to drop by was on the dresser with a card welcoming her, in script, to the Whistler.

Djuna Brown felt excitement as though she was having a rendezvous in a country she'd never been to before. This could be Paris. She dumped her bag on the bed and went into the bathroom. There were gold fixtures, a frosted glass shower stall, a triangular-shaped tub with jets, another telephone, a space-age hair dryer, and a woven basket of several bars of fragrant soap and bottles of high-end shampoos and lotions. Two bleached-white bathrobes with WH entwined over the pocket hung from the back of the door.

After she poured a bottle of bath salts into the tub and adjusted the jets, she unclipped her clamshell holster, stripped out of her travelling clothes, and went out naked into the living room. The mini-bar was in a faux Looie Katorz hutch. It was crammed. She selected two little bottles of Bombay gin, dumped them into a glass, and, ignoring the cans of tonic, added tap water. Halfway to the bathroom, she went back to the bar and added another bottle of Bombay. She carried the drink and her holster into the bathroom.

In the tub, with her drink balancing on the edge, she drank and told the ceiling, "Raymundo, you don't get away this time, not from me, bucko." She cackled, but felt a stirring of uncertainty. She should have called him, found out what his scene was before she came down to the city. What if he'd hooked up with some tall, blonde, helmeted traffic chick, a vanilla motorcycle rider in bug goggles, jodhpurs, and boots, who rode him like a Harley in a headwind? What if some headquarters clerk with massive knockers had detected the beatnik artist hidden inside Ray Tate and played to it, *oohing* and *ahhing* over a killer cop who carried a paintbrush in his holster and acrylics in his handcuff case?

Djuna Brown leaned out of the tub and picked up the phone.

"Yes, Inspector. How may I help you?"

"Is that Gail? Gail, is there a spa in the hotel?"

"Yes, Inspector, the salon is on the second mezzanine. Shall I make you an appointment?"

"Please. The whole nine yards, top to bottom. Say, in a half-hour?"

After getting a genteel pounding and pulling in the massage suite, Djuna Brown sat beside Gail from the check-in desk, who was wearing street clothes in the salon. A masked Vietnamese stylist hummed softly as she buffed. The salon had windows that overlooked the park behind the hotel. The park was abandoned. The salon smelled of emollients and creams. Two women in glowing robes slipped past in slippers, talking in hushed tones. Djuna Brown had only been in a salon once since she left the city the year before, a trip down to Chicago to pick up a Native felon. Before scooping him up, she'd window-shopped at the boutiques along Oak Street, then headed to the Fairmont and had her hair re-spiked and a full body massage. The next morning, the felon, chained to the bar across the backseat, had asked her to crack a window in the truck, saying she smelled like a white woman.

Gail the receptionist looked at the bulge in Djuna Brown's robe pocket and asked, "Do you have to wear that everywhere?"

"The gun? Yep. Regulations."

"Did, ah ..." The woman seemed fascinated. Djuna Brown thought she was going to ask to see it, to hold it. But she didn't. "Have you ..."

"Used it?" Djuna Brown lied: "No." Gail seemed disappointed, so she said, "I've pulled it a couple of times."

"Could you? Use it? I mean ..."

"Well," Djuna Brown smiled, "you never know until you need to know." She resisted the impulse to put Gail on. "How's it here? You guys busy?"

Gail shook her head. "No. Usually there are five of us working on the desk. Two of them are ... They started coughing? There's the bug, so management transferred them to Minneapolis. You've heard about that? The bug?"

"Yep. Some scary shit."

"And the other girl was ... She died?"

"The bug?"

"No." Gail looked around. "Some guy murdered her. She ... He beat her ... to ... until she was ..."

Djuna Brown was going to make a quip, but saw the woman was becoming distraught. She had been going to say, Men, you can't kill 'em and you can't use their bones for soup. She wasn't much of a cook, but she knew you could kill them. Ray Tate had said reassurance was one of the tools in the toolbox. She patted Gail's hand. "It'll be okay. He'll get dropped." To change the subject, she looked around and said, "You get to use this place much?"

"We're running about twenty percent, and those checked in are the guests who pre-paid." She seemed on safer, more stable ground discussing concrete facts. "Management want us all to dress civilian and use the facilities, eat in the dining room, make the place look normal, busy." Then she licked her lips and she leaned over and whispered. "Is that why you're here? The bug? They say it's a Chinese person, smuggled over from Canada, maybe."

"I don't know about that. They said, head down to the city, help them carry the water." She stood up when the manicurist finished her nails. They were perfect. In her arctic robe she was led down a hallway and ushered into to a quiet dark room. It reminded her of the sweat lodge. She wondered if the entire spa experience was based on Native healing culture, a rip-off of a sacred rite by a society that resold it as a frill for rich women at three hundred bucks a pop. *Why not*, she thought, *we've taken every other fucking thing.*

After the silent attendant massaged oils into her face, adjusted the temperature, dimmed the lights, and set a small pot of potpourri on a heating pad, she closed the door, leaving Djuna Brown alone and naked to decide if she should feel guilty. She lay on the softest of beds wrapped in the thickest of towels in the faintest of wave sounds and wondered if she was wasting State money, dolling herself up like a ga-ga high-school student laying a trap for the football captain.

Ray Tate had probably moved on, she decided. He was a keeper, if you could get past the crusted paint on his hands, his still angst about losing his wife, the absence of his travelling daughter, his bullet scars, and, of course, that he'd killed two black men and a dyke. She herself had never thought she could get past dead black men. They were good shoots, but the optics and the resulting riots had shaken the police brass and the mayor to their core. Ray Tate had been sidelined.

Near the end of the X-men case, a jealous ex-cop dyke had put a few rounds into her Raymundo. "You made me a cop," she'd told Ray Tate as she lay with him on his futon, careful of the tubes in his body. "Now I have to go back up there. They need policing, those folk. They need a gentle hand."

But the city did, too. Ray Tate loved his young cops, and feared for them operating in a police culture run by oily sharks, where experienced mentors had been retired off the streets early, leaving insurance adjusters with slide rules and spreadsheets to make life-and-death decisions for cops barely out of their teens.

So she went and he stayed. Both did, separately, what they needed to do, she thought. Neither did, together, what they wanted to do.

Back in her room she felt half her age. Boneless from the working-over she'd had, she lay on the bed, pulling half the duvet up over herself, cocooning. She would, she decided, have to be careful about how she approached Ray Tate. If he was into something with someone, she'd have to determine if their time the year before was a transient situation or something that had a life of its own. Worst case, she decided with a lack of enthusiasm or belief, was she'd snag some hot young charger, bang him stupid, and head back up north to Indian country where she knew love would wither dry like one of the arid pods the grim elders rattled at the hopeful sky.

The phone purred as she was nodding off.

Chapter 7

The task force brainiacs filed in in their power suits, carrying folders and briefing sheets and wearing masks as if they were real cops who actually went out among the public. In the array of chairs only one cop, a tall string-bean black guy from the duty desk, wore his mask on his face. The others, under their chins, on the backs of their heads, over their hair. One guy had it hanging over his crotch like a jockstrap, with a happy face on it.

Ray Tate heard feet shuffling behind him. Chairs squeaked as bodies dropped into them with exhaustion. Someone snored. Someone groaned. He smelled medicated soap and cheap drugstore colognes used to mask, or at least thin out, the sweat of double shifts in closed cars on surveillance jobs and gun-and-runs. As plastic lids were popped or ripped behind him, he smelled coffee. There, too, were girlish scents: emollients, shampoo, cheap perfumes. He felt a stirring and wished he'd gone up to the Projects, mauled the files of the overnight homicides, and found the girl cop with a clothespin on her cute nose. The thought of another night painting and drinking and smoking and waiting for morning depressed him.

As the brainiacs huddled at the front of the room, someone a few rows in front of him expounded on night-vision scopes as a tool to stop the migrants. "We anchor some barges out in the river, put some dead-eye musketeers on them with HKs and night scopes. A snakehead comes over the river with a load of Chinamen, *pliinkkkk*, we cooks his rices for him."

"Nice, Tim. Except we don't got night scopes. We don't got HKs. We don't got barges. We don't got anchors."

Someone else said, "The loony mayor got us nice new bicycle lanes up and down Martyrs' Hill, though. The loony mayor got us bicycle racks on front of the new buses. The loony mayor got us ..."

A breathtaking blonde clerk in a short skirt swayed across the front of the podium and opened a brown envelope. She tacked a photo of the latest victim to an easel and there was instant silence. The clerk stared at the photograph for a moment, made a choked sound, then quickly walked away with her head down. The victim's face was misshapen, her lips were ballooned, one eye was gone in a purple explosion above her left cheek. Her nose lay sideways on her right cheekbone. Ray Tate thought of nothing so much as the fractured mirror of a Picasso painting. Tubes ran from her nostrils and a thick piece of plastic was taped to the corner of her mouth.

Beside him, Brian Comartin muttered, "Fuck, fuck, fuck, that poor little girl. Ah, Jesus Fucking Christ." He took a shaky breath and seemed near tears. "I'm gonna *kill* this guy."

Ray Tate put a hand on his shoulder and wondered if he was looking at his own near future, a fat globe in upper middle age, not sure if he could carry the water any longer, living out a ghost life in the cavernous headquarters with a slide rule in his ankle holster.

The chief of detectives took to the podium. Reluctantly, he slipped his mask down. He gazed over the slumping, yawning troops in their rumpled clothes and couldn't keep the disdain off his face. "Okay, everybody wake up, have ears. We're keeping this one shrink-wrapped, nothing outside this room. We've got three dead women and we've got this one found unconscious today. All were beaten. No sex assault, no robbery that we can figure out. Today's survivor and one of the other dead three were found by the riverbank. The other two were at various locations downtown.

"The highlights are, as I said, all young female African-Americans, all beaten to pulp, no weapon used that we can tell, no apparent robbery, no molestation. So, no apparent motive. Which means we might be looking at the racial aspect as the connector. We like the Volunteers for this. They're out all over town in their stupid red caps, and down by the river. They're very, very viable.

"The current victim might be our breakout. She was found this morning when some boaters were walking along the river. Her prints aren't on file. She's not a missing.

"So, today's vic remains unidentified. She had no ID, just some house keys, locks unknown. The good news is she's alive. Bad news, she's comatose, possible severe brain injury, so when she wakes up she might give us something to go on, or she might start reciting Willie Nelson lyrics in Swahili." He smirked, shrugging in a boys-to-boys grin, and when he saw he was facing grim rows of iron faces staring at the victim and not at him, he cleared his throat. "Okay, anyway, we can't wait to find out. We're going to take this one apart." The Chief of Ds looked around the room. "The folks who found her said it sounded like she was asking about her dog, Harris, or something. If she was walking her dog on the banks, probably she lived in the area. If she doesn't live in the area, she drove, so a team of cadets from the academy will start doing licence tags on the surrounding streets, looking for something that hasn't moved in two days. Maybe look for abandoned bicycles. They'll also work the vets and clinics in the area, talk to dog walkers. Someone knows her, someone knows the dog, Harris. With a little police work we should be able to put a house around her.

"That's new, that's the fresh stuff. A Homicide team is setting up. We've got forensics down at the latest crime stage. The Volunteers were out last night patrolling for migrant boats and they left some beer bottles and other printable debris along the riverbank. That's at the lab.

We're doing canvassing. Intelligence is doing workups on the main players in the Volunteers and you'll be given targets first thing tomorrow. It'll mean double shifts, hard luck, kids, but there's nothing I can do about it. We're all maxing out, we're all beat, we suck it up. You guys are the enforcement arm of this thing. Don't worry about the investigative side. Concentrate the eyeballs on the Volunteers." He looked pleased with himself, a man in command. His cheeks were closely shaven, his eyes were clear, and he wore the power authority suit of the brass, a deep blue three-piece over a snowy shirt and solid blue tie that wouldn't strobe in television lights. "Questions, suggestions, obs, so far?"

A woman called, "We putting out a public notice? People should know there's a public danger. Especially black women."

"We're working around to it, Marty. We don't want to spook the Volunteers before we take them down." He looked around. "Anyone else? Got obs, ideas, questions?"

"No, Chief. No, man." The same woman called, again, sounding distraught. "We have to notify. We didn't do it back in '04 and that guy got more women before we got him. City's still paying the lawsuit by the families of those victims."

"I know, Marty, I know. We're working something out. Anyone else?"

"Yeah, Chief, I got some *obs*." A bow-legged, red-headed gunslinger from the robbery squad stood up. His Montreal Canadiens jacket was slung over the back of his chair, he wore a double brace of

semi-automatics in a worn shoulder rig, and the handle
of a compact revolver jutted from the back of his blue
jeans. He wore his mask backwards on the back of his
neck with OH FUCK OFF scrawled on it in grease pen. "I
observe I'm fucking whipped. We been going around
the clock, some of us, for more than a week with this
understaffing bullshit and doing gun-and-runs and I
further *observe*, Chief, that except for sleeping in my
car, I haven't slept at all. I *observe*, Chief, also that with
the plague out there we're down about forty percent
street manpower and I further *observe*, with respect,
this whole fucking thing is a dog's breakfast and we're
the fucking dog." The gunslinger wasn't big but he
was wiry and coiled with frustration and exhaustion.
He'd put three roving French-Canadian bandits toes-
up during a single bank robbery. The holdup squad up
in Montreal had sent him the hockey jacket. Except
for Ray Tate, who'd done a trifecta, although not all at
one time, he was the only other gunman on the force
who'd wiped three shadows off the wall.

"Okay, Steve, okay. Noted." The Chief of Ds
looked around for raised hands. "Anybody else?"

The ginger gunslinger remained standing and continued as if the Chief of Ds hadn't said anything. "And
I further *observe*, Chief, that you and that Chinaman
police chief and that fucking mayor all showed up this
morning on the TV looking pretty snappy, like you'd
been at a restful spa for a week or two, napping flat
out on your back like human beings, then getting all
barbered up for the cameras. You tired, Chief? You get
your beauty rest last fucking night when I was sitting

in the Brickworks pissing in a paper cup? *Observe* me that one."

"Ah, ah, also noted." The Chief of Ds licked his lips. He wasn't going to tangle with a gunslinger with three notches on his gun butt. He looked around and focused on the tall masked black detective seconded from the duty desk. "Marcus, questions, obs?"

The tall detective stood up and reluctantly slipped down his mask. "What are we supposed to do about OT? I got about a hundred overtime hours in and —"

Someone yelled, "Sit down, you fucking ass meat-ball."

Someone called, "You do-dick motherfucker."

The tall detective turned, "Hey, I know it's tough this girl's in a coma, but, hey, I'm not, and my family's gotta eat, right?"

A woman's voice from behind Ray Tate shouted, "Sit down, you fucking duty-desk hump-assed mother-fucker."

There were hoots and hisses.

Another woman charger yelled, "Yeah, have some fucking respect, you fucking double douche."

The black detective said to the Chief of Ds, "What the fuck was she doing, Chief, going out alone, down by the river? At night? How stupid was she?"

"Yo," a woman's voice from the back of the room said. "*Whoa* the fuck up."

The tall black detective turned his head and looked into the rows behind him. "You think she's bright, this one, Marty? The river? At night? She's a dumb enough to be a kiddie cop."

A uniformed black woman from the Youth Services team launched herself through two rows of chairs, her shoulder taking him in the kidney, sacking him as if he were a daydreaming quarterback. Both went down. Chairs clattered and skittered across the tile floor. The Chief of Ds stepped away from the podium and pulled up his mask as though he didn't want to be polluted by the scent of sudden cop violence.

"Ten bucks on the chick, Picasso," Comartin said to Ray Tate. "You think she likes iambic pentameter?"

Ray Tate laughed. He watched the Chief of Ds and the task force leaders look at one another. The woman from Youth sat on the detective's chest, her knees pinning his arms down, rocking it to him first-class with a measured metronome of thoughtful lefts and rights. It was bloody, there were teeth. It sounded like meat. "No bet."

Four buff heavies from the door squad casually stepped into it. It took three of them to move the youth officer off the duty-desk hump. She really didn't want to leave the job unfinished. Ray Tate could tell the doormen just loved the black woman, they were talking softly to her, calling her Marty, patting her over to make sure she wasn't injured. She was swearing and heaving. The fourth doorman slung the limp detective over his shoulder and headed for the door, whistling.

The chairs were marshalled up; the room buzzed with laughter and comments. The Chief of Ds banged the side of his fist on the podium. "Not a fucking word of this gets out. I see any of this in the media, everybody in this fucking room is riding a pencil until you retire." He shook his head. "Fuck sakes."

The chief hammer from Homicide whispered into the Chief of Ds' ear. The hammer's name was Bob Hogarth but he was called Hambone. A legend was that on his first murder, a hubby-on-wife bludgeoning with no weapon found and the husband bobbing and weaving pretty good, he'd tracked back a lengthy grocery list from two days previous and saw a frozen ham bought on sale. He got a warrant for the undisposed garbage and the contents of the house, detailing refrigerators, freezers, and other receptacles where frozen meat might be contained. After the search turned up the hambone in the garbage, he introduced himself to the husband. "Detective Robert Hogarth, of the … *Ham*icide Squad." "Fuck," the husband blurted, slumping.

The Chief of Ds stepped back. Hambone Hogarth had a different kind of weight: his team was four for four on taking down cop killers dead. No one who'd ever killed a city cop on his watch was alive and doing time. He was smart and he knew cops: he had no mask, his suit was rumpled, he had bed-head, and he hadn't shaved. He'd been seen in the streets, knocking doors, visiting victims' families personally because he had a lot of manpower off sick. He lit off a whistle. "Okay, kids, the program's over. Decision of the judges? Unanimous. Marty Frost gets the title, she goes to the welterweight finals."

Another round of applause and whistles and the task force began seating themselves.

"*Aw riiii*," Hogarth said, and the room quietened. "We're getting some help. State's sending us some bodies. We got some auxiliaries, some kids from the academy. There'll be teams listed up on the board tomorrow. Everyone report here, seven a.m. We'll have all the prints from the bottles back, and we'll have a roster up, once we see how many bodies are getting borrowed to us. We'll keep up Volunteers surveillance by day, catch them for anything, traffic, spitting on the sidewalk, public mopery. But we bring 'em in and sweat them for the murders." He looked around. "If the girl wakes up and fingers the mayor as the guy, we can all go home, done the good job. Until then ..." He simpered, "We *thuuuck* it up."

There was scattered laughter. One charger in the back said, in a high-pitched voice and a lisp, "But what about the moneys ... The *over-thime*? ... I needs a Bra-*thill*-ian waxing, I gots ex-*penthess*."

Another said, "Keep the money, dude. Just pair me up with that cool chick over there behind Ray Tate. Where you from, honey?"

And Djuna Brown said, "Paris, bongo. I be from beatnik life."

Ray Tate felt her light, fragrant hand on his shoulder and a soaring in his chest. But he made his face bland, twisted in his chair and looked at her deadpan.

For a moment her heart dropped. He'd forgotten her, moved on.

Then Comartin said, "Fuck, Picasso, that looks like the chick you sketched this morning."

Djuna Brown smiled.

Chapter 8

They stood with Brian Comartin and Martinique Frost in the parking lot. The youth officer used tissues and spit to get blood off her knuckles. She'd opened the skin pretty good. A broken bloody tooth fell from the cuff of her uniform tunic. They all looked down at it for a few moments.

"Wow, that was ... Wow." Comartin was in awe. "Ah, I'm Brian Comartin, half a traffic cop, maybe, but all poet. You, ah ... This is Ray Tate, and ..."

Djuna Brown was a little in awe, too, of the stocky black cop. She'd seen violence but never delivered with such righteous determination. "Trooper Sergeant Brown? Djuna? Ah, with the State?" She spoke tentatively, as if she needed Marty Frost's permission to be that.

Marty Frost, blowing softly on her right-hand knuckles, shook hands all around, awkwardly using her left. "Pleased." She looked pretty happy in the afterglow.

Comartin said, "You, ah ... Wow." He couldn't take his eyes off her and kept glancing down at the bloody broken tooth.

Ray Tate and Djuna Brown glanced at each other, amused. The fat policeman shuffled like a schoolboy. Marty Frost stared at him as though she'd never actually personally spoken to a stout white poet before. They were the about the same age and height, and about the same build, but Marty Frost had an easy muscular confidence in the way she stood. Even without the uniform, Ray Tate would have made her as a cop, would have recognized her as a charger even in silhouette. Her authority emanated.

She waited, watching Comartin. She seemed amused, too.

"You, ah, you like, like ... poetry?"

When she spoke, her voice was flat as if dealing with a suspect in the night. "*Po*-et-tree."

"Ah, yeah. You know. Moon, June, spoon."

"I'm into rap. You into rap, Traffic man?"

"Not so much. Yet?"

"We'll see. You married?"

"No. Not anymore. Just to my poetry."

Marty Frost turned to Djuna Brown and shook her head. "Hustlers, the both of them. White boys looking to score off us dark sisters."

"Really?" Djuna Brown made a sad smile of perfect little white picket teeth. "I heard of guys like that. But I never actually, you know, met one before." She looked up from under at Marty Frost. "We don't have that kind of stuff up in Indian country."

While Marty Frost made a show of looking Comartin up and down, Ray Tate read her. In angry battle she'd looked heavier and had thickened fixtures infused with anger, her grey-tipped cornrows held flat by tiny intricate African-looking barrettes. But now, outside the task force briefing, deflated back to normal size and calm in the sunshine with the violence out of her system, she was pretty and relaxed. Ray Tate figured she was into her late forties, maybe fifty, and he computed where she was on the job twenty-five years earlier. Tough days, he thought, tough nights. Any female cop who came out of those days in one piece and stuck it out was a little tougher than he could handle. He felt bad for Brian Comartin. He was in for an interesting time. He was going to miss his traffic surveys.

"Okay, Traffic man." Marty Frost nodded. She knew she had him cold. "First date, we double date, okay? Nothing on the first date unless I say so. Don't make me give you a beat down."

Brian Comartin looked insanely happy, as though a thorough beat down was all he'd ever wanted out of life. "I can get behind that."

"Yeah, we'll see." She turned to Djuna Brown and smirked triumphantly. "Two weeks, I bet, two weeks and I got him wearing gold chains and puffy Converses." She handed around her business cards and said to call her for dinner. "We'll go out and eat some food and we'll figure out how to get some justice for those poor ladies." She nodded at the geometric Jank

Center behind them. "Those pinheads couldn't catch their ass."

"Oh, let's do dinner at my place." Djuna Brown made a bright smile. "I'm at the Whistler. Great dining room. All in on the tab. Dinner's on the state. Ah, ask for Inspector Brown, okay? They got confused when I checked in. Seven o'clock? In the dining room?" She nodded to herself. "Marty, if you want, come by at six before dinner for a spa session. I'll book it. The state owes you a spa day. No charge, because your state government appreciates the contribution of municipal law enforcement in the maintenance of a safe and civil society."

Martinique Frost nodded. "It's about fucking time."

Djuna Brown knew there'd been no harlot with big boobs and no goggled Harley harpy in Ray Tate's immediate past. His need was unfulfilled. He had no new tricks, no new moves. He was a ga-ga schoolboy. In the Taurus racing to the Whistler he nearly cracked up a couple of times, glancing at her as if she might not still be there. In the elevator, the moment the doors swished shut, he had his hands on her; in the hallway he urged her along. The moment they walked into the bordello of the suite he was all over her. His breathing was heavy. The rough chintz of the loveseat rubbed on her but she hadn't actually removed any clothing and it was a just matter of friction and noise. Her little bra

ended up over a French lampshade, her Chicago pant-
ies around one ankle. She felt he wanted to devour her,
and afterwards, as she lay on top of him, finally naked,
she asked him about his habits.

"Well," he said languidly, "it's been a while.... A
couple of days, anyway. A chick in Records. Just physical. Nothing serious. You?"

"A guy from the new sawmill. He couldn't keep
his hands to himself. I had to cuff him up, get the
thing done."

"Fucking civilians."

"Fucking civilians. But, hey, when you got the need,
you got it, right?" She looked down at him to make sure
he knew she was kidding, that he was kidding. "Really?
You have someone?"

"You have a logger?" His hands were on her face,
as if to confirm the brown little face was actually under
the spiky hair and that she was this close to him.

"No. No logger."

"Then, no, no chick in Records."

"Okay, okay, then." She stretched luxuriously.
"I could get used to this. Paris must be like this. You
ever think about it, Paris, anymore? Running away?"
She trailed her thumb over the bullet scar near his hip.
"With me, I mean?"

"Yeah, yeah, I do. At night, mostly, when I'm
painting. But then, in the daytime ..."

"I want to see your new stuff, what you've been
painting. After dinner tonight, let's go to your place.
You still in the apartment where she ... Where you
got shot?"

"Yep. Gin in the fridge, water in the pipes."

"Gin and taps. I haven't had one since the last time I had one with you. Well, except a triple-o when I checked in." It had been a joke, a kind of inside joke between them back when they began seeing each other. One or both of them would have gin but neither ever had any mix, and if they did, they lied. A lime was heresy. They spent drunken soft nights sipping gin and tap water like fools and parsing their pensions for a lifetime in Paris. Djuna Brown thought of it as their beatnik dream.

She put her head into his neck and muttered, "Beatnik," and rolled over onto him.

She mixed their drinks and they carried their guns and robes into the bathroom. While the tub filled she called the front desk and made an appointment for Martinique Frost, a guest of the state government, in the spa at six, and a reservation for four at seven o'clock in the dining room.

Watching her standing naked, looking tiny and brown in front of his eyes, Ray Tate lay in the tub of bubbles and mentally engraved the moment for later at his easel, where he could conjure her presence, even in her absence. He had a mental catalogue of those gravure moments and they'd keep him painting and sketching for a lifetime in imaginary Paris. He was already becoming overwhelmed by the possibility of changing his life, of not being a cop but instead being something more internal.

When the phone rang at seven o'clock, they were still in the tub enjoying long conversations about nothing amongst long periods of contented silence. There was nothing left they could do. It was as though the year apart had been a long blink. The bathroom was dim and the water, emptied and refilled hot a half-dozen times, was again tepid.

She caught the phone on the fourth ring, standing at the wall phone, listening. The receptionist announced their guests were seated in the dining room. Djuna Brown, a dark shadow of form in a dark flat shadow, thanked the woman softly, although she wanted to scream abuse at her for bringing the real world of broken dead ladies into their Paris.

Chapter 9

Under the wide crystal chandelier in the dining room, Brian Comartin and Martinique Frost debated whether to order drinks or wait for Ray Tate and Djuna Brown. Comartin said if the state was picking up the tab, he was up for a bottle of Cliquot. He'd been researching wines, he told Marty Frost, in anticipation of moving to Europe, particularly Spain, living on his half of his pension and working on his poetry.

"Get the champagne, poetry man," Marty Frost told him. "They're upstairs banging. I know it. They're gonna be late or we might not see them at all, you ask me. You see how they looked at each other at the Jank? They've got history, those two. I bet they didn't even get the car parked before they were all over each other." Even though Ray Tate and Djuna Brown were only a half-dozen years younger than her and Comartin, she shook her head and smiled. "Kids."

She ran her eyes over his ill-fitting suit with amusement. She could tell he'd spent some time preparing: his hair was still damp, he was freshly shaven, and she smelled cologne. But his eye sockets still sagged, and he looked exhausted. Everybody on the job looked tired the last while. But at the same time he looked a little excited and shy and she felt a bit of it herself. No one had been interested in a long time.

She wondered how to handle him. Before being sidelined to the youth squad, she'd been a Sector Four detective, periodically detached to Homicide on sex cases. She was in demand for tough jobs that needed a certain hand. Now she was a just another brick in the wall. Being a brick wasn't bad, necessarily. It simply meant you were a nobody like all the other blue nobodies, competent maybe, but without the distinction or talent to stand out. You were interchangeable with all the other bricks, part of the average crowd, a blue grid of wallpaper. You'd never get ahead, you'd never fall behind. Not being noticed had become her status quo and she was confused about the shy interest from this fat white poet.

Her investigative specialty was conversation, although she never got to exercise it much any longer on the surly youths that came through her office. She hated the term *interrogation*. It was oppressive. Even *interviewing* wasn't what she did. Dialogue had been her specialty. For hours she could sit in a room with a murder suspect and chat the day away, never asking a direct relevant question, slowly bringing the conversation around to why they were really there. People found her likeable, and, before being handcuffed and led away, many seemed to want to hug her or shake her hand. She always closed. Now she tried to get children to explain why they were voids, why they murdered and beat and robbed and raped. But they had no vocal skills beyond yelling and threatening and whooping.

Brian Comartin was intimidated, knowing he was a cop in name only. He could detail how many cars on an average Wednesday in winter went through the intersection of Erie Avenue and Stonetown Way in any direction and at what average speed. He could tell you the gradient of Harrison Hill. He knew the loony mayor had the lights through the downtown timed so motorists never caught a break, forced to stop at each intersection, idling and fuming, then gunning to the next corner, only to be caught by another red light. There were twenty-seven miles of bicycle lane across the city, used for ten months, maximum, by two hundred people, maximum. He wondered what he could talk about to a real cop over a glass of wine under a crystal chandelier.

The sommelier came by and saved him, offering a thick wine list. Comartin, who had been to Champagne for two nights during a two-week vacation after his divorce, handed it back without opening it. "We'll have Cliquot. Chill it a little longer than you want to. Flutes, please."

The sommelier bowed slightly and went away.

"Flutes keep the bubbles longer, better bouquet," Comartin said for the sake of something to say. "If you'd prefer, I can get you a coupe."

Marty Frost recognized a suspect filling silence with babbling bullshit and began having the first really good time she had, except for acing the headquarters hump that afternoon, in a year. She stared at him without blinking.

"The coupe is the shallow glass." Comartin rambled. "They say it was modelled on Marie Antoinette's breast."

Marty Frost turned her head slightly to the left and raised an eyebrow.

Comartin licked his lips. "The left breast."

Marty Frost smirked a little cynical smile to go with her raised eyebrow.

"But, ah, it was actually invented before she was born."

Marty Frost watched him try to mine the arcane for a moment, then had pity on him. "Traffic man, slow down. You might got a shot."

Comartin felt a thrill. He had tales about how to uncork champagne, tales about the life and times of Widow Cliquot. His hold-back story of his adventures in the champagne world was when he beheaded a bottle with a long sabre, the only person on his tour to do so on the first attempt. It was a rare, almost accidental physical accomplishment and the wine company had given him a certificate.

He decided to save that for when he knew her better, when he needed the edge.

As the wine steward subtly twisted the cork from the champagne, Djuna Brown entered the dining room, alone. Her hair was spiked and glossy. She wore a pair of batik-brown harem trousers, a sleeveless batik-blue shirtwaist blouse, and her lucky red slippers with the little silver decorations. Turquoise good-fortune earrings that some children in Indian country had made to protect her from harm dangled from her earlobes. Her skin shone. Her gun hiked the loose batik blouse a little behind her right-hand hip, and she looked boneless, fluid. In anticipation of connecting with Ray Tate and possibly having to pry him off a city chippy she'd packed a short black skirt, a tight red silk blouse, a push-up bra, and high heels she'd picked up in Chicago. Where to keep her gun out of sight had been a problem, and she'd wished she'd looked into a garter holster. She was certain that her little silver automatic in a black garter when he ran his hand up there would put him through the roof. But clearly the skirt and push-up and garter hadn't been needed. The tight red silk blouse action could be kept in reserve for when he flagged.

She saw Martinique Frost and Brian Comartin staring at each other over the candles on the table under the sprawling chandelier. They looked like stiff kids on a date.

As she slipped into a chair, she looked around and said, "Oh, Ray's not here yet? Anybody seen him?" Her long cat's eyes were wide and innocent.

Martinique Frost made a cynical smile. "Gee, wonder where he could've got to. Sure you want to stick to that attitude? I've locked guys up who went with that. And I haven't seen a hickey in a long time."

"Well," Djuna Brown said, caught but fighting it out, her hand going to the light red mark on her throat, "probably he went home from headquarters to get a jacket or something? Caught in traffic. He lives up past the cemetery." She added, "I think he said."

"Traffic man here is telling me they modelled a champagne glass on a woman's boob. You ever had a guy hit on you like that? The boob in the glass shot?"

Comartin, carefully dribbling Cliquot into a glass for Djuna Brown, murmured, "If he was going directly from the Jank to up past the cemetery he'd been here by now. Twelve lighted intersections. Even with the signals timed against him, rush hour, the traffic off the Eight runs to about two hundred cars per twenty minute cycle, average, north and south. I figure, conservative, twenty-two minutes, unless he went to siren and lights."

"Yep," Martinique Frost said, nodding at Comartin. "A shower, ten minutes. Dry off, maybe five or six. Dress up for the dining room, five, maybe ten minutes. Drive back, the Eight is thin downtown-bound by then, well, I figure he'd've been here long time before us, ordering the champagne when we walked in. So, maybe not? Maybe he got into something else, didn't go home at all, lost track of the time, until late?"

Djuna Brown sipped the champagne, the bubbles tickling her nose. Happily, she looked from Martinique Frost to Brian Comartin. "Boy," she said, "I have a feeling that these guys dropping the women have no fucking idea what they're up against."

But she was pleased that her glow showed.

* * *

Ray Tate crossed the dining room, tucking in his shirt under his jacket, and dropped into a chair. "Sorry 'bout that. Traffic."

Martinique Frost nodded. "Djuna here told us you had to run back to headquarters."

"Ah, yeah, I forgot some stuff."

She looked at Djuna Brown. "Amateur."

Throughout dinner they talked about the city and the job, getting to know about one another without making declarative statements about who they were. You couldn't tell a story in which you were heroic or victimized.

Martinique Frost told about receiving a birthday card that morning, even though it wasn't her birthday. A sad tale of a man who killed his abusive girlfriend and, when he confessed, had wept and said he wished he'd had her for a girlfriend instead, but it was worth killing his girlfriend just so he'd meet her. So she didn't die in, like, vain, right? It had been six years earlier and she'd broken him down by saying she was going to miss her birthday dinner; her kids were waiting for her. But I'll stay with you, she told him as he cracked, because I know you're a good person who made a mistake. That did him and he rushed his confession so she'd get home for the dinner birthday party. He still sent Marty Frost handmade birthday cards from the craft shop up at Craddock.

Brian Comartin savaged the mayor for snarling traffic, ordering projections guaranteed to put more people on bicycles. When another guy in Comartin's office suggested the city issue bicycle licences, the mayor had him shipped off to the morning court run. It was a weak story and Marty Frost gave a small shrug to Ray Tate.

Ray Tate smiled and told about the cop ophidiophobia with who was able to respond to the py-py-pythons call because he'd overcome his arachnophobia.

Djuna Brown told a sweet story about when she and one of her troopers were chasing a drunken but very fast Native burglar across an ice field one night. The trooper jumped in the cruiser and drove around the ice field to head off the fugitive. While Djuna Brown, awkward in her mukluks, was in pursuit, she slipped on the ice and fell hard with a grunt. The Native dropped his loot, skidded to a stop and ran back to help her up, apologizing, make sure she was all right. I'm sorry, Miss, he said, please. Djuna Brown was smiling, fondly remembering. "We gave him the charge but we didn't beat him."

"Nice one, Djuna." Martinique Frost recognized the sweet sadness on her face, that she was, by her choice of story, letting everyone know who and what she was about. That she loved policing and she loved the people she policed. "I thought that was a bad posting up there, Indian country. Where the State Police sent you, get you to quit. What do they call it? The Spout?"

Djuna Brown nodded. "The Spout. Where they drop you in and they pour you out." She gave them all a gay grin. "They think sending you someplace to police folks who really need help, that that's punishment. That the work is punishment. You guys, when we get this thing down, with those poor dead women, you're all coming up there. My treat. We'll go fishing."

Marty Frost said, "Speaking of the poor dead ladies? I talked to a guy at Homicide." She took a leather-bound police notebook from her purse, then dug out a pair of half-frame bifocals and set them over her flat ears and on her perfect nose and began reading. She glanced up over them at Comartin staring at her. "What?"

Brian Comartin thought he was going to go into cardiac seizure.

She recited: "Belinda Clarke was killed first but her body was found second. She was a prostitute. Five-foot-two, one ten, slender, crack addict, single mother, soliciting, soliciting, soliciting, unarmed robbery against person, possession, possession, and possession. Found fully clothed and pulverized on the riverbank where she trolled for lonely men living on the boats moored offshore. Cause of death, massive trauma to left side of body, massive head injuries. Body found partially covered in shallow depression ten feet from the river's edge. A crack pipe and some rock and a hundred and forty bucks in small bills found in a hollow tree five feet from death site." Martinique Frost looked up. "This is a good lady. Eight men living on boats, three of them still married, all kicked in for her funeral. All attended. One of them opened a bank account for her two children. All were cleared as suspects. This lady never pissed off anybody, not for this. She was just dealt the low cards when she was born. Everyone used the same two terms: gentle and conflicted. One guy said she had a sweet soul." Martinique Frost kept her face in decided neutral. She didn't know them well enough to expose any emotional substratum. "If it hadn't been from the location and circumstances she was found in, the Homicide guy said it could've been a truck-on-pedestrian accident. She was punished."

It was work, now, no fun and games about breasts in coupe glasses or quirky little cop stories. They all gave Martinique Frost their attention. She demanded it. She was doing the good work.

"Ms. Clarke died overnight June 9th and was found June 12th, after victim number two was found on the 11th. There was a lot of rain and there was nobody on the riverbank to find her. The Volunteers hadn't gone public yet, that we knew of, they hadn't started their patrols and shit. So, number one, Ms. Clarke, was found after number two, Ms. Smith, was killed.

"Number two killed second, but found first, was Mariam Smith. June 11. Female, black, thirty, no criminal, no police interaction. Receptionist here at the Whistler, eight years. Married common-law to a hotel handyman, no kids. Ms. Smith is found in the alleyway between the rear of this hotel and that new complex of antique shops on Superior. Same COD. Massive left-hand body trauma, head injuries. No sex, no robbery. Her left-side torso bones had been pretty much powdered and her head jellied. Because victim one hadn't been found yet, and number three hadn't been killed yet, the hammers from Homicide went after the husband, your basic yawn theory. They work him up, sweat him a little, and then number one is found, Ms. Clarke, prostitute, cracker. And things get steered off that way."

Brian Comartin could tell there was more to what Martinique Frost was saying than a mere recitation of facts. She was spending something. He wished they were still alone in the dining room so he could ask, but all he could do was sit there and hope to understand it later.

"Now, after Ms. Clarke and Ms. Smith, they're thinking they've maybe got someone out there starting a run. And when number three, June Flowers, is found, June 19, they start to put them all together. Ms. Flowers, female black, single, twenty-two, waitress at the Stoney on Erie, night student in veterinary sciences at the university. She's found off Harrison Hill, in a vacant lot she cut through to get to the rear entrance of her apartment building. Cause, injuries, circumstances, all the same as the first two, powdered and jellied. But then the bug hits and right off three hammers are off the Homicide roster. An analysis guy is recruited to put the three into a frame, but he gets the bug and becomes the first known non-Asian fatality." She paused and tried to make a little smile. "Vagaries of life, right?"

Ray Tate knew what was going on, where she was going. "Marty, we can finish this later, you know?" He knew her story. "Don't go so hard."

"I'm okay, Ray. So, now, nothing happens. We've got the gang shooters up in Hauser dropping about one body every two days. We've got a run on domestics. We've got the contract killing of the State's ombudsman's wife. The Volunteers are running riot on the Asians. The bug is everywhere. Everything sucks energy and manpower from the ladies' murders. And it sits there, until this lady this morning is found. Something off-stage happens, probably because word's getting out that we're under white-power siege and these are all black victims, and they put together this task force. Me, I think it has something to do with the election coming up, there's some political agenda here. But, actually, I don't care. We're going to work for the poor ladies and this is going to be the good work."

Brian Comartin waited a beat. He saw Ray Tate and Djuna Brown glance at each other with sad knowledge. He was affected by the synopsis on some level, but couldn't identify why. He didn't have the ear.

After a moment of silence, Martinique Frost looked up, her mood changed up. She cleared her throat, dry. "Traffic man, we need a nightcap."

Comartin instantly decided against champagne. It didn't feel right. Champagne is for when we're happy, he'd been told in Champagne. He felt a lot of things, looking at Martinique Frost, but happy wasn't any longer one of them. Champagne was out of the question.

Without asking anyone, he subtly flagged a waiter and ordered a round of cognac.

The State paid for three rounds of cognac as well as the food and champagne. Djuna Brown signed the bill with an exaggerated flourish, adding a liberal twenty percent. The smallest of them all in body mass, she teetered a little. They trooped out of the dining room and across the lobby and out the revolving doors. The heat, even late at night, was heavy. Six Volunteers in their red baseball caps swaggered down the opposite sidewalk, looking wound up and deprived of someone to stomp.

Djuna Brown yawned. "Glad I'm already home. You guys okay to drive?"

Comartin said he was okay. "Genetics, I'm Irish. I can run these guys home. I'm Traffic man and anyway none of the guys is into doing road stops in case they inhale the bug."

Martinique Frost was tipply, but okay. "Traffic man *and* poet." She batted her eyelashes at him. "All in one cool package."

Ray Tate said he could hack it. "We'll all need cars in the morning anyway for the task force briefing. I'll swing by, pick up Djuna on the way in. So fuck it. Brian, we'll go in a convoy to the Eight, then make a run for it. You've got the crash car so you go first. Anybody red-lights us, you ram 'em while the rest of us scram. Every man for himself."

Comartin nodded solemnly. "Sounds like a plan."

They said goodnights and left Djuna Brown on the steps of the hotel. Ray Tate got into the Taurus, Marty Frost into one of the Chryslers, and Comartin into the traffic crash car. He led the way out of the driveway. Just before they hit the Eight, Ray Tate dropped back and circled back to the hotel, picked up Djuna Brown, and headed to his apartment.

"I can't believe you still live here, Ray." She remembered their nights the year before, especially their final night when Ray Tate, freshly shot and recovering with tubes in his body, showed sadness that she was heading back up to Indian country. They'd expected to be fired and had planned to head to Paris with their buyouts, where he'd wear a beret on the Left Bank and lean on an easel while she posed on a duvet and learned to cook cassoulet. "I'd've thought you would have moved out of here."

"Too much hassle. The light's great and I got a new ceiling, guy upstairs got a new patch of flooring." In spite of the new paint and plaster the ceiling showed bullet gouges that had been ineptly and cheaply repaired. He wondered why he didn't move out. But the apartment was the first place he'd ever lived alone. Before that it had been state orphan homes, the police academy dormitory, and the suburban house with his now ex-wife.

Djuna Brown looked at the framed prints on the wall. She could tell it wasn't Ray Tate's work. The pictures were almost cartoonish but done with a knowledgeable hand and they all went together in a distinctive kind of way. Ray Tate tended toward a more traditional sad hand, dark in charcoal and grim acrylics and less celebratory of life, kind of 1920s Paris before the Crash sent everybody back to America. These looked cheerful and deep at the same time. "This guy looks like fun."

"Canadian. A guy named Tony Calzetta. I went up to Canada and over to Toronto, saw an opening. I got a deal, so I got the three of them." He didn't say that he'd driven up to Canada through Indian country and couldn't make himself veer off the interstate to visit her. On the drive up he'd felt a thrill in his chest, tempting himself that he'd stop and see her and maybe never drive back to the city. Passing the feeder roads into Indian country he'd had a chest full of loss, almost of cowardice. But he pressed on, and in Toronto he'd visited a tiny gallery in Little Italy, fell in love with the prints, and dug for his wallet. He'd returned home, crossing at Buffalo, and suffered the cracked, broken highways across the bottom of the lakes, avoiding Indian country, avoiding temptation. He hung the three Calzettas for inspiration, to show different artists had different art, that there were places in life for colours and serious fun, far from the black moodiness of his charcoal.

She took off her clamshell holster, put it on top of a bookcase, and found a bottle of gin in the fridge. "We got any mix?" She laughed and turned on the cold water and popped off her batik top, staggering a bit in her little sports bra. She whooped, with a dirty leer, "Party time, sailor."

They were too excited to sleep much into dawn and just dozed to absorb the minimum rest they needed. At five-thirty, when light only barely thinned the darkness in the corners of the room, he awoke to find her looking at him.

"Ray? What do you think? Marty and her synopsis?"

"How long you been awake?"

"Little while. I was thinking about Marty, what she said. *Poor ladies. Ms.* this and *Ms.* that."

"I made a couple of quick calls. Martinique Frost is a very interesting lady. Comartin, who knows?"

That meant Marty Frost had been worth gossiping about and Comartin not.

"He's okay, though," she said. "He's got a good heart. And I think he might be crazy about Marty." She rolled onto him, more for convenience on the futon than for the carnality of it, but if it went dirty, what could she do? He was a bigger than her; she'd just have to ride it out. "What's her story?"

Ray Tate's apartment was on a lower floor of the old, squat apartment building, but it faced northwest to the distant East Chinatown. There was more light in the sky over there than there should have been, impossibly yellow throbbing and glowing in the northern sky, where the sun never rose. Sirens were raging at a distance. His cellphone, in the pocket of the sports jacket tossed on the floor on top of his ankle holster, began beeping.

Chapter 10

In the rear-view mirror Brian Comartin saw the Taurus peel off and head back toward the Whistler, just before the three-car convoy hit the ramp-on to the Eight. He smiled. He liked Ray Tate and Djuna Brown. Some cops could tell and re-tell their days of combat, how they put down the bad guy in a heroic blaze of gunfire glory and lived to tell the tale. They were intimidating, challenging in a seemingly bluffing but truly serious kind of way. But Ray Tate never referred to it, never mentioned the shootings or himself getting shot. That Djuna Brown in her batiks and little sparkly slippers had taken out an armed maniac was almost impossible to comprehend. He hadn't been in company of real cops for most of his career and usually felt a little intimidated. But these two were ditzy, it seemed, with thoughts of marathon banging in Paris. Brian Comartin's dream was the streets of Barcelona and long thoughts chewing on a poet's pencil. But it was the same dream.

The black Chrysler was gone from his rear-view and he thought that he'd outrun Martinique Frost. But then she was up beside his driver's door. She activated her inside light and pointed her finger ahead. He slowed and she pulled in front. They went past his exit at a steady speed. Well in time for the exit onto Huron, she activated her indicator and moved into the right-hand lane and onto the ramp-off. He followed, his mind a jumble of absent condoms, his overweight torso and body issues, and shortness of breath, having sex for the first time with a black woman. For a moment he felt like losing her accidentally on purpose.

But he stayed nailed thirty feet off her bumper. For the first time his life felt like uncharted free-form poetry.

Martinique Frost talked the night away in the kitchen of her duplex on the edge of Bricktown. He didn't make a move; he didn't know how and was waiting for an opening he knew he wouldn't recognize. She didn't call him poetry man or Traffic man. She was a little drunk and into herself enough to call him Brian. He was falling for her, she could see, and had a right to know, in case he wanted to pull back, give things a little thought. Ray Tate, she knew, would have done a casual workup on her if it looked like they'd be out and about together on the dead ladies case, but Comartin wouldn't know what to ask and if he did he wouldn't be able to parse the meaning out of the answers he'd get. Something as innocuous as someone saying, "She works hard; never missed a day off injured," could sound like a compliment to a non-cop ear. But in reality it meant, Look out, she won't get down in the blood and the mud and the beer, if it comes to that.

For a full half-hour Comartin didn't say a word. She spoke. He listened and tried to realize what his eyes were seeing across from him under the yellow light above the table that smudged sockets under her eyes. He'd had a wife a long time ago, a time of angry yells or depressive silence that had collapsed his marriage. He'd been uptight, frustrated, and only later realized he bore the blame because he never listened. Right out of high school he'd become a cop for the regularity of it, the constant paycheque, the protection of the union, early retirement. Not one day, he realized, had he actually liked being a cop. In spite of his square Irish body and red hair, his big freckled hands and his measured, lumbering cop walk, he'd felt there might be something else inside him. It was almost as though he became a cop because he looked like one.

His wife couldn't successfully contain a baby to term and he didn't want to adopt. She deteriorated under his autocratic decision-making, under his constant depriving her of the life she wanted. Unlike the poet, or at least the poetry lover he later detected faintly within himself, he'd become a violent, loud bully and not slow to shove her around when he couldn't articulate why his life was a failure. One day he went too far, and she filed from her hospital bed. On his divorce retreat, the trip to Europe where he'd gone to drink and unsuccessfully make love to slim young women, he discovered something hidden in himself when he found a book of poetry in English by Denise Levertov in the lobby of the Hotel Blu in Marseille. It was that easy. Picking up a book.

It spoke something to him, and he took it to his room and read it slowly and was so amazed that he almost phoned his wife. Instead, he sat on the lumpy bed and stared at the staggered lines of words in the book his hands. Words weren't only for threatening and browbeating and haranguing. He'd go home and remain a cop but he'd find a duty where he'd never have to put his angry hands on anyone. Administration. He'd learn to listen to both his own rhythms and the rhythms of others. Maybe, he thought, he'd find a poem of staggered lines inside himself.

In the duplex kitchen, Martinique Frost said she wanted just to talk, and it was going to take a while. He listened, and understood the human value of that.

She tried to keep her face as flat as her words. "You ever work Tin Town? Used to be there wasn't a cop down there that hadn't been battered or stabbed or shot. Not one. They'd send you out to direct traffic, you go with a partner, you both strap on the vest. You go for coffee fifty feet from the station, you strap on the vest, take a buddy. Guys down there carried shotguns, day or night. Everybody carried a bounce because when you get confronted you don't worry about escalating to lethal force, you just went straight to it and threw down your bounce on the ground beside the guy. Self-defence. Every cop that came out of there was either a super-cop or a mindless behemoth.

"Shitty people, shitty neighbourhood, but with some gentrification, which means tear them down, or burn them down, you could have nice condo towers, nice views of the river. So, in go the developers, the realtors. Buying land, buying up leases, out with old in with the profitable. Where there was a bail bondsman, now there's a real estate office. The cheque-cashing place? A café. Antique shops where the laundromat was, and then bistros and high-end designer food. A wine shop. A cooking school."

Brian Comartin felt like he had to say something, to show he was paying attention. "Like, a new Stonetown?"

She gave him that, but the Traffic man, she thought, didn't know the interrogative values of silence. "Exactly. So, straw men secretly representing developers start buying up the houses. Tin Town had great houses. Tin roofs, old stained-glass windows above the doors. But what they didn't have were firewalls. If one row house caught fire, well, up they all went. And they did. The bulldozers go in and some skyscrapers go up. Condos, mostly. A few rental buildings. Aimed at the downtown workers in their twenties who want to bicycle or hike to work, sit on their balconies over the quaint streets and the river, sip cappuccino after a hard day at the bank or the brokerage, whatever.

"So, I'm working Tin through a lot of this. Detective in the Sector office. There are still a lot of shitheads, so I'm busy, but there's an influx of yuppies into the condos. They form a neighbourhood coalition.

When there's a bunch of bicycle thefts, they're down to the Sector, complaining. When a flasher jumps out at the women doing yoga in the new park, they're down to the Sector, complaining. They're paying all this tax money for an expensive apartment, they want the policing they're paying for.

"The lieutenant, when the first complainants come in, yawns and nods, uh huh, uh huh. They don't like that, those coalition people, it isn't articulate enough for them, and a week later there's a new lieutenant. This guy listens. He forms a police-public coalition and they hold meetings in the party room at one of the condos. He calms them down."

For something to say, Brian Comartin said, "Community-based policing."

She let it go. "And one night after a meeting a twenty-year-old secretary is walking home and she gets jumped, beaten, and raped. We don't know about it at the time. And two weeks later, same thing, this time a twenty-two-year-old who came to look at a vacancy, she's jumped, beaten, and raped. She reports it, but a day later, at the Sector station where she was living then, up in Sector Two. And then another gets it. Some genius points out there might be a trend. We form a crew to work this guy. We don't say anything out loud, we don't want to spook him. We've got a lot of suspects, a *lot* of suspects, local area guys who are capable of this, and if they didn't do it, it was only because someone else thought of it first. We work through them. While we're working, bang, he goes off again. Nineteen-year-old student. We later learned there were three more unreported victims, they came forward much later, but hadn't reported it at the time of occurrence.

"By now we're down to one of two guys. We've eliminated just about everyone else. They're alibied. We've got two guys and one of them is named Adam Baxter Campbell. We like Campbell a lot. The other guy, well, maybe, but Addie Campbell is our first choice. He didn't leave much behind, when he was doing the women. He wore a condom. He was smart enough not to bite or smooch them, no saliva on the neck or ears. He wore a watch cap, so no hairs left for us. Just, bang. A blitz. And he liked his work. He beat some of them after he was done raping them. Like he was wasting time before moving on to someplace else he had to be. He had a history. This was him, ninety-nine percent.

"Word gets around. It always does. A woman in the coalition comes in to see the lieutenant. Hey, did we know there might be a serial rapist out there, operating in the condos? She wants to hold a community meeting, poster the area, alert everybody, start night patrols, self-defence classes, escort women from the bus stops to their front doors.

"The lieutenant sends me down to cool her out. Addie Campbell is due to go off, soon. We've got surveillance on him and he's getting wound up, scoping out women on the streets, following a few, making notes in a little book. A matter of time, and not much time, he's going. In the act is best. We've just tightened surveillance. 'Tell her we're close, we're dropping him in a day or two, the lieutenant tells me. Go cool her out.'

"So, I say I will, but I didn't feel right about it, I'd already said we should do a public notification and this might be the time. So, I'm gonna tell her, without actually telling her, to go public, scream her head off to the media. But just before I went to talk to her, one of the spin teams calls in. Addie Campbell just followed a woman from a coffee shop to an apartment building. So, the spinner snaps a photo of the woman. Then after she goes in, Addie goes up the stairs and watches through the lobby windows to see what floor she went to. He watches the elevator numbers and leaves and the spin team leaves with him. He goes to the factory he works at, goes in, comes out. One of the spinners goes in. Addie, the foreman said, came in and said he had a hot date, can't work the night shift."

Brian Comartin realized he had nothing to say, and the best thing was to not say anything.

"I go downstairs," she said, "and I tell the woman from the coalition that we're an inch from pinching this guy. I tell her we need him in the act, or close to being in the act. There's no way he'll beat it in court, if we catch him in the act. Easier on the victims, I said, if we get him dead to rights and he pleads out. She's okay with it. Not happy, but okay. She trusts me, I'm a woman.

"The spin team takes the photo of the woman Addie was working up to the superintendent of the building. The super looks at it and says, Molly Green, five-oh-two, back of the building. Single, a cat, a rental. Home most evenings, goes out Thursday after work to a Tai Chi class.

Lee Lamothe

"It's Thursday. Nighttime comes. Molly Green comes out in workout clothes and heads to the community centre at the foot of Harrison Hill. We're on her. We're on Addie's house. Addie likes the ten o'clock hour, thereabouts, home in time for the midnight movie. Addie stays home until nine-thirty, then he's out, he's in dark clothing, he's prowling toward Harrison Hill. We're up on him. We're up on her. Night scopes, multi-spin teams, the works. Because we've got a fix on his next target, the guys get a little sloppy, they play him loose. Too loose, but I mean, hey, we're on him. We're up on the victim. No way we're going to lose this guy. But of course, we do because he doesn't head to the community centre that Molly Green was going to.

"What we don't know is that Addie thinks ahead, likes to have a couple of treats in the freezer for when the hunger comes over him and porn on TV doesn't do it for him. Molly Green is for down the road, later, when something might not work out and he needs a quickie. She's a frozen pizza for when he doesn't feel like shopping.

"That night, that Thursday, he's got his eye on a Pilates instructor ten blocks away. And, because we think he's going to the community centre where the Tai Chi classes are and where he can bag Molly Green on her way home and we can bag him, we're sloppy, we play him loose because we're such smart guys. And of course we lose him. The next morning the Pilates instructor is found wandering naked out of a parking lot off Hedge Way. They get Addie when he shows up to work, smiling.

"There's a hat in this thing, and they need a head to put it on. The lieutenant shrugs and says he interviewed the coalition woman and attended to her concerns and sent her up to Sector detectives, and that's me.

"There's lawsuits. Big lawsuits. There's headlines like you wouldn't believe. These are yuppie folk, these are people who have access to the media and they're willing to use it. The city settled with all the victims. The Pilates instructor also practised some kind of martial art and got some skin evidence off Addie. He takes a plea, gets life. I get shunted to kiddie crime. The Pilates instructor needs a new face. The other women need counselling."

She saw Brian Comartin was trying to parse and process all the information, looking for something to say. But there was nothing that he needed to say. His role, in her life at that time, was to simply be there. Martinique Frost was amazed at how few people knew what they should bring. There was a lot more she wanted to say, but she felt she'd said enough.

"And I end up in my kitchen in the middle of the night with a red-headed Traffic man who writes poetry and tries the boob in the champagne glass line on me." Martinique Frost looked up at his wide sad Irish mug. "You can stay over, no point in heading out, it's late. But do you mind sleeping on the couch? If you've really got a need, I can deal with it. I think I like you, Brian, but tonight I'd rather not."

Comartin got up and rounded the table. He put his arm gently across her shoulders and touched his lips to the greying corn rows on her head. She'd spent something here, for him, he knew. In his chest he felt a swelling, the same swelling as when he'd discovered the Levertov book in the lobby at the Hotel Blu.

He thought of the perfect and flawed Levertov. *The beauty of deep lines dug into your cheeks ...*

Sirens sounded in the distance and slowly grew closer.

Ambulances whooped past outside Marty Frost's duplex.

Her cellphone rang.

Chapter 11

Djuna Brown didn't have a raid jacket, so Ray Tate gave her his. She struggled into it as he drove. It hung like a long dress down over her knees and she had to fold the sleeves back several times to free her hands. With her baggy batik trousers and sparkly slippers, she looked like a girl dressed up in a genie's clothes. Ray Tate looped his badge on the bead chain around his neck, activated the strobing Hello light on the dash, and swerved the Taurus up California Street. From there he sailed through the glowing gates of East Chinatown, keeping tight to the curb so that if ambulances and fire vehicles came up behind him they could get through. He parked half on the sidewalk.

It was bedlam. The smoke was a ghostly grey. The ground floors of a row of four buildings, two restaurants and two cheapo gift shops, were ablaze. Smoke rolled out of the two floors of flophouses above them.

Pumpers were farther up ahead in East Chinatown, working on fires burning two blocks away. Break-in alarms were blaring in rising and falling whoops. Wood crackled, windows blew out onto the road. People unseen were screaming for help. On the second floor over one of the shops, bleeding bare arms waved through jagged windows above the flames. Emergency lights strobed and throbbed, blue and red. The air smelled like searing meat and burning gasoline.

"Ray?" Djuna Brown came around the front of the Taurus, yelling above the chaotic noise. "Ray. Kids." She pointed at a woman and two children in the second floor above one of the restaurants. "I'm going in."

As she stepped away he grabbed her by the back of the yellow raid jacket. "Calm down, Djun'. Chill."

A high-rise unit with extra manpower hanging on the sides chuffed to a stop in front of the burning restaurant. A taxi screeched to a stop and a fire captain, half-dressed, tumbled from the front passenger seat.

Ray Tate shouted, "Sparky." He pointed. "Kids up."

The fire captain casually waved at him and yelled, "Okay, guys, we got kids in the sky, go get 'em." He started deploying his men into the adjoining building. The high-rise ladder swung out and up; two firefighters jumped aboard and rode it up until it clanged up onto the window ledge where the woman and children were. A pumper backed up to the rear of the high-rise unit and the crew started rhythmically running hose while a big man in fire boots, a T-shirt, and track pants ran with a huge wrench to a hydrant. There were a lot of auxiliaries arriving. In spite of their hale, the buffed-out fire department had suffered to the bug and had put out an all-hands.

Djuna Brown bit her lip, looking up into the smoke at the firefighters plucking the woman and children from the window. "Fuck, Ray, fuck."

"They're on it. They got to do their job, we got to do ours. Right now, we've got to secure those hats and those bottles." He pointed at several red baseball caps and intact bottles with scorched rags in their necks discarded on the opposite sidewalk. He took a tire iron from the trunk of the Taurus, crossed to a kitchen supply shop, and, with his left arm protecting his eyes, back-handed it into the window. The glass came down in sheets and an alarm sounded. A black Chrysler ghost car skidded into the curb and before it finished rocking four chargers bailed out, extending collapsible batons, leaving the doors open and moving on him in a wolf pack.

"Job, job, job," Ray Tate screamed, backing up and dropping the tire iron, putting his right hand in the air and holding out his badge with the left. "Job, job, okay, got it?"

"Okay, I know this guy," one charger said. "Tate. Tate, right?"

"Yes, I'm cool. I need all those big bowls and pots out of that display and I need one each on top of those baseballs caps, and numbered. Get something too, towels, to cover the bottles. Number everything. This whole fucking block is a crime stage."

Three of the chargers started a relay of plastic and crock-pots and towels. The red baseball caps and the bottles were covered. The fourth charger took business cards from his wallet and began writing numbers on them, slipping them under the bowls and pots.

There were no other recognizable ranks on the street. On the corner of California and Pike, three white men in T-shirts stood with their hands in their pockets, in a crowd of babbling, deranged, half-dressed Chinese, some of them running in circles. The three men were doing everything but whistling innocently and studying the fading morning stars overhead. An image came to Ray Tate, one he'd someday attack with charcoal: in the midst of the frantic residents, an elderly woman on her knees on the sidewalk with her head back, her mouth impossibly agape to show her broken teeth, pulling at her hair with her fists, silently screaming while one of the men in the white T-shirts stood behind her, laughing and pointing down at her with a heavily tattooed arm. He put that Edvard Munch image away.

Ray Tate collared one of the chargers. "My stage. Absent rank, this is my stage. What's your shop?"

"Billy Stiles, patrol, Sector Eight."

"Okay, Billy, those three white guys, behind me, there off to my left shoulder, T-shirts? They go in. If you can take them hard and make them bleed some DNA on your clothes, perfect. If not, put them in separate cells, let 'em smoke, let 'em drink. But you seize their cigarette butts, cups, and tins, got it? Document each item to the guy. Number one, number one; number two, number two. Don't lose track of what DNA belongs to who. We're gonna need a chain of evidence, here."

"They did this?"

"I'm thinking, yeah." He looked at the old woman on her knees. "Billy, that guy, there, laughing? Mr. Tattoo? Him, hardest."

"No problem." The charger turned his back to the corner and called his pals over into a huddle. "Those white assholes, T-shirts over my shoulder? We're working. Pile on, take 'em rough. Special attention Mr. Tattoo."

One charger, a young guy, said, "We don't got cause. What's the authority?"

"Him, Gerry, Ray Tate. He's a sergeant, this is his hoedown." He made a wide canine smile. "Okay, sack sack the quarterback. *Hu-ah*."

The men in the T-shirts saw them spread out and circle toward them, and tried to ease out of the crowd of frantic Chinese.

The chargers were on them and there was blood.

"Ray, Ray, hey."

Ray Tate turned. Martinique Frost and Brian Comartin were walking fast up the block, Comartin waving. Neither wore a raid jacket but both had their pieces visible in belt holsters, their handcuffs prominent and their badges swinging around their necks. White smoke from the soaked storefronts swirled around them. The infinitesimal water droplets in the air formed fine-meshed silver halos.

"We're running this. There's no white shirts here, there's no supervision. It's fucking chaos." Ray Tate looked at firefighters carrying limp bodies from the buildings, slapping oxygen masks on them and doing compressions and screaming for medics. Paramedics ran along the block with their bulky boxes, stopping, crouching and assessing. From deeper in East Chinatown, two ambulances sped down toward them, heading for the gates, and they jumped aside as a street-side open door of the ghost car was ripped off with a clang and sent spinning down the road.

An auxiliary firefighter on his knees gave up on a young girl on the sidewalk. He pulled her nightgown modestly down over her legs to cover her, then sat back on his heels, folding forward to pound the sidewalk with his fists.

"This is a murder stage. We have to get it right, until Homicide shows up and takes it over. Grab a charger or anyone else with any badge and assign him to a victim. They ask about authority, you tell them you're the chief's special task force and put 'em to work. Note their badge number. If there's a confirmed dead, assign one cop to the victim. He stays on it from here to morgue.

"Djuna, that fire guy over there, beating up the sidewalk? His victim is yours until you hand her off. Marty, Brian, you run it here, I'm going up the street."

A smoking body fell or jumped from the third floor above a restaurant and landed with the head making a dull *thonk*. "Brian, that's yours."

Comartin stared. "Uh, uh."

"Brian, take it. It's yours, man."

He didn't move. Martinique Frost put her hand on his shoulder. "Brian, c'mon, look after her."

Comartin nodded. His eyes were wide and he was hyperventilating.

"Brian, just go." Marty Frost started him with a gentle shove. "Go, man." He crossed to the smoking body and stood there, not knowing what to do.

"Marty, keep an eye on him, okay? Get a uniform to take it off him soon as you can." Sirens were building in the distance. He looked around. "When you guys get someone on all the victims, come on up the road. It looks worse up there."

A man in undershorts broke from the crowd across the street and toward a flaming restaurant, running over the shattered glass in his bare feet. A firefighter tried for him but the man darted around him and inside, screaming for someone. There was the creaking rumble of the ceiling coming down and the screams stopped.

"Marty, we need perimeter right here. Grab who you can and do what you can about crowd control."

He wondered who the man was screaming for.

It was worse up California Street. Four bodies lay in a line on the sidewalk in front of a karaoke bar. Two were burned past recognition of gender and looked like they'd been bubbled in boiling fat. The other two, young women, looked as if in peaceful sleep and seemed to be smiling up in fond remembrance at the reluctant yellow dawn. The smell of gasoline was sharp, the fire alarms had melted, and the block was quiet except for the rush and splash of dripping water out of the black maw of the building, the shouting of the workers, and the running of feet. The huge truck generators with their endless insect hum became part of his ears and he didn't consciously hear them. Everyone who was going to get out alive was out. A pumper poured water into the first and second floors of the karaoke. An aerial was extended over the building, and a hatless fireman in baggy shorts, no shirt, and rubber boots poured water down with precision as though he were strafing a hostile jungle from a helicopter. In the rising sun there was a glimpse of a rainbow over the building as the aerial shooter caught the light just right.

An auxiliary firefighter, a police cadet in his brown uniform shirt, and a security guard stood with two spectators and watched the arcing water make steam.

Ray Tate came up on them. "What the fuck are you guys doing?"

The cadet, who looked barely out of his teens, turned angrily. He was crying, snot running down his lip. "Fuck you. Fuck you, man."

"Sure. But fuck me later, okay? Right now you have to secure the evidence. Those bodies are the evidence. You don't have to look at them, you don't have to feel for them. But you have to be with them." He touched the boy cadet on the shoulder urgently. "Don't leave them alone, man, they're gone, but don't let them be gone alone, for nothing. Not here, like fucking garbage on the road. You have to protect them. I'll get someone to take transfer of evidence for you soon as I can. If I can't, when they go out of here make sure someone goes with them until the detectives get to the hospital or the morgue." He felt a hundred years old. He'd killed two men and a woman in the line and it had all been for this, to stand in a street of fire comforting a kiddie cop. "What's your name, cadet?"

"Jimmy Stiles. I'm at the academy. We were having a stag in the karaoke. My brother's on the job."

"Stiles? Yeah, Billy. Billy Stiles, right? In Sector Eight? A charger?"

"You know him? You know Billy?"

"Yeah, he's up the road, doing the work. Can you do the work, too, Jimmy?" He waited a beat, then nodded as if Jimmy Stiles answered positive. "Good." Above East Chinatown a helicopter appeared and hovered. "Anybody asks, you're with the chief's special task force. Take charge of this. These guys are your crew, you tell 'em what you want. Right now, you want one of these guys to go into those apartments across the road. You want him to get some sheets. You want to take them from him, shake them out as best you can, and you cover these souls. That's media fuckers up there in the chopper, looking for breakfast." Jimmy Stiles stood frozen. The other men watched. Ray Tate softly said, "Deploy them, Jimmy. Do what Billy would do."

Across from the karaoke fire a blocky Chinese man in a black suit, white shirt, and dark blue tie with a sparkling stickpin smoked a cigarette in a dim doorway, watching the wind-down of the fire.

Ray Tate saw only the glow of the cigarette and the reflection of the white shirt. He took his gun from his ankle and crossed the street, peering into the shadows.

"Mr. Wong?" The Mayor of Chinatown, the Wrong Wong, Mr. Presto. Every cop knew Willard Wong.

"Sergeant Tate." Willard Wong prided himself on being in the know about the cops. "Or is it Detective Tate?"

"Same rank, different clothes. Same pay." He holstered his gun. The doorway vibrated slightly from the rumbling of the engines of the big emergency vehicles.

Willard Wong was known on wiretaps as Six Fingers. Three on each hand, straight up. W and W; no one had to say his name aloud. He carried a block of mayoralty votes in his pocket and ran the rackets. He'd come up in the X-men case but left no fingerprints behind.

"You got another one of those?" Ray Tate's nose was full of burnt meat and his mouth was arid and he kept dry-spitting. Before he could accept one of Willy Wong's cigarettes, he turned, lurched away, and vomited champagne and cognac and bits of tenderloin against a wall. It all tasted like smoke. He pulled up his shirt-tail and dragged it across his mouth, and, as if nothing had happened, accepted the cigarette and stuck the tip into the flame from Willy Wong's lighter. He French-inhaled smoke out of his mouth and up into his nose and back out his mouth. It helped.

"It pains me, Sergeant, to see the sun come up on this. This tragedy." Willard Wong shook his head slowly then made a sad smile. "But, did you see the rainbow?"

"A lot of dead at the end of that rainbow, Mr. Wong."

"Yes, many I fear."

"Probably, Mr. Wong, if they weren't sleeping eight to a room in a building without working alarms, there'd be a lot less. Are we going to be able to find families to notify? In China? We're going to need a list."

Willy Wong made a little smile and patted Ray Tate on the forearm. "You should enjoy your cigarette, Sergeant. Everything will be taken care of. Have a rest break. Don't work so hard. There's always more work for a sergeant." He chuckled. "Better a bad sergeant than a good general, eh? Sergeants carry the gun in one direction, generals carry the gold in the other." He shrugged. "As it always is."

"And criminals carry the generals?"

"Of course, but not criminals, not always. Maybe once, long ago, in wild youth mistakes were made. But now, facilitators, guiding hands of the community." He softened his voice. "I heard you over there, speaking to that boy. The sheets. The souls. Why is it that in America they care more for the dead than for the living? If you passed them begging in the street or serving you in a restaurant, in life, you wouldn't even notice them. Coolies. Now because they're dead they get your compassion?" He stared at Ray Tate and asked, as if he really wanted to know, "If you weren't getting paid, how much would you care?"

Ray Tate knew there was nothing he could say to that. It was true and shameful.

They smoked their cigarettes.

Across the street order was being imposed on the stage. Detectives in suits and plainclothesmen in windbreakers were striding up the block and setting up perimeters. Chargers were directed to stretch yellow crime-stage tape. Men in shiny grey jackets with ARSON UNIT stencilled in yellow fluorescent on the back arrived and paced with clipboards and consulted with fire chiefs. The media helicopter noisily chopped up the pure blue sky. The fires were down but the firefighters stayed on the stage in case spot flare-ups broke out. The firefighter at the top of the aerial pressed his hand to the speaker on his ear, then swivelled his hose and aimed a hard flow of water. White smoke rose. Another brief rainbow. A dozen people wrapped in blankets or coats sat in a row on the curb across from the burnt-out karaoke, one of them a woman with wet hair holding a cat to her cheek and kissing it, another an old woman speaking to a framed picture of an older man. There was no breeze. Under the white sheets the bodies were motionless.

Ray Tate turned to Willard Wong and thought for a wild second about pulling his piece and shooting him a couple of times in the stickpin, both for being what he was and for being right. "Maybe. Maybe, Mr. Wong. But you carry a lot of the weight for this. You could take your thumb off their windpipes, even for a second. Let them breathe."

"You do care," Willard Wong chuckled. He took a tiny cellphone from his belt. "You care. What a crazy sergeant you are. I must tell a friend about you."

The morning sun was out and hot and it turned the puddles into low steam. Like someone walking through romantic mist, Martinique Frost came up the street, carefully avoiding puddles.

Ray Tate thanked Willard Wong for the cigarette and said, "I hope you fucking die," and stepped out of the doorway.

Willard Wong made a small dismissive gesture with his hand. "You'll get those who did this, Sergeant? It's important, yes. Chinese people didn't do this. Chinese people only died. As always." He made his small smile and tilted his head a little to the right. "A sergeant should be an example to the generals." He turned away, punching numbers into his cellphone. "I must tell my friend about you."

Brian Comartin was unlocking geometric gridlock at the gates of Chinatown, whistling sharply through his teeth and waving his hands to move ghosters and marked cruisers away from one another and out of the stage. Four coroner's catering trucks were idling patiently in a line outside the gates, waiting to get at the bodies. Comartin looked like he was in his element with cars and angles instead of bodies and blood. When he saw Martinique Frost and Ray Tate coming down the block, he trotted heavily over, trying not to gasp with the effort. They met in the middle of the street, greeting each other as if they'd lost each other for a long time, had lost each other in the chaos of a battle.

"Where's Djuna?"

Comartin pointed to a Chinese-American restaurant with its door open. "Some road sergeant came up and said to break it off, have some breakfast. He put his stick through the door window, opened it for business. The white shirts and the suits got the rest of it under control."

They walked across the road, Martinique Frost and Ray Tate a little ahead.

Ray Tate murmured, "How's Brian? He do okay?"

She nodded. "He settled down. He was a little shaky. I don't think he ever saw a body before. I'll keep an eye on him."

"You guys arrived together. You good?"

She gave him a smile. "I think you and Djuna did, too."

They stepped around the shattered glass on the doorstep. Inside the restaurant a television set showed live helicopter footage from above Chinatown. The road sergeant who had the beast's back, 667, was behind a flat grill with a stogie screwed into his face. A white apron was tied around his waist and he was frying toast and busting eggs. It was unthinkable to sizzle bacon or ham or any meat with the smell of the air outside. In spite of his girth, the Road moved like a ballet dancer, pivoting *en point* in his boots, his T-shirt stretched over his paunch, his suspenders hanging loose. A dozen chargers and firefighters sat on stools at the counter and more were in the booths along the wall. Rovers crackled questions and instructions and periodically a charger would mutter back a response into his shoulder microphone.

Djuna Brown sat with two young uniformed police-women, chargettes, at the end of the counter, drinking coffee. She looked up when Ray Tate, Marty Frost, and Brian Comartin came in. By the look of soft relief on her face, Ray Tate could tell she'd been worried about him. He felt a little guilty: he hadn't thought about her at all.

As he approached, he heard her merrily say, "Yep, batiks and slippers. State Police issue. They're giving us motor scooters next year, Italian ones with sidecars, so we can interact with the community, taken 'em for rides in the countryside." Her little even teeth grinned when the chargettes laughed. "We're learning to hug people, make them feel we're on their side, that we care." She stood up in the drapery of the raid jacket with the sleeves rolled back to the elbows. "Check this, let me show you, on, hmm, let's say, this random bearded guy here." She wrapped her arms around Ray Tate and put the top of her head under his chin and sagged a little. They stood for a moment, then she turned to the chargettes. "I don't even know this guy. But he smells like a beatnik, you ask me."

The chargers in the booths hooted.

He sat beside her on a vacant stool. "How'd you make out, Djuna?"

"It was bad, Ray. We had six dead at our end so far. You?"

"Six at least. There's going to be more inside when they can go in."

The Road came down the counter with platters of egg sandwiches up his arm and dealt them out. "This'll be a little better than the stuff at the Mex joint, Ray." He turned to Djuna Brown. "He tell you guys about the guy we were at that got shot yesterday morning? I asked the guy, 'Who shot you?' And the guy said, 'Depends what you mean by shot.'" He went back up the boards and came back with coffee cups and a pot and repeated, "*Depends* what you *mean* by *shot*. Lovin' it."

Ray Tate nodded. "John Smith. Citizen. Connoisseur of the pork chop. Fuckhead." He was ravenous. He felt Djuna Brown's hand on his thigh. As he chewed, he nodded up the counter where Martinique Frost and Brian Comartin were sitting quietly. "How'd they do, those two?"

"They're cool, Ray. They're okay. Brian was good until he looked at the woman who came off the third floor and landed on her head. He blew his dinner. But I think those two are working something out." She moved her hand in a small circle. "Like us, huh?"

Before he could answer, a charger in a wall booth called over. "Tate? Is a Tate here? Sergeant?"

Ray Tate twisted on his stool. "Yo, here, Tate."

"Just got some voice out on the air, Sergeant. Hambone Hogarth from Homicide is at the gates, wants to see you. You want me to ten-four you? Or wink you off?" WNK. Whereabouts not known, a.k.a. a fugitive.

"Yeah, show me rolling." He gathered his sandwich on his palm and stood up and yawned and almost sat back down again. He told Djuna Brown he'd see her at the briefing.

As he walked away he heard one of the chargettes say, "Is that *the* Ray Tate, the gunner? He looks pretty cool."

And he heard Djuna Brown answer proudly, "Yep, and you keep your horny city hands off my beatnik, city girl."

He felt pretty good about that.

Chapter 12

A Homicide crew was clustered just outside the gates to East Chinatown with their heads together and three chargers nearby to protect them from information pollution. They wouldn't let anyone approach to talk to them. The hammers from Homicide wanted to know what was up there inside the gates, but they wanted to know for themselves. Ray Tate had seen it before at murder stages. They wanted to go onto the crime stage with a fresh mind, with no knowledge that might taint their observations. If they went in with, say, an obvious detail told to them, they might look to confirm the expectation and miss the importantly obscure. They wanted to work pristine, without assumptions, and count their own bodies, draw their own conclusions. Some teams worked that way. All they had to know was that they'd been rolled out because someone had maybe died bad; they'd take it from there.

He went up to a protective charger. "Tate, Ray. They called me to see Hambone."

"Okay, be careful, don't queer things for them, okay?" He called, "Inspector Hogarth? I got a Ray Tate?"

Bob Hogarth detached himself from the group. He wore the same clothes he'd worn at the briefing the day before, when he pronounced Marty Frost the champ after she took out the headquarters hump, and he still hadn't shaved. He held up his cellphone. "Ray, you got pals I never imagined."

"I don't know nobody, Ham." Ray Tate shrugged. "I'm just an asshole."

"Well, you done good, anyway, here. Somebody noticed. We got your three viables down at the local Sector, we got blood off each of them. We got bottles that bounced off the windows, we got six baseball caps with hair evidence. Nice, nice freeze on the stage, you did." He shook his head. "Mutts. They thought they didn't need to wear gloves because the bottles would melt. Of course that presupposes minimum compe-tence in making sure the bottles didn't bounce back off the window. And too stupid to take the red hats with them. Guess they thought it would help them blend in with all those Chinese folk *not* wearing red hats. What ever happened to the diabolical criminal mastermind? I really miss that bygone era."

"Bummer, Ham." He yawned widely, tasting the vomit in his mouth. He wanted to book off sick and bang Djuna Brown into the Left Bank of the Seine. "So, I'm here."

"Who do you know? I just got a call that the chief's task force is expanded to include this mess. Take out the Volunteers for the women and this too. And someone at the Jank wants you prominent on the team."

Ray Tate thought, *That was fast.* Six Fingers Wong and his theory of sergeants, having to tell a friend about him. Willy Wong to the police chief, Pious Man Chan; Pi Chan to the Chief of Ds, Chief of Ds to Hambone Hogarth. He wished he'd parked a couple in Willy Wong's stickpin. He didn't know how long Djuna Brown would be in the city and he wanted to squeeze every Parisian minute out of the time they had. "Can you get me a pass, Ham? I don't need the profile. I got a life."

"Sorry, Ray. If they want you on this bus, then you get on this bus. Trust me, you don't want to know where the other one goes. I'll oversee it, if you want, but somebody wants your face above the crowd."

"Okay." Ray Tate had an inspiration. "Okay, but I'll need some people."

Hogarth shrugged. "Limitless budget on this. Pick who you want, out of what we got."

"That Statie, the little black chick, Brown. Comartin from Traffic. Marty Frost."

"I get the Statie, she'll be a good decoy if we still go that way. Marty Frost, sure, you put her in the room with white Volunteers and she'll have them slapping on black face and singing old Jolson tunes. Comartin? Why? You need valet parking?"

"You got a better place for him?"

"Good point." He looked around to make sure no one was nearby. "Am I going to have trouble with you,

Ray? No matter how this looks to outsiders and up at the Jank, I'm running this. We on the same page? You might have a good pal somewhere up the chain, but you've got a lot more enemies. You don't need another one. My advice? We break this in two, work the overlaps together. There's the dead women and there's this mess. Fifteen dead, so far. I want this."

Ray Tate thought of the gallery of photographs of the ladies on easels in the briefing room, their faces fractured into some kind of a demented Picasso art project, how one of them in life had evoked Djuna Brown into his mind, minutes before he felt her hand on his shoulder and turned to find her magically there. "I'll go at it from the women, then. I'm going to want to go at the guys in custody, first, see if they want to cop to anything on that. If they drop something about the fire, I call you."

Hogarth looked relieved. His crew had investigated all three of Ray Tate's fatal shootings and on the iffy middle one that Ray Tate himself wasn't sure of, they'd cut him slack. Hogarth didn't want to deal that card. It was something that shouldn't have to be said aloud, a debt never to be collected. It was enough, he knew, for Ray Tate to hear the echo.

"You go at them for the women until we get the fingerprints back off the bottles matched to Chinatown. And then they're ours. Don't ask a word about what went on here, though. If they go that way, head 'em off. I need them clean for my guys. We got a deal?"

* * *

There were media hordes in front of the Sector station. Marty Frost drove past and Ray Tate called inside on the cellphone. The duty sergeant directed them to the rear garage and told him to hold back. "If you don't want to have to tell a fib later, Ray, give me a minute to move things around in there. We'll put them in interview rooms. We'll get your guys in interviews A to C."

Two Asian chargers were coming out of an interview room when Ray Tate and Marty Frost emerged from of the door to the garage, walking slowly. One of the chargers had a split lip and was licking blood and ragging out his partner with good humour. "You're right-handed. I told you, stay on the right. I'm left-handed, I stay on the left. Nobody gets hurt except the guy getting the business. Police Fucking Brutality 101. Did you skip that class?"

Ray Tate asked, "He went off on you?"

The charger shook his head. "Naw. Bruce Lee here can't figure out left from right. We're getting basic bio-data off the guy in the garage, you know, chatting him up, and this hero here gets over on my left. In the middle of the interview his elbow takes me out on the back swing." Handing Ray Tate a sheet of paper, he burlesqued peering around and raised his voice. "Guy's not even Chinese. Fucking Filipino. They eat, like, dogs." He called, "Bruce, you eat dogs."

"Yum," the other charger said, "lunch on me."

"How are they, those three in the rooms? Anybody stand out real stupid?"

"Well, it's close. They've got one brain between them and I think they take turns thinking with it. Right now, I'd say the guy in the middle interview room has temporary custody."

They went down the hall bitching each other out.

"This is your kind of thing, Marty. How do you want to do it?"

"My kind of thing?" She smiled at him for a moment. "I figured you'd checked me out."

"The guy in B might have a clue, but the other two? Tweet tweet."

"Let's fuck with heads a little, okay? What do we really care about?"

"The dead ladies." He told her what Hogarth had said, to stay off the Chinatown arson murders. "The minute this becomes viable for them, the hammers come in."

"So, we do A first, we bend his brain a little. He thinks he's in here for the fires, right? He's anticipating, thinking, 'They'll ask this, and I'll say that. They'll ask that, I'll say this.' We don't have to be subtle. These guys are going for Chinatown anyway, we just want them to carry the dead ladies when they go. So, we go in and you work the preliminaries. You start out sitting, I'll eye-line him. But when I sit down, you step back, you stand behind him, just out of his eye-line. Humming, maybe, clicking your tongue. But real soft. If my hands are folded on the table, you can't talk, no matter how much you want to."

"What if I have to go to the bathroom?"

She smiled. "Put your hand up like a good pupil." She rubbed her face briskly for a few seconds. "Showtime."

A shirtless man with a shaven head was in A, slumped over the table, his right wrist manacled to a ring welded into the metal top. A fresh WPP, white people's party, logo was engraved on his right chest. Mom Forever Always was tattooed in a red heart over his left breast. He had a black eye and fat lips and was having trouble breathing through his nose and was coughing and moaning softly.

"Those fucking slope cops tuned me. I wanna lay a charge." He turned his face up to the video camera mounted in the corner of the ceiling and shouted with exaggeration, "Bru-Tal-It-ee-I-want-to-lay-a-charge." With his damaged nose he sounded like the guy in all the harelip jokes.

Ray Tate sat opposite him and put the page of bio data on the table. Marty Frost remained standing, moving just out of the man's eye-line, and folded her arms.

"I'm Sergeant Ray Tate. In the room is Martinique Frost, city police. We're conducting a multiple-death investigation."

"Fuck you. I want to lay a charge."

Ray Tate held up his hand. "We'll get to that. We'll get you a use-of-force complaint form, help you fill it out, if you want, okay? Let me read this over, correct me if I'm wrong, okay? I say something not right, you should help me keep the record straight. Before we start, do you need anything, a cold drink or coffee, or to use the bathroom?" He looked up at the guy as if having an afterthought. "Wait. That's a question. Rules say, before I ask you any question, I have to read you your rights, just to be safe, okay?" He took the square card with the poem printed on it from his pocket and held it so the camera picked it up. He read slowly, stopping at the end of each numbered sentence. "You get all that? I can read it again, if you want, slower."

The man was silent.

"You've got to nod for the camera, or say something. It's the rules."

The man nodded.

"So, you want a coffee? Use the bathroom? Anything?"

The man shook his head.

"Okay, let's go through this. Your name is Peter van Meister. You're thirty-one years old. Married, three kids. Work as a groundskeeper at the Riverview Golf and Country, nine years. No criminal record. We okay on this, so far? Peter? You have to speak or nod."

The man looked up at the camera and nodded.

"Okay. That's okay. I wouldn't say much if I were you looking at multiple murder charges. The charges, I have to tell you, are capital. The needle in this state. It might take a few years to get you through the appeals, but at the end of it? The needle. I'm going to ask you some questions. You can answer or decline. Some guys like to use this time to figure out what we know or what we don't know, to head us off later. Sometimes it works, sometimes not. Your choice. You can invoke at any time, just like I read you off the card. Like I said, I'd be careful. We good, man? Tell the camera." He stopped talking when Martinique Frost unfolded her arms and eased into Peter van Meister's eye-line and sat down. Ray Tate stood up, stretched, and moved slightly behind him. He very softly hummed the tune from *Dragnet*.

"This is very serious, Peter," she said, her hands folded primly. "If it was straight murder? You might dodge the needle. But multiples? With a hate crime add-on? Good luck with that. Very, very hard to justify to a jury, serial hate rape and murder. Juries, even in this town, can't get their mind around racial rapes."

His head jumped. "What? Rapes?"

"Relax, Peter. This might be the simplest part of your day. We know *how* you did the women, we know *where* you did them. But we don't know *why* you did them. Or who with. Maybe you've got a motive we haven't thought of yet. Maybe they asked for it. To start with, what were Belinda Clarke, Mariam Smith, and June Flowers to you, can you tell me?"

"Who?" The man was startled. "Belinda what? What the fuck?"

Ray Tate switched to the sound theme of *Law & Order* and softly shuffled his feet. He yawned and cracked his jaws but otherwise remained silent.

"Clarke, Smith, Flowers, and a woman to be named later. Your last victim. Serial sex murder. With a hate added on." She kept direct eye contact. Someone had once told her during an interview that she had beautiful eyes. You got great eyes, he'd said, I forgot you were a nigger. She'd thanked him very much, as it was the nicest thing anyone had ever said to her. "You got kids, Peter, any of them girls? Girls you want to beat to mush, Peter? Maybe do other stuff? How's things with your wife? Does she go along with that, you and your daughters fooling around?"

"Fuck. What are you talking about? I don't touch my kids. Those dead ones were all Chinese. Burned. I saw it. I heard them screaming in there, like fucking rats." He made a high-pitched singsong. "Fucking diseased rats."

"Peter, what are you talking about?" She spoke very softly as if she really wanted to know, to clear up her confusion. "All the victims were black females."

"No. In Chinatown. That's why we're here, right? The fires? Those diseased hordes that we burned up. Fuck 'em. I'm proud of what we did. As a white Aryan man I can hold my head up in my own country." In his honking voice he began chanting up at the camera. "Sink the boats, feed the fish, sink the boats, feed the fish," and pumping his fist in the air. "White power."

Martinique Frost leaned over the bio data sheet and pretended to read it. She picked it up and glanced at the back, as though she might have missed something. She folded her hands and shook her head, as if confused, and looked at the bio sheet.

Ray Tate tried humming the theme from *Hawaii Five-O*.

She looked up. "Peter, what the fuck are you talking about? There's nothing on here about fires. We don't do fires. Fires is some other department, the sparky squad. We do sex murder. Not fire murder. They bring us in for the real heavy on-hands stuff. The sick pervo shit." She made her face into confusion. "Sex murders, you know what that is, right? That's our game and we think you're our player."

The man shook his head and tried to push away from the table, to get away from her. The chain was tight from his wrist to the table. "No, no."

"You like the dark, Peter? It's okay. Even at my age, I get a lot of white dudes hitting me up. They can't help it. A lot of you white power guys have got some underlying desire to be the plantation man, jump the dark bones. I get that, that's biology. But why kill them all, after you got off? That's some sick shit. What you did."

He sat silent and shook his head as though she was hopeless to try to talk to. He twisted his head to see Ray Tate. "What's she talking about?"

Marty Frost's hands were folded. Ray Tate was out of TV themes so he moved to a slightly bouncy "Finiculì, Finiculà."

"Or maybe, maybe you're denying your own self? Who you really are?" She leaned forward. She was going at him now and her voice was even softer, confidential, sympathetic. "You got that dark crinkly hair. You shave it off your head, but I see it in your eyebrows, on your arms. You're pretty dark complected. Somebody there, in the woodpile. Is your family from down south? You ever do one of those ancestry searches, look for interesting relatives? You getting back some at big buck daddy?"

"No darky in me, bitch."

"If you say so." She shrugged and reached over to put her hand on his under the manacle. "My brother."

He snatched his hand away; the chain rattled.

Martinique Frost sat back and stared at him, her hands unfolded.

"Good motive, though, for the jury, if you want to go for it." Ray Tate said, moving into his eye-line. "Your mother was raped by a black guy? Fuck, man, who needs that shit? You suffered for it. Rejected by your own people, had to head north to make a fresh life for yourself as a white man. I can dig it. So you joined the Volunteers, you're just light-skinned enough, get some back for your mom. Who wouldn't? Natural you'd want to kill all those women after you raped them so they couldn't have any black sons to suffer like you. You're gonna have to work on that part, the rapes, and those mommy issues you got."

"Leave my mother out of this." Peter van Meister was getting wound up and confused. "I didn't rape no darkies. I wouldn't stick my dick in any of them. I didn't kill no black broads. That Chinatown stuff, okay —"

Ray Tate warned him, "Don't say it, okay?"

"Shut up about that Chinatown stuff, Peter," Martinique Frost said. "Don't go there."

"We don't want you to talk about that," Ray Tate said. "We're the fuck-and-kill squad. Some other guys might want to talk to you about that. But we're not those guys."

"Unless you banged the girls in Chinatown before you burned them."

"Then we got a game," Ray Tate nodded positively. "Definitely a game."

"Peter, just focus on sex crimes. Focus, man."

They were piling on. Peter van Meister seemed to shrink

Martinique Frost liked the rhythm and she folded her hands on the table. She'd found somewhere to go with him. His pride. "We don't want to know about Chinatown. Just shut the fuck up about Chinamen. I been all night counting dead bodies in Chinatown. I just come from East Chinatown. I've had a fucking lifetime of Chinamen. That's someone else's case. They can have it."

"Yeah?" Peter van Meister seemed happily curious. "Yeah? You were there?"

"Yep. All morning. You guys fucked my day. My day off, actually." She glanced at Ray Tate and arched her eyebrows, then crept into his shit; she'd read his pride and was going to poke it a little. "Three dead. Big fucking deal. I've seen three dead in a collision on the Eight."

"Three? We only got three? Bullshit. A dozen at least."

Martinique Frost unlocked her fingers and glanced at Ray Tate.

Ray Tate, out of his eye-line, glanced up at the camera. "Well, they're still counting them up. Three so far. Maybe it goes to four, five. That's your business, what happened in East Chinatown. My advice? If you're going to go down for something, Peter, go for the women. That's a man's work, a son's work. That's at least fucking normal, how they raped your mom and all."

"Don't talk about my mother."

Martinique Frost spoke to Ray Tate. "Except for the part, Ray, where he fucked them before killing them." She shook her head. "That might work against him. Rape is tough to explain to the family the best of times." She said to the man, "Do they know what happened to your mom?"

Ray Tate came into eye-line and before he could answer, he said to Martinique Frost, "Maybe he didn't know you weren't supposed to fuck them first? But he got overwhelmed, realized on some level they were sisters and needed his action? They were all good looking black chicks. I looked at their pictures, the ones taken before he got at them, and I got to say, I'm a red-blooded guy and dig blonde chicks, usually, but I'd have a little trouble keeping it in my pants."

She said, nodding thoughtfully, "That might work. You get one man with a working dick on the jury, Peter, maybe you got a shot."

Peter van Meister rattled at his manacles energetically and shouted at the camera. "I didn't do no dark. Those Chinese, they deserve what we gave them. Burn them rats out. Sink the boats, stop the plague. But I don't fuck black chicks. I'm committed to my heritage."

"Okay, Peter, okay." Martinique Frost patted her hands above the desk. "Calm down, man. We just go where it leads us, you know? They're racial rapes, no question. So, if it wasn't you, who among the committed might have betrayed the cause, the honest cause? You got an idea? One of the other guys we brought in with you? Likes the sisters, can't help himself?"

Peter van Meister was calmed that he wasn't on the spot for racial rape. "No. Those guys? No. We don't cross. We'd never cross."

She said, "We're going public tomorrow morning, Peter. We're going to put it on the Volunteers, all of it on all of you. Chinatown, the race rapes. And believe me, it'll be the rapes that you guys get famous for. You can head this off, if you've got a clue, an avenue we can pursue, so we can stop the press conference that'll make you guys look like perverts hiding behind the cause of true white America."

It didn't work. Proudly, he recited, "I know my rights. I-want-a-lawyer." He looked up at the camera. "Law Yer Now."

Ray Tate started laughing. "Get two, Peter. You're gonna need 'em both."

They waited in the corridor until they finished laughing like dazed fools.

Ray Tate shook his head in disbelief. "We're putting it down. More than a dozen homicides and we did it by begging him not to confess."

"But not our ladies, Ray. That's our mission."

"I know. But, you think about it, it's pretty cool. We could gag these loons and they'd blink out confessions with their eyelids for the camera, Morse code." He made his face straight, said, "Here goes," and opened the door to Interview B.

A muscular, shaven-headed man in a ripped T-shirt with blurry race and jailhouse tattoos on his arms and neck sprawled back in his chair and looked up at the camera with his arms folded and yawned. "Lawyer."

Clearly outclassed by a criminal genius, Ray Tate picked up the bio data sheet, and said, "Have a nice day," and stepped out.

"He shut me down." Ray Tate looked over the biodata. "Name, Ansel Partridge." He laughed. "Address: fuck you."

Martinique Frost said, "Been there, done that."

Chapter 13

In Interview C a bare-chested blond man with the fresh WPP tattoo on his chest looked up when they entered. He had long muscles and a workingman's tan up to his mid-bicep and down to the bottom of his throat. He clamped his mouth under a faint Hitler moustache.

He didn't say the magic words, so Ray Tate and Martinique Frost sat down facing each other at the far end of the long table, ignoring him for a few minutes. As if she had nothing better to do, she picked the sheet of bio data off the table and started reading. Ray Tate immediately got up and paced around as if his bones were stiff and stopped behind the man manacled to the table. He was afraid he was going to laugh from goofiness and exhaustion. They'd just solved a dozen homicides, but they weren't the ones they wanted.

When Martinique Frost looked at him, he shrugged and held his hands out, at a loss what to do.

"This gentleman is Joseph Carr, Ray. Forty-two, married, no kids, former car wash, former meat cutter, former video store operator, currently a dent-puller down at Bravo's."

"Who gives a shit?" Ray Tate yawned loudly. "I get my car fixed after-hours at the department impound. Twenty bucks and a bottle of Canadian Club at Christmas."

"You want to talk to him? None of us is leaving anytime soon. One of us should. I mean, he's here, we're here."

"Fuck no. That Peter, in the other room? Just yak-yak-yak. He'll be writing all day. We got all we need. Two for the needle, one for life." He moved out of Joseph Carr's eye-line on the left and came out on his right. "We're just going to hang out in here for a while, Joe. We're hiding out. There's bosses out there, looking for scalps because of what Peter said you guys did. He said you're the ringleader, but me? I doubt it. I like old Ansel there, next door for this. Your pal, Peter in the other room, there, he drove us nuts. He's got some serious issues, identity stuff. Too deep for me. Did you know his mother was raped by a black guy? Well, he said she was raped. Me, I'm not sure. And it turns out he's banging his own daughters. What's that all about? Anyway, he's got that dark skin and crinkly hair thing going on. Racial confusion, maybe. He's a watered down black guy, no question in my mind. What do you think?"

The man opened his mouth.

"Hang on, Joe." Martinique Frost held up her hand to silence him. "Nothing, Joe. Not a fucking word.

Don't talk to us, man. You oughta get a lawyer, you're going to need a lawyer. These are murders with a hate add-on and you're in needle-land and we don't want to fuck this up. Just sit there. We'll sit here and do up our notes, okay? When the coast is clear, and the white shirts have fucked off back to the Jank, we'll be out of your hair." She put her notebook on the table and took a pen from her purse and looked at Ray Tate. "They should all be this easy. I'd be fucking inspector by now, get transferred out of sex crime."

"Sex? What?" Joe Carr rattled his manacles to get their attention. "I —"

"Joe? Stop, okay?" Ray Tate said. "There's a procedure. If I want to ask you a question, if I want to ask you if you were beaten during arrest, if you want to take a piss or if you want to eat a sandwich, those are questions and before I can ask you *any* questions I have to read this to you first." He took the card from his pocket. "Okay, here goes." He read the Miranda poem. "So, you want a sandwich, take a leak? Been beaten?"

The man shook his head. "What's he saying? Peter? What's he saying?"

"You're going to bite it, for those women you raped and killed. Peter is going into a cell for life, when he finishes testifying, but you and your buddy there, Partridge with the Craddock tattoos? The strap-down and long needle. Rape-homicide. As bad as it gets."

"With the hate add-on," Martinique Frost added. "Those black women you raped, Joe? The mess you left of them? You know they were pulverized, right?

Half the bones in their bodies looked like they'd been hit by a car. You guys were out on the water that night, so, so long, Charlie."

Joseph Carr went, "Whoa, whoa, whoa. I didn't bang no black broads. Didn't kill no one. No one black, anyway. Chinks don't count. What the fuck's Peter been saying? He's a fucking mental. I'll go for the dead Chinks for the cause, but no way am I wearing banging some jig whore." A strange chivalry came up, suddenly. "Sorry, Miss, but you know what I mean?"

"Sure, I hear it all the time. Nothing personal." Martinique Frost shrugged and put aside his chivalry for later. "If you want to talk, get out from under the black chicks, tell the camera up there you want to talk to us, or not."

Joseph Carr stood as well as he could and said precisely, as if swearing an allegiance, "As an American patriot, I understand my rights. I want to straighten out this bullshit rape thing." He sat. "What'd Peter say?"

Ray Tate took out his notebook, flapped the pages loudly, and winged it, pretending to be reading. "He said, ah, here we go, he said, he didn't want to do the chicks, but it was, what he called, an action, proof of loyalty to the Volunteers? That you and your buddy, Partridge, there, next door, demanded it. Like an initiation. Peter said, 'We're gonna wreak havoc on all the lesser races, make a stand for the white nation. Tear down the walls, motherfucker.' The usual. He's in there now, writing up the details. How you beat them and beat them until their ribs powdered and their hearts were mush. How him and Ansel tried to stop you. I got to tell you, Joe, he's convincing. Especially after what happened to his mom."

Joseph Carr shook his head. "No, that ain't right."

"Well," Martinique Frost said, "you want to write it down and sign it? That you didn't do it? Get your position on the record? If you want, you can put in the stuff about Chinatown, how that was righteous action, but raping and killing women isn't what you're about." She flipped over the page of bio data and gave him her pen. "You do a man's work, now you get to defend it. I respect that, anyone would."

"Yeah, yeah, that's fucked, that stuff on women." Joseph Carr nodded. "I was raised Christian, you don't violate a woman. Even a jig. Never." He ducked his head. "Sorry, Miss."

Martinique Frost said, "Thank you for that, Joe. That's refreshing for me to hear."

Ray Tate managed to contain his laughter. Two out of three down. The third one was going to wear his ass for a hat for East Chinatown. There were at least three others who dumped the red caps at the arson scene, but they weren't his concern. He waited a couple of minutes until Joseph Carr had reached the bottom of the page, not wanting to put him off before he auto-graphed it. Joseph Carr slowed down at the bottom of the page as if he might be receiving a clue that he might be stupid. Ray Tate leaned forward over his shoulder and diverted him. "You've got a neat penmanship, Joe. Look at this, Marty."

"Sign it and pass it over, Joe. Let's see." He signed and proudly presented her with the paper and pen.

"Nice, nice cursive hand. You've been educated, Joe. Not a dummy like those other two. Where'd you go to school? You got high school, I can tell."

"And one year of state apprenticeship." He looked proud but a little sad. "I was going to be a master mechanic like my dad."

"It shows, you've got schooling. That'll look good, you go before the jury. Those other two? White trash. Losers. Trying to put you in. Don't let them, man, you've got some potential. Your life doesn't have to be over."

Ray Tate, with the money in the bank, picked up the statement and folded it and put it into his pocket. He could push a little. "If it wasn't you, Joe, any ideas who in the group went for the dark? Someone who might be a race traitor? Whoever gives the guy up, he can cut a deal with the State's Attorney. You got any idea? Someone with a thing for black chicks, on the down-low? Beats them to mush after?"

"Dunno nobody like that." He looked at Marty Frost and said earnestly, "If I did, Miss, I'd tell you."

Marty Frost said, "Because, Joe, if you did, you'd get first dibs on life with a chance instead of a needle with none. I'd like to see you get that chance, man. Turn your life around, get out from under that rape stuff. Anybody?"

He shook his head.

"Well, think about it, okay. If something comes to you, tell someone to contact me. Marty Frost. We can get together, chat. Make the best of this bad situation. Okay? Will you do that for me?"

Ray Tate stood up. He could push a little more for the team. "Look, Joe, there's some guys, Intelligence guys, they might want to talk to you. They got some stuff from Peter, but they think he might be making the whole thing up, that you're the boss in this. You want to have a sandwich and coffee with them? Get all this stuff behind you, come clean, not make your wife ashamed when it hits the papers?"

"My wife's gonna know about this? You got to tell her it wasn't us, did the nig —" He looked Martinique Frost. "I mean the black women."

She nodded. "We can try to keep all this between us, Joe. If you talk to the Intelligence guys, okay?"

He nodded. "Okay." He looked at her and then hung his head. "I'm sorry about the ... those women you talked about." He awkwardly put out his left, unshackled hand. "We just wanted to stop the Chinese plague. Protect the community."

"Well," Martinique Frost said, taking his hand in hers and solemnly shaking it. "You guys made a good start."

Hambone Hogarth came into the coffee room with DVDs in evidence bags under his arm. He wore a vacant smile but his eyes were sparkling. "Fuck. This is down. Shut-the-Fuck-Up Paquin just arrived and he's some pissed they didn't invoke, wait for him to show up, earn his retainer. You guys. That was fucking beautiful. Can I take you home with me? You want to come for dinner next Christmas? Eighteen homicides in Chinatown now, they upped the count after the canvass of the stairways, eighteen homicides. They haven't even started the autopsies and we're going to lay charges."

Ray Tate rubbed his eyes. "You want to get some of those smart guys from Intelligence in there, clean Joe out before he gets too-late smart."

"Yeah, we've already heard from Sally Greaves' spooks at Strategic Planning Analysis. The SPA wants to be copied on everything."

"But don't forget us, Bob. Our needs, right? We need a workup on the hierarchy, who in the gang might be a race killer, masking it behind that white power shit. I don't think it was the two mutts we talked to. They couldn't bang their hand. Third guy, Ansel Partridge, he's a strong viable. We gave you, now you have to give us."

"Done. We'll tee up at the task force office. Grab a couple hours' sleep, we're back at it at seven tonight." Bob Hogarth stood and turned to Martinique Frost. "I got to ask you, Marty, if I'm not outta line? All that nigger-this and jig-broad-that. That's got to wear. Didn't you just want to take him out?"

She gave him an even stare. "I've been called worse," she said, "by cops I've worked with, guys who didn't shake my hand after."

Djuna Brown and Brian Comartin spent the rest of the morning interviewing residents and witnesses. Because of the heat, she'd dumped the raid jacket in the restaurant and worked in bare arms, baggy trousers, and slippers. They were assigned a dour, young Chinese officer to translate. He gave them a lecture about there being no Chinese language, that there were several and the one they wanted was Mandarin. He was, he said, from a Fujian household, so he could help with the illegal immigrants in their own dialect.

In the middle of the fourth interview with a man who seemed to speak evasively in mutters and shrugs as if he didn't understand the question, the translator began shouting and pushing at him. "You fucking people," he said. "Send 'em back. Go home, go home."

Djuna Brown calmed him down and saw he had tears in his eyes. "It's okay, man. No hurry. Take a break. Get a coffee. Get a tea. Get me one."

He nodded. He left the immigrant with them and walked up the street and didn't return.

The immigrant man was looking across the street, trying to screen himself from view behind Brian Comartin, peeping over his shoulder.

Djuna Brown turned and saw a stocky, immaculate Chinese man in a dark suit and tie and a stickpin smoking a cigarette near the doorway to a vegetable shop, gazing at them pleasantly. Four men in open-neck white shirts and black suits stood a half-dozen yards away, doing nothing but idling. "Brian, I think those guys over there are making our witness shaky. You know Mr. Stickpin?"

Brian Comartin looked. "Willard Wong. Big man in Chinatown. The mayor. He's on the news sometimes. They say he's into the rackets."

"I've heard of him," she said. "He was in a case I worked, last time I was down here last year with Ray. I'm going to go make his acquaintance." She crossed the street, careful of broken glass and puddles in her slippers. It appeared she was dancing a complex step, or was a graceful child playing hopscotch. When she reached the other side of the street, she put her right hand on the butt of the silver automatic under her batik top and pointed her left forefinger directly at Willard Wong's face. "You, stand still."

Willard Wong watched her approach. Her dainty slippers seemed to amuse him. When she was close enough he examined the badge hanging around her neck. "Ah, State Police. Willard Wong at your service, Officer. I like the State Police very much."

She'd never seen him but remembered his name from a year earlier when she and Ray Tate had worked on the ecstasy and methamphetamine case. A warehouse tied to Willy Wong had been shot up, someone killed, and barrels of his precursor chemicals were hijacked. White badlands traffickers had wreaked havoc in his precious Chinatown, shooting and torturing his thugs. Willy Wong had almost lost his face because he didn't react strongly by leaving bodies in the streets, but after the two ringleaders were shot by Djuna Brown and a State Police sniper, things returned to normal. She'd heard he put the word out that he'd used his police connections to get them assassinated.

"I'm Sergeant Brown. I'll need to see some identification."

"As I said, my name is Willard Wong. W-O-N-G."

"Identification, bud. This is a crime stage and you're standing in it." She casually tapped on the pistol on her hip. "Or I can drag you through the filthy water and broken glass, take you for a drive in the trunk of my car."

This amused him hugely. Running his hands over his pockets, he looked up the block at the four men and smiled. He called something in Mandarin. They all laughed, and one man approached with a slim wallet in his hand.

"Mr. Wong's identification."

"Give it to him."

Willard Wong took the wallet and unfolded it. "My tailor said I must carry a … man's purse? Unseemly. Or make arrangements so my suits don't dis-align. He's in Hong Kong, what does he know of our American way? Fortunately, I have friends to assist." He gave her his state health card and watched her study it. "But I don't drive, either. I have friends for that. I have many friends for many things."

"You have a reason to be here, Willy?"

"Willard. I'm a local entrepreneur and benefactor to this community." He smiled modestly. "If I can be of assistance in this tragedy? I'm a friend of police."

"You can be gone, Willy, if you want to assist in this tragedy."

Willard Wong remained in place, smiling, confused.

Djuna Brown caught sight of Brian Comartin come up on the edge of her vision. She stepped back two paces and pulled her gun and held it straight down her leg. "Brian, frisk this friend of Willy here. He's got a lumpy suit. I fear for officer safety and the well-being of the community."

Brian Comartin told Willard Wong's companion to put his hands on the wall. The man stretched lazily, keeping his balance.

Comartin had to go to school.

"You can step him back a little and go wider, Brian, reach him a little higher."

"Step back, spread, hands higher." He seemed surprised that the man obeyed him and he got into it. He looked like he felt pretty good. "Don't you move." He thought that sounded weak. "*Don't* you *fucking* move."

The other three men came down the sidewalk. Djuna Brown took two more long backwards steps to make a wide controlling arc and put her gun up on them. "Okay, everybody, shadows on the wall."

Willard Wong said it wasn't necessary. "These men are all legally permitted to carry weapons in concealment. Signed by Pious Man Chan, the illustrious police chief. A personal friend."

"Well, Willy, I'm State. I don't give a fuck about Pious Chan and the city. He's just another Chinaman with an attitude, this city is just another shithole, you're just another douche with a stickpin."

"I know you, Officer. You were involved in the ... unpleasantness that hurt our community last year? You were on television for that. You shot a fat man. A bad fat man who tortured the children of Chinatown. A trafficker. I thank you. All of Chinatown thanks you."

"Just so you know, Willy," she said, not looking at

him. "I don't just shoot fat white guys. I'm no racist. First come, first served."

"Yes, you worked with Sergeant Tate. Ray Tate. Last year. Those drug traffickers. Now Sergeant Ray Tate is solving this trouble in Chinatown for me."

Comartin took a gun from a waist holster off the man on the wall. He didn't seem to know what to do with it.

"Secure the firearm in your belt, Brian. When you're done one, put him on his knees, hands behind the head, forehead on the wall. He's mine, then, I got him, you don't think about him. Concentrate and do the next one. " She shifted back to allow her gun arc to encompass Willard Wong and the men.

"Sergeant Ray Tate and I are friends. You should call him, Officer."

"Sergeant."

"Yes, Sergeant. You should call my friend, Sergeant Ray Tate."

"Sure, Willy, later, maybe. Right now we're removing firearms and bad elements from Chinatown."

"But, but the paperwork? The licences?"

"We'll sort it out, down at the Sector. If it checks out, you come down and pick them up. For now, just relax, Willy. Chill."

Comartin put the next two guys through the routine, taking a gun from each of them. He was running out of belt to tuck them into.

The last guy, spread up the wall like wings, cleared his sinuses loudly and casually horked on the ground, very vaguely in her direction.

Willard Wong murmured a warning.

"Oh-*kay* then." Djuna Brown said with exaggerated vivacity. "This fellow we'll do a little different, Brian. This guy is a bit more of a risk, with the health hazard, the horking and the like, in this time of medical crisis." She told the guy to keep his hands on the wall. "Good, good. Now, Brian you'd like him to step back for you, step back ... step back. Okay, perfect. You're a natural. Now tell him to lean forward for you, put his forehead on the wall. Weight on his palms and forehead. Nice, nicely done. Now, you need him to take his hands off the wall, to clasp his hands behind his head for you, lace his fingers." When the man was at a sharp angle, she said, "Brian, with your left hand gather his fingers, keep your arm straight, push, keep that forehead on the wall. Pat him down from the side. Now change hands on his fingers, go and do the other side. Very nice."

Comartin took a gun from the man's shoulder holster. He put it into the back of his belt.

"I observe he's getting agitated, Brian."

The man was calm, impassive, and almost good-humoured. It was a form of insolence, she decided. Disrespect.

"Brian? Scalp that guy."

"He's co-operating. He's okay."

"Brian, he's going to make a move. Officer safety is paramount. Scalp him. Swing him wide, both feet."

"Djuna."

"Right now, Brian. He goes down hard."

Brian Comartin used his right foot to sweep both of the last man's feet and at the same time let go of his fingers. The man's hands, still finger-locked behind his head were useless to control his fall. He'd been wall-scalped before; it was clear when he turned his head to protect his face and only the right side smeared down the bricks, but it left a lot of skin and meat behind.

Djuna Brown handed the wallet to Willard Wong. "Everything's in order, Mr. Wong. Your companions can pick up their weapons at Sector Eight. Thank you for your co-operation in this stressful time, and have a nice day." She smiled gaily at him.

Chapter 14

They walked the guns to the local Sector and gave them to the desk sergeant. "We got four pieces. Someone'll have to punch it all into the system, serial numbers. Some Chinese guys'll pick them up later. They said they worked for someone named Wong? Willy Wong?"

"Fuck. You braced Willy's boys? In Chinatown?"

"Sure. Chinatown is still in America and only we get to beat people there at random. This isn't Canada."

"I'm gonna hear about this, girl."

"Hey, they were acting suspicious. Intimidating our witnesses. Disrespecting."

"You know who he is? Willy Wong?"

"Yep." Djuna Brown nodded and said, "A local douchebag. How come your guys don't scoop him up?"

The desk sergeant stared at her. "You're not from around here, are you, honey?"

"Nope," she said, giving him the white picket smile. "I be from Bohemia." She had a thought. "You got a sergeant around here, Ray Tate? Hippie-looking dude?"

"He's in interviews."

"Marty Frost?"

"Black chick? She's with him, too. They're gonna be a while."

They went outside of Chinatown for something American to eat and found a deli with a vacant table in the back. A waitress came down with menus, saw their badges, and said, keeping the menus in her hand, "Brisket today. Not too lean, not too fat. Or egg salad. Rye or kaiser?"

They went for the egg salad. Meat was out of the question.

"On light rye," Djuna Brown said. "And a couple of Coors."

"I'll have to ask about the beer."

Djuna Brown said, "We'll pay."

The waitress shook her head. "Don't be silly," and went away.

"Nice, nice work, there, Brian. You slimed that mutt pretty good."

"I've, ah, I haven't done a ... takedown? ... in ten years." He looked back at her. "I'm Traffic, you know."

"Well, man, you're natural born cop."

He felt pretty good at that. "I guess you guys, you and Ray and Marty, do this all the time?"

"Brian. Let me tell you how it is. How it is with me, anyway. Guys like Willy Wong get nothing. Absolutely nothing. So, fuck them. Parasites. That guy horking on the sidewalk near my slippers? That gives me licence. They eye-fuck you, they give you licence. So you humiliate them, every chance you get. Guys like the immigrant that wouldn't talk to us? He gets every break we can cut. He's a victim. If you got any heart, that's where you spend it. With Willy Wong and guys like that, you do 'em hard, every chance."

"I thought, I wondered how it would be if Marty was there."

"You saw Marty at the chief's task force? Taking out that idiot from headquarters yesterday? Well, today was Willy Wong's lucky day."

"She's pretty tough, Marty. She's, ah ..." He didn't know what to say.

"You're digging Marty, eh, Brian? She's a cool chick, no question. She's cop." She sat back, pleased with the romantic drama. When the waitress put two bottles of beer on the table, she held hers up to clink. "I think she digs you too."

Marty Frost said she wanted to get home to get a few hours' sleep.

Ray Tate said he'd see her at the task force briefing that night. "We did good work today, Marty, or at least you did. No closer on our poor ladies case, but Intell or Homicide should be able to get us a suspect list. We'll go at them. One of them will break out. This is closing."

"I got to tell you, that wasn't very challenging, but it was fun." She frowned a little, harsh and painful but pretty. "In that room, with those guys? That was the real me. The girl driving around in the ghoster, playing kiddie cop? Not so much me. I can do that, but I just like to sit talking to people. You say the stupidest things, right off the wall, and it works, they relate. And they for some reason like talking to me. I don't get that much on the job."

Ray Tate stood with her near the desk sergeant's table. "Marty, I'm going to go off the wall here, okay? Tell me it's okay and I'll do it."

She gave him the same smile he imagined she had when she was in her teens. "Sure, Ray. Just remember, I got a gun."

"Comartin. You ask that desk sergeant for his cell number and he'll call the duty desk and get it for you. Give yourself an afternoon. I'll see you tonight."

He didn't have Djuna Brown's cell number. He called the Whistler and the woman on the reception desk said she'd check the room, then came back and said no one was answering.

The desk sergeant had a ghoster take him back to East Chinatown to pick up his car. On the way, the wheelman said he worked East Chinatown and it was a mess.

"Things are going to be weird down there for a long time." He suddenly stopped on California Street in front of an old woman dragging a bundle of clothing around puddles. "Just be a second, Sarge." He got out and helped the woman across the street to where a city bus was moving the homeless to a community centre. After helping her up the step and passing up her stuff, he reboarded the ghoster and looked at the wreckage of California Street through his windshield. "This makes me ashamed to be an American."

"How long you been working down here?"

"Two years. Punishment detail. I slagged my desk sergeant up in Sector Two." He pulled in behind the Taurus. "First six months? I was a hard-on. Pissed right off, how could they do this to me? Vegetable stalls impeding pedestrian passage? Hundred and twenty bucks, confiscate the cart, the bok choy, the whole shebang. Fuck you. Loiter on the sidewalk? Impede safe pedestrian passage, ninety bucks. Fuck you. I made a lot of fucking money for this city until I got trampled in a gambling raid and a kid pulled me out of the way of the exodus. That old lady, there, that I just helped? You know who she is, who I ticketed on my first day for a week's wages of selling vegetables she hoed in her backyard? Mae. She's the mother of a Hong Kong Homicide cop who put down the first nobody murder in the city's history. Guy was a hero over there until they killed him." He realized he was talking too much to someone he didn't know well enough to talk too much to. "Sorry. Babbling. That's your car, the Taurus?"

"Hey, hey, you're doing okay. You can show your heart."

"These poor fucking fuckers." He bit his lip, looking around. "I hope they get the guys that did this."

"Don't worry about that. As we speak they're dressing for the arraignment ball."

In the Taurus, he drove to the Whistler. People slouched along in the blazing sunshine, cowering, barely dressed except for shorts and T-shirts. And, in spite of the CDC experts saying the plague was coming under control, the masks. They looked like furtive spacemen, having trouble with the new gravity.

There was a perky receptionist at the hotel. It seemed she had no idea of the horror of Chinatown and, in spite of his wrecked street clothes, beamed at Ray Tate across the wide marble countertop in the freezing lobby. "Welcome to the Whistler, sir. May I help you?"

He picked his badge up from his chest and showed it to her. "I'm meeting State Police Inspector Brown in her room."

"I'll call up, sir." She waited out the rings. "I'm sorry, Inspector Brown isn't answering. You can wait in the lounge or the bar, sir."

"Get me house security, please."

She picked up the phone and spoke quietly.

A big, beefy man in a tight suit, with an earpiece coiling out of his jacket, appeared at Ray Tate's elbow.

"Is there a problem, sir?" His tone suggested there'd better not be.

"Ray Tate, sergeant, city police. I need to get into a room."

"You're Ray Tate? Fuck, I knew your father-in-law when I was on the job. He was Ident, photography. Great guy. Almost a cop."

"We're working the Chinatown fires. I'm teeing up with a State cop. I'm early and I'm fucking tired. Could use the shower."

"If Chinatown smells like you smell, man, the whole place needs a shower." The security officer asked the receptionist, "What's the room he needs?"

When she came in he was in the tub, having mastered the technique of adding water using his toes. He'd dozed and gained some rest, awakening only to warm up the water as it chilled. He'd avoided the bed; stretching out flat with the billowy pillows under his head would send him off for hours. There was some satisfaction that he and Marty Frost had put it to the Volunteers for Chinatown. But it hadn't moved the dead ladies case ahead except for maybe allowing Intelligence to drill into the group and maybe sight in on a good viable.

Laying in the smooth tub with the late afternoon light glowing outside the window, and a triple gin and double tap in a water glass on the rim, he had a strange sense of unreality. It was brought on by the realization that the bathtub and water and lotions and bathrobes could possibly be in the same world as the pain gripping Chinatown. Was it like a smell, he thought, how pain thinned as it gained distance from the source, thinned and thinned and finally was gone?

But it never was gone. Somewhere someone was being hurt. Somewhere someone's life was changing, probably for the worse.

Was it possible that only hours earlier he was in a world of smoke and burning flesh, thinking about shooting the tie pin of a Chinatown thug?

Was it possible that three hours ago he was in a room with brain-dead killers and having a good time, teetering on the edge of giddiness?

Was it possible that he hadn't seen Djuna Brown in six hours?

They'd love Paris, he knew. He'd paint and sketch and she'd find something for herself to do. When his ex-wife had bitched that she did nothing all day and night while he roamed his city with a gun on his ankle having adventures, he'd gone by the community college and picked up some schedules. None had attracted her interest. When he said they could take up something together, golf or tennis or a euchre club, she said no, you're patronizing me. In the end he'd realized that some people were only happy in a life they could complain about.

Djuna Brown might find herself to be a poet or a weaver or a memoirist or a photographer or a dancer in the dark. It was the possibilities of her, or them, that kept the dream alive. If only they could break away from their lives, turn their backs on the predatory burning cities that needed them.

In his mind were images of his life's work, most of it unpleasant but some of it not. Dim dawns with long streets of orderly garbage cans, of yellow square lights in windows above them. Men asleep on stoops, smiling dreamily in the dreamland of another place. Unlike his ex-father-in-law, he didn't need the day-to-day slugfest of pain and suffering to engage him. He could paint a tree, he could charcoal sketch a sad car at dawn, up on blocks, the hood yawning up, forgotten.

He could go blind and never see another image and the library of his mind would keep him busy forever, keep his knuckles black with charcoal, his shirt dripped with paint.

In the tub, his beard soaked and his long hair sodden, he was suddenly overwhelmed by his life, wondering if he could carry it any longer. That young cop who carried an old woman's bundles onto a bus and feared he'd revealed too much of who he was. The cadet cop unable to process what his eyes were seeing in East Chinatown, frozen in awe at the magnitude of what people could do to other people. The volunteer firefighter having failed to save a life, pounding his fists into the concrete. Marty Frost sagged in exhaustion outside the interview room, then rubbing something off her face with her brisk hands before they went in.

But there was also the sprite-like Djuna Brown in the restaurant, putting the chargettes on about her batik clothing and sparkly slippers, rising from her stool and wrapping her arms around him, calling him a beatnik in relief, that sweetest of voices. Momentarily, she'd sagged against him as if he were a lifeline.

And, on cue, the outside door of the suite opened and a soft voice called, "I detect a beatnik hipster in my house. Ooo, *oui, oui.*" He'd left his clothing on the bed, his boots by the door.

He heard the mini-bar popping open, the twist of bottle caps, the gurgle of liquid, then the running of water from the spigot into glasses. There was quiet for a few seconds, or almost quiet, anyway: the silent slide of her clothing coming off, the thump of her holstered automatic on the thick carpeting.

She came in naked, twirling, almost dancing, and put her holster on the toilet seat beside his. Without pause she stepped into the bathtub, balancing the glasses on her palm. She handed him both while she fitted herself into the tub, half beside him, half across him. He could tell she'd had an interesting day. Paris, he decided, as they shifted around. Somehow, sometime soon. If love felt like this in the chaos of the city, how great it could be in Paris. They'd have a room with a sloping ceiling at the top of a flight of steps, a place where they could close the world out.

This square tiled room, right now, was perfect in the moment.

They lazed in the tub. He told her about his run-up with Willy Wong, how he thought Willy had called the Jank and set him up to work the Chinatown homicides. "Don't know why. I mean, like he gives a shit about Chinatown. Probably he wants to show some people that he's got some control over the investigation."

"Yes, I met Willy today, too. Him and some thugs were standing around, intimidating witnesses me and Brian were trying to talk to. We braced them. I had to take some of his face, a little." She laughed. "Literally, in the case of one of his goons."

"Good."

"Brian did good. He's the one took out the henchman."

"What? He run over him?"

"Nope. Scalp-and-smear. Old Brian can sure get into it when he wants to. What did you and Marty get up to?"

"Not much. She solved the Chinatown murders. Like, eighteen of them. Got some of the guys anyway. They're going." He told her about the interviews, short and funny. "But she's a little unhappy. She's no further ahead on the dead ladies case, unless one of them cracks."

"Are we going to break it, Ray?"

"Well," he said, shifting her around a little, "not in the next ten minutes."

Martinique Frost called as Djuna Brown was in the bathroom re-spiking her hair.

Ray Tate picked up the phone.

"It's Marty, Ray. I guess you had the same idea, huh? Drop by, see if Djuna need a ride to the briefing?"

"Yeah, it was on my way from home to down-town."

"Not if you had to go through the Eight at Harrison, it wasn't, buddy. Truck on truck fatality. Nice try, though."

"No, I saw the slowdown and ramped off early at Erie."

She laughed and said, away from the phone, "Told you."

"Jesus, Marty, there's no wreck on the Eight, is there?"

"I've locked up guys went for that one, Ray. Heavy, heavy guys, so don't feel bad. Me and Traffic man, here, are heading in. We're going to pick up sandwiches and stuff, get some beer on the way."

"You guys are, ah, together?"

"Sure, Ray. That's what adults do. When you shy kids graduate high school, you'll see it's a whole different scene." She hung up, laughing, sounding young and carefree.

Naked, Djuna Brown came out of the washroom with her holster in her hand and pawed through the closet. Ray Tate, in his undershorts, watched her. He hadn't called in sick in ages, hadn't missed time at work except for when he'd been gunned the previous year. He felt like maybe a cold was coming on. Maybe a toothache.

"Marty and Brian are jammin'." He felt a little smug. "No question."

She gave him a secret smile. "Yeah, so?"

"Well," he said, "that was quick." He wandered toward her as she picked up his sweatshirt, smelling it. "They just met. Not like us." He reached out for her.

"Cool it, beatnik. I can get to my gun before you get to me." She looked at his rumpled clothes. "Those things smell like today. Smoke. What are you, Ray? Large, extra-large?" She picked up the telephone and pressed a button.

"Yes, Inspector."

"Yes, I need some things from the gift shop."

"I'll put you through, Inspector."

When a polite woman answered, Djuna Brown asked if they had any sweats, large. "Grey, if you got 'em. To bring out his eyes." She listened. "How about a light jacket? Sure, the hotel crest is okay, proud to show it off ... Great, send them up and you can charge them to the State room account."

They cruised the long way to the Jank. There were no Volunteers on the streets. At the gates of Chinatown a memorial was being created. Incense, candles, photographs, flowers. Buddhist monks in saffron robes waved incense in the air. A young man with a shaven head slowly tapped at a drum. The flowers were huge and colourful: traditional yellow chrysanthemums and pink lilies. Off to side was a group of a dozen masked young Chinese youths in kung-fu school T-shirts being harangued by a man in a black leather jacket. There were fists in the air. A black family of six in dark Sunday suits and church-going dresses kneeled on the edge of the memorial, bibles in hand.

"I can't believe what happened here, Ray. In this

day and age. It's the equivalent of lynching." Djuna Brown leaned past him to look at the growing memorial in awe.

"They're down, the fuckers who did this. Marty got 'em. They're fucked."

"That won't make this right, though."

"Nothing will make this right, except time." He shrugged. "We have to concentrate on the poor dead ladies. Marty needs it. She has to close it." He'd told Djuna Brown about Marty Frost wearing the hat for the fuck-up on the serial rape case back when she worked Tin Town. "I think she thinks if she gets justice for the dead ladies she'll undo what she didn't do, but should have done, with the serial rapist."

"Do you think the doer for the dead ladies is one of the Volunteers? One of the ones you guys got today?"

"Maybe, but maybe they're too stupid, the two guys that talked to us. They had no idea what we were talking about. But if it was a Volunteer, they probably know who did it, even if they don't know they know."

Chapter 15

The chief's task force showed up dressed for night work. Men in dark grey windbreakers over T-shirts, baggy jeans or khakis, running shoes, and women in track clothing and flat shoes straggled across the parking lot behind Jank. Most were carrying plastic or paper bags. Some furtively carried bright red-and-white styro coolers and stashed them behind the front seats. Everyone had a mask around their throats.

Marty Frost and Brian Comartin were leaning on the trunk of one of the ghosters. She wore a fresh beige pantsuit, but Comartin was in the same baggy stuff he'd worn all day. That told Ray Tate the story.

Marty Frost had a small smile for them as they climbed out of the Taurus. She ran her eyes up and down Ray Tate in his promotional Whistler Hotel garb, and her little smile turned into a smirk. Djuna

Brown was in a sleeveless dark blue sweatshirt, blue jeans, and her slippers.

"What's that?" Comartin pointed to a convoy of heavy black four-by-fours creeping into the lot, followed by five black crash cars, each with four chargers aboard. The vehicles stopped beside the fire doors and men and a few women in black head-to-toe fatigues disembarked. Most carried automatic rifles and duffle bags. Gas masks, helmets with visors, cord-cuffs, and other doo dads of police work hung from their utility belts. Their sidearms were strapped to their thighs. A few carried spare keys: long stainless steel battering rams with two handles on each.

"Suppression teams," Ray Tate said. "I think maybe those fools we took out of Chinatown gave up some intell." He looked at Comartin cheerfully. "Hope everybody got a lot of rest. It's gonna be a long night of knocks and locks."

In the briefing room, the chief of detectives and Hambone Hogarth were at the podium comparing notes. Five floor plans of residences were on the easels; the photographs of the dead ladies were gone. Nine photographs, most of them mugshots with numbers under the chins, of men with shaven heads and one woman were tacked to a corkboard, stacked like a pyramid.

Protocol dictated that the Chief of Ds had to speak first. He didn't have much that anybody with a radio or TV or Internet didn't already know. "There have been a lot of developments today, not least is the arson murders in Chinatown. We've managed to turn two of the suspected participants. Both have given up intell. Tonight we're going to act on it. The chief and the mayor are having a press conference at nine in the morning. They've got a lot to talk about. Three in custody charged with hate-murder by arson, times eighteen and more charges to come. We're shorthanded, we're all tired, but we have to close this tonight." He stepped back. "Inspector."

Hambone Hogarth had changed his suit into something just as wrinkled. His tie flapped from his pocket. He'd shaved, but with patches. His hair was a mess and his voice was hoarse. "We're breaking off the surveillance op. We know who we're after. We'll hold back on the decoys on the dead women ... the dead ladies case. Tonight we're hitting the homes of the main players in the Volunteers. We've got search warrants on their residences. This stuff is time-sensitive. We have to go, all at once."

Beside Ray Tate, Marty Frost stood up so quickly her folding chair flipped over. "What about the dead women, Inspector? What does this do for them? We got to put out a notification. What if the raids don't get the guy that did them? What if he's already out there and not at the addresses we're hitting? What if he's not a Volunteer? Who wears it, then, this time?" She pointed at the podium. "I want someone up there, right now, right here, to officially decline to notify."

The red-headed gunslinger from the holdup squad, with three notches on his grip, stood up two rows ahead. "Yeah, I'm with Marty on this one, Hambone. What's it hurt? We put out a public alert, we go out and do the job, and if we get him, great. If not, you don't have a bunch of citizens walking around like sheep and maybe he at least takes a break."

One of the Chief of Ds' sycophants stood up at the back of the room. "Downside is, he leaves town, takes his act on the road. What if he pops up in Chicago?"

The gunslinger barely turned his head. "Fuck Chicago. Chicago can kiss my red-headed ass. How about it, Ham, we going with an alert or what?"

Hambone Hogarth knew he was being fitted for a hat in front of four dozen witnesses. He was respected, but with four dozen pairs of ears hearing him decline to notify the public, there was absolutely no hope for secrecy. Someone would rat. Someone owed a newspaper reporter some favour, somewhere. Someone was banging a television producer. And if there was another negligence enquiry you couldn't expect dozens of people to put their hands on the black book and lie and risk their rank and job and pension. He stepped aside and turned to the Chief of Ds. "I'm operational, that's policy. Chief?"

The Chief of Ds gave him a simmering look but made a wide smile at the rows of faces. "Okay, we're a little ahead of you on this one, Marty. Public affairs is working on the alert. It'll be ready by tomorrow morning. If we get the guy tonight, it'll be moot. If we don't, then we'll be ready to go, we'll alert-out and go to decoys, show that we're on top of it. Personally, I think it's one of the dummies taken in this morning in Chinatown. If not them, then someone in the intell they provided." He gave Martinique Frost a friendly smile. "Nice work on that one, by the way, Marty."

"If he goes again, Chief, you're going to wear it. I'm gonna fuck you up."

"Okay, I know, Marty." He was patronizing. "We're all tired."

"Fuck you." She picked up her chair and sat down, ignoring him.

Hambone Hogarth stepped back to the podium. "Okay, we're taking doors tonight. We have five target premises and we're hitting them all at once. We have a warrant for each residence. Warrants include garages, sheds, doghouses, birdcages, everything. You'll each have to read the warrant so you'll know what you can and can't do, what to take and what to leave. But you won't be leaving much. Photograph everything before you take a room apart, then photograph it afterwards. Photograph every person in the residence. Everybody gets read their rights. We're going hard on this, but we're doing it right. Each raiding party will have a suppression team, with one officer designated as a bomb officer. The STs will breach, secure, capture, and remove occupants. They'll be turned over to uniformed transport. Children's welfare will have a male and female at each site in case there are minors on scene. Animal care services will have a team at each site. After the individuals are removed and sent to Sector Four, the STs will secure the perimeter and you guys go to work. Essentially," he said, picking up a copy of a warrant and reading from it, "we're looking for firearms and paraphernalia,

explosive devices and materials, documentation of conspiracy, and this includes address books, computers and
paraphernalia, manuals, right down to post-it notes
on refrigerators. If it's on paper and someone's written
something on it, we take it. Scorched earth. If you aren't
sure, the leader of your team will have a direct line to
a State's attorney. Don't just think of things related to
the firebombings in Chinatown and the murders of the
women. Think what *might* be. What *might* be planned.
We're stepping into homegrown terrorism territory, so
think dirty. When the *federales* get word of this they're
going to want in. We want it wrapped up and publicly
announced, then they can come in."

Someone called, "What about vehicles?"

"Vehicles are named in the warrants. We want any
GPS or documentation regarding purchase of gasoline
or on-road service. There'll be a fleet of wreckers ready
to hook them up and drag them away. If a vehicle
listed is on the property, it goes. If it isn't named in
the warrant, it gets seized anyway as an attached or
extended. If there's a vehicle not listed or described in
the warrant, say, parked on public roadway but possibly connected to the residence, not registered to a
neighbour, the vehicle will be secured and the evidence
officer will call the State's attorney to amend the warrant. Questions, obs? Yeah, Ray?"

Ray Tate stood up. "We don't want to forget our
dead ladies in this. I know this is a big deal, but the
Volunteers are coming apart, no matter what. Nothing
to do with the murders of the women goes into after-
matter, the oh-yeah file, an afterthought."

"Noted, Ray. You guys, everybody, flag anything you find that Ray's team can use. We're doing the Chinatown fires and the women murders as a hate crime, one big conspiracy. If you're talking to anyone stupid enough to talk without a lawyer, drop in a question about the women. Can't hurt. Okay, Ray, does that do it?"

Ray Tate sat down. Martinique Frost patted his leg. "Thanks, man."

"We dragged this whole thing in, we gotta get some slack. They'll go, Marty."

The Chief of Ds stepped forward. "Just two notes. We wouldn't have any of this without Marty Frost. She sweated and moved two of the Chinatown arsonists in record time today." He raised his fist in the air and made a short punch toward her. "Kudos and daps, Marty. And, you guys, when you're bringing your bodies into Sector Four and if you see some media there, don't think you have to hurry them inside." He looked smug. "I know on good authority the sally-port door is malfunctioning and won't open, so the arrested individuals will have to be walked across the parking lot. So that means, cuff 'em in the back. Nobody gets to play shy."

The plan was to set up an hour before the coordinated raids. Ray Tate and Djuna Brown were in the Taurus, and Martinique Frost and Brian Comartin rode in a black Chrysler. They were parked dog-end, driver's door to driver's door two blocks away from their target. A pair of Intelligence guys in a gas-company van, with a rotating light on the top, were down the block with an eye on a brick bungalow with an old red immaculate Reliant in the driveway. The Reliant was in the warrants. One of the Intell guys broadcast, "Site three set up lights in house and individuals in motion inside, note doghouse visible at east side rear of building."

"I got it." Martinique Frost called animal control on her cellphone and gave the address to a dispatcher. After a few seconds, she disconnected and went on the air. "Okay, all, pit bulls, two of them, noise and run-free complaints. The house is flagged as a hazard visit."

"Okay, thanks. First man in? Take a scattergun. Grind me up a couple of pounds, extra lean."

"Ten-four. No free bites."

"No free bites."

Marty Frost behind the wheel of the Chrysler reached behind the passenger seat and pulled up a shopping bag. "Mafia sandwiches. Sang-weed-ges, from The Boot. I got veal and peps, I got meat-a-balls, all on crusty, and I got, oh, I got a salad, no dressing. I guess that's for my poetry man." She gave Ray Tate, behind the wheel of the Taurus, a smirk and handed the salad and a plastic fork to Brian Comartin. "Next, the gold chains and the puffy Converses."

Djuna Brown said, "I dunno. You shoulda seen him take down one of Willy Wong's boys today. He spackled that wall with Chinaman cheek. All cop. If I wasn't stuck with the beatnik here, I'd give you a run."

"Keep your hands off my man, Statie."

Brian Comartin beamed.

They sat comfortable, eating.

Ray Tate said, "Brian, when you were in Europe, you dug it, right?"

"Barcelona's my place, but for you art types, Paris. City of Lights. You haven't lived, Ray, until you've sat on the Boulevard St. Michel at dusk, drinking champagne like water and eating oysters like peanuts. We get justice for the ladies, I'm booking all my sick days and vacations and I'm, we're, I think, over to Spain for two months."

"Think you can live on half a twenty-five pension? Not like a king, but maybe like an artist?"

"No question. A bun and coffee for breakfast, a sandwich for lunch, and at night you go for broke. Beef stew, cassoulet, some duck confit. Lots of wine. You get the prix fixe. Then you sit at a café and watch the parade." He looked at Ray Tate. "Ray, I'm not kidding. If you've got an artistic bone in your body, that place will spark it up. You thinking of going?"

"Yeah, I think, after this. Another twenty-one months, I go three-quarters pension. Hopefully my ex will be remarried by then, stop claiming the alimony. How about women? Will I have trouble getting hooked up in Paris? I hate being, you know, lonely."

Djuna Brown said, "Asshole."

"Hustlers," Martinique Frost laughed, "the both of them."

A few minutes before the appointed hour, they watched a taxi go past the front of the house and stop up the block. The brake lights flared three times and two men in raid jackets with shotguns exited the back seat. The gas-company van slid away and the taxi continued on. Immediately, a heavy-duty four-by-four pulled across the driveway, blocking in the Reliant, and four black-clad figures bailed out the four doors and raced up the steps, one of them with the spare key on his shoulder. From a block away Ray Tate, Djuna Brown, Martinique Frost, and Brian Comartin heard a voice scream, "Police warrant open up now." And then immediately the door went in under the key and without pause there were two shotgun blasts, boom boom.

Ray Tate said, "Dog food," and put the Taurus in gear.

The Taurus and the Chrysler sped up the block and screeched to a stop side-by-side behind the four-by-four. The two men from the taxi took up positions with a view to the east and west side of the house, with their shotguns to their shoulders.

Comartin went to get out of the Chrysler. Ray Tate called, "Wait, just wait. Let them do a census."

They all pulled on evidence gloves and waited.

A woman in black, her full utility belt swinging, ran from the house with a screaming child in her arms. She lit off a whistle in her teeth and a grey Dodge van marked Children's Protective Services came up the block.

Djuna Brown bailed and ran to the child. "You okay, honey? You'll be okay."

The child, a beautiful blond boy with gaps in his teeth, screamed spittle into her face. "Black bitch."

* * *

The female resident of the bungalow had gone to the Sector, the male resident was absent, and the suppression team had the perimeter of the house secure. Children's services had left; the animal control had removed the pit bulls' bodies, leaving a pair of long wide smears in the entryway to the house. A police department wrecker had removed the Reliant. Neighbours were milling on their porches and lawns.

A bomb guy came out and gave a thumbs-up. "The place is clear, attic, first floor, and basement." He chuckled. "Probably." He held up a digital camera. "We got pictures. Call me when you're done and we'll take aftershots. I'll be a block away with my fingers in my ears."

They trooped up the steps. The front door opened to a long hallway that ended with a kitchen at the rear of the house. The floor was original wood, scuffed one-and-a-half hardwood that had been oiled and buffed. The walls were plaster, creamy, original, and lined with religious pictures, as well as pictures of a couple and the child who'd been carried out of the home, with two pit bulls in the foreground. To the left an arched doorway showed a living room with a widescreen television. On shelves were books. Juvenilia, history, biographies. Nothing political or violent. The windows were dressed with lacy curtains. To the right of the front hall was another arched doorway, this one into a family room with a worn but tidy couch that had dog-bite marks on the wooden legs. In the kitchen was an old-style table and matching chairs. The chrome legs had been persistently chewed. The pit bulls. Through two doors at the back of the kitchen, Ray Tate could see into side-by-side bedrooms. One was a child's room with a crucifix on the wall, and under it a single bed with a lit lamp beside it. The other room contained a double bed with a larger crucifix on it and lit lamp on a low table.

He told Marty Frost to take the living room, Comartin the family room, and Djuna Brown the kitchen. "Bring anything you find to the kitchen. Anything really stinky, call the guy with the camera before moving it. We'll do the bedrooms, two by two, after."

The door to the basement, between a wall pantry and the refrigerator, was at the bottom of the basement stairs; the doorframe was splintered. A deadbolt was on the floor.

"Djuna, I'm going downstairs. Call if you find something."

He descended slowly. The house had already been searched and secured but he felt unaccountably spooked and took his gun from his ankle. Half of the cops that came out of the police academy were, by mathematical certainty, in the bottom half of their graduating class. He appreciated the bomb guy's dry sense of humour, but he didn't know him at all and the man could actually be a moron.

At the bottom he stepped over the door. The basement was low but long, with cement-block walls that showed no sign of leakage. A furnace was partitioned off by whitewashed particle board at the north end. A fuse box was mounted beside it. Washer and dryer facilities were on the east side beside a deep double sink. A workbench made of four-by-fours and one-inch plywood was on the left with a stool under it. Tin cans had been nailed to a sheet of plywood above the bench; they held an orderly array of screws, nails, nuts, and bolts. There were spools of wire, hinges, opened cans of paint, brushes in turps, and a full line of tools. The bare cement floor was swept immaculate.

Trash was kept in a big green rubber bin with the house's address neatly painted on the side with stencilled letters that read, HOUSEHOLD RENO WASTE, HEAVY, PLEASE RETURN BIN TO SIDE OF HOUSE, THANK YOU. Inside were elbows of wood, little cut-out pieces of half-inch-thick soundproof drywall sheets, empty packaging, carpet ends, a paintbrush crusted with light blue paint, and the detritus of a home project.

It was a workingman's home. A home handyman. A man with pride in his surroundings, in control of his environment.

Over his head were the lines of wiring for the place, carefully run through perfectly round holes in the eight-by-fours.

He could hear the rest of the crew moving around, banging drawers and doors, their feet sliding and thumping.

Ray Tate poked around the various shelves and closets. Sandpaper in various grits, a drill set with the bits in a vinyl wallet, a set of screwdrivers with yellow plastic handles in descending order in another wallet. A heavy leather woodworker's apron with deep pouches and splotches of light blue paint. Engraved in the leather was the lettering, DO IT RIGHT FOR AMERICA.

Ray Tate, when he was married and living in the suburbs, had a basement just like it but not nearly as neat and clean. A refuge, a hideout from domestic life.

There was nothing of the racist radical or the crackpot. He took a copy of the warrant from his pocket and made sure they had the right address.

He went upstairs. Having seen the basement, he was surprised at how big the ground floor seemed. In his mind he eye-measured the two bedrooms, the living room, the family room, and the kitchen. He went back downstairs, then came up again. No way, he decided, would all the rooms fit in the dimensions of the basement. He went to the foot of the stairs and looked around until he felt the hair standing up on the back of his neck.

Upstairs, he silently signalled the others, touching his finger to his lips and hooking his thumb at the front door. They tiptoed out and stood on the lawn while he told the suppression-team leader something was stinky. He punched in the chief's squad coordinator and identified himself and gave the address. "We need a home wrecking crew at this crime stage, downstairs in the basement. Maybe up in the attic, too. Measure the place off. There's a stash room down there, one end or the other. We gotta get it ripped up. I want the whole fucking house on the lawn. My people are out and someone could be having free-run in there. The suppression team is going to have to do it again by the numbers. And keep that idiot from the bomb squad on standby."

Chapter 16

Waiting for the home wreckers, Ray Tate told the suppression-team leader they were going to drive around the neighbourhood and they'd be on the air.

Parked in the Chrysler a block away, they cracked beers, limiting themselves to one each. He told them about the sheets of soundproof drywalling. "Someone's been doing a reno. There were cut corners in the garbage, stud ends, blue paint. I didn't see any sign in the house of soundproofing and nothing's been painted blue. Those walls are beautiful, real old plaster. Nobody who cares about their home would hang sheets of soundproof. And this guy loves his house. Plus, the basement is too small. You don't notice it until you look at the ground floor, then go back down again. Someone's built a trap down there. He might be in it, hiding and waiting us out, or he's stashing in there."

"Ray Tate," Djuna Brown shook her head in mock wonder. "Ray Tate, beatnik detective."

"Naw. Ray Tate, former suburbanite and home handyman. You guys find anything?"

She shook her head. "Nada, Dada."

Marty Frost said, "Zero, Nero."

Brian Comartin thought for a moment. "Fuck all, Paul."

Marty Frost patted him on the shoulder. "Nice try, guy."

They sat in comfortable small talk until the rover squawked.

"We got the Homicide hammers on the way, Ray, although it looks like a classic suicide. Hanging. To my amateur eye the rope scrape on the neck is consistent with a body drop. His hands are tied in the back and he used a slipknot so if he changed his mind, he couldn't, even if he wanted to. Tipped himself off a stool. Door was bolted from the inside. Goodbye and see you later. That's all I saw before I backed my guys out. The body hanging. And the porn on the walls. And the stash of DVDs. He really liked *Black Buxom Babes with Bodacious Butts*. He had a blow-up of the DVD cover above the widescreen. A true fan. But me? I thought it was poorly lit, the dialogue forced, and the character development was inferior." The squad leader of the suppression team shrugged. "I mean, I'm no critic, but ..."

"I guess he did it when we served the warrant."

"I think so, Ray. It all looked fresh."

"You see a note?"

"Nope. But it could've been in his pocket, or out of sight." The squad leader circled his fist over his head to gather his team to him. "Think this is your guy? Fuck, be nice to close the Chinatown case and your dead women, all in one day."

"Dunno. Our guy didn't bang them, didn't go for the bodacious butts. He just pulverized them."

"Maybe that's how he got himself up. Kill one, then go home and whack off to the bodacious action."

"Yeah, I guess. Maybe. Too deep for me. We'll see what the hammers find in there."

"Okay, we're rolling. Ah, look, I'm sorry my guys went in and didn't figure it out. It could've gone real bad for you guys if he'd jumped out with an Uzi and started strafing bodacious butts. We owe you one, okay? Somebody pisses you off in a bar or cuts you off in traffic, you just call, we'll roll a team, lay waste." He pulled off his leather glove and held his hand out. "We okay?"

Ray Tate shook his hand. "No problem. Who knew?"

"You guys hanging around? Want to go get a beer before we head out?"

"Naw. We're going to wait until the search team finishes scavenging."

He watched six cadets, led by a sergeant, gather at the foot of the stairs to the house. The sergeant stood on the top step. "We're only doing floor one.

The basement is a homicide scene, so don't go wandering. I'll assign you to rooms and you get every piece of paper, every notebook. If you see drugs or a firearm or a cellphone, call me. Don't touch it. Put your fucking mitts in your pockets and sing out. You guys are lucky. You're starting your career with the biggest mass murder in the city's history. You all get a good jump up. But if you fuck up? Apply to the fire department. They need more meatheads to run into fires."

Three teams from Homicide pulled up at the curb: two unmarked sedans and an unmarked van. They stepped out and stood on the curb, staring at the house. They were in no hurry. One of the team consulted a diagram of the house, the doghouse, the fence line and the porch, then disappeared up the side of the bungalow. The other five waited, holding satchels.

Ray Tate heard one of them say, "Bobby, you go in with the video camera. Call on the cell when you're done. Take your time. It's all time and a half."

Ray Tate wandered over. "Hey, Tate, Ray."

The hammer held up his hand. "Don't tell us nothing, okay? We're spooky that way."

"Not a problem." He wrote his cell number on a business card. "Call if you need us. We're cruising, or we'll be at the Jank." He stepped away, then turned back. "Hambone tell you how things are? What we're looking for? On our thing?"

"I got it. Now let us do our work, okay? We'll call."

* * *

Martinique Frost and Brian Comartin casually said they were going to cruise up to the Projects, maybe get a bite to eat. They'd be on the rover and available. They didn't invite Ray Tate or Djuna Brown to join them. They got into the black Chrysler and headed off the street. At the end of the block, without signalling, the Chrysler turned right, away from the Projects and toward Marty Frost's apartment.

Djuna Brown laughed. "I like those guys, Ray. Marty's all cop and Brian's just a teenager in love."

"She's got him eating salad already. Funny, huh? Talk about a mismatch."

She smiled, "Yeah, funny."

They walked to the Taurus. "It's going to be a long night," he said. "We should stay out. Ride the radios."

He drove downtown, the radio melodious. As a cop, Ray Tate's favourite time was the dead zone, when nothing was going on but something was going to happen. It had to. It was the nature of things. As a sergeant he could cruise relatively freely through the Sectors and cherry-pick calls to drop in on, notebooks to sign, share a coffee or a sandwich, collect gossip and funny tales. He loved the young cops out there, carrying the water, being faced with new situations that had to be parsed for them. There weren't many cops in his age range. A few older guys who wouldn't leave their streets and a lot of younger guys finding the tradition. He was, he felt, in the best of places, still learning subtleties from the old road sergeants and mentoring the kids.

Djuna Brown kept her eyes on the sidewalks on his side of the car, and he scoped the passenger-side pedestrians. Occasionally, creeping the curbs, they glanced at each other and smiled. It was the perfect date. They'd miss this part, when they were living in Paris. No matter what, he decided, he couldn't live another year like this past one.

There was a voice-out for a sergeant to attend a high-dollar commercial burglary. There was a voice-out for a supervisor to attend a collision at the foot of Erie Street. Both were scooped up by Sector cars.

There was a yawning voice-out from a lonely for a disturbance in Stonetown. "Desk. Urban Two lonely, I'm on view of a bar fight, several male individuals going hand-to-hand in front of the Stone on Drewry. I'm disembarking to referee." Then: "Windows are going in." Then, screaming: "Everybody."

The Sector cars dropped the burglary and the collision and responded.

"We're rolling that one, Djun'." He swung a sharp U-turn and accelerated toward Stonetown while she responded, "Chief's special plainclothes two on board with a shotgun we'll take that one, Desk."

He slapped the Hello light on the roof.

"Okay," the dispatcher said, a busy waitress reading back a complex order for a party of twelve. "We got the chief's special two with shotgun, we got Sector Four Adam lonely, Sector Four Bravo lonely, Scouts three, six, seven, eight, Sector Five visiting units Five Charley, Six Foxtrot lonely, Sergeant Four Niner lonely, and ... Thank you ... Mounted Units four and five on training closed band monitor only."

The Taurus shuddered as a chain of five Sector cars

screamed past it, almost close enough to adjust the side
mirror. Ray Tate got in line but dropped way back. He
fishtailed into Stonetown, two blocks from Drewry.
Two dozen Chinese teenagers in T-shirts were running
the streets, throwing garbage receptacles through windows, jumping up and down on cars locked in traffic. A
taxi driver revved ahead and a Chinese kid flew through
the air, over the taxi, and was run over by a panel
truck. Some motorists got out of their cars and went at
it hand-to-hand with the youths. Ray Tate saw one of
the rampagers go into a kung fu pose then launch himself into the air, swinging a graceful airborne kick at a
balding middle-aged man wearing a sports shirt over a
white T-shirt. He missed, and when he landed the man
swung a tire iron and the kung fu artist went down
with blood spouting from his head. The middle-aged
man dropped to his knees, stripped off his own shirt,
and immediately started staunching the wound. As Ray
Tate stopped the Taurus mid-block beside the bleeding
Chinese youth, he heard the middle-aged man say in a
remarkably calm voice, "You're okay, kid, you're okay.
We're with you." He said something in what sounded
like singsong language. He looked up into the strobing
red light on the Taurus, keeping strong pressure down on
the head wound. "Ambulances, I'm from St. Frankies'
Heart, call them and say Bronstein in Emergency said,
'Everybody Stat. Set a stage at Soldiers' Park.'"

Car alarms were screaming. Windows smashed in a
regular cadence down the block, whomp smash whomp
smash whomp smash. Entry alarms whooped in a building chorus. There was a gunshot, then a scream, and

someone yelled, "Got you, fucker slant cocksucker," in a thick Eastern European accent. Ray Tate got out to see if he could identify the shooting site.

The dispatcher was talking steadily but breathy. He couldn't make it all out, but it chilled him a little that she'd lost the edge of control in her voice, was a little overwhelmed.

When there was a break in the air he passed on the request from the doctor and said, "Chief's squad special, Tate, Sergeant. We need brass down here. We got gunshots." A shotgun blast came from farther down the block. "More gunshots."

There were five evenly spaced pistol shots and glass from five streetlight bulbs tinkled on the roadway. Ray Tate moved away from the Taurus, peeking up over the hood of an abandoned courier car, trying to spot the gunner.

Djuna Brown called out, "They're calling everybody in. Spot riots outside the zone. Equipment Supply will be at the command post at the east end of Stonetown with riot gear." The Taurus was doorlocked on the passenger side by an abandoned pizza delivery car. She climbed out by scrambling across the seat and out the driver's door. Her eyes were huge and beautiful in the stuttering lights and he loved her and saw she looked tiny.

A young man in a T-shirt with characters printed on it ran screaming between rows of abandoned cars, swinging a set of nunchaku over his head. Djuna Brown turned, saw him, and pulled her gun in a smooth jerk from her hip and centred on him in stance. Her voice was in full rising panic when she yelled, "Stop stop stop stop," and zoned in on him.

The doctor called a phrase in a singsong language. The youth stopped in shock and Ray Tate stepped around Djuna Brown and kicked him in the groin. He went down and rolled under the Taurus.

"Nice one, doc," Ray Tate said. "You *parlez vous* the lingo?"

"Ten years working medic in the camps in Asia." He looked serene and professional, as though chaos was his milieu. "This is fuck-all, in the fullness of the universe."

"Yeah," Ray Tate laughed, "but tonight it's all we got. Djun', you okay?"

"Yeah. He spooked me is all." She was frightened, but she laughed and was organized enough to have her gun pointing up. "Another nanosecond, that fucker was going to wear his ass for a hat."

"Get the scatter." He handed her the key. "We're writing off the car."

She holstered her automatic, stretched into the Taurus and unlocked the shotgun from under the dash.

Ray Tate caught the doctor checking out her butt. He went on the air. "Chief's special, we're abandoning our vehicle and heading on foot east into the command post. We have the shotgun, we're salt-and-pepper male female, plainclothes both."

"Units, be aware, chief's special moving on foot, black and white female male plainclothes, shotgun visible approaching command vehicles from the west. Have consideration."

Fifty feet up the block they saw a pair of Chinese youths in white T-shirts throwing outdoor tables and chairs through the window of Gratteri's Italian. Teens, black and white and Asian, were looting high-end clothing stores, running through the streets with armloads of designer goods. A car caught fire with a whoosh of heat. And another. There were chants and whoops. Two abandoned vehicles were flipped. There was more chanting. Sirens were circling Stonetown, tightening as the units gathered closer. More windows went.

Djuna Brown started moving toward the group attacking the restaurant.

"Whoa, Djun', fuck that. We only go to work for people." He took his gun from his ankle and kept it down beside his leg.

A road sergeant, standing back and watching a car burn with a disinterested look on his face, glanced up and read them as cops right away. He pointed down Parson's Lane. "Go around that way. You can't get through up ahead."

Ten strides into the tight, winding cobblestoned lane, a young cop with a high-pitched voice, wild eyes, and a noticeably bouncing Adam's apple above his collar threw down on them and screamed, "Halt."

They froze.

"It's cool." Ray Tate said calmly. "We're cops on the job."

"I'll fucking shoot you. Drop the guns. I'll fucking shoot you."

"Chief's squad special. Listen to the air."

The young cop opened fire. In the endless flash of firing his face was a series of instant images, each one with a look of panicked wet dread, his mouth agape as though he were howling.

Ray Tate heard Djuna Brown scream his name as she hit the ground, the shotgun clattering.

He felt his heart crack and he dropped to both knees. Before the kid could round-out whatever was left in the Glock into him, Ray Tate shot him two-handed three times in the middle of the chest.

Everything was still. The Lane was crowded with smoky humidity. The sounds of racing engines a block away, the wail of sirens, the shouts, even the erratic gunshots and smashing windows receded as if he were going deaf by the decibel.

It was weird, firing into the uniform, feeling so calm he thought he himself had been shot and was ceasing to exist. His greatest pride after graduation had been putting on the blue, no longer being different but being part of something. Not a foster home, not a number on a state welfare charge account, not being on a rotating roster of household chores. Now he'd shot the blue.

He watched the kid, suddenly on the cobblestones, twitching.

He turned his head, slowly, as if his neck muscles were locked.

Djuna Brown, wearing only one of her little slippers, was on her side, fetal, both hands on the right side of her head.

He heard the clumping of boots and the road sergeant rounded the bend in the lane with his piece out and up. He heard the Road go on the air in the patented calm urgency only road sergeants had: "Ten thirty three Parson's Lane shots officers down approach from the south." As he spoke he kicked Ray Tate's gun and the shotgun and the kid's Glock to the rain gutter on the edge of the Lane. "Weapons secure."

Ray Tate said, "Tate, chief's special, I'm okay. My partner."

"Gimme the outstandings."

"No outs. He shot her, I shot him. In the chest, I hope. I had to stop him. He flipped out."

The road sergeant went on the air. "No outstandings. Slow 'em down." He walked over to the kid. "You're one lucky fucker, kid." He reached down and slid his hand under the Kevlar vest and probed. The kid moaned.

Laying on her side, Djuna Brown giggled and sat up as though she'd awakened from a happy dream. Blood dripped from the bottom of her ear lobe, where only the twisted fastener that had held her magical turquoise earring remained.

The road sergeant went on the air. "All in order. Don't ask. It'll sort."

At the command post they waited for riot gear. Martinique Frost and Brian Comartin came up the line and stood with them.

Someone called, "Hey, back 'a the line, plainclothes. They ain't startin' the movie until we're all in our seats."

Without looking back, Marty Frost hung the casual finger straight up and there was laughter.

Djuna Brown was constantly touching her right ear where the blood was drying around the fastener. For the second time she said as if in a daze, "I saw it, Ray. It came out of the big light, heading straight for my face. It was spinning. I could hear it coming. Then at the last second it … it just veered and went for the earring. I saw it. It curved, like the earring was a magnet." She giggled. She couldn't stop giggling. Her head swung in giddy disbelief and the surviving earring shimmied.

Marty Frost looked back and forth at them and said, "What?"

Ray Tate told them what had happened in Parson's Lane.

"How's the kid?"

"Alive. That's all he can ask for. Hurting like a motherfucker though."

At the front of the line Ray Tate handed over his shotgun, gave his badge number, and made sure the issuing officer entered it into his notebook. They were given helmets, vests, and belts containing a baton, twist-tie handcuffs, and pepper spray.

The issuing officer looked at Djuna Brown's ear and said, "Hey kid, you know you're bleeding?"

"I bleed," she said, giggling again, "for my love."

"Cool, give me a call," he said, holding out clipboard for her to sign. You could tell she'd charmed him. He leered. "Name and home phone number. If married, hubby's work hours. If you want to wait for something that fits, we got Gap Kids sending over extra-petite vests." He glanced down. "What's with the slippers? We wake you up?"

Ray Tate said, "You got any stores on board, buddy?"

"Yeah, we got some pounders. Smallest'll be too big but better than those cute things." He called in through the open doors. "Boots, smallest, and better get a couple pair of socks." A hand passed out a pair of black uniform boots and two pairs of socks. Djuna Brown sat on the truck bumper and took off her embroidered slippers, pulled on the socks and the boots. She laced them tight in neat double bows. Ray Tate took the slippers, balled them, and put them into his pocket.

A gorgeous lieutenant in a white shirt was standing at the front of the supply truck, assigning troops according to a chalkboard mounted on the side. She had the black-framed glasses thing going on, with French-plaited blonde hair. Ray Tate remembered a lonesome breakfast spent gazing at her in the Jank cafeteria, mute at her beauty, wanting to cross the room and ask if she dug art. But she'd got up and left before he could, and she walked as if in her own pastel world of enduring beauty. She had no wedding ring on her ring finger, he noticed, but instead a twisted gold snake with a tiny ruby apple in its mouth.

Djuna Brown saw it. "Wow. That's nice. Where'd you get that? You get that made custom?"

The lieutenant looked at the ring. "Yes. Nice, huh?" She gave Djuna Brown a mysterious smile. "A unique symbol of love, undying." For a moment her face became sly.

Before she could saddle them with a hump detail, Ray Tate fastened on his belt and said, "We're chief's special. We're a four-man independent."

She nodded and made a mark on the edge of the chalkboard. The ruby flared in the electric light. "Okay, you're Chief's Special One. Roam. We don't have enough rovers, so don't worry about getting transport. Tie them up and leave 'em on the sidewalk, we'll collect them up later."

The remainder of the night was fire and thumps and crackling shattered glass. Rather than diminish, the rioters fed on the violence. The roving bands of angry Chinese kids grew in size and numbers and were joined by the socialist youth secretariat, mangy white kids in drab prole clothes and construction boots, masked anarchists in black fatigues, and more gangbangers out for some deep discount shopping.

Ray Tate led the way to the centre of Stonetown where they huddled up in a doorway. "Okay, rules of engagement. First, fuck property. Let them smash and burn, we hang back and keep moving, try to stay together. A cop gets in trouble, we go, all in. A civilian is in physical harm, we go to work. We go as a group. If any of us gets into the shit, we all pile on. No prisoners, then, no mercy. There's gonna be mistakes, we're all going to maybe see each other do stuff they shouldn't do. Deal with it later. If we get real busy, fuck that twist-tie stuff. Use the baton to disable and keep moving. If they're still on the street in the morning they'll get swept up; if they get up before that, they aren't going to do any more action."

Brian Comartin was licking his lips repeatedly, his head jerking in every direction.

"Brian? Brian, you okay, man?"

"Yeah, yeah, I'm okay." He made a little nervous laugh. He held his baton awkwardly and said with a weak smile, "This ain't traffic control."

"But it's still control. We have to control them but we're not here to cripple or kill them." He tried to remember his training. "Keep your baton swings low. Short and choppy. Thighs, backs of knees, shins. The order is like this: push baton, low baton, the pepper spray, mid-level baton, high baton, and the gun, last resort. If we all do it right, there'll be a lot of sore people in the cells in the morning but no one in long-term care with tubes up their noses."

They edged out of the doorway. A squad of riot cops came up the street in lockstep, three ranks of ten, fully decked out in insect gear, pounding their batons on their shields and grunting loudly. They went through the block like a slow black wall, pushing inexorably without pause, simply walking over the rioters who fell under their boots. Behind the riot squad a half-dozen uniformed and plainclothes chargers were on the victims with twist-ties and subtle knee drops. At the end of the block the riot squad wheeled west with the plainclothesmen following like bottom-feeders.

Djuna Brown was jumpy in her loose helmet and swamping vest. Her face was tiny in shadow. She wore

her utility belt bandolier-style, across her right shoulder
to her left hip. Ray Tate took her helmet and adjusted
the webbing. He adjusted the Velcro tabs until the vest
was almost snug.

Ray Tate took Marty Frost aside and murmured,
"Marty, if you can, keep an eye on her, okay? She just
dodged a bullet and might think she's supergirl."

"Maybe she is. That curving bullet sounds pretty
magical. Did it happen like that, like she said?"

"Yeah." He thought it was spooky. At that range
with the kiddie cop firing multiple rounds, it seemed
impossible he didn't take someone out. "Yeah, but she's
down to one earring and it's gonna be a long night."

The night was long on bedlam and his painterly eye
saw stark charcoal scenes of brutality, blood and tears
and debasement. He filed the images for a Paris easel
and went to work.

They attached themselves to undermanned squads
and teams when they could, helping clear rioters
from streets so ambulances and fire trucks could get
through. Mostly they twist-cuffed and stacked arrestees or shored up holes in the lines. Without gas masks,
when they smelled tear gas ahead, they moved away.

As the night drew on, discipline wore thin. There
was no supervision beyond what the cops found
among themselves. No white shirts were seen in the
streets. Sergeants and Roads spent most of their time
in defensive mode. Their shouted instructions were

ignored in the electricity of it. The rovers were shouted cackles no one could make out. There were cops with no radios at all. There were cops with no helmets or shields or batons. It was catch as catch-can. More than riot control, it was endless bouts of hand-to-hand combat. Suppress here, move there.

Better nature retreated before confusion, fear, and exhaustion. Wildfire rumours spread that a cop had been shot. That two cops had been shot. That a cop had been set ablaze. That a cop had been tossed from a roof. That a cop had his baton shoved up his ass. That a cop had been set on fire, shot, and tossed from a roof with his baton shoved up his ass.

Four rioters managed to isolate an old cop and they stomped him in chanting unison, trying to roll his body off his gun-side to get at his piece. They couldn't, and in frustration they kicked his rimless glasses into his eyes. Eventually, they were piled on by chargers, who dragged them into an alleyway and, one-by-one, broke their arms and legs in a most businesslike way with their batons.

A firefighter, carrying a heart-attack victim out of a shop, was swarmed by a pack and beaten, the heart-attack victim left to die gasping in the gutter. The firefighter reeled on the sidewalk, his eye out of its socket, cradled in his palm. A black-clad man in a ski mask ran off with the firefighter's hat on his head.

On one block a cut-off band of looters milled, kettled in by the riot squad on four sides with nowhere to go. Caught in the squeeze, they called for mercy. They were projects kids, laden with electronics boxes and

clothing. Four plainclothes officers in headgear stood
outside the kettle laughing at them. Then they threw
their helmets on the ground, and took out their batons.

One yelled, "Open the gate," and riot cops swung
open a hole.

The plainclothesmen poured through into the kettle. The gate closed behind them, and they devoured
the looters up like delicious crumbs off a cake plate.

No one was immune to their own nature.

With only one earring between her and death,
Djuna Brown lost it entirely. She had a wild and brutal warrior side to her, tending to two-handed, high
chopping swings and close-up shots of pepper spray.
Her movements were wooden, stiff. Sometimes Ray
Tate saw drool on her chin and she didn't stop smiling. Shock, he thought, or maybe she was proving
something to herself. In normal circumstances, after
dodging a bullet, she would have been given time for
reflection and counselling, the parsing of what might
have been her final moment, the blessing of continued
life and what to do with it. But there'd been no opportunity and she skidded. It didn't matter who had tried
to kill her, someone had, someone had no respect for
her life, she was garbage to somebody.

Twice he had to move into her arrests and cut off
the tight twist-tie restraints she reefed on screaming
youths. He saw her drop her face mask and powder
a looter's jaw with a lateral swing of her baton, then
start into him with her new boots when he was down
and unconscious, stomping him out. Ray Tate crowded
her up against a wall with his body and pushed up the

visor of her helmet. Her face was in gaping passion he'd only seen in their bed or in the bathtub. But on the street it was sick.

"No," he said. He grabbed her chin in his fingers and tilted her head back, hard until the back of her helmet touched the wall, and said, "I said, 'No.'" But he wasn't sure he'd got through to her.

Brian Comartin was in terror and that made him dangerous. Under the layer of fat were the jumping adrenaline-soaked muscles of a young cop, under the refinement of champagne and fancy glasses was a frustrated middle-aged cop. He became all elbows and knees and chesty swagger as he recognized the results of his power. Once, he went up the alley with a gang of chargers dragging a gangbanger. When he came out he had blood on his baton and a satisfied smile on his face. When he got a young girl in army fatigues in a headlock and sprayed pepper directly into her face, Ray Tate stepped in and calmed him by appealing to his shrinking heart. "Stay with Marty, Brian. She needs backup. I'm worried about her."

Only Marty Frost maintained. Her personal nature was strong; she had command. She ordered perimeters to be set up, supervised arrests, gave directions that were instinctively obeyed by wild cops. When there were outrageous beatings, she moved in and stopped them, but without making the chargers feel they were being over-controlled, that she was against them. Brian Comartin stayed close to her, keeping her back. They became a team and he seemed relieved that he had someone to obey, to feel he was protecting, someone to show his better angel to. Marty Frost took out a lot of shin, bicep, and thigh, and never touched a head.

They kept moving as a group. When they were alone, doing their own duty, they were mostly silent, breathing hard, moving through the lanes and alleyways, getting ahead of and cutting off groups of marauders. They found little groups of black-clad anarchists, veterans of street warfare, using the duck-and-jump. Hiding in doorways or under cars while police went by, then creeping out behind them and throwing bottles of gasoline or ball bearings or billiard balls. Ray Tate's little crew did a duck-and-jump of their own and attacked, yelling, leaving the anarchists on the ground.

It was a long night and, when the sky lightened imperceptibly, they made their way out of the grid of Stonetown streets.

They wound up in the aftermath, in the blue-grey gauze of pre-dawn, on a hillock in Soldier's Park, where the medical command post had broken down. There was the detritus of triage and urgent care: streamers of bloody bandages, ripped-off clothing, water bottles, eyeglasses, a wooden leg, a set of false teeth (uppers), a riot cop's helmet smeared with blood, a combat boot, wrappers from medi-packs.

But the air was sweet. It was sweet air up there, and on the softest breeze it came from the far-off lake to the north, carrying a morning smell and gulls silently scraping their backs against the bottom of the sky.

Ray Tate led his ragged little band to the top of the hillock. They were wooden, stiff. They stripped off their gear, tossed it away onto the ground as if it didn't have anything to do with them, and sat in a row like war survivors to look down at the smoke rising from the battlefield of Stonetown. The red and blue lights of emergency vehicles flashed in the low dawn in little flares. Lights from media cameras popped up white.

Djuna Brown sat staring at her hands. "Ray? Ray, what did I do?" She was weeping and constantly blinking and shivering in shock. "I want to go home." She had snot running down her nose. He thought she meant back up to Indian country, but she added, "I want to see my dad."

"Put it away for now, Djun'."

"Where, Ray? Tell me where to put it and I will."

Brian Comartin was staring at his hands, at the blood on his sleeves. "I'm no fucking poet."

Martinique Frost put her arm across his shoulder and said nothing.

Ray Tate had nothing to say. It was what it was. He spotted a bloody package of Marlboros, got up and, hoping against hope, bent stiffly to pick it up. Six crushed and broken cigarettes and a stupidly bright disposable yellow lighter inside. Straightening out some long butts, he lit up and handed the pack around. Djuna Brown lit up with him but didn't speak. Marty Frost and Brian Comartin had wandered off and stood with their backs to the smoky city, talking quietly.

Blowing a long plume of cigarette smoke down at

Stonetown, Ray Tate said to no one at all, "This used to be a pretty okay town."

They smoked or rested, and when they were done they picked up their gear and went down the hill into Stonetown, because there was nothing else they could imagine doing.

By morning's thin light, cars smouldered on the roads, the pavement was sparkled with long glass shards, and wreckers were righting flipped vehicles and dragging them away. Every business had been violated by rage or fire or both. There were four death sites, each bounded by yellow crime-stage tape. Cops were drinking bottled water, listlessly leaning on walls and sitting on cars, staring around in awe, looking at one another and going, "*Fuuuuuck*." Prisoner transport vans were prowling the intersections, stopping to pick up youths sprawled face down, their hands twist-tied behind their backs, their ankles secured. They were taken hair-and-heels and tossed into the vans with audible thumps. It was business-like work, with no pleasure or sense of fun or freedom of anarchy.

Ray Tate and his band wandered through the streets until they found the command post. They got at the back of the line, handed back their gear, and went looking for transport to the Jank to check on the results of the overnight raids on the Volunteers.

Chapter 17

There were no cars to take them to the Jank. A transport wagon was loading up and the driver said there was room with the cargo and they could make a stop. They climbed in. The cargo was four teenagers chain-cuffed together on a bench in the back. Ray Tate and his crew sat opposite them. They'd all suffered some kind of damage and they slumped, exhausted. All wore party clothes that smelled of tear gas and were soiled and ripped.

A blonde girl with luminous eyes, a split lip, one high-heeled shoe, and a tuft of hair missing from the side of her head asked if they were cops. They didn't answer because they weren't sure any more.

"We were just celebrating my birthday. We didn't *do* anything. When the windows started breaking we ran out and they boxed us in and put those twist things on us all night in the gutter. We don't even *live* down here." She was overcome with anxiety and began crying.

"We didn't *do* anything." She looked at Ray Tate. "I'm *seventeen*. It was my birthday party. *Please*."

He had to say something. "Calm down. You'll be all right."

The slot to the driver's compartment slid open. "All *aboarrrrrddddd* ... for the night train ..." The shotgun did a fair imitation of James Brown, "*Atlanta, Joe-Jah, Mia-mee, Flo-Dahhh ... and don't fo'get New Aw-leens, home a da bloose ... Yeaaaaaah ...*"

Djuna Brown wouldn't look at the girl. She said softly, "Ray?"

Ray Tate called out, "Where are they processing this bunch?"

"Sector Four's fully booked. We're going to Six. Home of the other blues. We can drop you guys first at Jank."

"I got to go to the Six. Drop my guys at Jank, I'll ride on up with you."

The girl said, "Can you help us?"

Ray Tate didn't answer. He stared at Djuna Brown's little fists balled up between her knees and down at her huge leather pounders with the double bow knots at the end of rolled up blue jeans. He took her little embroidered slippers from his pocket and handed them to her.

At the Jank, when she climbed out silently with Marty Frost and Brian Comartin, she left the slippers on the floor of the transport wagon and he stared at them all the way to Sector Six. It was a bumpy ride with angular sharp turns and the slippers moved silently around in their own sparkly, airless dance.

After the teenagers were led out, he picked the slippers up, folded them, and put them into his pocket.

Intake was swamped. Chinese kids, anarchists, 'bangers, and collateral passerby pick-ups were sitting in a line inside the back of the garage. All were sitting bound in the front with twist-ties, most had their backs against the cement-block wall. Some were sleeping with their heads on their knees. The chargers were having no fun with this. This was a day-after with the adrenaline rinsed out. This was hangover. They were almost gentle as they moved up and down the line in their black leather gloves, cupping the backs of heads while pouring swallows of bottled water into open parched mouths. The four teenagers from the transport van were seated closest to the garage doors.

The Road behind the beast, Road 667, was off to the side listening to a young, tough-looking black charger with muscles bulging out from under his uniform shirt. The charger's shaven head was infused with dark veins of anger and his neck was swollen with cords.

"This is fucked, Road. I didn't fight my way out of Hauser Projects to go downtown and beat down kids. It was fucking bedlam. My neighbour's fucking daughter had her front teeth clubbed out. She was heading home after shift at the Tower Mall. How do I fucking look him in the fucking eye over the back fence? Where was the supervision? Where the fuck were you, Road? Who's gonna answer for this?"

"I know, Carney." He was sympathetic around the unlit stogie stub in his teeth. "It was bad. It's been bad before. It'll sort."

"Sort? Road, are you fucking kidding me? Look at this, this bunch here. What, a concentration camp? That kid there's got to be twelve, thirteen." The charger shoved the Road in the chest with two hands, pushing him back against the wall. The stogie flew out of the Road's mouth. "They've fucking got piss and shit in their pants, you fucker."

Ray Tate took him down hard from behind, smothering his gun side, sliding the guy's baton out of the ring and getting it up under his Adam's apple, riding his back. It was like riding a bronco. The charger shifted his head to relieve the pressure on his throat and rose with slow ease. The Road knew there were no muscles for nose and shin, and he pulled his own stick and with mercy swung a low fluid lateral at the bottom of the charger's shin. The charger went back down, rolling and balling up. Ray Tate got up and stepped back.

"Fuck, Ray. I haven't had a cop go after me in twenty years." The Road stared at him, stunned, shocked, and suddenly old and afraid. This was a glimpse of the iron blue wall peeling like cheap wallpaper. "Twenty years, and that was because I banged his girlfriend. Not for work. Not in uniform."

"He's not wrong, Road." He thought of Djuna Brown, a brutal warrior, and the swaggering fat Traffic man going into an alley, and wondered where that came from out of them. That rage. That anger. That naked freedom. But this, too, rocked him. Since he'd joined the cops he'd had a vague idea, a hope, that whoever his father was, it was a fearless Road that gave him the blue genes. If not this one, then another. He felt shaken. He'd never seen a Road in fear. "This is fucked, all of it."

"I know." The Road bent over the charger. "Carney. Carney, you're right, man. But you don't shove the blue in public. You know that. You okay, kid?"

The charger sat, then got up using his hands and the wall. He hopped around on his good leg. The Road kept his baton down his leg, ready.

"I'm okay, Road. I'm okay." He tentatively put his hand on the Road's shoulder, finding balance. "Yeah." Shaking his head slowly, he limped past the prisoners and into the Sector.

It was enough for the Road. He tried to get back on game. "So, Ray, what brings you up here? I heard you were out and about in all this. You shot into a cop's vest? The fuck?"

"Just three times, Road, to calm him down." Keeping it light. Ray Tate nodded at the four prisoners he'd come up with in the transport van. "Those four, at the end? Can you do a discretionary diversion? They were in a club having a birthday party when the windows came in on them, so they ran out and right into it. Got caught up."

"Done. Get 'em gone." He didn't look as old anymore, but he didn't have the joviality of his command, either. He might not ever really get back on his game, but he tried. "Fuck, Ray, you want them all? I can do you a wholesale package price, kid. Why pay retail?"

"Thanks, Road. Tell the booking guy to skate them now, okay?"

"Done, Ray."

He went to the vehicle compound and told the civilian clerk he needed a car for the Jank.

"You got the requisition? Signed twice?"

"Chief's squad special." He was too tired to fuck around with the guy. "Anything'll do."

"Signed req, two sigs."

"I'm commandeering."

"You living in a Hollywood movie, or what?" But he put a set of keys on the counter and, turning away, said, "These might fit that blue Mercury up on the left. I didn't see nothing. I'm taking a piss when you come in."

Ray Tate cruised in a circular route to his apartment, avoiding both Stonetown and Chinatown. His clothes were rancid with smoke and gas and sweat. His hair was stuck to his neck. His beard smelled like his bad breath. There was blood on his fingers where there should've been dried paint. He felt like he hadn't seen his home in days and thought about heading to the Whistler, seeing if Djuna Brown had headed back there instead of the Jank, was curled up in the triangular bathtub instead of bailing out of the city and heading back to Indian country where life was just as hard but not as complicated. She might be gone, he knew. Maybe down to the capital to see her dad. But he didn't feel like arming a key off Whistler security and anyway he needed clean clothes, needed to stand in his own room full of canvas and charcoal sketches. It was his anchor, that apartment. His daughter's photographs from Asia on the wall, the Calzettas in their brightness, his small collection of art books in the bookshelf, his old uniform hanging in plastic in the closet.

He thought about the night in a detached kind of way. In the night he'd gone through two dozen twist-ties; he hadn't been particularly gentle, but he hadn't left anyone in the road with bone injuries and swelling blue hands. Dreamily, he felt the gun in his hand when he fired into the cop's vest. He made a small smile at the windshield. It had been genius and it would add to the oral history. The Road was right: it would sort, all of it. But maybe sorting wasn't enough. Maybe he needed to be sorted. He was sick of his gun, of his handcuffs, of living the life of someone he might no longer be. Brian Comartin, appearing at the river, had called him Picasso. Yo, Picasso. You got a reason to be here, Pablo? And: I, ah, I write, ah, poetry? Ray Tate smiled but was a little sad at the rapid change the love-struck traffic cop had undergone. Are we only that far from the worst of our natures? He wasn't worried about Marty. Marty was twice the cop of any cop. If she wasn't female and black she'd be a day away from being a Road. She'd see Comartin right even if it took the promised beat down. It looked like the dead ladies case might be down, down by suicide, but down, and Marty would be okay, she could go back to Youth Services or move to Barcelona and sharpen Comartin's pencils. There was that, any-way, the ladies might have their justice. You could retire with a good heart on that.

There were few people in the streets around him and most went without masks, or wore them around their throats. With the night the city had endured, the plague suddenly wasn't a plague. It was a bad cold. It was invisible, but the black coroner's catering trucks doing remains removal, the scorched buildings, the impromptu memorials, the clusters of cops on the corners, they weren't invisible. They were a new reality. The entire night would have been worth it if it meant the old was torn down and the city could start afresh, from scratch. But it would never be the same.

At his building he parked in the back lot, went in the service door, and strode up the steps three at a time with anticipation. Home. Upstairs in his apartment, without pause he kicked off his boots in the entryway, stripped his jacket and sweatshirt off in the pass-through kitchen, hopped out of his pants crossing the living room, and went through the bathroom door. He took off his ankle holster and threw it into the sink and stepped into the shower, where he punched the cold on full and finally let himself feel free.

He didn't dress. Naked and dripping, he called Marty Frost on her cellphone.

"Hey, hey, Ray. Where you at?"

"Home. I need an hour. Jesus, I need a year."

"Take a couple of hours. They're still processing stuff from the house. You know how they are, Hambone's guys. They're thinking this might be Mister Beatdown, did in our victims." She could be light, she could be dispassionate, she could be distant to it all. She'd done what she wanted to do, put justice out there for her ladies, the ladies who were now simply part of the unfortunate subspecies: victims.

"Where's Djuna and Brian? They with you?"

"They're around. Brian had a really hard time of it. He can't stop talking about it. We shouldn't've taken him out. Not a lot of rhyming couplets in Stonetown last night. That was no place for a poet."

"Well, now he knows. Djuna, where's she at?"

"She's okay. A guy from down in Missouri filed that his daughter living up here hasn't checked in for a week and he's worried. From what he said by description, Djuna thinks it might be the Jane Doe from the riverbank. He's driving up, should be here in the morning."

He gave her his home phone in case Djuna Brown had forgotten it. "Tell her to call me, okay?"

"You knew her before, hey, Ray? Before she came down for this?"

"Last year. We did a drug task force last year."

"How was she, then? Stable?"

"Well, she was weird with the slipper thing going on. She had white bleached hair. She had to take a guy out at the end of it. Weird, not crazy."

There was silence on the line. "Well, Ray, I'd be real careful until you get it straightened out. Not my business, I know, but she might be on the line of crazy right now."

* * *

He went to the acrylics and canvas. The charcoal sticks would snap under the tension of his fingers. He forgot to dress. When the north light of the room grew dim he turned on the light above his easel but couldn't remember doing it. He smoked some stale cigarettes he didn't remember finding or lighting and drank a couple bottles of beer he didn't know he had. The late afternoon air was warm and soft through the window and it dried him, left his hair in knots and his beard a bushy, damp mess.

It was almost full dark when the phone buzzed. He was so into what he was doing that he didn't connect the buzz and the device and the physical action it demanded. The painting was a mess of chaos, like an orchestra tuning up. The painting had started as a disciplined homage of red and yellow bars to Mark Rothko, an exercise to calm himself down, find focus. He'd seen an exhibit of Rothko paintings in Chicago and had worked through that style for a month or two. But today, as his mind wandered and he strove for Rothko, his hand went free into anger and shame, he dissolved into a maniac Pollock. The insane obscuring the disciplined. Which one, he wondered, was honest to him?

The phone buzzed and he located it. His mouth was dry in spite of the beer. With a rasp in his voice he answered the phone.

She said, "I lost you."

"I had to go up to Sector Six. When I headed for the Jank, the car just came here."

"Those kids. That girl. What happened to them?"

"They got kicked. They're okay." He listened to her breathe. "I got your slippers."

"Like Cinderella. I'm at the Whistler. Why don't you come by and see if they fit, if you're my Prince Charming?" She was trying to play light, to be seductive and gay. She was silent a moment. As he listened to the emptiness, he stared at the painting, seeing something there now, something original and of his own. He wondered: Which was she? Disciplined as Rothko or mad like Pollock? And what did the painting say about him?

He heard her inhale shakily. She choked and spoke all at once in a wet, blubbering stream: "Ray why don't you come here be with me I not me that the noise he shot me I saw it the bullet Ray and it just went sideways Ray I couldn't die in front of you that's not me I am —" She stopped and said, "I'm tired," and the line went dead.

He stood with the phone in his hand, looking at the painting he'd made. A painting that hadn't existed before he'd applied the brush to the acrylic and the acrylic to the cheap canvas and opened himself up like a tin can, and went to a place.

Who knew what you'd find when you opened that tin can? How did you know when to stop? When it was done?

Who but himself could judge its value, its honesty? If it said what he'd meant to say, even if he didn't consciously mean to say it, then it was successful, it had a value. There were mistakes, he could clearly see, where he'd layered too thick, thinned too much, shaken uncontrollably from inner tension when he should have been precise. But it was his, it was honest, and it was a step to somewhere. What more could you ask for?

He realized he wasn't thinking about the painting any longer, he was thinking about Djuna Brown, about himself.

He dressed fast in a clean sweatshirt and jeans.

There was, really, he knew, nothing else he could do.

She didn't answer when he knocked. He pressed his ear to the door. Nothing. He rode the elevator down to the lobby and had the receptionist call security. It was a different guy, a beefy barbered guy, and he had the mark of the fake cop. Ray Tate badged him and said he had to get into the suite.

"You got a warrant?"

"This is in-house stuff. Job stuff."

"Is there going to be something heavy in there?"

"No. Naw. I think she's just fallen asleep." He read the guy as a wannabe. He had to be careful. Middle-aged wannabes took easy umbrage. "We were in Stonetown all last night. A lot of weird shit. You know how it is." He shrugged and, as if told everything, he shook his head and said, "We need her at the Jank. She's a Statie. Probably grabbing a nap." Like: a Statie, what do you expect?

In the elevator the security guy said he'd been caught in a riot when he worked private for a chemical company downstate. "If last night was anything like that … Man, you saw shit."

"Oh, yeah, there was shit to see, no question."

At the suite the security guy tapped at the door. He tapped harder, longer. "Maybe she went out?"

"Dunno. Let's take a peek." He felt a deep dread.

"Look, I'll do the peeking, okay? We've got procedures, just like you guys." He cracked the door. "Miss? Miss? House security. Anybody home?" He peeked inside and ducked his head back. "She's in the shower. I hear the water."

"Staties. A little city riot and they fall apart."

The security guy, a pal in the rugged landscape of law enforcement, nodded wearily, "Tell me about it."

She didn't open the shower curtain to his call. The room was full of steam. He went to the minibar and mixed himself a double gin and taps and carried it back into the washroom. She turned off the water but made no sound.

He sat on the toilet seat and took his time. He thought back through time, looking for something she could relate to, something that was his, something he could give her.

"After I got shot, Djun', remember? You went and saw my kid, Alexis? She told me you guys met. A great kid, right? My kid? A gentle good kid. But how about this. When she was in the finals for the baseball team at school she came into home plate cleats first. She didn't have to. Her coach was calling that it was okay, windmilling her in. The shortstop

was still juggling the ball. But Ax just flew from third
into home. She was fast, I remember that, she was
flying. I felt good, seeing that. There was no way she
wasn't going to come in there and get the run. She
could've hopped on one foot, and she was crossing.
But for some reason, that catcher was in her way, in
the way of what she wanted to do. So she came in in
the dirt. And she took about a pound of meat out of
that catcher's calf. It was the winning run. I didn't like
what I saw, I didn't like what she did. But it was her
moment, she was in her moment, she was primitive.
I talked to her about it, afterwards. She said she was
lost in the sound of her own heartbeat, the screaming
from the bleachers. She didn't even think of mercy. It
wasn't about the run or the ball or anything. She had
to take out the catcher because she, the catcher, was
interfering with who she was, what she was going to
do. She never went out for baseball again. She was
ashamed of herself and I was more proud of her for
that than the winning run."

"So, what, Ray? You proud of me, the things I did?"

"No. Out there, in Stonetown, I don't know what
happened to you. I can't imagine. It was a you I'd never
seen, never imagined. But nobody died from anything
we did, you or me or Marty or Brian. It was bad, but
it was what it was. You're going to have to wear what
you did. Maybe baseball isn't your game."

He sat for a while sipping.

Her voice echoed in the silent room. "Ray? Ray?
I'm so ashamed. I don't do that. I didn't think I was
capable of that." She pulled back the shower curtain.

She was naked and her hair was flat to her skull. She was brown and beautiful and shivering from something other than cold. She wore the single dangly earring. She stepped out and sat back on the rim of the tub, her elbows on her knees, her face in her hands. "He shot me, Ray. That young cop. I thought … I thought I was nothing, I could have died, right there, killed by a kiddie cop. In front of you. We're not supposed to die in front of each other. I almost lost everything. I saw you, there, in the flash, alone in Paris, without me. Is there a Paris for you if I'm not in it? If you saw me dead on the road? Could you paint?"

He handed her the drink and watched her sip. He waited. It was her time.

She said, "It's so … it's so thin, what is and what could be." She looked into his eyes. "I'm not the same anymore, am I, to you?"

"You have to take time. You have to go through what you did, those things, to those people." He got up and sat beside her on the rim of the tub and took a swallow from the glass. "I've done the worst, Djuna. After the first guy I shot, I thought, that's it. I've done it. I won't have to do it again. I've crossed over. I know the answer: I can. But then, then there was the second guy. I'm not sure on that one, if I could have handled it differently. I've examined it every which way. I don't know. I'll never know if that guy died because he had to, or because I fucked it up and I couldn't control him. So I shot him dead. You might never know what happened, what came out of you. But you'll have to deal with it, you'll have to try to resolve it."

"But not if I quit, right? If we go to Paris?"

"You'll still have to know." He took her hand and stood her up. "I'll have to know."

"Can we go to bed? Not do anything if you don't want to. Just lie down for a while."

"Only," he said, "only if these slippers I got fit your feet."

Chapter 18

The chief's squad strategic room on four contained two dozen workers from the Wallpaper, the secretive part of Sally Greaves' Strategic Policy Analysis, the chief's mildly named dirty tricks unit. From the back of the room, where Ray Tate and Djuna Brown stood, forbidden from seeing their faces full on, the Wallpaper was a broad civic mix: they were young and old, black and white, Asian and Hispanic in various blends. Two were in wheelchairs, one had one leg.

By their posture, they all seemed pretty fresh and alert, as if the riots had happened in some faraway foreign land they never expected to visit but might have seen on television and might have found mildly interesting. Two were dressed in black, with hoodies up, wearing combat boots. Only those two looked tired, as if they'd been out running the streets in a riot. From the back of the room, Ray Tate and Djuna Brown could smell the tear gas off them. A young woman with a collapsed Mohawk turned to say something to her companion, an elderly woman with a collapsible walker. Ray Tate saw she had shrapnel in her face and a tattoo on the side of her neck. The old lady nodded and knitted with rhythmic clicks of her needles. It was as though the entire bland city had been brought to a conference to bore one another to death.

A furtive-looking middle-aged woman with tiny round eyeglasses, a severe overbite, and a slumping shuffle came into the room and walked to the front. Everyone straightened up. The woman had tragically bad skin that she didn't bother to cover with makeup, an artificially red patchy buzz cut, and she wore a man's suit coat with wide lapels over a T-shirt. She was braless and droopy and stocky. It seemed there was no effort she wouldn't undertake to display her unattractiveness; she'd given up or didn't care to begin with or she was just internal. Waiting for the room to quiet, she dug the nail of her right-hand baby finger deeply into her mouth, probing between her molars. When she took her finger out, she examined something on the nail, then flicked it to the floor.

Djuna Brown shivered. "Who's that creature?"

"The Graveyard. Sally Greaves. She runs SPA. Strategic Policy Analysis. Where Intelligence goes to die. Until it might be needed to fuck somebody up. She keeps the files for the Chief. Kind of nutty, but I like her."

Sally Greaves was the only person Pious Man Chan truly trusted, because she terrified everyone and wasn't terrified of him. She went from traffic cop to the

Jank in record time after she provided a roadside alibi for Willard Wong when a lot of people said he was killing two Vietnamese gangsters visiting from Toronto.

Sally Greaves stared over the assembled heads at Ray Tate and Djuna Brown and made a small nod. "Okay, shut up, kids. At the back of the room we have … ah," she consulted some writing on the back of her hand, "we have Ray Tate, the bearded one there, from the city, and that little thing, there, Djuna Brown, from the State. Don't gaze your eyes upon them, lest they gaze theirs upon you." Her voice was startlingly beautiful, deep but melodic, a little breathy; it was stunning dichotomy, like flushing a toilet and hearing a full symphony come up in acoustic perfection and wash over you in goosebumps and tingles. "And should they gaze upon you, children, your employment turns into a pillar of salt. You get fired and they get executed." She allowed her buckteeth to show in a little smile at this morsel of Intelligence wit. "Okay, we've got the take from five rez knocks, we've got five streams of product. Each rez is linked to the Volunteers. We want to sew the Volunteers up into body bags for conspiracy, but those two at the back like one of the homeowners, now deceased, for some murders." She smirked and shook her head disdainfully. "Murders." She consulted some writing on her other hand. "Some black women were beaten to death. No molestation, no robbery. Just beat downs. The only connector is they were all black, they were all beaten. They think it's about race. Does that about say it, dear?"

Djuna Brown said, "Yes. One was found dead on the riverbank, one comatose, when the Volunteers were manning patrols to keep the immigrant boats from Canada out. We're looking at race crime, hate crime. These were pulverizations of the victims. It was brutal."

Sally Greaves said, "If you say so, dear. So, kids, when you go through the boxes for conspiracy stuff, anything that might have to do with their case, put it aside, flag it. This is a favour for that Wishbone guy, Hambone, whatever, guy from Homicide. Any questions? And there better not be. Okay, go, next door, two to a take. We're not looking just for evidence, we're looking for intelligence. These two officers are going to hang around the building in case you turn something up. So, go ye forth and succeed."

The take from the raids had been separated onto five tables, most of it in clear-plastic stencilled evidence bags. Black markers noted the original bag number, the badge numbers of the cop who seized it, the location, the time of seizure, and the time of emptying. As the Graveyard's minions slowly went through it, scraps of paper were separated and assigned smaller bags of their own. Beside each table was a green metal cart where the small evidence bags were collected.

Ray Tate and Djuna Brown stood for a while, again at the back of the room where they wouldn't penetrate the anonymity of the Wallpaper, watching the green cart numbered Three. It was their house. Home of the hanging handyman, Corey Garnett.

They wandered over to the table, their hands carefully linked behind their backs, and looked over the searcher's shoulder at the take. The girl with shrapnel in her nose put her hand over her face, looked up shyly, and glanced behind them at the door where Sally Greaves had disappeared. She went back to work.

They could see six handguns and four scoped rifles had been tagged through the trigger guards, the tags reading FIREARMS COMPARISON. Some gaudy boxes of straight bodacious hetero porn, white on black, man on woman, were stacked in a bag. Hand-written labels on a half-dozen VHS boxes were a series: FUCK THEM WHITE, VOLUMES ONE THROUGH SIX. It was niche market porn. There were stapled tracts with swastikas stamped on them and thick red lettering calling white men to arms. There were maps, some hand-scrawled of the river, some of a compound with watchtowers on the corners showing lines of fire, escape routes, tunnels, fences. House-shaped symbols were marked HOME SCHOOL, CHAPEL OF WORSHIP, PANTRY, WORKSHOP, and DETENTION. Silhouette targets from a shooting range were perforated with bullet holes.

If those belonged to Corey Garnett, Ray Tate thought, he was a fine marksman.

"Too bad our guy didn't shoot the ladies," Ray Tate told Djuna Brown. "This guy's got the deadeye. I'd definitely go for him, if they'd been sniped off."

"And he didn't bang them, either. All this stuff." Djuna Brown shook her head. "A sex nut, no doubt, but does this add up to anything for us?"

"Here comes Hambone. We'll find out if there's anything else we can use from the interrogations if this washes."

They went down to the cafeteria. A metal grid screen was pulled down and locked over the service area. There were a dozen food and beverage machines beside it. Except for some maintenance workers eating sandwiches from bags, only Sally Greaves was there, sitting with a thermos, china cup, and a peeled banana in front of her. In spite of the cafeteria having long rows of empty tables, she sat only two away from the workers and was watching them surreptitiously. Occasionally, one of the workers, a thick potbellied Irishman with red hair, would look in her direction and make a comment to his colleagues. They snickered and she looked away shyly.

Hambone Hogarth fed coins into a coffee machine, then stepped back to let them make their selections. "Look at Sally, there. Always working." He had admiration on his face.

Djuna Brown glanced over. "What? Eating a banana?" She stared past Hambone in fascination. Sally Greaves seemed to have no gender, or to be of both. She wondered what kind of time of it she'd had, how she endured her life without going homicidal or suicidal. Had she ever tried to pretty herself up, got her teeth fixed, got contact lenses, done something about her skin? Shopped for flattering clothing or taken up sports? And that voice. Where had that voice come from? Did she sing in the dark when she was alone and imagine she looked as perfect as she sounded? As she'd often felt while working among the sad and angry faces in Indian country, Djuna Brown knew she was blessed being born attractive, desired.

"She's reading their lips," Hambone Hogarth said. "They're dissing her and she's getting most of it. They have absolutely no fucking idea who she is, what she can do to their lives. One of those guys, very, very soon, is going to be either fired for cause, or he'll be bringing the contents of other people's office waste buckets to her and thanking her for the opportunity to serve municipal law enforcement." Hambone Hogarth shook his head. "One of those bigmouthed guys has no idea that his life, as he knows it, is over."

They carried their coffees over to Sally Greaves's table. As if addressing a grand dame, Hambone stood back a little and politely asked if they could join her.

"Please." She waved her hand, her left hand, gently over the table. Even in the single word, Djuna Brown was entranced. If she'd been blind she would have fallen in love with the voice, male or female. It was full and seemed to go on for a long time, entering through her ear and reverberating pleasantly around her emotions. But it was the left hand, with the ring on it, that caught her attention. She glanced at Ray Tate.

"Sit here, Hogarth, and you, Tate? Here. I like to have attractive men on each side of me." She made her voice thespian and mocked a glare at the table of maintenance men. "Like my ruthless palace guard."

Djuna Brown sat directly opposite Sally Greaves, realizing this was the actual purpose of the arrangement. She knew a woman like Sally Greaves was always testing. Not judging so much as deciding. It would be very easy to look like Sally Greaves and pack a heart full of hatred and to lay waste in her wake.

"I'll bet your parents named you after Djuna Barnes."

Djuna Brown was surprised. Djuna Barnes was a relatively minor player in the Paris literary circles that had fascinated her dad, particularly the black Americans who travelled there to create, to live the *bon vie* away from an America that didn't mean them well. Everyone knew Hemingway, the Fitzgeralds, Gertrude Stein, and Alice Toklas, even to a lesser extent A.J. Liebling and Waverley Root, but Djuna Barnes was mostly a footnote in books written about the bigger players. She nodded and made a small smile of appreciation, "Yes. My father. I'm glad he wasn't a fan of Gertrude Stein."

Sally Greaves made a melodious laugh. She was a people person, perhaps by necessity, perhaps by trade. In any event, she drew Djuna Brown in. "These guys don't know what we're talking about, do you think? Except Hemingway. All the tough men know Hemingway." She looked past Djuna Brown's ear with the little crust of blood on the lobe. "My big strong Irish lover likes you. He's saying he'd break you open like a shotgun and horse-fuck you. Verbatim. I haven't heard, well, lip-read, actually, the word jigaboo since I was a youngster." She looked at Hambone Hogarth. "Sometimes I really like my job." She watched the maintenance workers get up and walk out, leaving their refuse in a mess on the table. They went out a stairway door. She blew a kiss in that direction and stared at it for several seconds.

Djuna Brown caught Ray Tate's eye and glanced down at Sally Greaves's left hand. A gold snake was wrapped around her wedding finger, in its mouth a tiny ruby apple. The same custom-made ring, she remembered, as the gorgeous blonde lieutenant at the staging area had worn. Djuna Brown felt very good about this, but she didn't know why. Ray Tate, she saw, looked confused. Ray, Ray, she thought, how can you be an artist when you miss the possibilities of life in front of you? She thought this might be profound in some way and noted to ask him that later. Someone for everyone, she thought, even brutal cops who forgot themselves.

Hambone Hogarth missed it all. He told Sally Greaves they were going to discuss the dead women's case. "If you'd like, we can sit somewhere else."

"No, it's okay. This is the case you like the suicided Volunteer for?"

"Well, with the white-on-black porn on the walls and the videotapes, yeah, we're thinking."

"But these weren't sex cases," Djuna Brown said. "He just beat them and left them dead. We're thinking a race killer."

"Maybe, maybe not." Sally Greaves thought for a moment as if remembering something. "On one of the

training courses at Quantico there was a lecture where
they said some men beat one woman to get aroused,
then go and find the victim they really want. Most of
the time the second victim isn't physically violated in
an exterior way. Raped, sodomized, terrorized, but left
in apparently normal outward physical condition, left
alive so he can come by later and observe her in her
afterlife. He uses the first attack, the fatal or sometimes
near fatal one, as an aphrodisiac. Could this be that
kind of case?"

Djuna Brown nodded. She could listen to that
voice all day. "It could be. It makes sense, you look at
it like that. A pervert, ramping himself up."

"These white power guys, they see themselves as
patriots, not criminals. I can't see one of them going off
without leaving a marking of some kind. A swastika
carved on the victim, that kind of thing. A way to strike
terror, send their message." She turned to Hambone
Hogarth. "Did anyone do a data drag to look for ancil-
lary straightforward rapes at about the same time?"

"Well, Sally, we were a little late getting onto this.
We're just getting into it now. Frankly, we wouldn't be
pushing it like we are, except someone high up put in a
word for Ray, here, on the Chinatown arson and gave
him magic powers. He's using them where he can. So,
he's got some temporary weight and we have to move
a little more aggressively."

She smiled. "Willard Wong." She asked Ray Tate
if he knew Willard Wong.

"At the Chinatown fires. We spoke a little. He went
on about generals and sergeants. I figure he, for some

reason, reached into his bag of contacts and put in the word. I don't know why. I just wanted to shoot him."

"Willard Wong is undergoing rehabilitation, self-rehabilitation. He's getting older, more spiritual, closer to meeting his ancestors and having to answer some uncomfortable questions about his behaviour." Sally Greaves spoke as if gossiping about a neighbour over the back fence. "We're all over Willy."

"Well," Ray Tate said, "for whatever reason, we got some weight, here. We did good work, or at least Marty Frost did, on the Volunteers who firebombed Chinatown. So I'm parlaying that goodwill, like Hambone said, into this case."

"Speaking of which." Hambone Hogarth took a notebook from his pocket. "We got little or nothing from the guys you had picked up in Chinatown, Ray. They're going for the arson murders, but on the dead women, nothing. After the raid on Corey Garnett's house, one of my guys went back at them with the suicide and the white-on-black porno. Both of them were convincingly shocked, my guy said. Garnett was a straight shooter, never catted around, was focused solely on building a compound up north where there were no blacks or Chinese or democrats or anything not God-fearin'. Raising his family right. We talked to the wife. No hope there. She says we made it all up to protect the Chinese and blacks who have corrupted the city. So, if it was Garnett, he was keeping it on the real down-low when he was with the cadre or his family."

"But he isn't ruled out, right?" Ray Tate asked. "The last lady, our survivor, was found on the riverbank the same night the Volunteers were out repelling boats from Canada. Maybe our guy hung around after the other boys left? An earlier victim was a black prostitute who worked the men on the boats. So there's a connection there, to two of them anyway. All blacks, no motive." He was desperate, reaching, and he knew it.

Sally Greaves knew it too. She asked if anyone did workups on the other victims. "Maybe the other women had some connection to the river, to the men on the boats? In their backgrounds?"

Hambone Hogarth shook his head. "Look, Sally, we fucked this one up. We've done it before and I'm sure we'll do it again. We get stupider, not smarter, the more we're in business. Reverse Darwinian. Another couple of decades and we'll all be testifying on all fours."

Sally Greaves gave them all a protruding smile. "We can put it on him, if we want. We can do anything, especially if he's dead. You want us to find something in his stuff, ties him in?"

Hambone Hogarth mused for moment. "But if the guy, the real guy, goes off again, then what? I don't mind charging a dead goof for this, but I'd hate to have to apologize to the goof's family."

"I guess. Look, why don't I put some of my kids into the files, see if anything comes up, might give you a point?" She looked at each of them, peering through the granny spectacles. "Give me a couple of days, get this Volunteer nonsense out of the way."

Ray Tate wanted to ask about the snake ring. He couldn't find a way into it. In his imagination the image of Sally Greaves grappling with the blonde lieutenant was disturbing and intriguing, both. He wanted to know how the relationship came to pass. He sat mute, trying not to stare at the snake and ruby.

Sally Greaves got up and gathered her remaining half-banana and her thermos and elegant china cup. "Let's see what my little wizards come up with. Maybe there's some stinko stuff from the other rezes." She made a crowded, goofy smile. "Me, with what you've told me? I'd go to the pervert side of the menu."

Hambone Hogarth and Ray Tate rose to their feet, well-trained schoolboys. When Sally Greaves was gone, Hambone Hogarth remained standing. "You guys can hang in if you want. Or I'll see you in the morning after Sally's people get done. I'm gonna fly. We're setting up a press conference tomorrow, announce the Volunteers' conspiracy."

When Hogarth had left, Ray Tate and Djuna Brown sat in the vast cafeteria, looking at each other.

"We okay to go home, Ray? The Whistler or your place."

"We're okay, Djun'. We talked it out. We'll put it away, both of us." Idly, he put his hand on hers. "Nice pick-up, by the way, spotting the ring. I couldn't have imagined that. I don't know if it's weird or not."

"I don't know. I like it. Look at us. Who'd have thought, this, us? This is strong, I know that. What Sally and the blonde have, they must have gone through some stuff to make it work. Just like us."

He stood up. He'd left the painting from that day out in plain view. It disturbed him that she might see it before he could look at it with fresh eyes and maybe decide to destroy it. "The Whistler. Let the State pay for the gin." He looked at his watch. "I should call Marty, tell her maybe it isn't looking good for the Volunteers. We're going to have to move out, wider."

"Let's hold off. I've got that guy from down south, Missouri, coming in that thinks his missing daughter might be the survivor on the riverbank. Maybe he'll give us a lead. Maybe Sally's kids will come through with a connection between the Volunteers and the poor dead ladies. Let's call Marty in the morning. You never know, right? Be nice to have a bit of good news for her." She made a small grin. "I'll bet anyway she's having a quiet night of poetry reading."

The Irish maintenance man was pushing a mop along the tile hallway in the lobby. He leered at Djuna Brown. She gave him a sweet smile.

They drank gin and taps in the tub, then they drank gin and taps in the bed. While he slipped asleep, she thought about the day. A bad time had confronted them, and they'd confronted it. A bigger problem, what to do when she was shipped back north, was looming. With the worst of the bug just about over, city cops would come back on the roster. The State wouldn't leave her seconded forever. It was unimaginable that she abandon the Spout. But it was imaginable not to stay with Ray Tate. She let her mind roam through the day, but not the night before.

She dozed dreamily and at dawn snapped awake and rolled onto him, and his hands moved over her body of their own volition. "Ray?"

"Ah, look, give me ten minutes more, okay. You're killing me. I got a gun."

"No, no, not that. How come Sally Greaves didn't offer to go into the background of the Volunteers for us? Dig for pervo stuff? Somebody with a free-range hard-on? She's been drilling into them for quite a while." She folded her arms on his chest, put her chin on her forearms, and looked at him until his eyes opened. "Did you get the feeling Sally was trying to steer us off the Volunteers?"

Ray Tate thought about it. "She and Hambone are friends, good friends. With a little help from Sally, he could just close the dead ladies case. That would be easier. Just close it between them, put it on the dead Volunteer, have a press conference. And if Sally wanted it done like that, well, she's a good pal to have owing you a favour."

"Maybe," she said, "maybe they'd close it dirty. Except we're in there, right? Someone up the chain of command got a call, probably from your pal Willy Wong, to put you into play, and now they have to be careful. You're not one of them. You have to be satisfied."

Chapter 19

Samual-with-two-A's Darius Evans looked like what he was. A scratch farmer who'd spent most of his life bent at the waist, putting in and pulling out. His hair was white and tight to his skull and his face was seamed. He wore the simplest of work shirts, tucked into clean but worn khakis, and a wide, old tie that was tied too short. His eyes were a little sunken after his all-night drive north. His hands were rough as bark, but his fingers were long and tapered like a pianist's. When he shook Djuna Brown's hand, the callouses against her palm were thick, but his long fingers gentle, wrapping softly and gently around hers. She read him as a man of huge personal strength and modesty. She saw a worn black bible, with pages edged in flaking gold leaf, in his coat pocket.

"Djuna? Is that a freedom name? That your parents gave you, if you don't mind my asking, Officer Brown?"

Tiny beside him in her little slippers, she guided him across the Sector reception room and shook her head. Strange that she'd have the same conversation in two days. "No. My dad read about a woman in Paris named Djuna. He liked it and I got it."

Inside an interview room she let him sit where he wanted. There was no percentage in controlling the format. She instinctively knew this man could do no harm except in back-to-the-wall defence, and even then he'd only use the minimum strength required. He reminded her of her father, a cab driver who parked with his inside light on and devoured books of any kind. Solid men. Men busting themselves the life they could.

She offered him coffee or a drink of any kind.

He declined politely and she knew he didn't want to inconvenience her.

"I'm getting myself a root beer."

"Well," he said. "They don't make root beers like they used to. No roots, I guess. And beer's a sin." He chuckled. "But I'd appreciate it if it's no trouble and I'm sure it'll be fine as long as there's no roots or beer in it."

He stood until she left the room, leaving the door open so officers passing would know he wasn't a suspect, that there might be a victim or a victim's bereaved family on site, to keep down the yelling and boisterousness.

She was punching buttons on the beverage machine when Ray Tate came in. He showed her a digital image on his cellphone taken from an awkward angle to show enough of the victim's face without revealing the full extent of the damage. It had been almost impossible. "He should be able to tell from this. If not, we'll have to take him down there. You want to work him alone?" He wanted her to deal with policing that was the opposite of the Stonetown riots. "I think you should, Djuna. If he can do it. If you can do it."

"He can do it, if he has to, Ray. So can I. He's got a strength to him. If that's his kid on the tubes, I just found out why she survived."

They went down the corridor to the interview room. He put his hand on her arm. "This is the real work, Djun'. That other stuff, that was the anomaly."

She looked at him with sadness. "I know."

"I'm going to meet up with Marty and Brian, at the Bottomless. Call me when you're done, come on over."

When she entered, Samual Evans stood and waited until she closed the door softly, put the cans of root beer on the table, and sat, then sat himself. He waited until she'd pulled the tab off her drink before doing his own. He waited until she'd sipped before he took a swallow. Ladies first.

"Mr. Evans, I need to recap. You reported your daughter, Eve, missing the day before yesterday. Your report, forwarded from Jefferson City, Missouri, PD, indicates you always spoke to her at least a couple or three times a week, that when she didn't call for more than a week, you went to the police station. You said Eve lived alone here in the city, that she was a documentarian filmmaker, that you didn't know if she had a boyfriend. Jefferson City forwarded the report to our missing persons unit." She looked at the follow-up, which was skimpy. A policewoman had gone to Eve

Evans's address, an apartment just on the dirty edge of Stonetown's development where artists and students lived in rundown rented lofts, and confirmed she hadn't been seen recently by either-side neighbours or the building's superintendent. The section on the form suggesting follow-up actions had been left blank. It was minimalist policing.

"Did you know, Officer Brown, the first two slaves off a slave ship were sometimes given the names Adam and Eve? I didn't know that when I named her. The history to it. I named her Evening. Evening Evans. Because when her mother and I were young and we bought the patch we'd sit on kitchen chairs holding hands in front of the house looking at evening fall, each night. I thought it was the most beautiful thing, to sit on land you owned, well, maybe with the bank, but you had a stake in it, and you could watch evening come down as if you owned it. My baby would be that beautiful and I'd name her after those happy moments. I didn't think how it would sound, when people shortened it to Eve. For a long time she got teased about being called Eve Evans, but she came to like it. She said it was a good name for filmmaker. For a long time she was Eve Evans, and then E.E., and when she did her first documentary about a cancer lady she brought it down to Jefferson City and they showed it at the film school and there on the screen was 'An Evening Evans Project.' I was so proud. Her mother had died the year before of cancer. At the end it was dedicated to the memory of her mother."

Djuna Brown recognized he was diverting. His all-night drive north must have been a babbling time in his mind. He'd do anything not to have to leave the interview room to find out if his daughter was one of the poor ladies. In his mind was a wispy cloud of hope that his Eve was off on a film expedition, maybe in Hollywood on a filmmaking course. You could live a long time in that trace of wispy cloud, even as it faded away. She wished Martinique Frost could meet this man. Marty could chat with him about all manner of various stuff and unearth from him what was needed to be known.

She softly cleared her throat. "Mr. Evans, the simplest thing to do is for me to show you a picture of the … the lady in the hospital. If you say that it isn't her, I'll take you to our missing persons unit and they'll do a more in-depth interview with you about your daughter. We'll get them to prioritize it, we'll get it in the media, on the Internet, on the film-industry related websites. We'll get it out to veterinarians, dog walking services, everybody. Wherever she is, she'll see she lost the rhythm for a bit and was a little careless and she'll contact you or us. Can I show you the picture?"

"Veterinarians? Dog walkers? No. She hated dogs, feared them." He smiled at Djuna Brown, relief apparent. "Before I moved to Jefferson City, we had the patch down south, she saw a dog chase down a gopher and rip it up and it made her sick, what an animal could do to another animal. When she tried to save the gopher, the dog nipped her pretty good, here on the hand. Did this lady in the hospital have a dog? It isn't Eve, then." He sat back relaxed, his stoic attitude softening into relief although not pleasure. "I feel sorry, though, for the family whose daughter it is. I'll pray for them."

Djuna Brown made a small happy smile. "Okay, then. It seems this girl was out walking her dog when she was attacked. She said the dog, Harris, saved her."

"Harris?" Samual Evans, his voice croaking, said, "Harris?"

She felt the case curve on itself. "Harris, we think it was her dog. She said Harris saved her."

Samual Darius Evans's shoulders sagged. "Could she have said Horace?"

"Who's Horace?"

"I'd better look at that picture, Officer, please."

Djuna Brown opened Ray Tate's cellphone and scrolled to the photograph of the survivor. She handed it to Samual Evans.

"It's Evening." He was finally overcome and his voice cracked. "My baby."

Belted in, Djuna Brown drove to the hospital. Samual Evans sat in the shotgun seat, unbelted, but she didn't comment on it as she did when Ray Tate was in the vehicle.

"I got it for her when she moved up north to go to school. A dangerous place, up here. We named it Horace because Horace Smith was half of Smith & Wesson, the gun people. Down home everyone has a gun. She was a good shot. She knew guns and wasn't afraid of them. I'm afraid I made her take it. She didn't want to. Up north, she said, was people who used their brains instead of their guns. But I insisted. I wouldn't give her my blessing unless she took Horace. I wouldn't sleep. And she wouldn't come up here without my blessing. So, she took it. When we spoke on the telephone, I'd ask, 'You keeping Horace nearby? Keeping him fed?' She'd say, 'Yep, Dad. Me and Horace double-date all the time.' She laughed. She was humouring an old man." He slipped into a reverie, his lips moving in recall of past conversations, and Djuna Brown drove slowly to the hospital while he nodded to himself at the windshield.

"Mr. Evans, I have to make a call, okay?" She dialled Marty Frost. "Hey, is Ray with you guys?"

"Nope. Me and my poet are having a healthy breakfast. We're hooking up with Ray later at the Bottomless on Ontario."

"I'm with Mr. Samual Evans, the father of the lady in the hospital? We're just heading over there now. He said Harris is actually Horace, named after Horace Smith, Smith & Wesson? Horace is a gun. It wasn't found at the scene, so probably the doer took it with him."

"Okay, good. Call us when you're done, come over to the Bottomless."

Djuna Brown clicked off and swung into the parking lot at St. Francis' Heart. Samual Evans saw some media crews set up at the Emergency entrance.

"Is that for us? For Eve?"

"No. You heard about the riots the other night? Those people."

Before getting out of the car, Samual Evans looked at her with huge sadness. "I made a mistake. I should never have let her come north. There are universities in the South."

She patted his huge hand with her little elegant one. "None of us is perfect. We're just people, like everybody else. Don't blame yourself."

At the nurses' station a harried doctor wearing a white jacket over a bulging T-shirt was flipping charts while a world of activity broke around him, as though he were a rock in a river. He looked vaguely familiar. She thought: *Bronstein.*

"Doctor Bronstein?" She showed him her badge. "You were out in the riot the other night? Chinatown?"

"I was. You were with that bearded officer. Last time I saw you, you were running down the street with a shotgun. A permanent image. Beautiful woman, slippers, and a gun. When you were a little girl, did you imagine that? That image? You, with a shotgun running towards a riot?" He rubbed his hands over his face. "Sorry. I'm having those kinds of thoughts lately. The mind has no neutral, sometimes, so racing the engine becomes the status quo. It protects itself with wide cerebral thoughts so it can ignore little physical realities that confront you. When I was in med school in Boston did I see myself in Burma, removing a bullet with a chisel and a pair of manicure scissors? And when I was there, did I see myself in the middle of an American street taking a Chinese kid out with a tire iron? That kind of stuff." He shrugged. "Are you here to lay some charges on my patients? Get in line."

"No, no. This is Mr. Samual Evans. His daughter came in a few days ago, she was found by the river? Head injuries? Massive body?"

"Yeah, she's one of mine." He shook hands with Samual Evans and said he was pleased to meet him, regretting the circumstances. "I meant to call you people, Officer, but, well, you know it got really busy really fast. Miss Doe, Miss Evans, briefly regained consciousness yesterday. Very briefly. Then she lapsed out. Then she did it again, this morning, this time for a minute." He said to Samual Evans, "I'm sorry what happened to your daughter, sir, but this is good news. She's got a long road ahead, there's some optical damage, there's some brain injury we haven't been able to fully evaluate. She's got the strength. I wondered where she got it."

"From her mother."

"I'm sure." Bronstein gave him a nod of appreciation at this. "Anyway, we've had to move people around. She's up on Five. Give me two minutes and I'll take you up there." He stopped a passing nurse and handed her a stack of files. "These ones we lose. We don't know where they are. They didn't come in and if they did come in, they didn't. Blame the filing system. Blame me." He glanced at Djuna Brown, turned slightly away and told the nurse. "The cops don't get these people." He picked up a phone off the counter. "Five-o-seven. I'm going in there with family visitors in two minutes. Clean things up. Make the lady as presentable as you can."

Djuna Brown saw in his lined face an inexhaustible, tough compassion. A multi-tasker of the physical and the spiritual and the practical and the emotional. She wondered how the night in Stonetown would have gone for her if she'd had his qualities and Samual Evans's strengths. She thought again about her father, down in the capital. She thought how much she was lacking as a person.

Bronstein took the remaining files to a frazzled-looking nurse. "These, Mavis, in this order, please. There are two more patients coming over from Mercy in about twenty minutes."

"We have no room, you know that." She shook her head, sternly. "We're all filled up."

He pointed into the nursing station. "Get maintenance up here, move those two desks out, swing some gurneys in, get some screens. We got lots of space. We can play tennis in here, if we have to, and still have room to dance, you and me, after work."

The nurse laughed and shook her head. "Okay, Doctor, okay."

He led the way to the elevators.

Djuna Brown asked, "What was that, about the cops not getting people?"

He wasn't evasive. "No record of them being here. They're gone." They boarded the elevator and he pressed 5 with his elbow. "Chinatown kids. Their addresses are in Chinatown, in the streets around the arsons. Students, restaurant workers. They were scooped up in Stonetown in the riots and pretty badly beaten. They paid a pretty heavy price for getting angry about their community being massacred. So, you don't get 'em."

When they stepped out onto Five, he led the way down the corridor past a waiting room crammed with people. "You guys didn't horse around."

She could say nothing to that.

At 507 he stopped. "Mr. Evans, I need you to listen to me for a minute, okay, sir? It's going to look bad. It's going to look a lot worse that it really is. There's damage you can see, there's damage you can't see. I need you to stay on the right-hand side of her. If you need to touch her, touch her on the right-hand side. Maybe her shoulder, maybe her hand. That's it. Don't touch her face, even on the bandages. You'll want to. I would. She's still a beautiful girl. But you can't, sir, okay? She can't move her head. If she awakens, you can move into her field of vision. Her eye won't move much. But don't get into the wires. Those wires are keeping her going."

Samual Evans nodded. He clamped his lips, took out his bible and clutched it in his hand.

Bronstein steered Djuna Brown away a couple of feet. "I can't stay. You've got five minutes before a nurse will come in. She'll evaluate Miss Doe ... Miss Evans. She'll kick you out or she'll give you more time. There'll be some crushed ice in there, he can rub her lips with it if she wakens. He can come back any time he wants, never mind that visitors' hours bullshit. Tell 'em at the nurses' station Bronstein said it was okay. I'll leave a note."

"Thank you." She put her hand on his arm and looked up into his eyes. He'd been in the riots, at the beginning, and he was dealing. He looked like he'd been in a lot of faraway shit, and he was dealing. "You're a good person, aren't you? In spite of all this? Of where you find yourself?"

"Not always, Officer." His face darkened a shade for a split second. He was intuitive and recognized she was asking something else. "None of us is at all times, in every place. We have to live with it as best we can."

She watched him stride down the dingy corridor past a garbage container overflowing with newspapers and tin cans. He veered into the nurses' station, took a plastic garbage bag from under the counter, and dumped the container into it, tying the bag with a flourish.

She could hear him whistling, swinging the bag, as he leaned over to hit the down button with his elbow.

If I'd gotten shot, she thought, if I'd gotten shot, boy.

Chapter 20

At breakfast in her apartment, Martinique Frost told Brian Comartin about Horace the gun. She made a show of relishing her buttered and jammed toast, sunnyside eggs, and crispy bacon, with endless *mmm*s and *yum*s. For fun, she poured extra cream into her coffee. Making his bran cereal with zero-percent milk last as long as possible, Brian Comartin watched her enjoyment morosely, but he was secretly pleased at this attention to his well-being. His coffee was black and sour. He had to get on top of his body issues. An advertisement for waffles came on the television in the kitchen. Brian Comartin groaned at the melting pat of butter, the pouring of syrup.

Marty Frost was sympathetic. "Twenty-nine more days, Brian, and we go to IHOP, my treat." She made a relaxed smile. "And, oh, three hundred and six days after that, I figure, we'll be eating breakfast every morning in Barcelona. Hang in there, man."

"Bar-*tha*-lona. In Spanish they pronounced the C as a *th*. Bar-tha-lona."

They were watching the waffles being devoured by insanely voracious children when the telephone on the kitchen table buzzed. Marty Frost hit the mute on the television and picked up the phone. "Who wants to see me? Joe who? Don't know him. Oh, wait, yeah, I know that guy. The firebomber, right? Okay, I'm gonna pick up my partner on the way in, we'll go straight to the secure lockup. Give us an hour, let them know I'm coming." She clicked off.

Brian Comartin said, "An hour? It's ten minutes, we take the Eight down to Huron, cut across the park, pop out a block from the lockup. Run a half-block the wrong way on the one-way and we're in the back of the parking lot. Twelve minutes, max."

She nodded. "But that doesn't allow for a detour in the shower, right? Diet without exercise is pointless."

He thought her greying cornrows and the grooves of life in her face were the most beautiful thing he'd seen. It was beyond sexy. There was a poetry there. He'd caught Ray Tate looking at Djuna Brown with what he imagined was the same feeling. There was life and possibility. Yesterday and today weren't the only available future. He saw her on Las Ramblas, sipping sweet, thick coffee; he saw himself, slimmer, fit, maybe a little ex-cop tough, sitting opposite in a ten-cent shirt and long, baggy shorts and espadrilles, reading an *El Periodico*, referring occasionally to a Spanish-English dictionary. At night after they had a good late dinner together, he'd sit by a window overlooking a town square and write poetry.

He had the perfect feeling that this part of his life was over.

Joseph Carr wore a full-body baby blue jumpsuit with wide belt loops and a waist-chain running through it to steel handcuffs, then down to shackles on his ankles. The slippers on his feet shuffled across the floor, and the chains clinked. Someone had been at him: he had a blackened eye, but his fists were scabbed and bruised. He was maintaining, holding his ground. He looked glad to see her, the familiar face who'd aced him into fatal declarations of guilty knowledge.

The custodian, specially trained in security of defendants in death penalty cases, sat him down, pushed Joseph Carr's cheek down into the tabletop, neither gently nor aggressively, slipped the waist-chain to the back, unlocked it, then secured it to the back of the chair. He fastened the handcuffs to an iron ring driven deeply into the metal tabletop. He stepped back, then used a chain attached to the chair to secure Joseph Carr's ankles to a ring in the floor. "He's all yours, Miss. Nobody that secure can get at you."

"Harry Houdini." Marty Frost smiled at him. As she always did, she tried to make a personal connection. "Harry Houdini. He'd get out of this. I saw it in a movie."

"Well, no. Harry didn't have me locking him down. Trust me, if Harry had had me in there with him, I don't care if he swallowed the key and puked it up, he'd still be trying to breathe through his ears." He tapped Joseph Carr on the shoulder. "Okay, Joe? Stay in the chair. Okay, Miss? I'll be behind that glass. I can see but not hear. The door lock is on a foot switch. I can be in here in literally two seconds. You just have to stand up, I'm in. Don't stand up unless you need me. Adrenaline kills."

When the custodian was gone, she asked Joseph Carr how he was making out.

"Okay. An awful lot of black people in here. I had a couple fights before they laid the charges and moved me to my own cell."

"Anybody I can call for you, Joe?"

"Naw. I mean, no, my lawyer called my wife. She knows about the ... those sex charges. That it wasn't me. She's standing by me on that. Chinatown, too. It had to be done. But she knows I wasn't in on any sex stuff. I'll go for Chinatown."

"Maybe, maybe, Joe, you've got some time in here, you might want to use that time to think things out? Maybe it isn't so cut-and-dried? This black, white thing? Chinese? Maybe people are just people, trying to bust themselves a living? I've seen everyone, black, white, Asian, Mexicans, everyone do the most horrible things. It always broke my heart and I admit I cried, but it didn't make me put it all on anyone."

She took a cigarette package from her pocket and held it up to the plexi-window where the custodian was watching. He shook his head sternly and pointed his finger at a No Smoking sign above her head. He wagged his finger at her, then closed his eyes for a moment and nodded. She lit two cigarettes with a plastic lighter and leaned across to put one into Joseph Carr's lips. She didn't smoke, much, but the companionship of it felt right. He took a deep drag, then bobbed his head down to his chained hands and took the cigarette from his mouth in his fingers. A second later he bobbed his head again to the cigarette, inhaling and exhaling. He seemed to have all the time in the world to think about what she'd said.

"People are just people, Joe. Like us, you and me. We're just people who need to make a human connection. Just like us, you and me. Are we race enemies, Joe? Do you hate me, want to beat me to death? I mean, you know me."

"No. I guess not. I dunno. No. I'm getting the needle for Chinatown, aren't I?"

"I don't know, Joe. Depends on your lawyer." He'd tell her, she figured, in his own time why he'd voiced out for her. "You can make some kind of a deal, I'm sure. If there's anything you need me to do, well, I can't promise. What you did was pretty outrageous. I'm not going to pretend it's forgivable. It'll take a lot of time for a lot of people, me included, to get past this, past what I saw you did in Chinatown. But maybe, maybe if you need something … Maybe." She sat smoking the cigarette as if she had all day.

"How come Ansel isn't in here? I'm here, Peter's here. I can't talk to him, but I saw him going to the visitors' room. I haven't seen Ansel. My lawyer doesn't know what I'm talking about, I ask."

"Who's Ansel?"

"The other guy, the one with the tattoos? Was picked up with us in Chinatown? He joined up about a month ago, Corey brought him in, said he was a righteous guy, a fugitive from Idaho. He's the guy that got arrested with us in Chinatown. Ansel Partridge. He was always off doing missions, he said. He'd be gone for a few days, then back with us. It was his idea, the firebombs. He brought the gas and the bottles. Let's make a strike for America. Burn 'em, burn 'em, burn 'em."

Martinique Frost felt a chill. "I don't know, Joe. Maybe they're holding him in federal lockup. The feds are hungry for this case. They aren't into making deals, but maybe they need this Ansel for something else."

"Yeah. Yes, I guess." He thought about that for moment. "So. They said Corey killed himself? In the raids?"

"Yes. He hung himself in a room he had hidden in his house. He was into porn. Black porn. It was everywhere. He never mentioned that, to you guys?"

"No. No, that's sick, Miss. Any kind of pornography is a sin. Women are to be respected." He bent to his hands and smoked at his cigarette until it was a stub. He looked around. She reached over and took it from his fingers and pinched it out. She pinched hers out, feeling a little nauseous.

"I guess, Miss, he was a troubled soul, Corey. The Lord sure don't make it easy."

"Joe, let me ask you one, okay? With what you know, this racist porn he had, the suicide, do you think Corey was capable of beating black women to death? Was he that hateful?"

Joseph Carr thought about it. His face went through several changes and she believed what he was going to say would be the truth. Most liars operate off the face of confusion or innocence. One or the other; lying can get complicated, best to stick to a simple set of expressions. Joseph Carr was actually processing. "No. No, I don't see it, but how do we know what's in the hearts of others?" He nodded to himself as if he liked the phrase he'd come up with. "In the hearts of others." He took a deep breath. "Look, can I talk to you about something? I don't want Corey's family hurt any more than already."

"I'll listen, Joe, but I have to tell you, my entire focus right now is on getting justice for the poor ladies. That's my mission, my duty. We're thinking it was Corey, some twisted race thing. He went off. If what you tell me is going to get me there, I'm going to use it. If what you tell me doesn't do that, then I have some leeway, what I do with it."

He nodded. "Ansel. After Corey brought Ansel around, they'd go out sometimes, just the two of them. That was weird. Corey was afraid of Ansel but Ansel was all chummy. Once, Ansel made some crack, like he was teasing. An inside joke, you know, how a guy says something that nobody else understands? And they laugh between themselves? Well, with Ansel, that time, it wasn't for pals laughing. It was Ansel laughing and Corey getting all white in the face. He was terrified. But Ansel just went off on something else, another plan, another action."

"You remember what it was about, that Ansel put to him?"

"It was nothing, really. Ansel was always trying to push us into buying some guns off him, guns he'd bought and needed the money back for. Corey said he didn't ask Ansel to get any guns. Ansel said something like, 'Well, we're gonna need guns to tear it down, you guys agreed, and I went out and spent nine hundred bucks to get these things and you don't want them? What am I gonna do with all these guns?' And Corey said, he was a little pissed off and trying to stand up to Ansel, he said, 'Take 'em up to the projects, sell 'em to the gangbangers.' Ansel didn't like that much, arming the enemy. He said, 'Well, maybe I can take 'em down to Smoketown, I got a pal spends a lot of time down there, hunting up black cooz. Can't remember the race traitors' name but it'll come to me.' Next day Corey sold a snowmobile he had just bought last winter and we had a bunch of guns."

"You think Corey went beyond the porn? That he was into black women, sexually, like, physically? Down in Smoketown? And Ansel worked him off that?"

"I don't know, Miss. I'm just sayin'. If Corey had that ... kind of stuff going on, there's no way he'd kill them, after. Corey was no killer. And Ansel, well, if the women were killed and not ... had things done ... then maybe Ansel. But no way is he gonna ... do stuff to them."

"Well, Joe, we weren't exactly square with you. The black ladies were beaten to death, but there was no sexual assault. No rape. We made that up to move you. It had to be done, you know? It hurt me to lie, seeing what it did to you, to make you worry for your family. But I have to speak for those poor dead ladies. That's my job, my calling. If you want, I can call your wife and explain it to her. So she doesn't have bad thoughts about it. Women can take that kind of stuff hard."

"No, no, it's all right. She knows me. She knows I'd never —" He went silent. Then, "I'm glad they didn't suffer all that before they died. Those women."

It was time to move him again. He'd ramble all day with her to avoid going back inside the isolation cell. "So, you remove the rape part of the attacks on the ladies, what do you think? Ansel? Someone else in the group?"

"Like I said, I don't know what's in other folks' hearts. But if, like you said, the ... women were killed and not ... had stuff done on them, then maybe Ansel. Ansel could kill anyone. He told us stories about things he did. How he stone-cold capped asses, he called it, for America."

In her mind, she organized all that he'd said. She wanted to leave him, but she wanted to leave on good terms. "Okay, Joe. I was glad to hear from you, so I could come in and clear up that sex stuff. I was going to come in, see how you're doing, but we got really busy. The people in Chinatown, I guess you heard, were pretty upset about what you guys did. They did a lot of damage over in Stonetown. That's sorting out, but we still haven't conclusively put the dead ladies on Corey or any of your people." She leaned forward gently. "Anything else, before I head out."

"Yeah, yes, maybe. I was thinking. You said one of the … the ladies was killed by the river? The night we were patrolling?"

"Yes. We don't have a timeline, that last poor lady is still in a coma. She was just a girl, Joe, about as big as a kid. A girl out for a walk. He grabbed her up and just …" She shook her head as if she couldn't comprehend it.

"Well, Miss, I was thinking. We was out on the water, about ten o'clock to after midnight. Having a few beers. Nothing came over from Canada, so we packed it in. Just about midnight. There was me and Corey and Peter."

"No Ansel?"

"No, not that night. He said he had another action to do, he'd hook up with us later. But we didn't see him for a day or two."

He wanted to please her, to give her something. She wondered if, in his life, he'd had any exposure to black people, had had a coffee with one, or a meal, or even a chat on a street corner. Or with a Chinese person. Or any person unlike himself. Somehow his life had become ghettoized. He'd barricaded himself from the people of America, people who weren't much different from himself. Frustrated sometimes. Happy sometimes. Exhausted and worrisome about their children and elderly parents and finances. He had access to all of America and he'd limited himself, or been limited to, a narrow, hateful slice. Cops did it too. They cut themselves off from their own human nature, made themselves separate and different. They barricaded themselves. The thought of Barcelona with her poet was becoming attractive, even urgent, for the survival of her sanity.

"If that's true, Joe, that means Peter, and especially Corey, aren't who we're looking for. You're sure, right? This is the truth, just between us?"

"Me, Peter, and Corey. We was on the water, we beached the boat on the shore, we went back to Corey's."

She waited a minute. Her instinct was to lay back, but to give him something. She couldn't give him approval. That would be too much, even for her. "Maybe, Joe, maybe you're making up for all that other stuff, now with this. There might be some strange roundabout reason, man. If you hadn't gone into Chinatown that night we wouldn't have met. If we hadn't have met, I wouldn't be getting this information for the poor dead ladies."

He looked over her shoulder and seemed to be thinking about it. "Yeah. I'm gonna have to go to school on that. But maybe it sounds about right." He mulled and nodded to himself. "Did this help? With those … poor dead ladies?"

"I think so, Joe. If you and Peter and Corey were in the boat, then maybe Ansel is the guy. Did he ever mention any place? A restaurant? A bar? Where he worked? Girlfriend? A car or truck you might have seen him in?"

"Nothing. He always showed up with Corey and he left with Corey. He never talked about nothing except actions. Actions, actions, actions."

"This is good. You've done well for me and I appreciate it." She looked at her watch. "Joe I have to take off, follow this stuff up, find the justice."

Then he said why he really wanted her to visit. He'd rehearsed it to get it right, to let her know clearly, she could see. He spoke almost formally. "You know, Miss, if I had someone like you, black or white, in my family, talking like this together, I think I'd'a done okay, wouldn't be in this mess." He awkwardly half-stood, bent at the waist. "I just wanted you to know that."

Martinique Frost looked at the Plexiglas window, made a thumbs-up motion, and raised her eyebrows. The custodian nodded. Slowly she rose and came around the table and gave Joseph Carr, held hunched over in his restraints, an awkward hug. "Good luck to you, Joe."

"You're a good person," he said, "and I think I might'a been a good person too, if things was different." He sat back down as the custodian came in, a tiny can of pepper spray subtly hidden in his hand. "Would you tell those Chinese folks I'm sorry? If they'd'a stayed over there we could'a been friends. I really like their food."

"I'll tell them, Joe."

"Head down on the table, Joe. Relax."

He put his head down with the custodian's hand on his head, but he kept his eyes cut up into hers. "If I see them in heaven, things'll be different. I promise you."

She couldn't think of anything to say to that and left him being re-shackled.

Chapter 21

Samual Darius Evans, with the worn black bible in his hand, sat silently with his daughter for the five minutes until the nurse came in. She checked the monitors, made some notes, and said they could have five minutes more.

The moment she stepped out of the room, Samual Darius Evans excused himself to Djuna Brown. "I know when you're a police officer, it's hard to believe, with all you see, I know that. But I'd like to pray, here, with my girl. I don't want to embarrass you, Miss, if you'd like to leave."

He was goodness. He was her father. He was what Ray Tate had in mind when he said to keep your heart for the victims. She said, "Even police pray. May I stay? And pray? With you, for her?"

He laboriously got on his knees with a heavy sigh and the crackle of cartilage. She stood behind him, erect with her head bent, and folded her hands at her waist. Feeling like a bit of a fake, she was surprised to hear Evans's voice in her ear: "Pretend to believe when you don't believe, and you'll be ready to believe when you do." That was the essence of his faith.

The room was quiet. Machines beeped. A car engine roared outside the window.

She closed her eyes.

And then there was a convergence inside her, a gathering. Maybe because she was exhausted and her posture allowed her to finally relax. Maybe it was some osmosis of the tensile strength of Bronstein or Samual Darius Evans, strong fathers both. But there was something happening. It wasn't a vision of God, but it was a diverse confusion of elements, not unpleasant, not demanding to be calmed, but only to be recognized, endured. It was the smell of sweat-lodge smoke, the caw of a raven, it was the flash of Ray Tate's face in the instant before she'd been handed the email calling for help down in the city, it was the sound of the curving bullet taking her earring off with a buzz and a clink.

She was warmed, flushed, as she listened to the rhythm of Samual Darius Evans's voice and while she couldn't hear the words, she recognized the pacing of The Lord's Prayer.

There was a pause after he said a strong, loud, "Amen."

Then he starting singing what sounded like a lullaby.

Then he stopped.

Then he cried, "Evening."

Alarmed, Djuna Brown reached out to comfort him, to restrain him if necessary although she couldn't imagine anyone with enough strength.

Evening Evans's uncovered eye was open, flickering toward the sound of his voice.

Djuna Brown felt pretty good. Maybe her little portion of the praying had paid off in the God scheme of things. She left Samual Evans with his daughter, left the hospital to stand in the sunshine. She called Ray Tate.

"She's awake, Ray. We were … we were just in the room and Mr. Evans was praying and she just woke up. She can't talk yet, but the doctor, Bronstein, remember him from Stonetown? Doctor Tire Iron? He's her doctor. He said maybe later this evening we can take a really soft run at her. Simple yes or no stuff. Nothing too confusing."

"Great, good, that's good news, Djun'."

"And that Harris thing? We thought was a dog? It was Horace, a gun, named after Horace Smith, Smith & Wesson. She had it with her. Looks like the doer took it. I told Marty."

"A mystery solved. What are you up to? Now?"

"Nothing. You, ah, want to meet? At the Whistler? Have lunch?"

"Marty and Brian are on their way here. They've got stuff. I'm at the Bottomless on Ontario Road. Why don't you come over here? We can strategize, maybe … ah, I dunno, head to the hotel after for lunch?"

She didn't have a car, and asked for directions. He said to take a cab, it was easier.

But she didn't. She asked a passerby for directions to the Bottomless on Ontario and in her little slippers started a twenty-five-block hike. Her path took her through Stonetown. It still reeked of smoke. There was a lot of damage. Every window had been shattered. Shopkeepers and restaurateurs consulted with insurance-claim adjusters waving clipboards, or listlessly swept the glass and debris from their storefronts into the gutter. Some buildings had been burned. She stopped and watched and bummed a cigarette from a passing woman.

She smoked, remembering her wild night there. How she smelled on herself terror, how the burning gasoline burned at her eyes. This is the place where everything that was me evaporated, she thought. I got caught up and found myself to be a stranger to me. I was afraid and was almost killed in front of Ray, breaking his heart, and ...

And then in front of her in Stonetown there was a moment, a moment of validation she needed.

A dozen Chinese youths in black kung fu pants, work boots, and white T-shirts came up the block, two by two, followed by two creeping car-loads of chargers. The Chinese teens wore work gloves. They stopped in front of a narrow bistro where a woman in a white chef's jerkin, black-and-white checkered pants, and wooden clogs stood surveying the damage, shaking her head.

One of the Chinese kids went up to speak to her. She hugged him and Djuna Brown heard her say, "I'm so, so very sorry." And the crew moved into the restaurant. Four chargers in their black leather gloves disembarked their ghoster and followed them in.

A battered U.S. mailbox was carried out by two Chinese kids and stood upright at the curb. One of the chargers moved to the broken window and, with his baton, scraped the shards of glass remaining in the frame. Two chargers came out carrying a newspaper box; they set it up near the mailbox. One kid came out with a broom and swept the patio meticulously. Two others carried out broken chairs and tables. The woman in her chef's outfit set up four tables on her patio and went inside. She came out with a tray covered in foil and a case of beer.

Snapping caps, she saw Djuna Brown smoking at the edge of the railing. "Are you okay? You're crying."

"So are you."

"Sometimes, sometimes … this really is America." The chef laughed and sniffed. "Go figure."

Djuna Brown moved on, thumbing at her eyes. Reconstruction efforts were everywhere. She saw Willard Wong in pressed blue jeans and a white buttoned-down shirt with a thin cardigan over his shoulders, like a cape, directing a crew of workers at a furniture store. He aristocratically smoked a cigarette, holding it near his mouth as he inhaled and exhaled. From inside came the rip of a power saw, the hammering of nails. As she passed, he spotted her and wagged his finger at her with a smile. She waved gaily and paused at the foot of Parson's Lane. There'd be bullet pockmarks in the brick walls, a shattered earring on the ground, and there'd be the cobblestones where she'd curled up and was afraid to look at Ray Tate, fearing the bullets meant for him hadn't curved in magic. Where, when she heard his voice talking to the old Road, she'd started giggling and proceeded to fall apart.

She moved on, avoiding Parson's Lane. She carried a melancholic feeling of hope with her. Not wanting to spoil it, she added five blocks to her trip to the Bottomless and avoided Chinatown, not wanting to push her luck. Chinatown would still be forensics teams and flower shrines.

The blue Mercury and a black Chrysler were parked illegally in front of the Bottomless, curb-side wheels up on the sidewalk. Through the window she could see Marty Frost and Brian Comartin sitting close together at a wire metal table. They looked, she thought, like a middle-aged couple planning their day, maybe discussing going to a movie, maybe planning a late dinner. Ray Tate was at the serving counter. When she walked in he looked and gave her the old sly Ray Tate smile, and then told the barista to blow up another cappuccino, his simple sister was here, on leave from the asylum. The barista laughed aloud.

When they were settled in around the table, Djuna Brown went first, relating the miraculous reviving of Evening Evans, leaving out her own effort at prayer. In barely concealed wonder, she spoke at length about Samual Darius Evans and his strength of character.

She spent some time on Bronstein, his easy command of his staff, the collecting of the bag of garbage, the rearrangement of the nursing station into a hospital ward. She detailed her walk through Stonetown, told of the Chinese kids and the chargers working on the bistro, the owner weeping. "Amazing how in the light of day everybody's humanity comes back, how we all recognize each other again," she said, speaking of the neighbourhood and, maybe, about herself.

Essentially, she added nothing to the dead ladies' case, except that Harris was Horace and Horace was a gun, and Marty Frost and Brian Comartin looked at each other in amusement as if Djuna Brown were indeed a slightly simple-minded sister in her little spangled slippers.

"Cool." Ray Tate appreciated all of it. He could tell she was back. "Now, about last night at the Jank." He told them about the suspicion he and Djuna Brown had that Sally Greaves, the head of the SPA, wasn't being straight with them. "She seemed to be more interested in putting the hat for the ladies on a sex deviant. They want us to look elsewhere. We got the sense that the whole discussion was a set-up, maybe by her, maybe by her and Hambone Hogarth. They don't want us jumping into the Volunteers' shit. We didn't know why, then." He sipped his coffee and said, "But I think Marty might know why. Ansel Partridge. Marty?"

Martinique Frost went over her conversation with Joseph Carr. He'd made alibis for himself, Corey Garnett, and Peter van Meister. "The only player we know wasn't there is Ansel Partridge. Mystery man. He comes, he goes. Picked up with the firebombers in Chinatown but not in custody, not anywhere in the system. I checked." She looked around at each of them. "Ansel Partridge. Cop or informant, living the cartoon life. And maybe, in his spare time, killer of the ladies."

"Not something Sally Greaves would want out there in the press." Ray Tate nodded appreciatively. "Nicely done. We can use this. It answers a lot of questions. Sally Greaves wouldn't want us uncovering that Ansel Partridge might be a rogue, working undercover on the Volunteers by day, killing innocent women by night. All on the city payroll. Hambone wouldn't really care. At any time he can hang it on Corey Garnett, solve the whole thing without a messy trial. And he gets a favour from Sally, in case he needs it down the road. Neat. Sweet."

They figured Ansel Partridge wasn't his name, but back at the Jank Martinique Frost put him through Google and several search engines. There were no hits. The media drag came up negative except for Ansel Adams, the photographer, and the Partridge Family. She did a search on the Aryan Nations and several other white power groups. "No hits for Partridge, Brian. But when in doubt, go to the chat rooms. People will say anything about anyone."

"Do you want me to do a driver's licence on him? Put him through the computer for a criminal record?"

"Nope. We hold off on that. Once we do that, we're gonna hear about it, fast, if he's a cop. If he's on the job, or an agent for the job, there'll be a red notify on his working name in case he got burned or someone is checking him out. Someone'll come at us, asking why we put him in. We hold until we're ready to tell them." She peered at the screen then rubbed her eyes. "We get everything we can, then we make an official move." She took her glasses from her purse and put them on.

Brian Comartin stared, captivated. She looked real and beautiful and thoughtful.

She said, "What? I'm old, okay?" She gave him a sad smile. "Brian, you're not getting some twenty-year-old cadet, okay? Deal with it, *amigo*"

His heart soared a little.

She said, "Here we go. NARC-W. The National Anti-Racist Coordinating Workshop. 'Beware of these agent provocateurs.' Look at them all." She shook her head, "Oh, I like this one, this is a great site. I wouldn't trust any of them." Then she laughed. "I bet this is one of Sally Greaves's operations. She runs pictures of actual revolutionaries as cops, gets the black marble thrown on them, puts 'em out of commission. Diabolical."

There was nothing on any of the sites. A lot of the men had the shaven head and tattoos, but none were Ansel Partridge.

Billy Stiles, in civvies, was in the parking lot at Sector Four doing start of shift. He was yanking his duty bag out of the trunk of his personal car when Ray Tate creeped the Mercury up off his bumper. "Hey, Stiles. Billy Stiles, right? Ray Tate. We met at the Chinatown fires."

Billy Stiles dropped the bag and put out his hand. "My brother, Jimmy, told me about some fucking hippie cop that helped him out. The kid said he froze, you woke him up."

"A good kid. He did the job. How's he doing?" Ray Tate got out of the Mercury. "He saw some shit that night."

"Good, good. I 'preciate you looking out for him."

"Not a problem. He'll do good."

Djuna Brown got out of the car and Billy Stiles looked her over. Ray Tate introduced them. "We're following up on those three bozos you guys took in from the fires? Joe Carr, Peter van Meister, Ansel Partridge?"

"Well, we separated them right away, took their shirts, or in the case of the tattooed guy, a piece of it. And boy, did we have to negotiate with both hands and a stick. A scrapper. We called for transport but we only got a car for van Meister. Too bad for him it was a couple of Chinese chargers, and they were some pissed. I can tell you about Joe Carr; I took him in. He cried all the way. Oh, what did we do, oh, what did we do? The Chinese guys took van Meister. Gerry Martin took the tattooed guy. That would be this Partridge, I guess?"

"I guess. Where can I find Gerry Martin? He on shift?"

"Naw. He hit the jackpot. Transferred out yesterday to Admin Fraud. Straight days, Monday to Friday. I didn't even know he'd applied. His wife just dropped a frog and I guess he wants to be around for her and the kid." He shrugged. "Some guys aren't made for the street."

"Okay, we'll find him down at the Jank."

"Not this month. They don't need him on shift until next month so he's taking his time-in now, now that the plague's let up a little and guys are coming back. He's got a place down in Delray Beach. Next time we see him he'll be tanned and happy, chewing on a pencil, wearing a suit from Bummy's."

"Did he say anything? About Partridge, about the transport?"

"Nope." Billy Stiles slung his duty bag over his shoulder. "I want to say again, thanks for that with Jimmy. You ever get caught drunk driving in Sector Four, have 'em call me." He nodded to Djuna Brown. "You're the girl that got her ear shot off by the cop, right?"

"Yep, I be that very girl." She made a dreamy smile. "Magical stuff. Woo."

"You see the bullet curve, it was coming at you? Did you go, 'Fuck, how did it miss me?'"

She was startled and gave him a suspicious look. "How'd you know that?"

"I had a guy throw down on me, open up. Five feet away. Bang bang bang bang. I saw it too. One bullet came spinning right at my fucking eye, then at the last minute veered and got me here." He pulled his polo shirt collar down and showed a shallow groove like a burn mark. "Nothing. Took out a bit of flesh is all. I don't remember moving. I'm sure I didn't."

"It took my earring off. Amazing, huh?"

"Not so much. I wasn't wearing my earrings that night, but I'd just met my wife the night before and knew we were going to get married. Love makes you lucky, she says, I'm lucky for you." He stared at her, looking a little embarrassed. "I, ah, think about that a lot."

"Thanks for that." Djuna Brown put her little hand on his thick arm. "I needed that."

"No problem." He stepped away, then turned back to Ray Tate. "You know, on Gerry Martin? That took the tattooed guy in? Last thing he said to me when he cleared out his locker, was, 'I never thought I'd want to blow a guy with that many tattoos unless I was in Craddock, starved for love.' Funny, huh?"

Ray Tate made a thin smile. "Not so much, maybe."

They went inside Sector Four to the intake desk and gave the body snatcher the date and approximate time the three Volunteers were brought in from Chinatown. "Three guys," Ray Tate said, "Carr, Joseph; van Meister, Peter; and Partridge, Ansel. Came in by Stiles, Martin, and two Chinese chargers."

The body snatcher was a hump who looked for every reason not to do something. He sat like a lump, vacant, vapid. He was expert. "You got their badge numbers? I can't do a search without badge numbers."

"Just go over the chronology of intake that night." Ray Tate smiled, trying to reach into the guy, who looked vaguely familiar. "Three Anglo guys you got that came in that night together, that don't have Chinese names. They'll do."

"We took a lot of people through that night. That's a lot of names. If you have a badge number?"

Ray Tate stared at him. "One second." He went to the sergeant's table and asked for Billy Stiles's badge number. The young sergeant tapped at his computer and wrote it on a piece of paper. "You get any duty out of that old hump motherfucker over there, let me know. I'll get you a combat citation."

Ray Tate gave the number to the body snatcher. The hump stared at the piece of paper for a few minutes, as if the five digits were a code he needed to break, but not too quickly. "Is that a five or an eight? It looks like it could be either."

Ray Tate looked at the paper. "Eight. That's an eight."

"Okay, if you say so. But you better be right. I don't like to do things twice. It lowers my overall productivity and could jeopardize my chance for advancement. And if it turns out to be a five 'stead'a a eight, you're going to get a whole different guy's name popping up. I don't know if I'll have the time to do it over again."

While the hump figured out which keys to press on his keyboard, Ray Tate looked at Djuna Brown and shook his head, smiling in appreciation of a master. It took a while for the hump to coordinate his fingers. He warmed them up like a pianist, readied himself, sighed deeply, and began the ordeal of tapping in the five digits. Ray Tate looked around. He loved the sameness of Sector stations. The smell, the noise, the lighting.

Even humps like the body snatcher, they were good for stories. They were artists, masters of the do-dick. Ray Tate remained patiently good-natured about it. It was a process. It had to be endured.

"Okay. You're right. That's Stiles's number. William F. Stiles. That would be Billy, right? Short for William, I guess. It *was* an eight. I was sure it was a five. But you're right. It's an eight. You look at it a certain way, it's a crapshoot, five or eight. But, when you're right, you're right." The hump waited.

"Terrific." Ray Tate resisted laughing, "And what did we find?"

"You were right again. He brought in a guy named Carp."

"Carr."

"If you say so." He signed out of the screen. "Anything else I can do for you today?"

"Yeah, we already know about Carr. We want one of the other guys that was booked in with him."

"You got a badge number?" He sat back, triumphant, and folded his hands over his belly. "We took in a lot of people that night, you know."

Ray Tate was dizzy. Djuna Brown laughed. They stood in the smoking area on the side of Sector Four, sharing a cigarette, trying to decide what to do next. The hump had eventually said there was no third arrest. Just Joe Carr and Peter van Meister. When they left he was examining the mid-air between the ceiling and the floor as if looking for clues to the miracle of existence.

"We know, Ray, he came in. You saw him, right? In the interview room?"

"Well, they say not. Someone, I think, is scrubbing him. Gerry Martin going to Admin Fraud is a fix. Sally Greaves. The Graveyard."

"We should head to the hotel, Bongo, and talk about it. In the bathtub."

The hump came out the door, lighting a cigarette. He was rotund and had a skin condition on the back of his neck that he rubbed at absent-mindedly. He saw them, then wandered over to the garbage receptacle and tossed in a rumpled paper bag. "You handled that pretty good. Most guys I can make pig-biting mad in about thirty seconds. You're Ray Tate, right? The gunner." He held out his hand. "George Meyers. Hump and do-dick extraordinaire." He nodded pleasantly at Djuna Brown. He was an entirely different person. The look of vapid, mean stupidity was gone from his face and he almost beamed upon Djuna Brown. "Don't know you, Miss." They shook hands.

Ray Tate knew who he was. Everybody knew who George Meyers was. George Meyers was a legend. "Meyers. I met you with my father-in-law, ex-father-in-law, anyway, Harry Cane, back when I came on. He took me to a retirement whip-around. For, ah, a Road that pulled the pin. You came out of a cake in garters and fishnets."

"Well," George Meyers said, simpering, "I was a lot slimmer then." He ran his hands over his hips and addressed Djuna Brown confidentially. "I eventually had to accept the fact that I inherited my mother's thighs."

"Sorry, man," Ray Tate said. "I didn't recognize you."

"'S'ah'ri'. Most days *I* don't recognize me." He glanced at the door to the Sector. "So, what you want: They came in, some college kids from SPA. Evaporate Ansel Partridge, they said, he was never part of your life, they said. Or your pension'll be gone like he's gonna be, if he isn't, they said." He shrugged. "What do I give a fuck? One less hump."

"But he was here, right? And Sally Greaves's crew came and disappeared him?" Ray Tate bit his lip "Nothing left lying around, notes, meal slips, anything? Scrap of T-shirt?"

"Nope. And Gerry Martin, well he's on the way to a white shirt at the Jank. Good luck finding his notebook for that night. I'm no swami but I predict he's going to have a garage fire, where he keeps his notebooks. I thought there was more to that kid. Billy Stiles was bringing him along." He looked over their heads where surveillance cameras panned the parking lot. "I bet they're watching us right now. The cameras see everything. The hallways, most of the garage, interview rooms, the booking table. If someone wanted to vanish someone, they'd have to get all the tapes, well, the disks, they use now, I guess. Just like those SPA kids did. Not just the tapes up there and in the interview room and the booking tapes. They'd probably get them, too. Then they'd have to get the tapes of the cars entering the property at the gate. The brass installed

them for the summer because off-duty guys were going
to the pumps out back, loading up on free city gas on
their way for a weekend in the country. Those tapes,
probably, the kiddie cops from SPA didn't know about,
didn't ask for when they went up to a decorated officer
and treated him like a fucking douchebag."

Ray Tate put it together. "I guess I should look in
the garbage bin?"

"I would. And you oughta know, after you left, the
guy on the desk with the big mouth made a call on his
cellphone. He said, 'They're here,' and hung up. But
this isn't a freebie. I need you to do something for me."

"Name it, George. It's done."

"When you get this guy, find out where he was on
September nine, nineteen ninety-four."

Chapter 22

Djuna Brown called Marty Frost and arranged for a meeting at the Whistler in two hours. Ray Tate said, "Tell her to make sure they didn't do a records or motor vehicles on Partridge. We're not ready yet."

Djuna Brown passed it on, glanced at Ray Tate and shook her head. "Okay, Marty, in a couple of hours have the front desk buzz up that you're there. We'll do in that mini-bar."

After she clicked off, Ray Tate said two hours was a long time. "How we gonna fill it? You got pay-per-view?"

She smiled. "Asshole." She read the streets and spoke without looking at him. "You notice, Ray, almost nobody's wearing the mask? Plague alert is winding down. That means they're gonna send me home. How are we going to handle that?" She put her hand on his thigh. "I can't handle another year, like this last one. I ..." She looked out the windshield. "I see why you love these streets, Ray. I can't ask you to leave them. But I think I'm afraid of them. You know? What happened to me, what I did?"

"Maybe we should find something down here, something to keep us both working but off the streets for a while until we sort us out, get another year of pensionable time. You could get assigned to the State headquarters, down in the capital. Hour and a half commute." He cruised in the direction of the Whistler and picked up speed. "Maybe we need a vacation. But where to go? Disneyland? You down with the Mouse?"

"You're an asshole, *ma cherie*."

In the suite they resisted the bathtub until they ran the surveillance video through her laptop. There he was, a three-quarter face, a little blurred but recognizable, in the back of a police car, his mouth open, talking.

"Beautiful," Ray Tate said. "Now we just need a printout."

"But after, though, Ray, huh? I need a long bath. Why don't you have a nap while I soak? I'll wake you up when Marty and Brian get here. You rest, buddy. You had a long day."

He smiled into her sly cat smile. "Asshole."

They took their guns into the washroom and dumped them in the sink. They had time to waste while the tub filled and they wasted it. They climbed in and arranged themselves and then got stupid again.

"George Meyers was on Homicide," Ray Tate told Djuna Brown when they'd calmed down. There was water on the floor. There was water on the walls. She was brown and boneless on top of him. I am, he thought, getting good at this bathtub stuff. He felt dreamy. Could skin possibly be so smooth? She was a cool chick. She made him bigger than his job. He never felt white before, he never felt any colour, not before he put his hand on her skin.

"He was an ace detective. I know people say that about a lot of Homicide guys. Pure cop. Sherlock blood. That kind of bullshit. But George Meyers actually was one. Maybe the only one in my lifetime, the only one I ever met. You know the motto, We Speak for the Dead? With George it wasn't a motto. He actually felt he did. Out of forty-one homicides, he cleared forty. The twenty-first broke his heart. Broke him. Simple case, really. Four-year-old girl goes missing. Gets found dead. Raped. Little black girl. Fuck, it shames me I can't remember her name. I was one of the blue suits doing the canvass, doing the dog's work. He works a suspect list, works it down to one really good viable. This takes him a couple of years. He stays in the rotation, takes fresh cases as they come. Solves them. Moves on. But all the time he's focused on this one, the little girl, poor little black girl."

"Sounds like Marty. Obsessive. Her ladies. Obsessive, but good obsessive."

"Yeah. The cop gene. So, anyway, every time I saw him around the Jank, he was a little smaller. It was like some joker snuck into his house and kept replacing his suits, each time leaving a suit a size larger. He works his viable. He's married, no kids, and so he rents a room in the neighbourhood where the little girl lived. He moves the case file in there, sets up his own command post. Copies of everything. Photos, reports, arrest reports, suspect files, you name it. Then he starts sleeping in there. Two years he's got this secret life. The wife leaves him, he's never home. He doesn't notice. All he thinks about is the girl. The girl, the girl, the girl. If you picked up a perv, anywhere in the city? Next day there's George on the phone. 'See what he was doing on September nine, nineteen ninety-four. See if he's got an alibi.' 'Alibi for what, George? This guy was wagging his wiener at a dog.' 'September nine, nineteen ninety-four. Get back to me.' And if you didn't get back to him in due time, there he was at your desk when you came in one morning. 'That pervo, kid, what's up with him?' People got so when they saw him coming, they just went, 'Oh *fuuuuuck*.' Relentless."

"Looking at him, you'd never know. He was really like that? Mr. Go Fuck Yourself?"

"Yep. George Meyers. Hump and do-dick." Ray Tate asked if it was a smoking room.

"We're cops, Ray, we go armed. We can smoke anywhere."

He stood naked and climbed out of the tub. In his jacket he found some stale cigarettes from a Native reserve. Da Rez. The Reservation. He lit two and took them back into the bathroom. He'd always been a little shy about being naked. The personal residue of living in foster homes with no privacy. You slept in your clothes. Not anymore.

He got back into the tub and lay down beside her. "So, he, George, has his good viable. But he can't move the guy. He harasses him. The guy loses his job. The guy loses his wife. The guy tries to commit suicide, he's going to jump off a ledge. George shows up at the scene, tells the fire guys to catch him in the pancake, no matter what. 'I need him alive. Kill him later if you want, but right now, get that fucking mutt down here in one piece. I got questions.'

"This goes on and on. Finally, he breaks. Perfect homicide record, except for one. You know how many guys have that record? Exactly none, ever. Except George.

"So, he breaks. Neighbours at the rooming house hear screaming one night and call the cops, somebody being murdered in there. Door team goes in. There's George, sitting on the bed, slumped. There's his viable hanging upside down on the closet door. All fucked up. Teeth on the floor under him, blood. The viable gets a big whack of dough, a settlement. George goes into the void, they rinse his head, park him in dreamland. Which is where we found him today."

Djuna Brown saw the sadness on his face. "But, Ray, he came through, right? For us. He dollared up."

"Yeah, yeah, but except for that murder that got under his skin, ruined him, made him care too much? He'd have Hambone Hogarth's job. And this SPA bullshit wouldn't be going on. We wouldn't be doing this at all. He'd never let them protect a killer. He'd burn the fucking house down around them." He shifted and she put her head under his chin. He said, "George spoke for the dead. And he spoke really loud."

* * *

It was coming together in fragments.

Ray Tate called Brian Comartin and told him what they had. Comartin gave him his private email address and said to send the file over. He'd drop by his place, make some prints and bring them to the hotel. Ray Tate asked him to crop the prints in various ways, some tight so they didn't look like they were taken by the gate camera.

He stared at Ansel Partridge as he sent the email on Djuna Brown's laptop. Ansel Partridge definitely looked like trouble. From the shaven head, the solid muscles, and the gallery of tattoos, he was the quintessential ex-con. Even in the shadows, filmed through the window of the ghost car, his eyes glittered. Crank, Ray Tate decided, or crack. Commander Freebase. He wondered how tight Partridge's handlers were, if they even had a handle on him at all. "This is our guy, Djun', I feel it. This mutt's a killer."

When the front desk called up to say they had guests, they were drinking gin and taps from water glasses, sprawled in towels in leather chairs in front of the window, imagining the Left Bank was out there, waiting.

Ray Tate held the phone in his hand, his palm across the receiver. "We could get them to wait in the bar, fuck our brains out for another half-hour. Who knows when we'll get the chance again?"

* * *

Brian Comartin looked around the room and said it reminded him of Marseilles. Martinique Frost asked if she could move in and sleep on the couch.

Djuna Brown picked up the phone and asked the front desk if there were any more rooms available in the State block. There were; hers was the only one in use. She reserved one for Inspector M. Frost, State Police Barracks Six. "She's going to stay down here for a few days. Thanks. Four-oh-nine. Got it. Can you arrange for her to pick up a key card at the concierge? Thanks. Is that Gail? Thanks, Gail." She hung up and told Marty Frost, "Four-oh-nine. Key at the desk. Just sign any name you want. Except mine. Maybe Sally Greaves. That's a good State inspector's name. Use Sally."

Brian Comartin spread out a half-dozen prints of Ansel Partridge. Some were loose, showing Gerry Martin behind the wheel, Partridge in the back seat. Some were cropped tightly of just Partridge's face. Those ones could have be taken anywhere by any surveillance camera.

Djuna Brown went to the mini-bar and fished out little bottles. She sang out, "State-Police Bar is open for business. May I take your drink orders?"

Martinique Frost went for Heineken, with a Coors Lite for Brian Comartin. Ray Tate went for gin and taps. Djuna Brown mixed drinks at the little bar table and took out bags of mixed nuts and some Toblerones. She laid everything out on a tray on the bed. The hostess.

They sat and drank and nibbled, feeling pretty pleased with themselves. Justice for the dead ladies was possible.

Martinique Frost finished off some beer. "Okay, we've got a good suspect. We've got pictures. How do we want to play it? How we gonna make them break cover? I say a media leak, leave it at that. Once Sally Greaves sees it on the front page, she'll have to bring him out, just so they can have a press conference to say they've ruled him out. Or we do a little blogging ourselves, put it out anonymously. Watch out for this guy. Anybody seen him?"

"I'm not crazy about that," Ray Tate said. "If by some longshot he's a cop, we're basically burning him. We don't know if he's drilled into other covert operations. If we're somehow wrong about him, I don't think we want to wear it. I say we go to Homicide and request an alert. Once they see that every cop in the state is looking for Partridge, they'll put a stop to it, come around asking us questions, try to cool us out, maybe bring him out to us. Open a dialogue. We're told someone at Sector Four called down to the Jank and gave them the heads up we're onto him."

Brian Comartin said, "Or we could just do a records search on Partridge, maybe just put him through motor vehicles. If he's flagged with that red notice thing, they'll come to us, show themselves." He shrugged. "Simple. That still leaves us with alternatives if we need them."

Martinique Frost shook her head in wonder. "Brian Comartin. Poet detective."

Ray Tate was appreciative. "I like it. We start a paper trail on this guy. Make them come to us. But we'll need a badge number, an innocent party, from out in left field. 'Fuck,' they'll go, 'what's this all about? Another cop looking at Ansel?' They've got a clue now that we're drilling into them and if they see one of our numbers pop up, they might lay back, try to wait it out. But, me, I think they're going to move on us, as more people get involved."

George Meyers said Billy Stiles was assigned to Sector Four, Area Two, due for a meal break in six minutes. "You find your guy? Where was he September nine, nineteen ninety-four?"

"We're still looking for him." Ray Tate smiled at Djuna Brown and shook his head. "You got a cell number for Stiles?"

"You got his badge number? Can't check without a badge number." But he laughed and read it off his computer screen. "I'm off shift in an hour. I'm gonna give you my home phone, just in case your guy looks good for my girl. September nine, nineteen ninety-four, don't forget."

"I'm on it." Ray Tate wrote down the number.

He called Billy Stiles. "Hey, it's Ray Tate. You're going for a meal break?"

"Yep. Cosmo's, down in The Boot. Lasagna tonight, little salad on the side. Cosmo emails the menu to the

night shift Sector sergeant. Why, you get caught boozin'
and cruisin' already?"

"No, naw, we're just doing a thing, thought maybe
you could help out."

"You were talking to George, I saw you. Did
he ask where you were on September nine, nineteen
ninety-four?"

"Nope."

"Well, he asked me to find out where you were.
'That Tate character. Nice guy, father-in-law's a cop, but,
look, Billy, if you bump into him again? If you can without arousing suspicion, ask him where he was that day.'"

"He ask where you were?"

"Oh, yeah. High school. Detention. He actually
checked and ruled me out." Billy Stiles laughed. "So,
you wanna meet up? Cosmo's?"

"There's four of us. Good lasagna?"

"You leave a buck each on the table. How bad can
it be?"

Billy Stiles was rolling lonely. He sat alone in his big
vest at the back of the Italian restaurant, with a white
napkin tucked into his tunic, a plate of lasagna, a glass
of red wine, and a basket of garlic bread in front of
him. His shoulder mike was in his epaulet, making
sounds only he could understand.

Ray Tate and his crew walked through the thin
evening-dining crowd. The cashier read them right off
and shouted into the kitchen, "Four specials."

When they approached the back table, Billy Stiles rose to his feet and shook hands all around. He waited until Djuna Brown and Martinique Frost were seated, then sat himself, the host. Djuna Brown and Marty Frost gave him sweet smiles. He blushed a little.

"Dunno you," he said to Brian Comartin, "but you're rolling with the right crew. But you, I know. Marty Frost. I was transport on a guy you sweet-talked about killing his wife and had her head in a bowling-ball bag. I remember, we was taking him to the lockup and he said, 'That black woman with the beautiful eyes? Think she'll wait for me, while I serve my time?'"

"Jerzy Markovic." Martinique Frost laughed. "Old Jerzy made a mess of his wife's face. I remember you. You were a boy."

"Still a boy." He turned to Brian Comartin. "I'm gonna ask you one, okay. You don't want to answer, you want a lawyer, okay. But I'm askin'. Where were you on September nine, nineteen ninety-four?"

Brian Comartin said, "What the hell?"

"Don't worry about it, Brian," Ray Tate said. "Figure it out, let him know. Important stuff."

Billy Stiles shrugged. "Unless you don't want to say." He leered up an eyebrow. "For *some* reason?"

A dour, heavy waitress wearing a black skirt and long-sleeved thin black sweater dealt out four plates of lasagna, salad, another basket of garlic bread, and poured some red wine into water glasses. Billy Stiles thanked her politely but she didn't say anything. As she walked away, Billy Stiles watched her. He was the host and had to have something, a story, an observation, gossip. "Her family are Calabrese, were farmers down at the toe of Italy. There were nine children in her family, eight boys and her. Her old man churned out a boy a year until they had a girl and he retired his dick. So she's the youngest. When she was eleven there was some kind of long-standing feud with a neighbour came to a head. Over a goat or a fence or something. One night the guys from the neighbours decided enough was enough and came by and there was a gun battle. Dad, died. All the brothers, died. All of them. Shotguns. Traditional weapon for *faida*. Feuds. Three male cousins in the next village got whacked and they killed a baby boy sleeping beside the mother. They killed all the males in the family, to head off revenge down the road. Boom, boom, boom, boom. The grandmother, mother, and daughter all moved here, never go back. This is a great restaurant, but you don't want to be in here on the anniversary of the murders."

It was a pretty good one. Billy Stiles was a good host. They sat in appreciative silence for a few moments, thinking their thoughts, making mental pictures. Ray Tate thought about the charger who'd driven him to his car in Chinatown, after the riots. Pointing out the old bent lady with her bundle of rescued possessions, the widow of the cop that solved the first no-body homicide in Hong Kong, then was whacked. One day, he knew, he'd be cruising that Sector with someone and he'd see her. He'd say, "See that old lady there, shuffling along, looking like nothing? Well, back in Hong Kong ..." It was the way. The city was built on layers of stories, each story a citizen or a cop or a crook. It was oral history, it was human context. If you didn't love it, or at least recognize it, it would crush down on you.

They started into their lasagna, and Djuna Brown was eating fast with her face over the bowl and her mouth full, cheese strings down her chin. "This, man, I needed this. They make this here?"

"Yep. She starts it every morning after church. Every morning. Lasagna *al forno*. You see *al forno* on a menu it means it was baked in an oven."

They were finessed. Billy Stiles was the perfect host.

"So, you guys come down here for an Italian cuisine lesson, or...?"

"Well, not really, although it's the usual first-rate night out in Sector Four." Ray Tate drank some of the wine. "You know what we're up to, right? Finding this mutt, Ansel Partridge that got disappeared. Reason we want him is we like him for some murders, some black ladies that got beat to death. Might be an undercover cop."

"And the job's protecting him?" He thought about it. "No. Naw, no way for that."

Ray Tate thought he was being naïve. "Billy, c'mon, you know and I know there's cops and there's cops."

"Oh, jeez, Ray, I don't mean a cop wouldn't do something like that. Just, if it was a cop, there'd be no body to find. A cop'd know the body's the best piece of evidence, he'd scram it where you wouldn't find it." He leaned confidentially toward Martinique Frost. "I got this hole, can't tell you where, but I dug it deep. When the wife goes too far some night ..." He smiled.

"That's how a cop thinks. This guy dumping bodies? No, not a cop. You sure he's not an asset of some kind? Freelance asshole for Intelligence, SPA? I could see that, they get some sketchy guy, turn him loose, don't check him too good."

"Well, he could be. Makes sense. Anyway, we got his name, for sure a cover name, and we got his picture. We want to drill into him, but the moment we do, it's going to be raining Sally Greaves on everybody. We want to make them come to us, shake 'em up a bit, make them panic a little that more people are onto this guy. Maybe bring him out to chat."

"Well, that works." Billy Stiles mopped up his tomato sauce with a piece of bread and popped it into his mouth. "That's why you're here. You want to put him through, right? Maybe a bogus traffic stop. Tap his name into the on-board computer. But then the bells go off at the Jank and they come wondering why the guy was put in, then some poor fucking ground pounder is wearing the what-the-fuck." He smiled at Marty Frost. "You guys want me to be that poor fucking ground pounder."

"Well, we could do it ourselves, but they might be watching for that. One of our badge numbers comes up on the on-board, they go, 'Oh those smart guys from the chief's special, trying to draw us out.' And they stay away, bury him deeper, assign us all to the morning court bus."

"Not bad. Your way doesn't leave much cover for the ground pounder wearing the brown helmet, though, when they come around."

The sad lady in black came and cleared their dishes silently. Billy Stiles slipped his chair back an inch, respectful, and nodded thanks. He ordered five espressos. When she was gone he said, "How about this. I'm sitting in my ghoster and some plainclothes comes up and badges me. Says he needs to put a name through. I make him sign it in my notebook, that he requested access on my unit. He puts the guy through. SPA or whoever comes to me and I say I was parked when one of you guys came up asked to use my on-board, your rover battery is dead, or something. Well, why wouldn't I? So, I do. That's all I know, here's my notebook, this is the plainclothes badge number, he signed the act. Leave me the fuck alone. What do I know? I'm an asshole working a night shift. They come at me, you come at them. I can get behind that. Then, you got them out in the open, you can tail them home or you can brace them, you know who you're up against."

Ray Tate looked around the table. Everyone nodded. It got the job done without jeopardizing Billy Stiles.

The woman in black dealt around five tiny cups of espresso in saucers with little spoons. Djuna Brown looked at the surrounding tables for sugar.

Billy Stiles said, "Sugar? No. They already put the sugar in the cup before the hot coffee goes in. It caramelizes it. Gives it a deep body." He sat back, pleased, and swallowed his coffee in one shot. It was his table, no question. He was the host.

Ray Tate decided Billy Stiles was going to make a great Road someday, if they didn't get him fired.

* * *

They did it for real. Billy Stiles put himself in front
of the bank on Shirley, a well-lit spot that would let
the surveillance cameras pick up the action. Ray Tate
walked up to the car, showed his badge, and spoke
through the window, asking Billy Stiles to run a name,
his rover was flat. Billy Stiles wrote Ray Tate's badge
number and request in his notebook, handed it out,
and Ray Tate signed it. Then Billy Stiles swivelled
the on-board computer to the window and Ray Tate
leaned in. A few seconds later, he walked away. Billy
Stiles drove off, slowly, and stopped farther up Shirley.

Martinique Frost and Brian Comartin parked the
Chrysler three blocks ahead with the ghoster in their
review mirror. Ray Tate parked two blocks back. "No
point in all of us sitting here like lazy cops. Anything
you want to do, Djun'?"

"Maybe check on Evening Evans." Djuna Brown
used Ray Tate's cellphone to call St. Frankie's Heart. She
got Bronstein and asked about Evening Evans. Could she
come in, maybe ask a question or two? Bronstein said
she was mostly awake, praying with her father, badly
wanting a cigarette, so come on by, but no cigarettes.

"I'm gonna go, okay, Ray? You guys got this? I'm
going to take a photograph of Partridge. Maybe she
got a look at him, maybe checking her out, earlier."

"If she puts it on him, call me right away, okay?
That would be good to know when we get into it with

Sally's people. If we got an eyeball from a victim, she's going to have to play it straight with us, let him go for the murders, ride out the aftermath."

She got out and flagged a taxi.

Ray Tate called Marty Frost in the Chrysler on the cellphone, advising he was riding lonely.

Chapter 23

Doctor Bronstein was on the telephone headset in the nursing station. He waved cheerfully as Djuna Brown passed, and she noticed that he was wearing the same T-shirt as earlier in the day. He was unshaven but showed no other signs of the length of his day. In fact, she thought, he seemed energized, his hands in motion as if illustrating some complex procedure.

Samual Darius Evans was in the corridor outside his daughter's room.

"They're just doing ... some stuff. Hygiene, they said."

"How's she doing, sir?"

"Better, they say. To me she still looks pretty bad, but they say better." He clutched the bible in his hand and closed his eyes briefly. "So I thank the Lord for that. And you for your prayers."

"The doctor said she's talking. Wanting a cigarette? That's a good sign."

"I always bothered her about that. The smoking. She liked to tease me, say she was down to three packages a day. Even when she was bad, she was sweet." He made a fond smile. "If the man who did this knew her, even a little bit, he'd never have done this."

The door opened and a nurse came out. "You can go in. But not long, all right? And no cigarettes. She said if I got her a package of Kool menthols she'd give me a hundred dollars." She shrugged. "Going rate on the ward is two hundred. We're negotiating."

Evening Evans was barely visible under the bandages. The machines beeped rhythmically. Her eye moved when the door swished open and she lifted her hand slightly when she saw her father. He sat beside her and held her hand, still clutching the bible to his heart in the other.

Djuna Brown introduced herself.

"Eve, I'm looking for the guy that did this. I have some questions. I want to show you a photograph. Are you up to it? If not, no problem, I can come back tomorrow."

Evening Evans's voice was soft. "I fine. Dad here. I fine now."

"Okay. I'll try to keep my questions to yes or no answers as much as I can. First, can you tell me if you've ever seen this man before?" She held the photograph of Ansel Partridge in front of her face, moving it in and out to be sure the single eye focused.

"That man?"

"We don't know. Is he familiar to you?"

Eve Evans shook her head slightly.

"Did you see the man that night? Or maybe before the attack, on the street, anywhere?"

Eve Evans shook her head slightly.

"Did he say anything?

"Dog. Call me dog."

"Before or during? Wait. Let's do it the quiet way. Before?"

Evan Evans shook her head.

"During?"

She nodded.

"Did you get any sense of how big he was?"

Evening Evans nodded and licked her lips. Her father gently rubbed an ice cube across them. She spoke. "Pick me up neck held me one hand. Big man."

Djuna Brown waited while Samual Darius rubbed another ice cube on his daughter's mouth.

"Did you have a purse, to carry Horace in? Or your ID."

"Just Horace pocket. Key. Just quick walk. Purse home."

"Did you see anything on the river?"

She nodded. "Vol'teers think. Lights water."

"Now, I need longer answers to some of the questions. If you can, good. If not, like I said, another time."

"'Kay."

"Why were you down there that night?"

"Film."

"Did you have a camera? Did he take that?"

"No 'quipment. Look see. Scout. Out."

"What were you doing when he ... got you?"

"Noth'." She paused. "Stop lit cig'rette. He came."

"Is there any chance, any chance at all, that it was someone you knew? Who knew you? Might have followed you?"

Evening Evans shook her head.

"Boyfriend? Old boyfriend? Anyone who might have targeted you?"

"Not."

Djuna Brown couldn't think of anything else to ask.

The nurse came in quietly and checked the monitors. "How you doing, Eve? You want some privacy? Some rest? Just say so."

"Fine. Dad here." The hole in the bandages where her mouth was made a small smile. "Two hundred. One pack. Kool menth'. And lighter." She inclined her eye slightly to Djuna Brown. "Find my luck lighter?"

"I'll check, Eve. I'm going now. I'll come back, soon, maybe with good news."

It didn't take long to come over the rover.

"Sector Four, Two, come up."

"Sector Four, Two."

"Your ten-twenty?"

"In front of the bank, Shirley Street, north of Manitoba. Idle and available."

"Maintain and hold, Four, Two."

"Ten-four."

Five minutes after Ray Tate heard the maintain-and-hold on his under-dash radio, they came up Shirley in a black Volkswagen Jetta, slowed at Billy Stiles's ghoster, then continued on. Two minutes later they came the other way, slowed again, passed by.

Ray Tate, slumped in the Mercury, called Billy Stiles's cellphone. "That might be them."

"Well, they do that again to me, I'm interacting. That's creepy. You want me to stop 'em if they don't stop next time?"

"Well, Billy, officer safety is always a foremost concern. Find your comfort level." He clicked off and called Marty Frost. "I think that's them in the Jetta. I'm afraid Billy's gonna act up here."

"Okay. I like this guy." She laughed. "That was pretty great lasagna. He's a great host."

Five minutes later the Jetta came up the block and stopped with its headlights on, twenty-five feet off the front of Billy Stiles's ghoster. No one disembarked.

On the rover, Ray Tate heard him broadcast. "Desk, Sector Four Area Two solo unit immediate backup Shirley north of Manitoba suspicious auto black Jetta possible officer jeopardy I'm out interacting at gunpoint."

Billy Stiles activated his overhead rack lights and, with his shotgun, was out of the ghoster, around to the trunk side, with his flashlight up on the windshield of the Jetta and the short shotgun up, one-handed to his shoulder.

The rover was crowded with responses. Lonelys, the Sector sergeant, a transport van diverting from a night-court run. Cars from the surrounding areas and one from Sector Eight.

Ray Tate began laughing. It would have been better to follow the SPA people back to Sally Greaves and have the upper hand, some control, but this was okay. This was creative anarchy. He stopped laughing when the Jetta started rolling slowly forward and Billy Stiles parked a sparky load of pellets into the front-left wheel and grill, about a second before he yelled, "Halt."

The driver's door opened.

Billy Stiles yelled, "Stay in the vehicle shut off engine do it now hands on your head do it now."

Ray Tate went on the cellphone to Marty Frost. "You guys seeing this?"

"Yeah. I'm really liking this guy. I guess we ain't followin' no one nowhere tonight. And ... here come the troops."

Sirens running, three unmarked ghost cars fishtailed onto the block, wedging themselves around the Jetta to block escape. Behind them came a sergeant's marked car that hit the turn too heavy. It crashed square into the back of the Jetta, jumping it forward. Two people in the Jetta jacked forward into the dashboard and the air bags blew up. Car alarms went off.

Billy Stiles went around to his dash radio. He was very calm, almost indifferent. "Desk, we got at least three injured in departmental traffic event, one an on-duty sergeant and two civilian suspects and we have shot fired by one on-duty, ambulances and fire requested this stage asap and supervisor. All calm this scene."

* * *

Hambone Hogarth and Sally Greaves sat opposite Ray Tate in a conference room in the Intelligence offices at the Jank. The shooting and takedown had gone out on the radio, that two of Sally Greaves's amateurs had almost got aced by a real cop. Rumours were wildfire that the bosses were trying to shut down a serial killer investigation because a cop might be involved. The chief might be involved. The temporary mayor might be involved. The media centre had already received a dozen enquiries. It was suddenly going public and damage control was going to kick in.

Sally Greaves looked depressed, sucking at her bucked teeth, frantically rubbing the fingertips of both hands into her scalp as though she had a rash. "Hambone, I don't know where to start with this guy. This guy's a ... fucking ... fucking menace." She glanced down at the flakes of dandruff she'd snowed onto the table, and looked up at Ray Tate. "You're a fucking menace."

Ray Tate felt sorry for her. She was still a cop. She was ugly and tragic and she'd just had an example of how she wasn't all-powerful, didn't control the world around her, not the real cops out on the real streets. And, he thought, she's scored herself some primo blonde lieutenant action. There must be something more to her than that voice.

"Look," he said, "you guys came up with the Volunteer angle to the ladies murders. You set up the task force. Hang it on them, you said. So we looked around in there. And we find Ansel Partridge but then he disappears. None of the other goofs we've come up with has it in them to just kill women. And then you try to steer us away from the Volunteers with some sex-perv Quantico bullshit." He shrugged. "All I did was put through a suspect in multiple homicides. That's my job. Ansel Partridge." He had a buff envelope on the table in front of him. "This guy." He slipped a photo out, a tight three-quarters of Partridge, with no references to suggest the location it was taken.

Sally Greaves looked at it. "Where'd you get that?"

"It was taken by a surveillance camera near the scene of one of the murders, just before."

She shook her head. "No, that's impossible."

Ray Tate told Hambone Hogarth he wanted to conduct an interview with Sally Greaves and Ansel Partridge. "We can go off the record, if you want, with Sally. I don't give a shit if he organized the Volunteers and caused that mess in Chinatown. But I've got dead ladies and she's hiding my viable."

"You know, Ray, the chief's gonna shut you down first thing tomorrow. Willy Wong or no Willy Wong. You're fucking with in-house stuff, now."

"I don't care, Ham. I got tonight. What more can any of us ask? If Sally co-operates we can have three homicides down by dawn. This thing is going public, I promise you. Other people on my team are willing to leak this to the press and wear it, take early retirement." He looked at their faces. "What you don't understand, living up here in Jank, is there's cops on the street who give a shit for victims."

"You've got to put a stop to it, Ray. What do you want? A bump? Station sergeant? Done. Your team? Whatever they want. Let's just hang the dead women on that lunatic Volunteer. Corey Garnett. If there's someone else involved, we'll take care of it. You got my word."

"What fucking happened to you, Ham?" Ray Tate felt a rush of anger. "What happened to fucking you? Nobody walks on murder. Not even in this town."

Sally Greaves said, "He isn't a cop. Ansel. Ansel's an operator." She looked for a few seconds at Hambone Hogarth and licked her lips and then asked Ray Tate, "What do you want? End of the day, what makes the happy you? Not the crazy you."

"An interview with Partridge. Maybe strap him to the truth machine. I don't know. What I do know is I've been given this thing, and even though it turned into a steaming piece of shit, it's mine."

"I want to be there, Sergeant. He won't lawyer up, but I need to be in the room. Does that work for you?"

"Time, place, up to you. You want to sit in, sit. I'll have someone from my guys there. She'll want to work this. She cares. Imagine that."

"Two hours," Sally Greaves said. "In the conference room. Best light on this, I guess, is you'll have him ruled out and you can go look for the real killer."

"More like, Ray," Hambone Hogarth said, jovially, "you'll be driving a prisoners' bus, in the wee dawn hours, picking weevils out of your beard with tweezers.

This was your chance back, man, out of the wilderness. Somebody was pulling for you in the chief's office. But now? Now you've gone nuts. Fuck, Ray. Cops shooting at cops? Cops crashing into cops? I know you were the ringmaster behind that little circus on Shirley. Man, you are so fucking fucked."

Sally Greaves shook her head. "Let him run it out, Ham. He's right. We forgot something. We'll do some back and fill, after, once he gets off Partridge as a viable."

Chapter 24

Just after midnight Ray Tate and Djuna Brown met up with Martinique Frost and Brian Comartin at China-Mex, an all-night bucket of blood where the outskirts of Chinatown was being squeezed by Little Juarez. The place was almost empty; what was there were dregs who recognized the Chrysler crash car and the Mercury and the cops and choreographed a not-so-subtle moonwalk out the rear door. Two women slept at tables with their heads on their arms. The guy behind the hot table was black and looked pretty miserable about it. An espresso machine was set up beside a percolator holding a glass pot with sticky-looking sludge at the bottom.

Djuna Brown went up to the counter. "Espresso. Double." She looked at the others. "Everybody?" They nodded. "Make four."

The black guy took some little paper cups from a shelf and started jerking a lever.

"Whoa, there, my brother." Martinique Frost leaned on the counter, friendly, ready to pass on global cuisine wisdom. "In Italy they put the sugar in the cup, then shoot in the coffee. It caramelizes it."

"Yeah," the guy said. "But this ain't It-aly, I ain't no wop. And you ain't Mario Ba-*fuckin*-tali. This is Mur'rer City. Here you put your own sugar in. I ain't paid that rate, do no special orders. So, you want four *ax*-pressos or not?"

They sat at a booth in the front window watching their cars. Cop shotguns were a prime item on the street. Not worth going hand-to-hand with chargers for, but an empty cop car was an enticement and might be worth the risk. If you lost a scattergun it was bad. If that scattergun was used to take out a cop, you'd be wanting to apply to a teachers' college out of state under another name.

The guy behind the counter called, "Yo, you *ax*-pressos are ready for pickup." He loomed massive and leaning against the counter behind him and waited. "You wanna eat?"

Djuna Brown said, "You got any *forno*?"

"Girl, I got *hor*-no and I got *por*-no but none of that *for*-no."

"Then we're okay."

"You gonna pay? If you ain't gonna pay, I won't ring it in."

Brian Comartin got up and gave him a ten. "Keep the change."

The black guy didn't ring it in anyway and put the ten into his pocket. "This time of night, it's all change."

Around the table they chatted for a while about the night. About Sally Greaves's little minions being pulled out the van through the windows, one of them visibly pissing his pants. Billy Stiles becoming the hero of the Sector when it was learned he'd braced two SPA goofs from the Jank, opened up on them, made 'em eat an airbag and shit their pants.

"Man, Billy." Martinique Frost said, "If Billy Stiles had already killed his wife, and if he could speak Spanish and write poetry like Traffic man here, well I dunno. If he was this cute, I mean, as my poet. That boy is on wheels."

Djuna Brown, who'd heard the story from Ray Tate, said she wished she'd been there. "Yeah, Billy Stiles is fab. So, Ray, what's the deal?"

Ray Tate shot back his espresso and made a face. But it was coffee. He called, "Yo, another round. This time we don't pay, so fuck you."

Martinique Frost called, "Don't you be spittin' in there, my brother. I got my eye on your ass." She was only partly kidding and watched him work.

"So," Ray Tate said. "They know we've got a picture of Ansel Partridge. I told them it was a surveillance photo from near one of the body dumps. Sally didn't like that much. She's been around long enough to know that there's never one picture of anything. She says he's one of hers, an operator, but he isn't viable for our poor ladies. Word's getting out. They've been getting press calls about a serial killer cover-up. They're clamming, but she's bringing Partridge into the Jank at one o'clock. We can go at him, but she wants to be there, in the room. I said okay."

"Are we all going to do him?" Marty Frost asked. "All at once? I don't like that. That tells him we think he's so smart it takes a bunch of our brains to keep up with one of his. That won't work."

Ray Tate shook his head. He went to the counter and got the espressos. After he sat and poured a bag of sugar into his, he said, "I figure that, and if you guys have a problem with this say so, that Marty and I'll take him first. Mostly Marty after I do the prelims, set the scene for him. Then, if we don't go anywhere, after we take a break, Marty stays and Brian goes in. He looms in the background in and out of the guy's eye-line. Marty, you can give him some pointers on the eye-line thing. Last resort? Djuna goes in. She's the same colour and body type as the victims. Maybe she sets him off." He looked around. "I've got to tell you, I told Hambone and Sally we're dedicated to our ladies. We're ready to go all-in, go public, take early retirement, rather than let it go. Was I out of line?"

They all shook their heads.

"Okay, that's that then. Djuna? Anything from the victim, Eva? Evans?"

"Eve. For Evening. The most beautiful time of day." She took out her notebook. "Down and dirty. Evening Evans was out walking on the river, close to midnight, looking over sites for a film about the Chinese migrants on the boats from Canada. She's a filmmaker. She sees something, she thinks are Volunteers on the river, waits, and when they're gone she goes to light a cigarette and he gets her. Holds her up by the throat against a tree and just goes to work on her with the other hand, his right, I guess. Calls her a dog. After that, she doesn't remember nothing. She had no purse, just the gun, her house keys, her smokes, and her lighter. He's away with the gun. Presumably the smokes and lighter, too. When I left she was offering the nurse two hundred bucks for a pack of Kool menths."

Ray Tate asked if anyone had anything to add. "Okay? We go. We're only going to have one kick at this fuck. After that, we lose him and Sally sends him back under."

They went to the Jank in two cars so everyone would have flexibility when the Ansel Partridge interview was completed. Only two of them would have to stay to book him over to a body snatcher. Ray Tate pulled in at an all-night mom and pops to get some Kool menthols. When he came out he stood on the sidewalk and lit one. He made a face, but kept smoking it. He thought his way through the case. Something itched him. When the cigarette was half gone, he pitched it, tried to spit away the minty taste, and got in behind the wheel.

"What, Ray? You were off in space-land there. Maybe we should put off Partridge until tomorrow, go at him fresh."

"Naw, no I'm okay. Just something rubbing me the wrong way."

Martinique Frost and Brian Comartin were leaning on the Chrysler in front of the Jank. "He just went in," Brian Comartin said. "This is one scary-looking dude."

"Who took him in? Was he chained up?"

"Nope. Hambone from Homicide and a little woman, ugly. Scratching at her head. They were just going in when we pulled up."

"Sally Greaves."

A red Porsche Carrera came up around the Chrysler and slid expertly into the duty sergeant's vacant slot. A woman got out and trotted in flat slapping heels up the handicap ramp into the Jank. It took Ray Tate a minute to recognize her. The beautiful blonde lieutenant with the glasses and the dreamy smile, but without the glasses or the smile. Half of an impossible love story that illustrated the possibilities of life. Of anyone's life, of everyone's life. It would be great, he thought, to know her and Sally Greaves well enough to be able to have a thoughtful conversation with her about their hearts' processes. Through the glass doors he saw her flap her badge at the night desk team, then rush through the security arch. Moral support for Sally.

"Okay, let's head up, get this guy in chains." He thought for a few moments, getting off the blonde and onto the dead ladies. He had to get his mind right. "When we go in upstairs, I go first. I'm gonna go hard, set the tone. Brian, you've got a shotgun in your vehicle? Get it."

When Brian Comartin returned, Ray Tate led the way up the ramp. Inside the doors he badged the security team.

"You can't bring that in here," one guard said, staring at Brian Comartin's shotgun. "Not naked. You'll have to bag it."

"Chief's special squad," Ray Tate said. He felt himself getting wound up. "Our motto is, Fuck You. How many guys you got on tonight?"

"Six, usually, but we still got guys out. We're four tonight. We got one guy racking out."

"Wake him up, get him out. I'll need one of you. You pick."

"What's going on? A lot of heavy hitters through here tonight."

"I need a guy to come up to Intelligence, let the people in the conference room see him, then stand outside the door. Light duty."

"I'll take it." He came around the counter, yawning. "Sounds almost like police work."

The door to the conference room was ajar. Inside, sitting at the top of the table, Ray Tate could see Ansel Partridge, sipping at a cup of coffee, relaxed back in his leather armchair as if he were sitting in his living room with buddies, planning some radical social engineering. He looked like the inflated essence of brutal. Pounding a little woman to jelly would be his standard pick-up line. Yellow foolscap notebooks were stacked in the centre of the table with a scattering of yellow pencils.

Ray Tate told Marty Frost to pull her piece but keep it down her leg and Djuna Brown to stay out of sight. "If we need you to spark him off later, better if you come as a surprise, okay?"

She gave him a wan smile. "But when we beat him later, I get to help out?"

"You got dibs." He made a fond smile. "Here goes."

As he came through the door, Ray Tate heard Ansel Partridge laugh at something. Sally Greaves and Hambone Hogarth were seated side-by-side to his left, mid-table.

He took the shotgun from Brian Comartin, shouldered up and walked quickly down the room. He stopped ten feet from Partridge, took stance, racked the shotgun and put it up into his face. "You. Up. Turn around. Hands on your head."

The front desk officer said, "Holy fuck."

"Go outside, secure the door. We need you, we'll call you."

Ansel Partridge looked at him dreamily, glanced with good humour at Sally Greaves, and slowly rose. He clasped his hands at the back of his neck and turned to face the wall.

Sally Greaves stood up. "Hambone ..."

Hambone Hogarth said, "Ray, Jesus ..." But he was smiling, and sat back in his chair as if watching a complex routine by his favourite hilarious comedians.

"This is a murder suspect unsecured," Ray Tate said. "I fear for officer safety and the security of this building. Brian, search him and chain him in back. Marty, you take the top chair at the top of the table, inside the door. You're the writer."

"*Don't* you fucking *move*." Brian Comartin went through his lessons. He didn't cross the shotgun. He put Ansel Partridge through, backing him off the wall with his forehead touching, told him to put his hands down behind his back, one at a time, then chained him up, and patted him down hard. He put him back in his chair with a thump and glanced down the room at Marty Frost; she batted her eyelashes in admiration, holstered her gun, and took out her notebook.

Ray Tate cleared the shotgun sleeve onto the table, left it racked open, and picked up the shell and pocketed it. He sat down, smiling pleasantly at Sally Greaves and Hambone Hogarth. "Marty, in the room we've got me, Brian, you, Ansel Partridge —"

"Wait," Sally Greaves said. "Wait. Not in a notebook. You can take notes on paper, but nothing on the numbered pages. Once this foolishness is over and Ansel walks, you give me the notes. If you decide to charge him, we'll sign them off and staple them in the book."

Marty Frost said, "Ray?"

"Okay. Do it that way."

She picked up a yellow pad from the table and sat back down at the long end, opposite Ansel Partridge. He stared down at her and licked his lips.

"Okay, me, Comartin, you, Sally Greaves, and Robert Hogarth. Ansel Partridge." He turned to Partridge. "I'm going to read you something, your rights. Don't stop me, even if you've heard them before. Humour me." He read the poem. "You got it all? Want to hear it again?"

"Nope. I'm hip."

"Okay. I'm Sergeant Ray Tate, chief's special squad. The short strokes are, we're investigating the murders of three black women, and the attempted murder of a fourth. We believe you may have involvement in those events. Do you understand what I'm saying? That we're investigating you as a suspect in three murders? The victims were black. You're a racist. If this is a deemed a hate crime there'll be enhancement add-on that will make you eligible for the death penalty. Do you want to reconsider exercising your right to a lawyer?"

"I'm sure," Ansel Partridge said, nodding, "the victims will be missed by loved ones back in Afri*coon*."

"I'm saying again, you're aware this might lead to a death penalty resolution if you're found guilty."

"Yep. The needle."

"Right on that one. The long yawn." Ray Tate folded his hands on the table. "First, what's your name? Your birth name?"

Ansel Partridge glanced at Sally Greaves, then said, "Ansel Skineard."

"Related to Lynyrd Skynyrd? You play music?"

"Only on people." He smiled in appreciation of himself.

Sally Greaves said, "Ansel."

"You want to spell it for the record, Ansel? And give me your date of birth? Home address."

Ansel Partridge spelled his name. He was thirty-two years old. He had no fixed address that he wanted to talk about.

Ray Tate nodded at Marty Frost. She made a note and handed it out the door to Djuna Brown, who stayed out of sight.

"Are you a racist, Ansel? Belong to any groups?"

"American. I'm a proud American. A proud, white American male. I'm not a racist. I love, embrace, and believe in the white race."

"Criminal record?"

"Nothing heavy. Some actions, you know? You'll have of file on me in there for some assaults, a gun a couple of times."

"You pull any time? Serious time?"

"Nope. Few days here, few days there."

"Those look like long-term prison tattoos to me, you got the yard muscles thing going on."

"My cover."

"We'll get to that."

"No," Sally Greaves said. "We won't."

"Well, let's wait and see, okay? You have a job, Ansel?" He almost said, "You a workingman?" He got that itchy feeling again. Like déjà vu. "What's your trade?"

"Patriotic American white male. Full time." He smiled with a glitter. "I do a lot of overtime."

"You work nights on that job? Around town, down by the river?"

"Well, Oh-*Bah*-Ma Hu-*Sane*'s America needs help all the time, everywhere."

"Good man." Ray Tate took some three-by-five photographs of the murder victims in life and in death from his pocket. "You know any of these women? Bumped into them, maybe, when you're out defending the flag?" He separated the living images from the others and arrayed them on the table. "Beat them to death, that kind of thing?"

Ansel Partridge glanced at them indifferently. "All look the same to me."

"Those are the before pictures." He tapped the remaining photos, but kept them face down. "These after ones are a little different."

"Can I have a peek? Just in case, you know ..." He made a beatific grin. "Well, you know. For later."

"Later, maybe, if you're good." He boxed the edges of the photographs into one stack and left them face down on the table. He looked over Ansel Partridge's torso. "You still working out? You do any boxing, anything like that? The guys that took you out of Chinatown the other night, they said you were a scrapper."

"Yeah, yeah, I boxed a little. Back in the day. But they only wanted blacks from shacks, not whites with rights."

There was a timid tap at the door. Marty Frost leaned to open it, then nodded to Ray Tate. He said, "One minute," and went out. Djuna Brown showed him her notes. "Assault, assault, gun, gun, possession meth, we got a rape, two weeks ago, no disposition."

"Can we put a car under him?"

"Driver's licence, no plate attached to his name."

"Okay. Get the badge number of the arresting officer on the rape. Get his off-duty phone number from downstairs and give him a call. Get what you can, particularly the date. If Ansel used the beat-down to get it up, like Sally says our killer might've done, we're close to getting him. And we need the race of the victim and the general circumstances."

"Okay. How's it going? He going for it?"

"We haven't done alibis yet. We'll take him in there, let him wander around, see how he lies." He stepped back into the conference room, closing the door. He sat and took out the Kool menthols. "I got the shotgun, I declare this a smoking facility." He offered the package around. Hambone Hogarth and Sally Greaves didn't respond. "Ansel? Light up?"

"Don't smoke," Ansel Partridge said. "Respect the body as you respect the nation."

"Except the meth, right?" He lit up and blew some cool smoke at Ansel Partridge. "The all-American white trash ride? How much are you shooting. Like, each hour?"

"You found out about that, huh? Bogus. I was working an op when —"

"Ansel, stop." Sally Greaves said, "Ray, he was working a drug conspiracy. He got scooped up and was charged. We let the charge stand, for now. We have to keep him dirty in case we have to pull his bail and put him back in the jail, do some operating on the conspirators. Open case ongoing. Off limits."

"Like the Volunteers?" Ray Tate laughed. "He's pretty dirty on that. That was nice."

"You agreed, Ham, we're not here for that op. That op is off limits, too, pending. We're here for murders."

"Yeah, c'mon, Ray, get on focus."

"Sure." He smoked his cigarette as though he was enjoying it. Ansel Partridge didn't react. "That rape, that was an op, too, I guess."

Ansel Partridge shrugged. "She'll recant. They always do."

"Ansel?" Sally Greaves had a tone in her voice. She wasn't warning him to shut up; she was genuinely surprised. She said to Ray Tate, "That didn't show up when we vetted him. That must have been after. I didn't know about that."

"Must be really recent, then, Sally. How about that? Guy's a fucking drug addict and a rapist. Nice white trash specimen you got here. We're looking right now, and if the victim there was black and beaten ... Well, you said it yourself before, our killer might use the beatings to get his dick hard for doing the rape victim." He needed a few minutes to figure out how to steer Ansel Partridge around. It was more difficult than it seemed, to run an interview with natural flow. He wondered if it was time to let Marty Frost do her thing. "Kids, I need a health break. We're gonna get some coffee. Marty, you want to babysit Ansel here?"

Sally Greaves shook her head. "If Officer Frost is staying, then I'm staying."

"Sally, she isn't going to talk to him. Promise. Marty, not one word, okay? Not even small talk. Don't ask if he needs to piss, have a nap, or wants to beat you to death to get his dick hard. Just sit. We come back, you can go out, get coffee or personal maintenance, whatever." He picked up the shotgun but left the photos stacked on the table. "Don't fuck this up, Marty. We're close."

Ansel Partridge said, "Bullshit, close."

"I want it in her notes," Sally Greave said. "And she notes that, too, that I requested it. She writes 'interview in abeyance' and notes the time. Then we all sign it and we can step out, taking the notes with us."

When Marty Frost finished the notation, Ray Tate, Brian Comartin, Hambone Hogarth, and Sally Greaves signed the ruled line under the last notation. Everyone left the room, Sally Greaves taking the foolscap pad, leaving Martinique Frost and Ansel Partridge at opposite ends of the long table.

Sally Greaves was pleased to see Djuna Brown standing in the anteroom.

"Sergeant Brown," she said, "a pleasure to see you again."

"And you, Miss Greaves." She made a hesitant smile. "I hope this isn't too stressful for you. If it wasn't so many murders."

Ray Tate, passing behind them on his way to the washroom with Hambone Hogarth and Brian Comartin, gave her a definite nod and tapped the wedding finger of his left hand. He mouthed, "Go." Aloud, he said, "Coffee on the way."

When they were alone, Sally Greaves said, "I looked into your background, Sergeant Brown. I hope you don't mind. A habit. I've put my mailman through, my dry cleaner, the owner of the local bistro. You never know."

"No. No, I don't mind. Was it interesting for you?"

"That lesbian thing? That you pretended to be gay so you could work and be left alone by the men? Pretty creative. But you weren't gay, and now you're hooked up with Ray Tate. That must be a chore, for you. He's killed two men, black men. Doesn't it concern you, that he might be a racist? Aren't you a *little* concerned?"

Djuna Brown made a disappointed little smile. "You don't have to come at me this way. Ray's okay. I think you know that, already." She gave Sally Greaves a sad look. "You don't have to try to do me like this. I know what I know about Ray, same as you know what you know about the blonde lieutenant." She saw the look of surprise on Sally Greaves's face. "The rings. The gold snake and the ruby apple. You want to hide it from other people, but not deny it from yourself or each other."

They sat side by side on a leather couch.

"You're very observant. Very ... keen." Sally Greaves was almost disarmed. She stared at Djuna Brown as if at a canny creature she thought she might have to be careful around. "So, you know."

"I don't care. Can I be frank? Okay. You are what you are, and you look like what you look like. You accept it and you demand that everyone else accepts it, too, whether through fairness or fear. I can tell because you don't try to hide it. You enhance it. Fine. I look like I do and I try to enhance it, too. Men and women? For some reason I attract them both. I have to accept that. And I have to be very careful. I can't make a mistake with anyone, send conflicting signals. With Ray I know I'm on the right path for me. I look at you and I see an unattractive woman, but a woman in love. But you must have something. You've attracted love. Did you ever imagine?"

Sally Greaves looked at her closely with a hint of bitter suspicion. "I saw, from the corner of my eye, he,

Tate, made a signal at you a moment ago. What was that? To work me?"

"Yep. Ray mouthed it to me. 'Go,' he said. But he knows I won't. I can't. That's not my style. That would be like surrendering who I am to a State pay-cheque. A welfare case in a round hat and a uniform. That's not me." She liked Sally Greaves and felt it was important for her to know she wasn't being worked. She felt sorry for her, but she liked that she was willing to confront others and that was admirable. "I'm going to talk, here, and let you know how things are with me. I don't want you to say anything, okay? When I'm done, we'll sit here and wait for the coffee. I won't ask you a question about this case. I can't stand that you think what you think I'm doing. Someone more secure than me wouldn't care, I guess. But I've made some mistakes. I've been shaken. Ray saw me make those mistakes. He looks at me different than before. I think he's okay, now, but you know what? He can't ignore what he knows, what he's seen. He'll love me, he can't help that, but he'll never look at me the way he looked at me before I shamed myself."

"What did you do?" Sally Greaves made her face into concern and patted her hand. "Would it help to talk about it?" But her heart wasn't really into it.

Djuna Brown laughed. "Nice try." She took a deep breath. "I spent the last year after I left Ray down here up in Indian country. You think being a dyke is a tough go in the city? Try being the only black up north with knuckle-draggers, crazy Christians, and poor Natives with nothing left to lose. And being a

sergeant where the troops have to do what you tell
'em. So, I got nobody to take my back. I've been beaten
shitless while those fuckers working for me drove in
the other direction and yawned. At least you've got
the gorgeous lieutenant you can go home to. I made a
mistake going back up there, I know that now. I went
home alone every night. It was good, I think, for the
people I police, that I was there for them, but every
night I cried." She looked into Sally Greaves's eyes. "I
was lonely. I … withered."

Sally Greaves stared at her. "You look like you're
going to cry. You're not much of a cop, are you?"

"Nope." She dried her eyes on her sleeve and
made a small laugh. "Right now, I'm barely a cop.
We're quitting, Ray and I, after we put this case down
and each get a little more time in, bump up the pensions or the buyouts. We're too good for this. I can't
give any more, and I won't let him. He's a painter, you
know. We're moving to Paris." She made a little laugh.
"That's in France." It was an inside joke on herself.
One of the first comments she'd made to a task force
sniper after she'd downed a fat drug dealer the year
before. She'd said she and her city cop, Ray, were moving to Paris. "That's in France." But now it was a year
later and here she was, back in Murder City, working
a case too big for her skillset because she'd been lonely.

Sally Greaves got up and walked to the window.
She stared out into the darkness and down onto the
parking lot below for a long time. She turned as Ray
Tate, Hambone Hogarth, and Brian Comartin came
into the room with coffee. "Ham, I need the room."

"Sally, be careful, now." Hambone Hogarth looked suspiciously at Djuna Brown sitting on the couch. "Take some time, think about it, Sally."

"Ham?" Sally Greaves stared at him. "Just go, all right?"

Djuna Brown nodded at Ray Tate. Without saying a word, he put the coffee cups down on the table and left with Hogarth and Comartin.

Chapter 25

In the conference room Ansel Partridge and Martinique Frost ignored each other. Marty Frost could listen to her own heart beat all day, could imagine she heard her eyelashes moving. What mattered was putting down the poor ladies' case and heading to Spain with the traffic poet. She knew the face couldn't truly hide the mind, so she thought pleasant romantic thoughts to give Ansel Partridge something to get wound up about. She'd done some research on Spain. Much bigger than she thought. Diverse in every way. Barcelona, which her poet pronounced with a *th*, seemed infinitely more interesting than the places to the south. Marty Frost liked food. One of the food articles she read described Spain as the new France and Barcelona as the new Paris. Cooking had always been of interest to her, but being alone for so long she'd stuck with take-away and a lot of frozen trays of meat and potatoes with a giant, healthy, white lumberjack on the packaging. The wildest she'd ever gone out of a recipe book was a spaghetti carbonara and it had been a gummy tragedy. As things developed with Brian Comartin, she hoped she wouldn't have to try to cook him a meal before they pulled their pins and flew away.

"What are you smiling at?"

And then Marty Frost had his number. If he'd sat in brooding silence, she would have started making small disturbing observations, drilling into his reticence. But Ansel Partridge wasn't used to not talking. She could see him in his op life and in his actual life, verbalizing the entirety of himself. His beliefs, his exploits, his possessions, his connections, his dick and his fists and his tongue. Probably he could sit in a room for hours without speaking, but only if there were no one there with him and he could think up cool things to say when they arrived. It was ego-shattering to him if he was present and wasn't talking or being talked to or being talked about.

She looked up as though she'd forgotten he was in the room. "Sorry?"

"You're smiling down there. I'm in handcuffs up here. What's so fucking funny?"

She had nothing for him. He was like the big muscular stupid kids she dealt with in the youth unit. Soon a thing of the past. That assignment had shaken her faith in the turnaround ability of any living soul. Giving up on kids was hard. But there were some people who were voids, and you had to avoid spending yourself on them, wasting yourself. No reason to be circumspect, make them want to marry her, tell her she had beautiful eyes, for a black person. Ansel Partridge was nothing to her. He'd go for the murders of the ladies or the Chinese.

She winged it. "I'm thinking, and I don't know, so I'm guessing, that it takes a few minutes, the needle. Not when it goes in and they start piping in the drugs. At that point there's no hope, no prayer. But leading up to that. The formalities." She laughed, nasty. "You'll have to let me know, after."

"I ain't getting no needle."

She spoke as if he hadn't spoken. "You got some buff muscles going on there. Nice big snaky veins. I heard they sometimes have trouble with those veins and all that muscle work, the needle breaks off, they have to put things on hold for a half-hour while they fish it out with a pair of tweezers, go find a new needle, start the procedure all over again. All while you're strapped to a gurney, waiting. I'm not thinking about the time after the needle finally does the job. That half-hour, waiting, that's what I'm wondering about."

"Fuck you, bitch."

"Fine." She relaxed her face and thought about *paella*. In an article she read about it, *paella* sounded pretty good, easy. Rice and seafood, some saffron. Even she couldn't fuck that up, she'd thought. But then there was a detailed note in a sidebar article about the type of pan needed, the degree of heat, and the creation of something called *sofrito*. That didn't sound like simply opening a can of tomato soup, that *sofrito* action. Brian Comartin had been to Spain.

He'd know if the *sofrito* was done right. Maybe he could cook.

"You fucking people don't know who you're dealing with. This is an SPA op. This is way above your pay grade. You're all going down, when this is done. Your lives are over."

"I'm sure." She kept her face right. Lots of shrimp in *paella*. She'd always eaten shrimp without checking that someone had removed the black thread, the guts, down along the back. The shit sac, it sounded like. She wondered how many she might have eaten in her life, without knowing it, before reading the *paella* recipe. Shrimp shit. That sounded bad, worse than fucking up that *sofrito* stuff. What if she made *paella* with shrimps and he started running his knife down the back, stripping out the shit sack. Even by candlelight on the terrace of their little apartment overlooking a square, not romantic. She smiled.

"You want to ask me something. That's why they left you here. What? Ask me. I can tell you stories, curl your hair." He laughed. "But you already got that conky hair going on."

She gave him a small smile. "You want to answer my questions? Even though Sally told you to shut the fuck up and you don't want a lawyer? You must be pretty stupid, An-Sell. Just sit there and wait, okay? I'm just the secretary on this case. Taking notes. No coffee for me. I don't get any credit when they charge you, I don't get any crap if they don't. They don't make muscles for the kind of shit I have to put up with, okay? Not from you, from them. But it's all pensionable time so leave me the fuck alone."

"Pension. Fuck that. What you make, last year? Overtime, all in?" He waited and she saw the opening. It was the comparison game. How much more valuable he was than she was, how much more he made, how free he was, unrestrained by rules and regs. But she waited until he said, "What, thirty-six grand. Then taxes. Then union dues. Credit union. Then fuck-knows what else?"

She knew where he was going, another comparison of value. She said, "Forty-one-six. Overtime. What do you care? You made, what, a fast five grand from Sally? Another couple grand for testifying? Except whatever you got, you don't get to spend because of that pesky needle." She wanted to wind him up. It was unusual for her. Usually, she was the mother. The good wife. The achieving daughter. Someone you could relate to. "When I'm spending my pension in Spain, your toenails and hair will be growing inside a casket."

"No way. No fucking way." He looked a little off-balanced by the image. It was a good one, she had to admit. The specificity of it. "I made forty-one grand the last four months. Tax free. A white man's wage, before you people started sucking off the welfare money, leaving the cities in debt. Fuck you, you fucking bitch."

"White man bullshit." She pretended to be outraged at what he'd said. "No way Sally gave you that kind of dough. More like, she got you for a case of Bud, a TV with rabbit ears, and a bag of crank. You fucking trash asshole. White nigger. She'll go on banging her hot chick and you'll be forgotten. Ansel Who? Oh, that guy that killed all the women, tried to make it look like an action, but he just liked to do the dark because no decent white woman would have him."

He glared at her. Before her eyes, he seemed to inflate. She feared the handcuffs would pop, that he'd come howling down the tabletop like a storm. She wondered if Brian Comartin had cinched the cuffs tight enough. Casually, she put her hand near her gun. She felt a little anxious. She hadn't known Brian Comartin long enough to know if he did it right. "Calm down, An-Sell. Just chill. They'll be back in a minute."

"You wish, you hope. I saw that. I got to you. You're fucking afraid. The white man. You people recognize it. Like a dog seeing the whip and pissing himself. I fucking got you." He was satisfied.

He had, a little, but she had to try to work it. "Well, you're a scary guy, An-Sell. You're a fucking nut. I seen what you did with those women there," she nodded at the stack of photos, "and I see whoever did that is a fucking animal. You should be put down, what you did." As she spoke, she felt her fear blossom in to real anger. She casually put her hand on her gun. "You know what, Ansel? I hope you walk out of here tonight. I don't give a shit whether you did it or not. I want you out on the parking lot. I'm going to save the state the cost of a needle."

"Yeah, yeah, yeah." He was still happy. "But check this, Jemima. What if I didn't do them? And if I didn't do them, then somebody else did, right? And when you find out it maybe weren't me, *maybe*, you're gonna realize that even if you get the real guy that did it? There's still me and guys like me out there. Makes no difference. Maybe if you go back to A-*free*-ca you'll be okay. But here? No. Your black ass will never be safe in my America."

"You'll go. Guys like you always go. America's going to get you. We'll get you in the courtroom or we'll get you in the streets. Down, down like dogs." She got her game back and laughed. "Think about this, An-Sell. Your pal Sally, there, she's got a job, she's got a chick, she's got a pension. She going to give it all up so you can get in a courtroom and start telling your lies? I guarantee you, I guaran-fucking-tee you, you die before this gets to trial. This, or the Chinatown fire murders. You're a fucking menace to a lot of people. Sally won't want you anywhere in her life."

It had the wrong effect. She saw that. Something she'd said.

He sat back against his handcuffs. "Old Sally, that old dyke? Not a problem. Fuck her pension and her job." He laughed aloud. "You ever see that ring she wears? The snake and the apple?" He made a satisfied smile and stopped talking. "Make sure your phone's on. Anytime now."

Martinique Frost didn't know what he was talking about but she felt something had just been busted and that was enough. He'd mentioned Sally could lose the job and the pension, but not the love. She wondered what he knew about the love.

And what was that about the ring?

* * *

Ray Tate, Hambone Hogarth, and Brian Comartin went back down to the cafeteria and punched out some coffee. The crew of maintenance guys were at a table, thumbing through a skin magazine and passing it around with vocal relish. The Irish guy was the loudest, saying what he'd do to what part.

Hambone Hogarth looked at him and said, "Dead man walking. Nice to know one guy's getting it, anyway."

Ray Tate said, "You okay, Ham? You covered in all this? When Sally's thing comes crashing down?"

"I'm square, Ray. You have no fucking idea how square my ass is, this thing ends."

They sat for a few minutes in the anteroom. The security desk guy was yawning uncontrollably, repeatedly. Djuna Brown asked him to go yawn in the hallway for a while.

"Sure, dear. Sing out if you girls need me."

Sally Greaves told Djuna Brown, "I hired him because of Monica. We were out one night and ran into him. They're cousins. Ansel had had some trouble, but was trying to get straight, he'd been running with a bad crowd. Into racist stuff. Knew the druggie players. Gunrunners. Monica was very big on family. If I could find work for him. He looked the part. He acted the part. But he had a good heart, she said, he'd seen the light. So, I had some ops on the go and we could use a guy like him. We can always use a guy like him. We paid him a thousand a week against a bonus for the bodies he set up. He scooped up a lot more money, I'm sure, running action on the side. Meth, hydroponics, whatever. Guns. He delivered the goods, so his little sideline was overlooked.

"We saw the Volunteers were getting pretty active. With the plague coming on, we thought there's going to be trouble. But we've got Ansel. We fire Ansel in there, he gets them active before they're ready, and when they go we got them before they can get the idea themselves. Right off, he spotted that Corey Garnett had some weird sex action going on. Down to the bars in Smoketown, hiring black hookers. Ansel turns that back on him, but like a buddy. Says he knows, but he doesn't care. Forget that separatist stuff, the compound up the Badlands. Ansel wants them to take all of America back and Corey's a natural leader. Textbook stuff. Frighten, then reassure, belittle, then praise. Tear down, then support. Now, he's drilled in to the Volunteers, especially Corey. They're all afraid of him and he works that. They start buying up guns, they start training. Before, they're just white power goofs, talking big and planning their own dream city up in the Badlands. Marginal, but they could go off, if the right cause comes along. And the backlash against the Asians could be that flashpoint. If they've got it in their hearts to go, then we want to choose the time and place. So, Ansel gets in there. Ansel's what you might call a catalyst for change."

Djuna Brown wished Ray Tate or Martinique Frost were there, sitting in. She didn't know what to ask. Sally Greaves was open for the taking. She was waiting for questions, she was waiting to justify or confess. Djuna Brown went with what always worked for her. Honesty. "Ah, look, Sally, I don't know about these ops things. I don't know if there's something going on with them that isn't right. I hope you covered yourself. The money and stuff. I think you probably know how to protect yourself. I hope so. Really, I do. That's not my kind of policing. But the women, the dead ladies. And Ansel. Do you think he's capable of doing that?"

Sally Greaves sat in thought. "At first, no. When I met him he was strange, but charming. No racist talk, no swearing. He came around with Monica for dinner and ... he was trying to turn his life around, like she'd told me. Now, now after the charge he's got, I think he's capable. I think he's maybe viable." She took a shuddering breath. "If I'm responsible for him doing ..."

"Don't say anything to me about that, okay?" Her cellphone rang. She answered and listened for a few seconds. "The victim, is she black? We're looking at him for some black ladies ... When did she come forward? ... Is the other one laying charges? Anything tying them together? Any good M.O.? That's creative ... I need the dates. Got it. No, no, we're looking at him for murders. Okay, thanks for or getting back to us." She clicked off and then punched a number. From inside the conference room she heard Marty Frost's cellphone emit. "Marty, ah, you guys getting along?"

"Me and An-sell, we're buds. We're going to change the world together."

"Well, good, let me know if I can help out with that. Look, I just got a call back from the guy investigating that rape, that old Ansel is charged with. There's actually two victims, both white. After the first one heard the second one had reported, she came forward."

Marty Frost spoke away from the phone, "An-sell, you've been a very bad boy. Very, very bad." Back into the phone she said, "The dates? Do they fit ... ah ... with our thing? That maybe he used our ladies to get himself ramped up?"

"No. They're off, happened earlier. One was a year old."

"Maybe practice runs? How'd he ... You know."

"Both were taken from a skating rink. He slammed into them, came back and helped them up, took them for a drink, calmed them down. Put rohip in their drinks and the next thing they know, they're face down alone in the bathtub at home. He put both through a thorough cleaning, inside and out. Just letting you know, in case, you know ..."

"Nice to know, nice to know." She clicked off.

Djuna Brown stood up. Sally Greaves looked pale. "Sally? You okay? We should get the other guys back in there, let them get back to Ansel. And you might want to talk to Ray. You can trust him. All he cares about is the poor dead ladies."

"I'm going to sit for a while." Something had changed. Sally Greaves seemed defeated, suddenly. Her overbite gnawed at her lip. "I'm going to sit, okay?"

"No problem. You want another coffee?"

"No. Just to sit." She looked into Djuna Brown's eyes. "Thank you. For this."

Djuna Brown went out into the hallway. The duty desk officer was asleep, standing up against the wall.

"Hey, snoozy. Wake up, man. Go back in there, secure the conference room door. Nobody in, not even the lady, until we get our team back up here. Stay awake."

"You know who she is, right, the dyke? SPA. She outranks me by about six."

"Yeah, but this is chief's special business. You want Pious Man Chan to explain the chain of command to you?"

She went down to the cafeteria. The maintenance crew saw her come through the door and stared, all of them turning in unison as she passed. There were sounds, little lip noises so subtle she thought she might have not heard them at all. It was people like this, she thought, that made people like Sally Greaves have to hide, made them targets for opportunists and driven into lives of secrecy where they could be preyed upon with impunity. For a second she thought of throwing down on them all, put their shadows on the wall, scalp herself some stupid night-shift face. But instead she smiled and gave them a pleasant look as she sat down with Ray Tate, Hambone Hogarth, and Brian Comartin.

"What was that all about, Djun', up there, you and Sally? Sisterhood stuff?"

"Ray, Ray, Ray." She felt pretty okay. The end of it all might be near. Paris was around the corner. She'd done good by being good. "Dream them dreams, bucko."

Hambone Hogarth said, "Did Sally say anything stupid?"

"Nope. But she doesn't have any problem, now, I don't think, if we want to hack old Ansel's nuts off. She thinks he might've done it, is viable for the women. She overheard me getting the lowdown on Ansel's rapes. There were two of them, the first reported after the second. Rohypnol, both times, same M.O., took them out of a skating rink, home for a boning and a bath. I got the duty security guy on the conference room door. Nobody in, nobody out, until we get back up there."

Ray Tate said, "Is Marty still in there?"

"Oh, yeah." She laughed. "Oh, yeah, I heard them through the door. They're talking up a storm. A little tense, it sounded, but they're good buddies by now, I think."

Hambone Hogarth said, "Whoa, whoa, whoa. No talk. You told her not to talk to him, Ray. You made a deal."

Ray Tate stood up. "Yeah, you're right, Ham. I'm going to have to sit Marty down after this. No fibbing, I'll tell her, and make her stay after school. Chicks, what are you going to do?"

"You know, Ray, this doesn't have to go farther. Corey Garnett is still viable. Ansel goes to trial and a lot of dirty stuff's going to come out."

"We'll be in Paris," Djuna Brown said. "Write us and let us know how it sorts."

Chapter 26

When the elevator doors opened they could smell the gun smoke. The duty desk security officer was sitting on the floor in the anteroom beside the door, his legs splayed, painfully gasping, "Holy fuck holy fuck," looking down where his vest had four evenly spaced tears. His gun was in his hand and he stared at it with deep curiosity as if it was an exotic food, as though he was wondering why he'd be holding an eggplant. The door to the conference room was closed and there was no sound from inside.

Ray Tate came up on his right side and secured the gun away. He told the guy to relax, the vest had absorbed it. "Who did what? Who's outstanding?"

The duty desk guy had trouble speaking. "She outranks me, by about six. She said she was going in. I said no. She pulled her piece and got me, point-blank."

"Buck up, how many outs?"

"Nobody outstanding. Her, I guess. I dunno. I went out for a second, couldn't breathe. She could'a left."

"How many shots, inside?"

"Dunno dunno dunno. Some. Fuck."

"Ham," Ray Tate said, "roll the gun trucks. This could still be live."

"Easy, Ray, easy. We don't need tacticals here yet. Let's see what we're dealing with."

"This isn't going to sort, Ham. This is major fuckup incident." He called out, "Marty, Marty, you okay? Sing out for me."

The conference room was silent.

Djuna Brown moved toward the door, her gun out. "Marty?" She sounded panicky. "Marty, please."

Behind her, Brian Comartin stood frozen.

The duty desk officer moaned loudly. Djuna Brown told him the shut the fuck up. "Four in the vest, suck it up, man. I'll give you one in the ear, we can compare. Button it, Alice." She cocked an ear to the conference room door. She shook her head.

Brian Comartin was a slow processor. But when he figured things out he went for the door, shouting, "Marty? Marty?"

"Chill, Brian. Take it easy, man." He didn't stop and Ray Tate took him around the waist. Brian Comartin still had chops like a young cop. He kept moving like a ship, dragging Ray Tate in his wake.

Ray Tate yelled, "Ham."

Hambone Hogarth took a collapsible baton from

his back belt and pressed the button to extend it. He took Brian Comartin across the shin with a back-handed whip and he went down, Ray Tate wrapped around him. "Cool it, Brian. Don't make this worse, okay? You cool?"

Brian Comartin rolled, clutching his shin. "Okay, yeah, no. No, Ray, we gotta go in. She could be bleeding out."

"Chill. Let's see."

The conference room was quiet. In the anteroom the duty desk guy was breathing hoarsely. Brian Comartin was clutching his shin, moaning. Djuna Brown was constantly licking her lips.

Ray Tate and Hambone Hogarth looked at each other.

"What the fuck, Ray?"

Ray Tate took his cellphone from his pocket and punched a number. Inside they could hear a cellphone emitting.

Then it stopped. "Officer Frost."

"Marty. Marty, Ray, what's up, hon'?"

"He's dead." Her voice was flat.

"Are you hurt, Marty? Can you get to the door, come out and see us? Let us see you're okay?"

"I can, Ray, but you know what? I'm just too tired. Come on in, it's okay."

"Marty? Any unsecured guns in there? How many people down? Is Sally still in there, with you? You need ambulances?"

"No. I know a dead man when I see one. An-Sell bit the big one, trust me."

"Come out. Brian's out here, he's worried about you."

"Tell him I'm okay."

"I'm sending him in, unarmed. Is that okay? Should I worry about him? About Brian coming in there, unarmed?"

"Brian's okay. Send him in." She sobbed. "I'd never let Brian get hurt." She laughed. "Brian. How about that? Me and a poet."

"One second, Marty. He'll just be a second." He told Brian Comartin to take off his jacket. He yanked at the Velcro to free the duty desk guy's vest, then put it on Brian Comartin and secured it. "Brian, I don't know what's going on in there, if Sally's holed up with her. I told her you're unarmed, but I want you to put a piece down the back of your pants, okay?" He stuffed the security desk guy's Glock behind Brian Comartin's belt. He put his face close to his. "She said she loves you, man. You're a lucky guy." He thought for a moment, wanting to get it right. "But if things go to shit, use the piece. I mean it. At the end of the day, you go home and cry."

"She said that? She loves me?"

"Yep. Crazy about you." He tried to read Brian Comartin's eyes. "We can wait. The guys on the gun trucks can do it."

"Okay, Picasso. Okay. I'm going in." He seemed dazed. "You guys should move back a little, just in case Ansel's got a gun. When it's clear, I'll sing out."

"She said he's dead. But he could be making her say it, to get us in there. Or Sally."

"Marty wouldn't do that to us." He got angry. "What's the matter with you, Ray?"

"Okay. But, Brian? End of the day, you go home. That's number one. Use your training. Do what you have to do. *End of the day, you go home.*"

Hambone Hogarth said softly, "He's shaky, Ray, maybe you're right. Let's back off and get the boys with toys."

"Yeah. Yeah, this is bad." He held up his hand. "Brian, hold, we're getting the gun trucks."

Brian Comartin turned and took the gun from the back of his pants. He loosely held it in Ray Tate's direction. His eyes were shining.

"No, Brian," Djuna Brown said. "Not Ray."

Hambone Hogarth moved in front of her, completely blocking Brian Comartin's view. He held his right palm up, then slowly moved his hand to the skirt of his jacket. "Go on in, Brian, okay? Slow, though, okay, man? I'm going for my phone, okay, she might be hurt in there and we need some help for her, all right, man, just going for my phone, if you want me to stop moving say so, okay, I'll stop, we'll talk about it, look slowly, slowly." He took his phone from his belt, keeping his eye on Brian Comartin and the gun. From behind him he heard Djuna Brown's automatic slip from the leather holster. She held it flat against his back; he could hear her breathing through her nose. "Let me make the call, Brian, get some help for her up here. Okay, they're picking up ... Hogarth, Homicide. We have a red incident. Roll the gun trucks and ambulances, a couple at least. Seal the building, man the elevators. No one to this floor unless they're in full combat, including tactical paramedics." He paused a moment, glancing sharply at Ray Tate. "Yes, I got it. I'll deal with that later."

Brian Comartin wiggled the gun. "Back, Ray, you too, and hang up." He waited until they'd moved well away from the door. He stood with his hand on the knob, then let go and stripped off the vest and threw it on the floor. He tossed the gun onto it.

He opened the door and the strong smell of gun smoke came out. He limped inside, a thick fat man with red hair and a hope of poetry.

He called out, "Marty?" as if he were yelling hopefully down a well.

At the top of the room, Ansel Partridge was face forward over the conference table, his face in the array of photographs of the poor dead ladies. Slightly on his left side, his hands were secured behind his back.

Brian Comartin didn't know so much blood came out of a gunshot to the head. There was a lot of it. On the wall behind Ansel Partridge at about head height there was spatter of unrecognizable stuff. It amazed him, in a detached kind of way, what a vast carrying vessel a skull was. He'd once taken a wineskin about the same size full of red to a bullfight near Seville and, holding it up and squeezing it, he thought it held an impossible amount. Spain, he thought, it won't be like this there.

Marty Frost was sitting in a chair midway down the conference table, her cellphone and her gun in front of her.

Otherwise the room was empty.

"Marty? I'm going to let them in, okay? Ray and Djuna are worried. They think you might ... you know." He made a laugh. "You might shoot me."

"You better take the gun, Brian. Secure it."

"No. No, you keep it there." He sat down opposite her. "I'm gonna sing out, okay? Let them know we're okay, we're okay."

"Yeah. Djuna sounded pretty freaked out. Sensitive girl. A Statie, you know?" She shook her head. "That girl and her beatnik."

Comartin called out, "Ray, hey, we're okay. Ansel's dead. Sally's gone. We're just taking a break, okay? A minute or two, then you can come in."

"Okay. Ah, Brian ... ah, what's my name. The other morning on the river? Tell me something."

"Picasso." He thought for a second. "'Hey, Picasso, you got a reason for being here?'"

"Okay, Brian. But I'm gonna open the door. Just gonna push it open a little, okay, we won't come in, but we have to see."

"Okay."

Martinique Frost gave him a wan smile. There were pinches of white in the brackets around her lips. She nodded at the gun on the table. "That's not professional, Brian, leaving a weapon around. Bad policing."

"Yes, well, we don't do that stuff anymore."

Hambone Hogarth moved to the edge of the door and quickly ducked his head around. Then he did it again, memorizing the scene. "They're sitting at the table, she's on the far side, he's on this side. There's a gun out on the table." He ducked his head again. "They're holding hands. Fuck's that all about?" He ducked around again. "Partridge is down and out. Three serial homicides cleared. Two rapes. Eighteen mass murder. What a fucking week."

"Let's give them another minute, Ham." He turned to Djuna Brown. "Djun', holster your piece. When the droids on 'roids come in here in their tin hats they're not gonna want to see anyone with a gun out."

Hambone Hogarth held up his cellphone. "Ray, they told me downstairs, outside in the parking lot there's a Porsche with a dead woman inside. A blonde. In the duty sergeant's slot. The guys ran out when they heard the shots and they took Sally into custody. Fuck man. What a fucking mess."

"The blonde, I don't know her name, but she's, was, the hottie with the black-rimmed glasses. Lieutenant Somebody. She and Sally were … together?"

"The one with the slow walk?" Hambone Hogarth said, "Well, there lies a busted dream."

Djuna Brown walked softly to the door. "Brian? Can I come in? I really want to see Marty's okay, man. Just for a sec. I'll leave my gun out here with Ray. Brian? Please, Brian." She looked around the door. "They're getting up. They're coming out. There's a gun on the table, they left it. She looks okay, Ray, she isn't shot."

When they came out, Djuna Brown tried to hug both of them. "You guys, you guys."

Out in the hallway there was a rattle of equipment. A gun barrel with a mirror attached to it peeked around the open door.

"You all cops in there?"

Ray Tate called out, "Yeah. We're good."

"We'll be the judge of that. Any unsecured firearms in there?"

"We're armed and there's a handgun unsecured on the table in the conference room. Police weapon."

Hambone Hogarth identified himself. "This is a homicide stage. Come in careful."

"Don't think so, Ham. We're shy. We want you to come out to play with us. And today we're playing the Simon Says walk backwards on your knees with your hands on your head game or get shot." The mirror moved around. "That guy on the floor, the officer, what's his story?"

"Took a bunch in the vest."

"Been there, done that. If he's bleeding, we'll come in and get him, but otherwise he gets to go last." The mirror moved again over them. "Eenie meenie minie moe." The mirror stopped. "The little lady there, I spy with my little eye a telltale bulge, so the jacket comes off and she comes out first." He laughed. "Didn't know there were children present. Somebody call child welfare, we got a waif in her sleepy slippers."

Behind him someone laughed and said something.

The voice behind the mirror said, "Okay, Miss in the magic slippers, stop me if you've heard this before but ..." It was an old joke, it sounded like from the laughter outside, among the droids on 'roids. "... First you get on your knees ..."

It took a while. The tactical guys were humorous throughout but patient and very specific. Everyone, even Hambone Hogarth, came out on their knees backwards and had their faces held to the floor while they were frisked, relieved of their weapons, and made to sit under a machinegun.

Once they were all out, a two-man sweep team went through the anteroom and past the duty desk guy still looking at his vest, seemingly amazed at the great strides in Kevlar technology. The sweepers did the peek and duck at the conference room door, then went in. A moment later, one lit off a whistle; two tactical paramedics in combat garb scooted into the anteroom and started on the duty desk guy. They lit off a whistle of their own, and two guys in ambulance outfits and vests came in and ran the duty desker out on a gurney.

"We got to separate you guys," the man with the voice behind the mirror told Ray Tate. He looked very young and had acne under his helmet. "Big brass balls are on the way and they're calling the shots." He made a smile. "But, you know, we're just out to kill people, not tell them what to do."

He gathered his guys and they trooped out.

Ray Tate said, "Marty, you okay? Brian? What happened?"

Marty Frost rotated her neck as if she had a cramp. "I heard gunshots outside, in the waiting room, then right away the door came in and Sally had a gun. I could've shot her, but how do you shoot a cop? She was screaming something. By the time I figured it out and went for my gun, she'd unloaded a bunch into Ansel and ran out. Why'd she do that, Djuna?"

"Ansel's her lover's cousin. I think the two of them whipsawed her, got a bunch of city money, used her up. She was sad. She thought a goddess loved her and that made her as beautiful as her voice."

"Okay, kids," Hambone Hogarth said. "We shouldn't say nothing to contaminate the interviews."

Ray Tate said, "Fuck you, Ham. Kiss my *fucking* white ass." He asked Brian Comartin if he was okay.

Brian Comartin didn't say anything to him. He put his arms and around Marty Frost and said, "I thought you'd killed him."

She leaned back and gave him a smile. "If I'd'a shot him, *amigo*, I'd'a shot his fucking *cojones* off."

"You speak Spanish?"

"Just the good dirty stuff." She ran her hand over his face. "We're done, right, with this business? We going to Barcelona?"

"Marty," Brian Comartin said. "Bar-*tha*-lona. Jesus."

He looked insanely happy to be hooked up with such a dolt.

* * *

Hambone Hogarth's team showed up after the tacticals had left. Ray Tate, Djuna Brown, Brian Comartin, and Martinique Frost collected their guns and were escorted out by teams of Sector detectives to separate locations.

Through the open door, Ansel Partridge was still visible, sprawled on the table. Blood from his head wounds had soaked the stack of photos of the poor dead ladies and audibly dripped off onto the floor. It looked like he was examining the photos close up and taking his time about it.

Hambone Hogarth gathered the Homicide team. "Okay, guys, here's what we got —"

The detective-sergeant leading the team said, "Ham. No. Don't dirty us up. Let us go to work."

"This investigation is going to fly high, Tommy. You gotta know —"

"We don't care. We don't wanna hear about it. Let us go to work. You know the drill. Go downstairs and bug the guys doing the dead one in the Porsche, let them tell you to fuck off. Just make yourself available for interviews, okay?"

"Tommy, this guy in there —"

The lead detective put his hands over his ears and chanted. "I can't hear you, I can't hear you ... Danny, take Inspector Hogarth down for a coffee." He paused a beat. "You heeled, Ham? Where's your piece?"

"Fuck, I dunno. The tacticals put us through and took it. Probably it's down at Peter's Pawn and Loan by now."

"Goodbye, Ham. See you in about an hour."

* * *

Ray Tate told the interviewing officer they were working a serial killer case. Ansel Partridge had emerged as
the prime viable. He was an agent for Sally Greaves,
and had been drilled into the Volunteers. "We told
Sally we wanted to talk to him, that he was viable, and
she brought him here, upstairs, for an interview. She
thought he didn't do it."

"In the middle of the night? You want to re-think
that?"

"Nope. One a.m. Privacy, I guess. So, we went at
him a little, then took a break. I went downstairs with
Hambone and Brian. I left my partner with Sally in
the anteroom. I left Marty in there with the suspect.
Sergeant Brown, my partner, came down to the cafeteria and told us Sally was on side, that she'd moved off
her position. Ansel was viable. We could go at him raw
and dirty. We all came up together and walked into
what we walked into."

"Some guys are going to come at you harder than
this, Ray."

"I could give a fuck. We got the guy killed some
poor ladies."

Djuna Brown was so forlorn that the interviewer felt
bad for her.

"It's okay, it's okay," the interviewer said. "Just

formalities, you know? Why don't you give me a run-down, tell it as you like it. We'll get to questions afterwards, okay?"

Djuna Brown went through the structure of the case. The poor dead ladies. The Volunteers. How Ansel emerged as a viable, how Sally Greaves was running him, how an after-hours interview was set up. "Ansel Partridge had gone wild. I think Sally came to know that."

"She could have shot him anytime. Do you know why she waited? Why she picked that time? And not before she brought him in for the interview? Or at the first chance, here?"

"I don't know. Maybe she wanted no witnesses."

The interviewer stared at her for a moment, then added, "An officer was in the room when she did it."

"All that matters to me is he was a serial killer, a racist creep, and she smoked him. Good job, too. I don't care why. The fucker wore his ass for a hat. We all wanted to put him down." She looked up at the interviewer. "I mean, what good was he?"

"You don't get to decide that."

"Yes, really? Who does?"

Marty Frost told the interviewer about how she was working Ansel Partridge up, when she heard voices out in the anteroom. Then gunshots. Then screaming Sally Greaves with a gun in her hand came through the door and put three directly into Ansel Partridge's face. "That's all she wrote."

"You were armed, Officer. Why didn't you take her out? You were guarding the suspect, the suspect was your responsibility."

"Too fast. It happened too fucking fast."

"The suspect was in your care and control. You let him get wasted."

"My bad." She shrugged. "He can sue me."

Brian Comartin didn't know anything. He was upstairs, he was downstairs. If Marty Frost said anything, he didn't hear it. He didn't care about anything. Marty was okay. Fuck you.

"You've got to give me something, man. I can't go out of here with an empty notebook."

"Well," Brian Comartin said, "those speed bumps that loony mayor put on the side streets, to slow down traffic, piss off the motorists? Bad idea. What do you think happens when a cop car or a fire truck hits them, on the way to an emergency?"

"That's not going to cut it. We got dead cops here."

"And too many bicycle lanes. Not enough cyclists, and what about in winter when the Express comes down outta Canada, drifting snow to the roofline? Who's riding a bicycle then? Nobody, that's who."

Hambone Hogarth waited in front of the building. By rank he was allowed to look into the Porsche. The blonde lieutenant behind the steering wheel had no remaining face, it was all blood and bone and stuff and an eye on her cheek. Sally must have reloaded on the way down in the elevator, he thought. No face. Not so beautiful now, he thought. He said, "Not so beautiful now."

One of his Homicide hammers said, "That's what the dyke said, when the duty desk boys chained her up." He looked into the Porsche. "Looks okay to me, except for that fucked-up face. A hockey mask and we're good to go."

It was noon before the preliminary interviews were finished. As each of them signed off their statements and were told to keep available, they headed down to the cafeteria. The day-shifters and white shirts watched them crossing the room like a lost patrol, sitting in the table farthest away from the sunlight. They were ragged. They looked at one another. No one said anything except, "Wow," or "Fuck." Djuna Brown watched the doorway.

When Ray Tate, the last one out of the interviews, came in and sat down, he immediately stood up and said loudly, "I'm going. I've had enough of cops and cop bullshit."

Brian Comartin said, "I'm outta here, too. I'm stopping at Personnel."

"Me too, poetry man." Marty Frost nodded. "Can't take another year of this shit. Just pay me off. See you guys back at the hotel? We still got a suite there?"

"Seven for dinner, the dining room." Djuna Brown smiled. "We might be late, so wait for us." She linked her arm through Ray Tate's. "We're banging, you know."

The front of the Jank was jammed with media vehicles, camera crews, and reporters thumbing iPods. The Porsche Carrera was covered with a yellow sheet, a wide area of the parking lot marked off with crime-stage tape. Ray Tate's Mercury was inside the stage.

The sunlight hurt their eyes. It was the light of another world. Ray Tate linked his arm tighter with Djuna Brown and they went along the west wall of headquarters, looking for transport. Two chargers were inspecting their ghoster for damage from a previous shift before signing it out, one of them consulting a clipboard.

"Yo, taxi."

The wheelman looked up. "Ray Tate. And a little friend." He held out his hand and introduced himself. "Quite a night you guys had."

"Yeah. And our car's inside the stage. You guys want to cruise the Whistler, look for miscreants?"

"We got a run up the other way. Sorry."

"Chief's squad special." Ray Tate put his hand on the guy's shoulder. "We're commandeering."

"Well, you put it like that, hop aboard. Who the fuck am I?"

Chapter 27

They went into the shower and did nothing but shower.
They yawned and shook their heads at each other.

"Does this mean we're getting old, Ray?"

"Tell you what. We dry off and get into bed. If one
of us is still awake in five minutes, then we'll see."

"I'm asleep now, Bongo." Wrapped in a hotel
bathrobe, she sat on the bed and called the desk.

"Yes, Inspector Brown."

"No calls to up here until five o'clock, okay?"

"Yes, Inspector."

"Is that Gail? How are you?"

"Fine, yes it's me. I saw on the news you got him.
The one who killed Mariam?"

"Sorry, who?"

"Mariam Smith. She worked here? I mentioned
her in the spa, that day. And the other women? You
said you'd get him."

"Oh, yes, I'm sorry. We got him. He's dead."

"I'm glad. You won't be disturbed."

Djuna Brown hung up and lay back on the bed and fell asleep in the middle of a vast yawn. Ray Tate came out of the washroom in a towel. He looked at her, then stared at the print of *Whistler's Mother* above the bed.

I can do that, he thought, closing the thick drapes. And I'm going to.

The staff in the lobby knew who they were. The concierge thanked them. The woman on the desk said Mariam could rest in peace. In the dining room the maître d' showed them to a sparkling table beneath a crystal and silver spider chandelier.

"Please be our guests for dinner this evening," he said. "The Cliquot is on the way. Miss Mariam was a very good person."

Brian Comartin looked fresh and scrubbed. He had a suit and tie on and was closely shaven. Marty Frost sat beside him in a gay blue dress of white polka dots. She was made up carefully and there seemed to be less grey in her cornrows.

They all sat, pleased with themselves and one another. The wine steward brought and poured the champagne into flutes.

"Well," Brian Comartin said, "I guess we should toast something."

Martinique Frost said, "The poor ladies."

They gestured with their glasses, not clinking, and drank.

Brian Comartin raised his glass, "Retirement."

After they drank, Martinique Frost said, "China-town." And then she said, "Stonetown."

Djuna Brown sipped and held up her glass. "Poor Sally."

The looked at her, but they knew she was a little different. They toasted.

Hambone Hogarth called in at seven the next morning, waking them up.

"Brown." She put her hand on Ray Tate's shoulder. He was still dressed. She was still dressed. They'd collapsed after dinner. She'd been dreaming that Ansel Partridge had done the shooting and he'd taken out Ray. The bullets came out of the gun, destined to miss, but they curved toward him in slow motion, homing in on him as he dodged. It was taking them a very long time. She was glad to be awake. "What is it?"

"Hogarth. I need you to come in. Homicide offices at Jank. Sally wants to talk to you. She's exercising her rights, but if she gets to talk to you, she'll talk to us."

"Not my case. My case is down. You've got all you need. You got a witness, you got a gun. What else do you want her to give you? I'm tired, man, I've had it. I'm checking out today and going someplace else where they eat snails and drink champagne for break-fast. *Au 'voir.*"

"An hour. Give me an hour. I'll have a car waiting down front in fifteen minutes. Bring you in, drop you back."

She thought about him, in the anteroom where he'd shielded her from Brian's gun with his body. Casual heroics, instinctive. Cop. "Okay. Okay, but I'm not taking a statement from her. I'm not softening her up for you guys. I just listen."

"Anything you want. Just talk to her, maybe that'll move her."

"Gee." Djuna Brown sat up. "I hope not."

She quietly dressed in clean batiks and her slippers. Before she went out the door, she shook Ray Tate's shoulder. "Raymundo, they need me down at the Jank for a bit. Okay?"

He rolled over. "What for? What time is it?"

"Sally. She won't talk unless it's with me first."

"Fuck it, Djun'. That's not our case. Our case is down. We should be pricing tickets to Paris."

"We'll make it, Bongo. I'll be back in time for breakfast."

When she arrived at the Homicide office, Hambone Hogarth walked with her to the interview room and said Sally Greaves was on suicide watch, chained waist and wrists and legs. "You talk to her, then we'll put some guys in. They're taking her to arraignment and then, I think, a mental lockup. How'd you guys do, last night? Get much sleep?"

Djuna Brown felt like she was floating in her slippers down the fluorescent corridor. A headquarters security guy was standing in front of the interview room.

"If you're taping us," Djuna Brown said to Hambone Hogarth, "I'm not reading her her rights."

"No problem. They'll get me when you're done."

When Djuna Brown came in, she saw that Sally Greaves was too small for her jumpsuit. The sleeves and the cuffs were rolled. Sally Greaves was staring at her hands, twisting the gold-and-ruby ring around and around.

"Can't get it off. My knuckles are swollen. It won't come off and I really want it gone. It's strangling me."

"One sec'." Djuna Brown opened the door. Hambone Hogarth was talking to the security guy. "Ham, I need a bar of soap, a bottle of water, and some paper towels."

Hambone Hogarth said to the security guy, "Do it."

While they waited, he said past Djuna Brown's shoulder, "Sally? Coffee? Anything?"

"I'm fine, Ham. Sorry about all this."

"No worries, Sal'. It'll straighten."

The security guy brought the soap, water, and paper towels. Djuna Brown took them into the room and closed the door. She lathered her hands and took Sally Greaves' ring finger in her palms and worked it. She felt Sally Greaves staring at her face. The ring, with a little more work, slipped off.

"There you go." She put the ring on the table and dried her hands. "I'll voucher it for you."

"No, I don't want it. Can you take it with you? Get rid of it. Make sure no one ever wears it, promise."

"Done."

"They're taking me to arraignment, so I'll be fast. Ham's guys want a run at me. I made a deal. If I talked to you, then I'd talk to them."

"Fuck them, Sally. Let me read to you, invoke."

"No, I want this behind me. My life's over, I know that. But you said something, upstairs, there, before … it happened. About being loved. Let me tell you about that."

At eight a.m. the phone in Martinique Frost's suite rang. She forgot who she was supposed to be and just said hello.

"Ford, down at the lockup? You know Joseph Carr? He wants to see you."

"That's not my case."

"Whatever. He said it's important. About the Riverbank?"

"Okay." She hung up and shook Brian Comartin. "I got to go in, Joe Carr wants to talk."

"I'll go with you."

"You don't have to. Sleep."

"Five minutes."

They took a cab. The driver wanted to talk about the shootings at the Jank. They ignored him. At the lockup, Brian Comartin sat on a bench in the morning sun while she went and signed in. She surrendered her weapon.

Inside the interview room, Joseph Carr was already seated, chained hands to the table and feet to the legs of his chair. A face was framed in the window of the door.

"I hear-ed Ansel is dead. That true?"

"Killed last night, Joe. He was a police informant. At least he can't testify against you, right?"

He shook his head. "Guess not. But I'm going to tell them what they want to know. I want to plead guilty. I'm responsible for those people in Chinatown. I'll stand before God."

"It's good that you feel that way, Joe." She waited a few seconds. "I had a couple of tough days. What's up?"

He was off in thought, his forehead knotted. "I been thinking a lot, a lot about that night? On the river? When we was ending our patrol, the night you said that ... that lady of yours got beat? Well, I heard, like, a gun shoot. It weren't loud, like a varmint gun. And I hear-ed a noise, a pinging, like *piiiing*, you know? When I was a boy my father taught me to shoot an old twenty-two rifle. I missed the target and the bullet skipped off the bumper of his truck. It was an old truck, with a metal bumper? I thought he was going to whip me, but he just laughed." He shook his head. "I'm glad my dad's dead. He didn't like the blacks, but he'd be ashamed, what I did." He seemed very sad, thinking about disappointing his dad. He shook himself and came back. "So, anyway, that night, the river, I hear-ed a gunshot up the hill and I think that shot hit something, I think it hit that metal sign was up there. No Fishing? No Swimming? The same sound." He looked sheepish. "I don't know, important or not."

"Joe, thanks for this."

"There maybe was someone yelling, running? But it might'a been another night. It sounded like a man, and your lady was ... Well, beat, right? And not shot, right?" He looked into her eyes. "If I remember more, maybe next time you can stay, longer? Talk some?"

"I'll try." She stood and put her hand on his shoulder. "I'll do my best for you."

He looked at her. He was crying. "My dad didn't like the blacks, it was down south. But I think he'd like you."

Sally Greaves said at first she was sure Ansel Partridge wasn't their serial killer. "Not until I heard you on the phone. In the anteroom, about how he got his victims. The rink? The bump? That's how I met Monica. I was at the skating rink, up on Marlborough one night. I love skating. Went every night. When you're going really fast, no one looks at you too closely, they can't see if you're ... you know. Ugly? Different? You're a graceful blur. One night I was up there and this guy went past, so fast he ran me into the boards. Kept going. I didn't even see him. Monica skated up. I recognized her from the job, I was like all those guys I see in the cafeteria, in the hallways, lusting. I felt as hopeless as they looked." She laughed. "Men, women, we're all the same, we all want the same things, but to a different degree." Her eyes were away, out of the room for a moment, then they came back. "You've seen her, right? Monica? Before I ... before she died?"

Djuna Brown said, "Just the one time. Two actually, just for second. She was doing assignments during the Stonetown riots. That's when I saw the ring. I saw her arrive that night, at the Jank. In the red Porsche. She was a beautiful girl."

"I bought that for her. I stole the money for ghost informants. Stupid. Jewellery. A sports car. She was half my age."

"We can all fall in love with the wrong person, Sally. Although sometimes it turns out to be the right person. You don't know. You never know until you know."

Sally Greaves smiled. "You mean you falling in love with Tate?"

"No. I mean him falling in love with me."

"You have to get past that, whatever you think you did wrong." Sally Greaves nodded. "So. I heard you on the phone in the anteroom, how Ansel got his victims out of the skating rink. And then raping them on the rohip and the cleaning up of the victims. I told him how to do that. He came by one night for dinner with Monica and I and I had too much wine, talked about cases, one of them a case where the doer drugged his victims, cleaned them up afterwards to get rid of evidence. I gave him his M.O."

"You were a victim, too, Sally. They used you. They set you up and they whipsawed you."

"I guess, I guess. But I'm not going to hide behind them. I killed them —"

"Sally, no. I haven't given you your rights. Tell it to Hambone's guys after they read to you. They're waiting. My case was the poor dead ladies. And it's down."

"I was thinking. You never got to the alibis, did you? Where Ansel was at the time of the murders."

"Doesn't matter now, Sally. You've got more important stuff to deal with."

"Do you know the dates?"

Djuna Brown didn't, offhand. She had a vague timeline. "Ah, I'd have to check. June, first week or ten days, that was for two of them. I don't remember the other one." She thought for a moment. "June ninth was one. My father's birthday. Another one, a few days later."

"Then there might be a problem. I got a call from the Maricopa County sheriff's office that they were holding Ansel down there on a gun charge. He told them he was doing undercover work for us, he was operating. I confirmed it, but I had no idea he'd left town, was out there. I think it was around that week. You should call Arizona, check the dates they had him."

"I'll give them a call, Sally."

"Or not. I'm not telling anyone."

"That won't work for Marty Frost. She wants the right guy."

"However you like. You do what you want with Arizona." She gave Djuna Brown a beautiful buck-toothed smile. "If I'd met you, well ... If you were that way, I mean, my way. I don't get to meet a lot of humanists."

Djuna Brown stood up and knocked on the door. "You can't be all things to all people, Sally. But ..." She gave Sally Greaves a small sweet smile, "sometimes you get to be what you are."

In the hallway Hambone Hogarth asked if Sally Greaves gave it up.

He got a small sweet smile, too.

When Martinique Frost left the lockup she found Brian Comartin sitting on his bench, looking like the retiree he was destined to become, soaking up sunshine. She thought, starve some of the extra weight off him, reduce the jowls, grow out a Hemingway beard. She sat on the bench beside him. It would be good not to have to move until they needed *paella*. "Traffic man, we need wheels. We have to do some cleanup. There might be a problem with Ansel."

"I'm retired soon as I sign the final papers. I don't have problems. I make problems." But he got up. "Let's walk over to Sector Four. They got a ton of cars there, and nobody to drive them."

They strolled down the streets like a long-time married couple. There were few masks being worn. People bustled. They stopped to look into windows. At Sector Four they went to the lot.

Brian Comartin whistled up a clerk. "We need a car."

"You got a req? You need a req. Two signatures."

"Chief's special squad."

"Chief's. I guess, then, you're commandeering?"

"How'd you know?"

"There's a black Chrysler over by the fence. Keys in. Abandoned traffic car. That do?"

"Perfect."

"But I didn't see nothin'. I was taking a piss when you took it."

They found the car and boarded, and Brian Comartin rolled out of the parking lot. "Did he have something? Joe Carr? Or was he just lonely?"

As the car went past the lockup she glanced back with a little sadness at the pattern of tiny cell windows in the brick wall of the back of the building. She wondered if it made her a bad cop, to care about the victims and to care about the doers. She felt Joseph Carr was a victim of something, and that made all those dead Chinese people victims of something, too, something beyond him. The Chinese people were dead and without hope of change; Joseph Carr was alive and change was a possibility available to him, although he'd never walk free again.

Change was all around, some of it generated internally, some of it imposed externally. You had to deal. Djuna Brown had almost lost it in the dark streets of Stonetown, Marty Frost knew, not so much because she was afraid, but because she'd almost become a victim. Cops aren't supposed to be victims. As much as there was sympathy and caring for an injured or even dead cop, there was an underlying feeling that he'd failed. Djuna Brown had got off light with an earring shot off the side of her head, but she was young and had an imagination and she had Ray Tate. A couple of inches to the left. Dead in the street. Her lover watching her bleed out. Poor girl, they'd say with harsh sorrow, how'd she fuck that one up?

"Marty?"

"Ah, yeah. Sorry. Off on a little voyage." She turned down the radio. Unlike Ray Tate, she wasn't a radio rider. Ray Tate liked to find action, to check on the young cops, to find scenes in progress. She preferred to go from A to B, do her job, then wait for the next one. Do her little piece of a case. She liked to be in the aftermath when things were less crazy and the human element emerged, not the wild, spitting anger that preceded it. "So, our man Joe. Joe was out on the river the night Evening Evans was attacked. He heard a gunshot. He told me he heard what might have been a bullet hitting a sign along the river, a man yelling."

Brian Comartin turned the Chrysler into the entry to the Riverwalk. They cruised slowly; Marty Frost got out a couple of times to examine the signage. On the fourth stop she returned to the car and told Brian Comartin to park it, they'd found the place.

"We got a No Swimming sign with what might be a bullet skip off it. There's a bit of blood on it, I think. Ground's all churned up. We'll need some guys down here to do a scrape."

She called the Homicide Squad and told one of Hambone Hogarth's minions where she was, that she needed a vampire to do some blood work on Riverwalk, and gave the location of the sign.

"They're pretty busy, Officer."

"Chief's special squad. You tell it to Hambone."

Chapter 28

They saw Ray Tate slumped on the terrace drinking coffee. Even from a distance his eyes were shot. Brian Comartin parked the Chrysler in the driveway. The valet came down the steps; Marty Frost showed him her palm and he nodded and backed away.

"Ray, you look like you had a bad night dancing with that slut, Widow Cliquot."

"That stuff, Brian. Goes down good, comes out pretty raw through the nose."

"Oysters, you need oysters for breakfast." Brian Comartin was jovial. He held a chair for Martinique Frost and got a sweet smile, then sat. "Djuna still out of it?"

"She got called to the Jank. Where you guys been?"

"Detecting." Marty Frost put her cellphone on the table, and poured coffee for herself and Brian Comartin from a carafe. "Just cleaning up." She told him about

Joseph Carr wanting to see her and what he'd said. "So we went down by the Riverwalk. Found the sign. Found what looks like blood spatter."

Ray Tate thought for a moment. "Oh, oh." He pointed to her phone. "Gimme." He squinted at the number pad and punched in the Homicide number. "Ham? Ray Tate. Djuna leave there, yet? Well, look, are they done with Partridge down at the abattoir? I need to know if he had any gunshot wounds, other than what Sally parked in him. Okay." He asked Marty Frost the cellphone's number and passed it on to Hambone Hogarth. "We'll stand by." He clicked off.

"So, maybe Sally was right. Ansel Partridge might not be good for our ladies, if he has no wounds and Eve Evans got one into the guy that jumped her." He poured more coffee. "Fuck, two good viable heads and no one with the right hat size. This is the case that wouldn't die."

A taxi pulled into the roundabout and Djuna Brown got out. Ray Tate lit off a whistle and she skipped up onto the terrace. "Bongo, you look like you been shot at and missed, and shit at and hit." She gave him a sympathetic kiss, sat, and greeted Marty Frost and Brian Comartin with a smile. "A city guy. I'm going to own his ass in Paris." She poured herself a cup of coffee. "So, we might maybe got a problem."

"Huh." Martinique Frost said, "Tell me about it."

"Why, what's up?"

"You first. We're waiting for a call from Hambone about something."

"Well, our old pal Ansel might have an alibi after all. We didn't get to alibis before Sally shot him. But if we had we might've found out he wasn't in town for at least one of the poor ladies. Sally says he was behind the pipes in Arizona. Gun charge. I'm going to call the Maricopa County sheriff. But she was pretty sure."

Marty Frost's cellphone buzzed. She answered.

"Hey, Marty," Hambone Hogarth seemed happy to hear her voice. "My guys tell me you're down on the Riverwalk, want a blood scrape? We got a vampire heading down there now. What's it about? Your case is down."

"Well, maybe, maybe not, Ham. The last victim, the survivor, might have put a round into the guy as he was beating her. That's the blood on the sign. Ansel have anything like that?"

"Nope. Three .38 loads in the face. That's it."

"They did it right, right? Armpits, body hair? She only had a little .22."

"They gave him the full service massage. Nothing but Sally's rounds." Hambone Hogarth made a bitter laugh. "You guys just can't be satisfied. Each time you get a viable, he dies, so you clear him. Just pick one, we'll make it fit him, and we'll go out and get a beer."

"And it gets worse. Ansel might have an alibi for one or more of the murders."

"Goodbye, Marty."

"A good official alibi."

"Been nice, chatting, Marty. Glad you chief's special guys took this case and not us. Goodbye. Good luck. Write if you get work." He laughed and hung up.

"So," Djuna Brown said, "we wait on the blood work, we check Arizona. Anything else we can do?

They got a good pool here, let's get some bathing suits in the gift shop, go for a swim."

Martinique Frost looked depressed. "Fuck, fuck, fuck, fuckity-fuck-fuck. Where did we go wrong? What did we miss?"

"Maybe it was one of the other Volunteers?" Brian Comartin bit his lip. He wanted to help but all he had were maybes, no fresh ideas. He was glad he wasn't going to be a cop much longer. "Maybe it was just random nut after all."

A black Buick with a lot of gleaming chrome wheeled into the roundabout. A woman got out of the passenger seat and opened the rear door. She took a garment bag out, started to head to the revolving doors, then turned back.

When the driver powered down the window and leaned across the passenger seat to speak to the woman, Ray Tate had a holy-fuck moment, the cop version of *satori*.

"Djun', who's that? The Buick?"

She leaned to look. "Gail the receptionist. Coming on shift, I guess."

"The guy?"

"Don't know. She said she'd started seeing somebody. Him, I guess."

"I know that guy. Marty? Brian?"

They looked. The man lifted his hand and waved goodbye to the receptionist, sat up and powered up the window. He rolled to the edge of the sidewalk, pausing to let people pass.

Neither Marty nor Brian had seen him before.

"Brian, grab the plate, okay? Djun', see if you can catch Gail on her way in, chitchat, girl stuff, maybe ask about the dude in the Buick. Casual, like."

Djuna Brown headed for the lobby door and Marty Frost asked what was going on. "Is he a Volunteer?"

"Dunno. Dunno, but I know I know him. From someplace. He's a wrongo." He sat, thinking, running things though his mind. Through the door he could see Djuna Brown and Gail gabbing, Gail doing all the talking. Laughing. "Run the plate, Brian, see what comes back."

Brian Comartin called in, gave his badge number and put the plate through. He dug out a pen and they waited. It took a while. "Yep, still here. I'm ready to write ... Really? I never met one before ... Got it." He hung up and said, "I never met an actual John Smith before. I met a Joe Doakes and a John Hancock, but never a John Smith. Anyway, that's who he is. Middle name Harold. Fifty-five-fifty Harrison Hill. DOB February 14, 1970, born on Valentine's Day, six-foot-two, two-thirty-five, blond and blue. No unpaid moving traffic or parking citations. One parking violation, not paid, but still in the discretionary grace period. He's got to get it in today."

"Okay. Okay. We're working." Ray Tate felt his heart racing a little. "We need some stuff. Marty, put him through for nation-wide criminal. Brian, we need the photo off his driver's licence and we need it sent here. Can you access email off your phone? Do it that way. And we need to know when and where he picked up all his parking tickets, rolling stops, whatever." While Brian Comartin was on the phone loading it in to Records, he added, "And his previous addies, every place he's ever lived."

"Who ever lived?" Djuna Brown was at his shoulder. She sat down. "What I miss?"

"Maybe a viable. Maybe not. I think so, though. John Smith. Guy that dropped Gail off."

"Yeah, Johnny. Gabby Gail's beau. Real love going on there, Bongo. I should be so lucky."

"Tell us what you got from her. About John."

"Well, it started in tragedy. John's wife, Mariam, was killed, she was actually the second poor lady killed. She worked here, with Gail on the desk. Killed up that alley around back, heading to her car after work."

"So what else did she say?"

"She said Johnny and Mariam were married. They'd met here. He did some contracting, plumbing, they had a lot of trouble with the sauna, the showers, the swimming pool. So Johnny's around and he hooks up with Mariam. And they get married. Mariam, when they met, was doing rooms and linens. With Johnny she blossomed. Took night courses in hotel management, moved eventually to the desk. Started dressing better. She was in line for middle management when she was killed. No kids. They lived in an apartment on Harrison Hill. Gail was really distraught after the funeral and had to take some time. Mariam was her only real friend at work. She was an example. Gail admits she has some self-effacement issues, but, she said, if Mariam could do it, then so could she. With Johnny's love and support."

"How'd Gail hook up with Johnny?"

"They saw each other at the funeral. She said the usual, you know, if you need to talk to someone, to call her. So he did. They talked. Hambone's guys were still all over him. See, the first poor lady hadn't been found yet, so Mariam looked like a one-off domestic, maybe. He got fired from here. Then they found the second. And then the third. So he moved off viable. And then the plague hit and everyone had newer fresher cases. Meanwhile, Johnny and Gail took things real slow. He does odd jobs, now. He'd worked in a slaughterhouse but quit. She was real happy when he didn't come home stinking of hog shit. They kept themselves on the down-low until just recently, but they're going slow, just breaking cover a little, now." She looked around, brightly. "So, what I miss?"

Ray Tate took out his cellphone and scrolled through the images. He passed the phone around. "That's him, right? I'm not nuts? That's the guy doing the poor ladies and I'm a fucking asshole."

They looked at the image on the screen of the fella who'd been shot in the shoulder, ducking away from the cellphone, the fella who wondered if he could be a weatherman, even if he didn't have the big head action going on, the fella smoking Kool menths, careful of his ash.

They took over the table on the terrace into the lunch hour.

It came fast. The motor vehicle licence photo was the same John Smith. He came back from criminal with an of-interest flag attached to his name, put up by Homicide when he was still viable in his wife's murder, to notify them of any incidents or contacts. A couple of paired drunk-assaults, bar fights, it seemed. That was it.

His parking tickets were all around the city. Overtime parking. Fail to pay meter. They mapped the locations on a napkin and crossed them with what they knew of the poor dead ladies. There was a hit. June Flowers, victim number three, waitress at Stoney's on Erie, killed cutting through a vacant lot on her way home to her apartment on Harrison Hill. John Smith had an overtime parking the same night, two blocks away.

His employment record from the State showed several plumbing jobs: he was unlicenced, he had no union membership, he'd worked in a car wash, a restaurant kitchen, a lumberyard, and at Bradshaw's animal processing plant.

They were winding it down when Hambone Hogarth called on Martinique Frost's cellphone. She handed it to Ray Tate.

"Ray, a heads-up. We're doing a press briefing at four this afternoon. On the shootings at headquarters and an update on the Volunteers conspiracy, tying the serial murders into it, hooking it on Ansel."

"I'd hold off on that, Ham, if I were you. We got a viable."

"Bullshit. Who?"

"We got a good guy and we're working it."

"Gimme something, Ray. I gotta call the chief's office."

"A guy you guys had, Ham. And you let him go. You let the case go." He didn't say he himself had let the killer go.

"Ray …"

Ray Tate hung up.

Brian Comartin and Martinique Frost went to the plumbing contractors that had employed Johnny Smith to talk to bosses and workers. Only one worker, at a small firm on the outskirts of town, remembered him.

"Pussy hound. He'd'a fucked a U-joint if we let him. Mr. Lube, he called himself. Really liked a black chick that used to work in payroll. He said black chicks always had issues, needed some guidance from Mr. Plantation Man. One day he showed up with rips down his face, the boss came out and told him the black chick was more useful to the company than him. Fired his weird ass."

At the carwash where Johnny Smith used to work, the owner said he was a loon. "Most of the time he was okay. Always reading on his break. Those books. How to build your self-esteem. Be the person you can be. I said to him, one day, you trying to better yourself? Give the fucking windshields an extra wipe. He said he didn't need to improve, but a lot of people did, especially chicks, and he wanted to help them. I fired him when an NFL player's wife said he asked her about where she saw herself going in life, as a black woman. Her husband's a fucking quarterback and she's getting sacked every night by ten million bucks. Where's she gonna wanna go?"

Ray Tate and Djuna Brown went to the local Sector and muscled a car. Chief's special, Fuck You. In a new fleet Ford 500 they headed out to Bradshaw's.

Aaron Bradshaw was a predator. He preyed on the new immigrant, the down-and-outer, the guy needing a job for bail or probation or parole. He worked them like dogs. It was said he turned the better-looking young females over to a cousin who ran a chain of massage parlours. If anyone complained about anything, Bradshaw dropped a dime and the worker was back in Mexico or the clink or on his ass on the street in record time. Ray Tate had run into Bradshaw several times over the years.

Bradshaw's Pork was just outside town. It was a huge facility of metal huts and loading docks with picnic tables scattered around the property. Bradshaw processed a lot of pigs and nothing went to waste. A rendering house was away to the edge of the property.

When they pulled up in front of the offices, the air smelled like a fresh and bloody crime stage.

Inside, Aaron Bradshaw was consulting with a secretary. He was big with a huge pot belly that held his trousers down near his crotch. His hairpiece was bright red with grey sideburns down into his jowls. The secretary had big breasts, looked Central American, and was biting her lip and shaking her head as he whispered into her ear, his hand moving on her shoulder.

"Bradshaw." Ray Tate moved quickly to the desk. "Back off her."

"Warrant? No? Then get out."

"I'll get a squad of Homeland guys in here, shut you down."

"And in a fucking hour I'll have full roster, at a quarter of a buck an hour cheaper each. Do me a favour." He leered at Djuna Brown. "You looking for a job, dear? Big pay, short hours. Overnight shift."

Djuna Brown gave him a saucy smile. "Another time, maybe. Looks like a cool place to work. You actually get anything done here besides boning?"

Bradshaw laughed. "That's more like it. This guy? No sense of humour. Ready to believe the worst lies about anyone."

"Well, he's a city guy, right? Me, I'm State. To me, all people come fresh."

"What can I do for you? You looking for a wetback did a robbery? How many you want? I got a bunch."

"No. We're interested in John Smith."

"Johnny?" Bradshaw's mode changed. He licked his lips. He became cautious. "I had a guy with that name. Long time ago, month or maybe two. He came, he went."

"He have any friends here? Guys he hung with?"

"Well, no. Not I can recall. What's he done?"

"Can't say. We're just looking around at his shit."

Aaron Bradshaw looked at Ray Tate, then back at Djuna Brown. "I'll talk, but not in front of both of you."

Ray Tate went to the door. "Stay in the window where I can see you both. Djuna, if you have to plug him, plug him. In the nuts."

"Fuck you."

"Soon, Bradshaw, you fucking deviate."

"Get the fuck out, the both of you."

"C'mon." Djuna Brown patted the air. "C'mon. Ray, go the fuck outside, man. Let us talk."

Ray Tate went out. He stood on the walkway looking in the window.

Ray Tate was pissed off and Djuna Brown insisted on driving. She made sure his seatbelt was fastened. "You know, Ray, in this down economy more people eat pork than anything except pasta and chicken? And macaroni and bird get old, real fast. The worse things get, the better it is for Bradshaw. Busier it gets, he said, the more poor migrants he can help make new, prosperous lives in America, giving them work, feeding their families. He's a humanitarian; guys like you just don't see the big picture."

"That's always been my drawback, why I'm stuck at sergeant. I just don't dig it. But you did, right?"

"Sure. Perfect economic sense, once you have a pro explaining to you. He provides jobs, he provides nutritious food. A good guy, that guy. Unless, of course, you're a victim. Then, maybe not so good. We didn't get into that part."

"So, Johnny Smith."

"Interesting, our Johnny. In the pens he was the guy who got 'em out, sent them on to the next step. The butchering, the rending. Easy job, white man's job. He kept on top of the pens, made sure everything was okay. He did the separating. No dirty bloody jobs for Johnny, that stuff was for the beaners. Did a good job. Great employee."

"So, why'd he let him go?"

"Great employee, except for one teenie weenie habit. He'd get a young pig, string it up by the neck, and have some fun with it."

"He fucked them?" Ray Tate looked at her, amazed. This was choice. "He's a pig fucker? Holy shit, Djuna, I've heard of that but never met one of those guys before. Banging a pig. That's a little odd, even in this town. I once busted a sheep shanker, funny story. This guy —"

"Some other time, Ray." She was happy he'd calmed down and was having fun. "No, he didn't jam them. He hung them up and went to work on them with his fists. Just demolished them. How long it went on, Bradshaw didn't know. But he caught him at it when one of the inside guys refused to work with Johnny. How come, Bradshaw asked, how come you're risking going back to Guatemala in handcuffs? Because, the guy said, he beats the poor animals."

"Fuck."

"Yep. He just hung 'em up and pulverized them. Bradshaw caught him, booted him."

"The hogs. Eve Evans said he called her a dog. Maybe he said hog."

"I like this guy, Ray."

"Djun', I love this fucking guy." He sat back, watching the streets. "You know, he wants to be a TV weatherman."

"He got a big head?"

Marty Frost loved John Smith, too. He was viable. She listened to Djuna Brown tell about the interview with Aaron Bradshaw.

"How you want to handle it, Marty?" Ray Tate signalled a waitress. "It's all of ours' case, but the poor dead ladies are your weight."

They sat at a corner table in the hotel bar, drinking cold beers. Each round, the waitress said, "Compliments of the house."

Martinique Frost thought about it. "First, we should confirm he's got a gunshot wound. Then we get the vampires to do a quick blood type, his and the stuff off the sign at the Riverwalk. DNA will take a while. Djuna, can you work that Gail girl a little, somehow find out if he's wounded, hurting?"

"Lemme think on that. She might be off shift by now." She got up and went into the lobby area.

Brian Comartin said he had an idea. "Stroke of midnight, the discretionary period passes on the last parking violation. We can take him."

"For traffic?" Marty Frost stared at him. "Brian? We want him for multiple murders."

"And failure to attach seatbelt. I noticed he drove off unsecured this morning. Maybe he's got a bad habit."

Ray Tate said, "That's heavy, heavy shit. Unsecured. Yikes."

Djuna Brown came back into the bar. "She's just going off shift, he's picking her up. I got her chatting, said me and my man here want to go bowling, did she know a place? She said up on Chester. I said, 'Hey, you want to come with us?' She said she dug bowling, but her beau got hurt at work the other day, his arm was fucked up."

"*Okay*," Ray Tate said, "okay, that'll do it."

Chapter 29

When Gail the receptionist got into the Buick and pulled out of the roundabout, Brian Comartin and Martinique Frost, in the Chrysler, and Ray Tate and Djuna Brown, in the 500, played them loose. The Buick went directly to the Eight and headed north.

Brian Comartin went on the air. "Eight to Park, west to Harrison Hill, his place. Eleven minutes, traffic flow and road conditions."

The dispatcher came on. "Rambling units out there, identify."

Ray Tate went on the radio. "Desk, we're chief's specials running an op. Two vehicles, four officers. Assign a band, please."

"Ten-four, chief's special. Dial over to channel nineteen. It's all yours."

"Ten-four, Desk. Official time check?"

"Nine-forty-two at the twin tones." She waited until random units came on with various ding-dongs. "*Thank* you, children."

They dialled over and came up to make sure both units were in sync.

"Brian, put him through again, make sure he didn't go pay the ticket today."

"'Kay, Ray." He came back a moment later. "Still open." There was a moment of silence. "You know, when he got in, I'm pretty sure he didn't secure his safety belt. If we don't want to wait until midnight."

"Can you roll up on him, take a peek? Wait for a pod of traffic and get inside it?"

Ahead, Ray Tate saw the Chrysler change lanes into a cluster of cars. It went up beside the Buick, held the same speed for a few seconds, then dropped back. "Unsecured, Ray. Moving violation. Ejection of a motorist through the windshield in event of collision? Public hazard."

The Buick was four exits from the Park Avenue exit.

"Okay, we let him take the ramp. Remember there's a gun outstanding. Eve Evans's twenty-two. We'll get in front. At the top of the ramp, Brian, you put the sunrise in his mirrors. When he's over to the side, we'll roll back, hold him. You bumper him up." He dialled over the Desk. "Desk, chief's special, we're doing a traffic stop at the top of the Park eastbound ramp off the Eight." He read off the descriptors of the Buick. "Monitor the band, please."

"Channel is being monitored by a supervisor."

Ray Tate went back to channel nineteen. Two lonelys came on and said they were in the vicinity of Harrison Hill and might drop by.

"Be aware there might be firearm onboard."

The monitoring sergeant came on. "Chief's special? Cause to stop?"

"Seatbelt violation. Vehicle operator observed unsecured while in motion."

"Got it."

"Marty, Brian. I'm going up front, you guys put the sunrise in his mirrors. When he rolls to a stop, I'll reverse to block him tight."

"Yes," Marty Frost said. "Ray, if we find Eve's gun …"

Ray Tate swung out and passed the Chrysler and then the Buick. Djuna Brown obscuring her face, sat sideways as if talking to Ray Tate. He got into the exit lane, watching the Buick's lights in the rear-view mirror. It swayed over the broken white line without signalling.

"Fail to indicate a change of lanes on marked roadway," Brian Comartin said. "Hundred bucks and demerits. This guy's a crime wave."

Ray Tate led the way up the ramp. The traffic signal at the top was red and there was minimal traffic. The Buick stopped behind him, indicating a right hand turn. In the rearview, he could see John Smith and Gail laughing. The Chrysler came up behind the Buick. He went on the air. "This is perfect right here, Brian. You light 'em up and Marty you sweet-talk them out. Put them on the road." He undid his seat belt and took his gun from his ankle. He wished the 500 was equipped with a shotgun. A good shotgun was a mood-setter. "Arm up, Djun', showtime. We get out, you go wide. Watch for crossfire with Marty and Brian."

She pulled her little automatic and put her hand on the door latch.

He saw she was wearing only one earring, the dangly one, in her left ear. He smiled. She was weird.

The grill lights on the Chrysler began flashing. Brian Comartin gave the Buick a shot of roof music, then crept right up on the bumper. Martinique Frost got out with a microphone on a long curly cord and stayed behind her door. She told Brian to rotate around the back of the car and watch the passenger's hands. When he was in position, she announced over the loudspeaker, "Driver of the black Buick, put your vehicle in park and shut off the ignition. Good, now, throw the keys out onto the roadway. Good, now, driver and passenger put both hands out the window and wait. Keep those hands out. You don't want me to not see both hands. Very good, people."

Ray Tate climbed out, with his gun up on the Buick. "Djuna, tell Marty to get them out, driver first, onto the road, knees then face. You chain him up."

Through the windshield he saw John Smith looking at him. His mouth moved and he smiled.

Over the loudspeaker, Marty Frost called, "I'm missing a driver's hand."

John Smith stretched his hand out, as if to touch Gail's face.

There was a snap of noise and a flash of light off his fingertips.

Ray Tate saw her slump against the passenger door.

There was another flash and snap and John Smith's head jerked back against the headrest.

After the Homicide detectives were done with them, they were each sent to wait in Hambone Hogarth's office. When they were all gathered, he took them across the street to a greasy spoon. They sat at a round table in the back. The cook brought down a carafe of coffee and left them.

"Well, it looks like you guys got the right guy this time. Took you a while, a bit of a body count, but Smith looks good for all the women. The twenty-two belonged to the surviving victim. Blood type on the sign matches with Smith, DNA pending. He had a gunshot through and through in his shoulder. With the murder in the car, that's four up and four down. But I sent some guys to do some prelim work. Seems Smith wanted to off his wife, hide her in a crowd of dead black women. She was too uppity, he told a guy at the local bar. He spent all his time building her up, getting her to go to night school, being supportive. And then she starts to outclass him. She's on the rocket to management in the hotel chain, he's beating pigs to death and laying plumbing. He told the bar guy he created her and she forgot that it was him that carried her, that made her what she was. He was going back to white chicks who appreciated him. We wouldn't have looked at him too hard at all if the first body had been found first. As it was, when the third popped up it looked like a nut on a run. We were off him." He shrugged. "It's all been done before, but we would have circled back on him eventually."

"That's it?" Marty Frost sipped her black coffee and shook her head. "That's it? A domestic? He was just an asshole?"

"Yep. No race killer. No right-wing crackpots. Just a guy with a wife that pissed him off."

Djuna Brown said, "But why kill Gail? She was crazy about him."

"We went through her apartment. There were new clothes in there, still with the tags on them. Business suits, new shoes. There were brochures from the university with some courses, hotel management, public speaking, that kind of stuff, circled. She was improving herself to death."

"Gail was good people," Djuna Brown looked sad. Brian Comartin patted her hand.

Martinique Frost was still dazed. "A fucking domestic."

"C'mon, Marty." Brian Comartin said they had to go pack. "We leave tomorrow, we're so outta here." He stood up and said to Ray Tate, "This is no place for people like us."

Ray Tate wondered who he meant.

Epilogue

The Center for Disease Control people isolated Patient Zero, an elderly woman who'd come across the river from Canada. She was dead when they found her, long-dead in a rooming house owned by one of Willard Wong's front men. By then most of the plague had evaporated from the city. Willard Wong paid for a traditional funeral for Patient Zero and had her ashes shipped home to Fujian Province. He built a shrine on California Street at the gates of East Chinatown and every day he stopped and lit incense.

Joseph Carr sent long letters to Martinique Frost. No one told him she'd retired and moved to Barcelona. But he wrote the letters to her daily, care of the Jank, and never realized he was actually writing to himself.

Sally Greaves entered a plea of insanity. It was accepted by the judge, who had an older brother with bad habits involving teenaged girls and party drugs.

Hambone Hogarth had a search team and lock-smith with a blowtorch in Sally Greaves's home within hours of her arrest. When the detectives doing the follow-up investigation went to gather evidence for the case file the following week, they found a hidden compartment in the back of the closet had been burned open with an acetylene torch. Pious Man Chan appointed Hogarth deputy chief in charge of SPA, Sally Greaves's vacant job.

Evening Evans only went home with her father long enough to undergo rehabilitation at a clinic. After eight months of rehab she headed back to the city and began her project on the illegal migrants, getting used to her eye patch and her cane, which she thought made her look daring and mysterious. "I am," she said to a colleague, "truly a camera on a tripod."

Cops slowly drifted back onto the duty roster. Administration staff were gradually taken from the streets and put back on their asses behind their desks. They had stories to tell. They'd seen shit and didn't mind if they didn't see it anymore in their current lifetime.

Ray Tate received in the mail a folded menu from a Barcelona restaurant. On the back of the menu, written down the middle of the page, was a ragged poem, written in pencil. The title was "This Is No Place for People Like Us."

The poem reminded him of a recent call from George Meyers. "Kid," he had said, "that fat guy, the traffic guy you was with? Comartin, right? You ever find out where he was, September nine, nineteen ninety-four?"

Ray Tate booked his accrued vacation.

The State Police wanted their lone volunteer, the midget black sergeant from Indian country, back. She couldn't be located. When the bills from the Whistler hit State accounting someone noticed two inspectors, which the State cops hadn't sent, had gone deluxe.

When, in the following month, hotel bills from the Elysees Mermoz Hotel in Paris came in, the all-in State card was cancelled.

In the taxi to Charles de Gaulle to catch their flight to Chicago, Djuna Brown looked out the window at the cafés and intersections and people dressed in cool chic clothing, at the deliverymen hauling goods from vans, the shopkeepers hosing down their sidewalks, and the waiters setting up tables on patios.

She caught a glimpse of the Seine, of the bridges they'd crossed daily, their arms around the other's waist, losing themselves in the romantic warrens of streets and alleyways, in the galleries and restaurants of the Left Bank.

She put her hand on Ray Tate's leg. "I really like this place, Bongo. When we get out of prison, let's come back."

ALSO BY LEE LAMOTHE

Free Form Jazz
978-1-55488-696-8
$11.99

Disgraced city cop Ray Tate and outcast state trooper Djuna
Brown track down a wealthy sexual sadist and a depressed
career criminal flooding a Midwestern U.S. city with killer
ecstasy pills. Mismatched and mutually suspicious of each
other, Tate and Brown hunt the mythic Captain Cook and
his henchman, the homicidal Phil Harvey. But as Captain
Cook sinks deeper into a spiral of sexual depravity, Phil
Harvey begins to question his role as a lifelong gangster.

Tate and Brown discover, as they sift through the rub-
ble left by their targets, that no one is what they appear to
be — not even themselves. Travelling through the Chinese
underworld, clandestine drug laboratories, and biker-ridden
badlands, the troubled duo encounter murder, political corruption, police paranoia, and psychosis, but can they find
redemption?

MORE GREAT CASTLE STREET MYSTERIES
FROM DUNDURN

Daggers and Men's Smiles
Jill Downie
978-1-55488-868-9
$11.99

On the English Channel Island of Guernsey, Detective Inspector
Ed Moretti and his new partner, Liz Falla, investigate vicious
attacks on Epicure Films. The international production company is shooting a movie based on British bad-boy author
Gilbert Ensor's bestselling novel about an Italian aristocratic
family at the end of the Second World War, using fortifications
from the German occupation of Guernsey as locations, and
the manor house belonging to the expatriate Vannonis.

    When vandalism escalates into murder, Moretti must resist
the attractions of Ensor's glamorous American wife, Sydney,
consolidate his working relationship with Falla, and establish
whether the murders on Guernsey go beyond the island.

    Why is the Marchesa Vannoni in Guernsey? What is the
significance of the design that appears on the daggers used as
murder weapons, as well as on the Vannoni family crest? And
what role does the marchesa's statuesque niece, Giulia, who
runs the family business and is probably bisexual, really play?

She Demons
Donald J. Hauka
978-1-55488-763-7
$11.99

How can an enterprising newspaper reporter sell his Babji dolls when there's a beheaded street youth, a Rave Messiah battling a berserk "God Squad," and a conniving new editor to deal with? Especially when he's suffering all the symptoms of dengue fever? Hakeem Jinnah is back and as politically incorrect as ever. The chain-smoking, headline-chasing hypochondriac is in a race to find a killer and help save his buddy Sergeant Graham's career. But a bevy of She Demons bedevil him at each turn. Soon Jinnah is entangled in a cultic web that threatens his friends, his family, and his life.

Fast-paced, funny, and suspenseful, this is the second Mister Jinnah novel featuring the larger-than-life crime reporter. Just as in his debut adventure, *Mister Jinnah: Securities*, the flirtatious and always resourceful Jinnah has to use every ounce of his investigative genius to solve a crime … and make a few extra dollars on the side.

Available at your favourite bookseller.

DUNDURN
www.dundurn.com

What did you think of this book?
Visit www.dundurn.com for reviews,
videos, updates, and more!